Praise fo

"A delicious roma   ers whose wit, passion,   he adds a mystery and h   ers into the tale until they are completely captivated. It's another keeper from a talented storyteller."

—*RT Book Reviews*, 4½ stars

"Fun and passion-filled Regency… readers will savor the numerous red-hot love scenes as Grant finds his way to maturity and love."

—*Publishers Weekly*

"Lee has a definite flair for creating engaging characters, and the latest installment in her sexy series will delight readers who relish experiencing a different side of Regency life."

—*BooklistOnline.com*

"A wonderful love story… at times poignant, wickedly funny, and sometimes just wicked, I did not want to put it down."

—*Romancing the Book*

"Be warned, this book sizzles. The chemistry… is explosive. If you want a read that will keep you up past bedtime having to know what will happen next, then this is the book for you."

—*Long and Short Reviews*

"Written with a deft hand… With a tortured hero, a strong heroine, and a touch of mystery, *What the Bride Wore* will become an instant favorite of Regency fans!"

—*Debbie's Book Bag*

"Very entertaining historical romance with wonderfully eccentric characters and a nice mystery... I found myself enthralled from the very beginning."

—*Book Lover and Procrastinator*

"With thrills, romance, madness, and secrets, *What the Bride Wore* was a fantastic read. Lovely!"

—*Imagine a World*

"Exciting, fast-paced Regency romance... just a plain great read. Ms. Lee is a wonderful storyteller."

—*My Book Addiction Reviews*

"This story had it all, troubled hero, beautiful, brave heroine, and frightening villain... Time seemed to fly by as Ms. Lee is able to pull a reader into her imaginary world and not let go until the last page."

—*Librarian Blog Spot*

"Sweet, original, and suspenseful... Fans of heated romance with a touch of mystery will enjoy *What the Bride Wore*."

—*Caffeinated Book Reviewer*

"A delightful and unique series... Lee likes to delve deeply into her characters' minds, making the reader feel that they really know them."

—*Ramblings From This Chick*

"I will definitely be adding Jade Lee to my auto-buy list."

—*Books Like Breathing*

What the GroomWants

JADE LEE

sourcebooks
casablanca

Published by Sourcebooks Casablanca, an imprint of Sourcebooks,
Inc.
P.O. Box 4410, Naperville, Illinois 60567-4410
(630) 961-3900
Fax: (630) 961-2168
www.sourcebooks.com

Printed and bound in Canada.
MBP 10 9 8 7 6 5 4 3 2 1

One

WENDY DREW CLUTCHED THE SMALL SATCHEL TIGHT to her stomach. She held it as Freddie pulled open the heavy office door. Then he gestured her inside, a smirk on his thick, flat face.

She ignored it. After all, she'd been coming to this gambling hell for months. Or was it more than a year now? It didn't matter. Her time here was done, and she felt a surge of mixed feelings at that.

Part of her would miss the excitement of the gambling hell. The thick air, the turn of a card, and the rattle of dice had their own allure. Money, desperation, lust—all those intense emotions—had played out a nightly drama before her, enticing enough that she'd been tempted to play as well.

She never did. She was there to work and to pay back her idiot brother's debts. But now she had the money in hand. All of it.

She and Bernard were finally free of Demon Damon. Or at least they would be the moment she handed over her satchel of coins. So with a surge of relief, she stepped into the luxurious office. Damon was there, his hair dark, his body languid, and his smile like a temptation from the devil himself.

Wendy wasted no time. "I've got it all," she said clearly. "I'm here to pay back everything Bernard owes."

If anything, the man's smile widened, though there was something horribly feral about the look. "Really?" he drawled, and Wendy felt a shiver of excited fear skate down her spine.

"Yes. Right here." She showed him the small stack of coins.

"Then by all means, my Wendy, come closer. Show me exactly what you have, and I shall tell you if it is enough."

She didn't hesitate. To pause in front of the Demon was asking for disaster. So she walked confidently forward, though her heart was pounding in her chest, and began to neatly line up her coins on his desk. It was all there. And in case he questioned her, she also set down a page of foolscap with the debt, her payments clearly marked. It included the money Bernard made in his job as a footman for the Demon and her own work at his vingt-et-un table.

He raised his eyebrows at that, and perhaps she caught a flash of admiration in his eyes. She hated that his approval could spark happiness inside her. She knew Damon's true character. Had since she'd been a young woman. She knew better than to want anything from the man.

"Sorry, luv," he said, deliberately making his accent coarse as a way to remind her of their shared childhood. Like her, he could use the King's English or the roughest cant. "But you're one hundred twenty-four quid short."

"I am not!" she snapped as she thrust forward her page of accounting.

He smiled, then pulled out the ledger kept locked in his desk drawer. He opened it easily to the page detailing Bernard's debt and turned it for her inspection.

Everything was there, identical to hers, except for two things. The first was obvious, and she pointed to it immediately. "What is that?"

"Your brother's dinner for the last two nights. Added to his tab."

She shook her head. "I told him I won't pay another quid more than his original debt."

She watched the Demon's eyebrows rise in surprise. "You won't pay for his meals?"

"Or his gambling or his clothes or his women. The original debt. Anything else, you take up with him." She lifted her chin as she said it. A sign of clear determination, though inside she shook. It was a hard thing to cut off her brother, but she would not be held hostage to the Demon. Not any more than she had to. And that meant standing strong for any extra debt— including something so small as Bernard's meals.

And while she thought on the responsibilities of a sister to her younger brother, the Demon carefully crossed out the dinner tab on this sheet and created another for Bernard.

"I won't pay any more of his debts," she said clearly. "You cannot get to me through him anymore." She had little reason to suspect that Damon had used Bernard to get to her. After all, he had dozens of women for the asking. But lately, she had begun to wonder. And certainly the way the Demon looked at her made her think that he wanted something specific. Something dark and exciting.

"There. That's done. A hundred twenty-one quid short."

She shook her head. "I don't understand."

"It's in the interest payments," he said, his accent now as fine as brandy. "You rounded down, whereas I rounded up."

"To increase the payment."

He didn't bother to deny it.

She bit her lip. She didn't have it. It was breaking her to give him this much. "How many more days work to pay that off?" This schedule was crippling her. She was the seamstress and co-owner of A Lady's Favor dress shop, but she'd been skimping there to work here.

"One night," he said softly.

"One night?" she gasped.

"In my bed."

She reared back. Even knowing that he wanted her—he'd made no secret of his desire—had not prepared her for such an offer. One night. A hundred and twenty-one quid. Exorbitant. "I'm no whore. Not for you, not for Bernard, not for anybody."

He reached for her face, his long finger smoothing her cheek. At first, she had hated that her skin prickled with awareness whenever he touched her, but it wasn't his touch—or at least, not only his touch. When she was in the Demon's presence there was danger, almost a visceral thrill, and she knew other people felt it too.

She flinched back.

He let his hand drop to his side, his lips curved in amusement. "Very well, then. Man the table every night for a month and—"

"No." She couldn't do that. She'd collapse. She was already so tired she struggled at the shop to see her own stitches. She caught herself just today sewing a line in a gown that weaved like a drunken sailor. "I'll give you another option. Dinner. At my table. Every night."

That would declare her as his mistress for all the world to see. She might not care for herself. What did it matter what the world thought so long as she knew the truth? But the toffs who came to the gaming hell would know. And they might tell their wives and their daughters to stop coming to the dress shop for their clothes. No one wanted a fallen woman sewing the dresses of their virginal debutantes.

So she and Damon set to dickering. The Demon seemed to like a good bout of bargaining. Sometimes, she did too. There was always a way to balance the scales that would work for both sides, but the exhaustion was wearing on her. She just wanted this done. In the end, she agreed to four *private* dinners and another seven nights as hostess in the gaming hell. At least he hadn't demanded that she work at any of his half-dozen brothels.

Once the bargain was sealed, she turned to leave, but his words stopped her cold. He spoke casually, as if just remembering something. But Wendy knew it was a ruse. The Demon did nothing casually.

"I was sorry to hear about your lodgings. Where will you live now?"

She froze, feeling an icy shiver down her spine. "There's nothing wrong with my home." She and her mother had lived there for years since the building in which Wendy had spent her childhood had burned to the ground.

"Oh, perhaps I heard it wrong then."

She turned, anger making her fists clench. "Tell me, Damon."

He leaned back in his chair, a feral grin on his face. "I'm sure I heard it wrong—"

She spit out a curse, a word she hadn't used in a decade. "I am too tired, Damon. What have you done to me now?"

He frowned, and for a moment he looked confused. As if he hadn't realized that she was at the last of her strength. "It's that blighter Lord Idston. He's declared you unsuitable tenants."

She shook her head. She and her mother were the *most* suitable tenants there! They paid their rent on time, brought some respectability to the building, and kept an eye on their neighbors.

Damon simply shrugged. "You should go home and check. But first…" He stood from behind his massive desk, moving with that grace he'd had since he was a small boy. She waited in silence, knowing he would tell her what he wanted in his own time. Demanding answers only made him draw out the tension simply because he could.

He stopped directly in front of her, his smile gentle—an obvious lie.

"I have a set of rooms that would work for you and your mama. Close by, but still safe. Just two blocks from here. It's a grand sight more plush than what you've got now."

She shook her head, wishing she could avoid getting deeper into this man's clutches. The way he looked at her—like she was a sparkling prize set before him—was in its own way heady. No other man looked at her that way, and the Demon always made it easy to give in to his offers.

"I can show it to you. The rent's fair, and I'd have my men help you move."

"How fair?" she asked before she could stop herself.

He shrugged and named a reasonable rent given the location. But she just shook her head. "I don't want to move from where we are. I don't—"

Her words cut off as he stroked her neck. Again, he used only one finger, but the touch went from her jaw, down her neck, and to the edge of her bodice. A slow, feathered stroke so light she might not have noticed, except that she saw him do it. His eyes darkened, his nostrils flared, and she saw triumph in his gaze when she didn't flinch away. How could she? If she weren't looking right at him, she wouldn't have been sure he touched her at all.

"You can't seem to get ahead, can you?" he asked, his voice thick. "Just when your business begins to profit, your brother acts the idiot, your rooms get taken, and now you mistrust every boon as if it contained a hidden snake." He shook his head. "But this one doesn't. I have a place to let. You need one."

"I don't—"

"You do. Lord Idston will have served noticed to your mother this morning."

She winced. "You did it. You made him do it."

His arched his brows, his expression insulted. "I'm powerful, Wendy, but even I cannot predict the vagaries of the gentry."

It was the way he said the word "powerful" that hit her. He slowed it down when he spoke, as if liking the taste of the word. She closed her eyes, cutting off the sight of his dark eyes and chiseled face. And in that moment—when her view was cut off—she felt a tingle in her left nipple. She gasped, her eyes flying open, but he simply stood there as if he hadn't done anything.

"No," she rasped as she backed away. "No!"

He smiled and shrugged, as if her answer meant nothing. The idea left her reeling. One minute she was his prize, the next she was less than nothing.

"As you wish," he said. "Go home. See what your mother says. You can always come back to me. Though don't dally. I can't have the place standing empty on your pleasure."

"I understand," she lied. She didn't understand any of what that man thought or did. And that was the worst of it. Because part of her truly did want to learn. After all, she was a woman six and twenty, never having been kissed by a man. Never touched the way a woman wanted.

Why not accept his moderately priced rooms? Why not have dinner with him? Why not spend one night in his bed for a hundred twenty-one quid? Then she would know what other women knew. Then she would understand the dark promise in his eyes.

But that way lay madness. And likely disaster.

So with a last shake of her head, she fled.

Radley Lyncott stood at the prow and closed his eyes. Weariness dragged at his body.

Moored at the London dock, he couldn't hear his own thoughts, much less the soothing sounds of the sea, but he stood here nonetheless with Matthew beside him. The boy stood like a captain born, not an eleven-year-old cabin boy, and Radley couldn't help but smile.

"You needn't stay," he said. "Your mother will be wanting to see you."

"She's busy," was the boy's terse reply.

Radley didn't look at the boy, but he dropped a hand on the child's shoulder. He felt the stiffness there and waited for the tension to ease. Then he spoke quietly enough for only Matthew to hear.

"Even whores love their children. And all ladies like receiving gifts. She made sure to give you a chance at life, Matthew. One that gives you a good future and a home on the sea. Don't doubt her love just because you're ashamed of her."

Matthew's shoulders tightened as he listened to Radley, but in time the boy's shoulders sagged. "I'm not ashamed exactly."

Radley didn't answer. He had no right. After all, his parents loved him and had provided for him. There was no shame in his parentage—well, not for a few generations—and that made him one of the luckiest men alive. But he saw this struggle in many of his sailors—the shame and the hunger for a better past. "Show her how much of a man you've become, Matthew. Let her be proud of her boy."

He felt Matthew twist to look at him. "You think so?"

The question was vague. Did Radley think he was a man? Did Radley think his mother loved him? Either way, the answer remained the same. "I do. Now go. I can't leave until you do."

The boy frowned. "But lots of captains leave the moment the watch is set."

Rad shrugged. "Aye, but I'm not a captain yet. And this ship is a prize. Have to wait until Mr. Knopp tells me what to do with it."

Matt straightened with pride. "You'll captain it for sure, sir. You brought it in here limping along. No other man could do it better. Mr. Knopp'd be a fool to—"

"Yes, thank you," he said, cutting off the boy's rampant enthusiasm. The boy's words were merely an echo of Radley's private hopes. A captaincy. The chance to make his own fortune in his own way. He was more than ready for the challenge.

And while he shooed the boy off to see his mother, Radley's thoughts turned to his own family. His father was gone now, so he had a mother, a sister, and a woman not yet his bride. She was almost more memory than real, a creation of nights spent dreaming. She had an elfin face and an adorably determined set to her jaw, and he'd wanted her since before she was old enough to be wanted by any man. Her name was Wendy Drew, and he had a fine gift for her in his gear.

It hadn't been proper for him to court her before. And truthfully, he hadn't wanted to brave his parents' disapproval back then. But he was old enough now, as was she. And with a captaincy, he'd have the means to treat her as she deserved.

But not yet. Not until he spoke with Mr. Knopp and gave a full accounting of the cargo, the ship, and the repairs that were needed. And not until the last of the rigging was squared away. He'd be at it now, but it wasn't proper. An acting captain gave the orders. He didn't tie the knots himself. But the inactivity chafed. He wanted to be at his courting.

It was hours before all was set to rights. Mr. Knopp listened to everything Radley had to say, took the log-book and the accounting, then in the way of so many owners, gave no indication as to his thoughts. He was a fair owner and not a fool. With a fleet of boats at his command, there were other hopefuls in his employ. Radley would just have to wait his turn and pray that his work spoke for itself.

He had almost despaired of the promotion until Mr. Knopp's final words.

"Good work, Mr. Lyncott. Very good work indeed."

"Thank you—"

"Oh, and there were some solicitors asking after you. Misters Chase and Pelley. Know what that's about?"

Radley shook his head. "Never heard of them."

"Didn't like them, personally. Nose in the air and all that. Could tell they didn't like talking with a German. Refused to tell me anything about what they wanted with one of my future captains."

Radley barely kept himself from leaping on those last two words. Knopp was watching him closely—as were the sailors on watch—so he kept his expression as calm as he could. "I'll need their direction, if you wouldn't mind, sir."

"Oh right." His employer fished around in a pocket

until he produced a linen card, somewhat the worse for wear. "I promised to send them word when you arrived, but I suppose you could stop by all on your own." The man narrowed his eye. "You'll want to find out from the clerks what's what before you meet with the legal men. I don't need to tell you that I don't like my employees in ugly with the law."

Radley frowned. Disquiet grew in his belly. "Did it seem that there was trouble?"

"No, else I would have told you sooner. But those types are nothing but trouble, if you ask me. Probably some lord wanting something." Again, he eyed Radley with a hard stare. "Could be about a woman," Knopp said, obviously fishing.

Radley shook his head. "No woman, sir. Not that would have a solicitor." Unless it had something to do with his sister. She was housekeeper to a Scottish lord.

Mr. Knopp studied his face for a moment longer, then shrugged. "Best find out what you can, soon as you can. Those types don't relish waiting on the likes of us."

"Yes, sir. Right after I visit my mother."

That was it. A short conversation that was more an attempt to find out information. But Radley was as much in the dark as Mr. Knopp, so he set it aside in his thoughts. He was finally free to do as he willed, and that would not be chasing after some high-in-the-instep solicitor.

By the time he finally made it to land, the afternoon was far advanced. If he saw his mother or sister first, it would be too late for afternoon callers. The idea was ridiculous. After all, Wendy would be at work now as head seamstress for A Lady's Favor dress shop, which she co-owned. She cared nothing for proper visiting hours. But it was one of the ways he could show her respect. A true gentleman followed the rules of proper courtship, and in this way he showed that he valued her as a lady.

Which meant that he had precious few minutes to get to the lodgings she shared with her mother. He would pay a quick call, do the pretty with her mama, while arranging a better time to visit—one where he could see Wendy—and then be off to his own mama.

He walked briskly, knowing the route by heart. She'd moved after the fire, but not out of the neighborhood. He had grown up in London and knew the byways from the dock to this quarter better than anyone.

He mounted the steps to their rooms two at a time. He hadn't slept above a few hours in the last three nights, but the weariness was fading fast as he neared his destination. He'd just knocked once when he heard it: a woman's sobs, deep and gut-wrenching.

He frowned, wondering for a moment whether to proceed when a small voice spoke from behind him.

"A sad tale there," said a young girl of about eight. He didn't remember her name, but he knew the type. She would know all the neighborhood gossip and would share it for a price. A small price now—as she was young—but in a few years, she could turn bad if someone didn't take a strong hand in her rearing. "And look at you, just back from the sea. Have you seen your mama yet?"

Did he know her? He hadn't a clue, but obviously she knew him.

"What happened here?" he asked. She got a canny look in her eye, but didn't have time to capitalize on his question. The door was wrenched open by Wendy's mother—her face streaked with tears and her hair a mess.

"Henry! The most terrible thing has happened!"

He shook his head, apologizing even as she recognized him. "Not Henry, Mrs. Drew. I'm sorry—"

"Radley! My goodness, look at you!" She sniffed and wiped her eyes. "You haven't seen Henry today have you?" she said with a slight hiccup of a sob.

"We're on different ships. He came in with *The Northern Glory*, likely a week back. But I followed afterwards on—"

"Yes, yes. He came back over a week now. But I've sent for him. I…" She hiccupped again, and then her words were lost.

Radley was all too aware of the girl standing behind him. Whatever the tale was, there was no point in declaring it to the world. "If I might come in, Mrs. Drew? I'd love a spot of tea. Then you can tell me what you've done to find Henry. I'm sure I can locate him, if you give me a little time."

She nodded and was just stepping back to let him in when they heard it: footsteps running hard. Light enough to be a woman's, fast enough to be desperate. He knew without looking that it was her. *Wendy*. He knew, and yet he still had no time to brace himself as he turned to look.

There she was, her eyes wide, her bonnet askew, and her skirts stained with mud. She topped the stairs in a leap, and then skidded to a halt before them. Her gaze caught for a moment on him, then narrowed on her mother's distraught expression.

"I'm going to kill him," Wendy cried. "I'm going to kill him and feed him to the dogs. And you—" she said as she pointed a finger at Radley. "You're going to help me."

Her mother was as shocked as he was. "Wendy!" she snapped even as she wiped away her tears.

He rocked back on his heels while a smile tugged at his lips. That was his Wendy: fierce, passionate, and impetuous. And now he could finally start courting her.

Two

"PERHAPS WE SHOULD STEP INSIDE."

Wendy grimaced as she looked at the one man she'd never expected to see standing in front of her door. He was gesturing her inside. And lest she be confused, his gaze shifted to the shadows behind her where Little Lucy stood listening to every word she said.

Damnation, this was *not* what she needed. Radley Lyncott was head and shoulders above other men. Rumor had it that he'd been born to the nobility, though on the wrong side of the blanket. Whether that was true or not, his mother had done her damnedest to make sure everyone knew they were related to the Duke of Bucklynde. Truth be told, Radley had never seemed concerned with that. His heart and soul had always been for the sea. And seafaring he had gone, appearing every once in a while bearing gifts that were the envy of everyone in the neighborhood.

There was a time when she'd thought to catch his eye. A time when she had dangled herself before the prince of their little pocket of London. But whenever she'd tried to put on airs, he had been the one to point out her deficiencies. She hadn't had the polish his mother taught to lucky girls in their neighborhood. And by the time Wendy had learned it, the man was gone.

At least she'd managed to get him to take Henry with him. Otherwise, she might now be dealing with both her idiot brothers' problems instead of just Bernard's. Unless she was wrong. Unless this had nothing to do with Demon Damon. And that, of course, was what she needed Radley Lyncott to help her with.

But first—yes, he was right—they needed to be inside and away from Lucy's prying eyes.

"Of course," she said in as polite a manner as possible. "Pray, Mr. Lyncott, would you come inside? Mama, please put on some tea. I'm sure Mr. Lyncott is thirsty, and it is teatime, after all. I would like a cup myself."

Then she brushed straight by them both as she went inside. She was putting on airs, of course, acting a great deal more elevated than she was. But she needed to get inside before he did to make sure their home wasn't in a state of disarray. She and her mother kept things as neat as possible, but Henry was home and had been for more than a week. She needn't have worried. Apparently, shipboard life had taught her brother something. Everything appeared in its place—most especially Henry's seaman bag, set in the corner.

"Where is Henry?" she asked as she pulled off her bonnet and tried to neaten her hair. It was impossible. She'd run nearly the entire way from Demon Damon's, so even if her bonnet had kept her hair from the worst of the wind, her skirts were stained with mud, and her chemise was stuck to her skin like a wet rag. She felt completely done in, and it if weren't for the fury that burned in her blood, she'd collapse right here and now.

"I don't know where he is," her mother said as she put the kettle over the grate. "I sent messages to you at the shop and him at the pub. I hadn't expected you yet. You must have run like the wind."

"I wasn't at the shop." And wasn't that just like her mother to send two neighbors—likely two gossips like Lucy—to find them. It would set the neighborhood to talking for sure. But of course, given what she feared had happened, they would be talking in any event.

She sighed and folded her hands against her belly. It was the only way she'd learned to hide her fists. "But I'm here now, Mama. Tell me the worst of it."

Her mother managed to pull herself together. She dried her tears and spoke in a clear voice. "A man was here. Said he represented Lord Idston, who owns this building, and that he's turning us out. We have until tomorrow night to be gone."

Wendy felt her teeth grind together. So the Demon was right. "Did he say why?"

"Said we're terrible tenants. I told him we pay our rent on time, keep everything clean, and that we've even helped our neighbors when they couldn't pay. He should ask people. Everyone knows what good people we are. He didn't care. Didn't want to hear any of it. Nine years we've lived here. Nine years! And now..." Her voice choked off, and she looked at

Wendy with watery eyes. Her next words were half sobbed. "Where will we go?"

"To my mother's," said Mr. Lyncott in a firm voice. "She's got plenty of room with Caroline living out as a housekeeper. Henry can sleep at his berth, and I will too. You'll have to bunk tight—the two of you in one room—but my mother will be pleased to have you."

Wendy turned to him, relief at war with dislike. She was enormously grateful for the offer, but he'd just returned home. How like a man to assume that his mother would take in guests without even asking.

"Really?" she asked, trying to keep the anger from her voice. It wasn't aimed at him, but she had all this fury boiling inside her. She didn't know what to do with it, so it leaked out in her words. "And have you talked to your mother in the last year? How do you know she has room? How do you know she'll be pleased to have two strays in her home, and worse, in her son's room?" What she remembered of Mrs. Lyncott was that Radley's room was as sacred as a cathedral. No one could stay there but the man himself.

Radley's cheeks flushed a ruddy red, but he still held himself as high as Prinny himself. "She'll greet you with open arms. You can rely on me."

She swallowed, nodding in acceptance. He'd said those words once before, and he had done right by them. He'd sworn he'd look after her brother, and Henry was as fine a man as she could have expected. Certainly, her brother had done the maturing himself, but he was healthy, whole, and apparently a fine seaman, if his pay was anything to judge by.

She had no cause to cast aspersions at Mr. Radley Lyncott now. So she forced herself to nod her thanks. "Just be sure please. Go ask your mother now, and if it's all right, we'll come tomorrow. With gratitude."

He flashed her an easy smile, deepening the weather lines in his face, and making him all that much more handsome. There was a joy in him when he did that— had been since he was a boy. And not a female around could resist him when he flashed those white teeth with a sparkle in his copper eyes.

"So I won't be needed for a murder?" he teased.

She snorted. "Oh, there may still be one, never you fear." Then she quieted. She shouldn't be talking so breezily about killing the Demon. Certainly most people would know she was blustering in her fury. And those same people would assume she meant Lord Idston. But she knew the truth and so would Damon.

"Who's talking murder?" asked a laughing voice from the door. Wendy spun around to see her older brother, Henry. He and Radley were the same age, but couldn't be more different. Unlike the proper Mr. Lyncott, Henry was a man written in sloppy lines. With his brown hair mussed, circles under his green eyes, and his clothing rumpled, he was an easy man to disregard. And yet, somehow he managed to find companionship wherever he went, be it male, female, or even canine. Everyone seemed to like him. He was her brother Henry, and he filled the doorway with his carefree presence.

"Henry!" their mother cried with relief. "I'm so glad Lucy found you."

"I found her, actually," he said. "On the way home." Wendy noted that he didn't say home from where, and she didn't want to ask. "What's this about being thrown out?"

Their mother nodded as she wiped her tears. "Nine years—"

"'Bout time to find another place, then, right?"

"But nine years—" she said again.

Henry waved away her concerns even as he clasped hands with Mr. Lyncott. "Radley, old man! Didn't realize you'd made it in. Nine years in one place makes it smell bad, don't you think?" He turned and sniffed the air. "Bad odor here."

"That's you, you lout," said Wendy as she cuffed her brother affectionately. Some days she thought the man completely useless, but on days like today, his easy acceptance of... well, everything, made her worries fade a little. The Demon made her feel like a worm on a hook, but Henry could make her think that every setback was a good choice.

Her mother chimed in with her own sniff. "Where were you, Henry? You smell like a brothel."

Her brother's eyes widened in horror. "A brothel? Never you say that!" He sniffed at his sleeve, then held it up to Mr. Lyncott. "What do you think, Radley? I think I smell like a garden of roses. Roses and Lilies and Emilies and Marys. Ah, sweet Mary..."

Mr. Lyncott rolled his eyes. "I think we'd best forget that. I told your mother she can stay with mine."

"What? Right generous of you. So you'll be staying on the prize ship then while my mother kicks you out of your bed? Smart man—sleeping elsewhere. Mamas tend to ask too many questions." He waggled his eyebrows for emphasis.

Meanwhile, Wendy took a deep breath. "Henry, could you help Mama pack?"

"Pack?" he cried in mock horror as he picked up a pillow she'd made when she was ten. "It's all trash. We'll just throw it out."

"Throw it out!" exclaimed her mother with gratifying horror. "You put that down. We'll pack it for our next place."

"This old thing? Whatever for?" Then the two set to bickering. It could have been horrible, but with Henry, Wendy just shook her head. It was noisy and sometimes uncomfortable, but he'd gotten their mother to stop crying. And as they bickered over the crockery next, Henry paused enough to shove Mr. Lyncott.

"Make her stop doing that, will you?" he said as he gestured at Wendy. "Damned uncomfortable sight to see my sis doing that all the time. Makes a brother jumpy."

Wendy frowned at her brother. "What are you talking about?"

It was Mr. Lyncott who answered, his voice a soothing rumble beneath the higher notes of her mother's diatribe about ignorant sons.

"You're rubbing your chest," he said gently. "Does it pain you?"

She looked down in surprise, and sure enough, there was her fist planted above her heart, pressing down. She dropped it with a self-conscious shrug. "I ran too fast coming here."

He didn't argue. Instead, his expression softened. "You'll find a way through, Wind. You always do."

She blinked, startled by his use of her nickname. He'd started calling her that on his first leave. He said it was because she blew about like the wind, then he'd tweak her hair or her cheek or her nose. She'd cry out in indignation, and he'd just laugh, saying he was trying to catch the wind.

"I haven't heard that name in years," said her mother.

Wendy nodded. She'd been thinking the same thing. Meanwhile, she looked about her home, her heart in her throat. Where would they go? Even if Radley's mother allowed them to stay, they couldn't rest there forever. They needed a home.

"Do you still want this?" her brother asked, as he held up her spare chemise. It had been drying in her bedroom, but for some reason, Henry thought it best to bring it out for everyone to see. "Looks a bit small, if you ask me," he said as he peered at her chest.

"Henry!" Mama exclaimed.

Mr. Lyncott turned a snort into a cough, and Wendy shot her brother a murderous look. "You just like touching lady's things. Now put that back!"

He shrugged. "Just saying you should toss it in the rubbish if it don't fit anymore."

He was right, damn him. It was too small, but she'd be damned if she admitted that now in front of company. So she glared at her brother, then pointedly turned her back.

"Mr. Lyncott, would you mind escorting me back to the shop? We can discuss my plans to murder my brother along the way."

Both men laughed, the sound beautiful in a way she hadn't experienced in a long time. It was so full and open that it made her think of the wide, blue ocean, which she'd never even seen.

"Well, at least you have come to the right person for advice. I've been planning ways to gut your brother for years now."

"Then, we do have things to discuss," she said as she grabbed her bonnet and headed for the door. He joined her quickly enough, but her thoughts were faster. By the time he'd made it to her side, she'd left behind all thoughts of packing and chemises that were too small. Her mind was back on her growing list of tasks for the day.

There was work at the shop, a new home to find and lease, and then there was the growing problem of Demon Damon. It was that last one that had her mood souring. She meant to be done with the man, but she didn't know how. She shuddered at the thought of turning into the man's whore or spending her life at his vingt-et-un tables. She didn't fool herself into believing that one more month's work would have her free. After all, she'd thought she'd be done today, but he'd found another way to hold her. What would be his next gambit? And the next?

"You are doing it again," Mr. Lyncott said softly as he caught the fist that rubbed her chest.

She flushed as he gently pressed it down. "I was just thinking—"

"Of something terribly unpleasant," he said in a low voice. He released a low sound that was half sigh, half growl. "You can't commit murder, Wind. I don't care what has happened or why. It will change you in bad ways."

She swallowed, wondering for a split second if she could tell Radley the truth, if somehow he would help her. The Demon had to be stopped one way or another. It was bad enough that he ran gaming hells that had half the aristocracy in his pocket. But she suspected he was behind all the terrible things that had happened lately. Not to her, but to her friends. Murder, attempted murder, and any number of small harassments. Could it really all be laid at the Demon's door? If the answer were yes, then she and her friends would be in danger as long as the man lived. But could she really kill the bastard?

She swallowed and looked away. She didn't like it when the laughing prince of her childhood turned dark and serious. And she didn't like it that he knew what she was thinking even before she did.

"Very well then," she said airily. "You shall tell me exactly what follies my brother Henry committed while at sea with you. Every single one, mind you, so that I can tease him when I next see him."

"Oh my," he drawled as he held out his arm. "We shall have to walk very slowly then. This might take a while."

Good. And while he kept her laughing, perhaps the ache in her heart would ease, and she would indeed find a way free. But she doubted it. The dark and serious side of her personality knew she was caught, and it was that side that made her say her next words.

"And if there is murder in my future, Mr. Lyncott, then you needn't fear I'll involve you or my brother. I shall need someone with more experience." And at that moment, her mind flashed to her younger brother,

Bernard. It was true that he'd gotten her mixed up in this problem in the first place, and she'd long since suspected that there were hidden depths in him. And that they were hidden for a reason.

Meanwhile, Mr. Lyncott stopped walking and looked down hard at her. "What have I missed, Wind? What has happened since I have been away?"

She didn't answer because he had hit on the problem exactly. He had missed too much. After all, he was the prince of the neighborhood, destined for great things that took him outside London to the world at large. She on the other hand was stuck here. That had always been true for them both. So no matter what had happened in the years since he'd been away, her path was set.

&

Radley didn't like this silent Wendy. She walked beside him, her hand on his arm and her manner poised, behaving now nothing like the wild thing he remembered from his childhood—always dashing one way or the next, always with big ideas and detailed plans. How far had she gotten with those dreams? And at what cost?

When she didn't answer his first question, he tried a different tack. "How is the dress shop doing? Have you made it into a success?"

"It's better and better every day," she answered with a smile. "Helaine is married now to Lord Redhill. She brings in the nobs like no one else. She frets, of course, given her past, but she's a worrier."

He nodded, not truly remembering who Helaine

was beyond her relationship to Wendy. She was co-owner of the dress shop and the designer. But beyond that, he had no idea what Wendy alluded to about Helaine's past.

"We've got a lady's shoemaker too. A woman, who designs for women. Married just a week ago and…" Her voice trailed off on a shudder. She tried to suppress it, but he felt it nevertheless.

"What happened?"

"Someone tried to murder Irene. It happened…" She shook her head. "Doesn't matter."

"Was the man caught?"

She nodded, but in slow motion, as if she wasn't quite sure.

He narrowed his eyes, slowing their steps even further. "What aren't you telling me?"

She shrugged, trying to be casual. "What if… well, what if the man apprehended wasn't responsible?"

"I don't understand what you mean. He attacked, didn't he?"

"He did but… what if someone put him up to it? Someone made him—"

"Made him attempt murder?" He pressed her hand where it rested on his arm. "No one can be forced to kill. There's a moment before you strike when the decision is all yours. Doesn't matter the cause or the pain or the reason behind it. When it comes to striking that death blow, it's a choice."

She frowned as she looked at him, and he felt the shift in her thoughts in the air around him. She had ceased thinking about her problems and now looked at his.

"Wind—" he began, but she cut him off.

"You've killed more than fish," she said. A state-ment not a question. But he answered it nonetheless.

"We were attacked by pirates on this last voyage. It's happened before, but I was young the last time. Green and caught flat-footed. But this time, we saw them coming." He looked away. This time he'd been in charge. Their captain was down with a fever, barely functional, though he tried. Gave a good accounting of himself given the circumstances, but the man could barely stand much less direct a defense.

Which meant as first mate, the command had been in Radley's hands. He had given the orders to kill, to destroy their attackers without mercy.

"Battles on water are ugly things. Hours waiting, seeing them coming, and then it's all a blur until it's finished."

"You survived though," she said, her voice barely audible.

He nodded. "We won. Crippled the pirates, took their ship, and I sailed their vessel home as prize." He'd also sliced a man's throat open and barely noticed the warm spray of his blood. He'd watched dispassion-ately as five men plummeted to their deaths, a result of his order to fire. And worst of all, he'd judged their leader guilty and performed the execution with an icy calm. "I'll likely gain a captaincy from it."

"You don't seem happy about that."

"Oh, I am. I've wanted it all my life. My own ship, leading the men to profit, the freedom to choose the best course." He turned to her. "But I've changed, Wind."

"You've grown up. We all do."

He shook his head. How did he explain how different the world was at sea? The deprivations, the unending wet, and the capricious, brutal nature of his life there. And yet, he loved it. There was beauty there. A call to his soul that he didn't understand but couldn't deny.

"What are you thinking?" she asked. "You look sad."

"That I'm a sailor, Wind. And when I chose that life, I gave up the part that could live quietly here."

"But do you want to live here?" she said. "You're to be a captain, master of your own ship. That's better than anyone from the old neighborhood. That's like being a king."

He smiled. "You own a dress shop that caters to the *ton*, Wind. That's a miracle that puts me in awe."

She smiled, and her whole face brightened, even though her words seemed contradictory to her obvious pride with her achievement. "Constant worries, constant work."

"But you love it?"

She nodded. "As you must love the sea."

"Yes."

They walked in silent accord then, skirting the trash and the people that clogged the streets. He didn't like the crowd of buildings, hated the disorganization of London now, although he hadn't as a boy. At least on the ship, there was a pattern and a rhythm. If there was anything like that here, he didn't discern it.

But Wendy obviously did. Even though she was a woman, her fingertips light on his arm, it was she who led them through the streets. She knew the direction to her shop, but more than that, she understood the dance of people on land. And in this, he was content to follow. He wasn't going to ignore, however, the protective instincts that Wendy's plight had ignited in him.

"You have yet to tell me the real problem, Wind. Why have you been suddenly thrown out of your home?"

She sighed. "I'm not sure. That's what I hope you can find out. You're a man and can ask questions that won't get answers coming from a woman. You're to be a captain and can talk to solicitors so that they'll answer."

"I would not be too sure of that, but I can certainly try."

"And…" She bit her lip, looking suddenly nervous for a second. He wouldn't have caught the look if he hadn't been watching her so closely. Then she lifted her chin and spoke her mind. "Perhaps you could meet with Lord Idston. He's the one who will have the truth."

"Do you know where I can meet him? I don't have any connections to the world he frequents."

She nodded. "I have a guess where he'll be. There's a gaming hell he likes."

There was extra tension in her voice, and he wondered what she knew of gaming hells. How close to that world had she wandered?

"I'm a sailor on leave," he said quietly. "It would be the easiest thing to wander into a hell."

She looked at him, gratitude in her green eyes. "I need to know. I need to know if it's an unlucky thing or something more."

"I'll do what I can, Wind." For her, he would do that much and more.

"Thank you," she breathed. She stopped their steps then. It took a moment to realize that they stood in an alley beside a back door.

"Is this your shop?"

She pointed to the door. "The workroom is right there."

They stood facing each other then. They were close. She was a small woman, almost tiny. But there was nothing small in her character or her bearing. So when he bent his head, it was as much a bow to her regal nature as it was as a man staking a claim to her lips.

She didn't expect it, which was nearly laughable. He had thought of her as his wife for so long, he'd forgotten that she knew nothing of his intentions. His gifts these last years had been given under her brother's name. Tokens of affection from Henry to his sister, or so the packages claimed.

So when he pressed his mouth to hers, she gasped in surprise. Her eyes widened, her lips parted, and though she might not have invited his advances, he was too far gone to stop. He had to kiss her. He'd been waiting nearly ten years to do so.

He took her lips, and before he could stop himself, he wrapped his arm around her back and pulled her close, plundering her mouth with his kiss, putting all his love and desire into it. In this way, he declared his intentions to marry the wind.

Three

Wendy realized his intention early, but she could not believe it was possible. The boy prince from her childhood standing before her now as a man? And with desire in his eyes? Such a thing wasn't possible, and yet he was touching her face, his calloused thumb a fiery stroke across her cheek. Then his mouth descended, and she was shocked enough to gasp, but not so shocked that she refused him.

He was everything she'd ever wanted, and so she opened herself to him. And when his fingers trailed into her hair, she swayed toward him. Her hands pressed against his chest, and she felt the muscles underneath his clothing—banked power in a broad expanse. But most of all, she felt his mouth growing insistent, his tongue sweeping inside her lips, and the heat of him as he plundered her mouth.

She was submissive at first, enthralled by the sensations he gave her. But she soon grew bolder, twisting her tongue with his, clutching his shirt beneath his coat. And the closer she got, the more their mouths fused, the less she thought about Damon or moving or even the sewing she had to do. Her thoughts fled into the rhythm of his kiss, into the grip of his arm around her waist. And into the sweet, wonderful scent that had nothing to do with London and everything to do with fresh air and clean water.

Then he ended the kiss in a slow withdrawal that pained her. As his intensity lessened, her worries crowded back. Each second of his withdrawal added more to her burdens, and she whimpered at the weight. To be free for even a few moments made the return of her cares all the more burdensome.

"Wind," he murmured, his voice low and gravelly.

She didn't respond, except to clutch his shirt harder. She was not ready to return to her list of tasks, and he had just shown her the perfect escape.

But he wrapped his hands around hers and stilled her frantic motions. "Wind," he repeated, his voice growing clearer. "May I call on you tomorrow?"

She blinked, confused by his formality. He wanted to call on her? Like a high-born gentleman to the likes of her? She nearly laughed. In her jumbled thoughts, she wanted something a great deal more carnal than a gentlemanly visit.

She closed her eyes, trying to gather her wits. For all that she had little experience, her time in the hells had exposed her to a myriad intriguing words and ideas. Some of them burned in her memory and made her wonder. It was that curiosity that had her lifting her head to his.

"Yes," she said. Or she thought she had. Instead, the word sounded more like, "Why?"

His lips curved into a smile. "You kiss me like that

and then ask me why?" He touched her jaw, another fiery caress across her skin. "Wind, I have thought about you often over the years."

She looked at him, trying to understand. She had thought of him relatively little, except as a half-forgotten wish. Her life was too full, too busy to spend time on what might have been. But on a ship, she supposed there were long hours of doing nothing but staring at water. Of course he would reminisce about the days of his youth.

When she didn't answer, a flash of worry crossed his face. "Wind? May I?"

So compelling was his gaze that she nodded before she thought deeply about it. The hows and the whys were impossible. "I will be working." She was not someone who sat around waiting for afternoon callers.

"We could walk through the park."

She bit her lip. She did love to walk through Hyde Park at the fashionable hour. She wore something gray and ugly, then sat on a bench watching as fashionable ladies paraded by wearing the dresses she'd sewn.

"I would like that," she said, a smile curving her lips. She could show him her creations on a countess or a baroness. Would he like them? Would he be proud of her? She had no need for his approval, but she'd like it nonetheless.

He grinned. "I'll come here tomorrow afternoon to take you to the park. We'll sit and watch the peacocks strut by."

She nodded, feeling awkward and excited all at once. It had been years since she felt this giddy uncertainty, and she wasn't sure she liked it. But she was powerless to stop the simmering heat that built in her chest and slowly climbed to her cheeks.

Then she heard a noise from the workroom. Someone was coming to the back door. "I need to go," she said.

"Of course." Then he took her hand and kissed it, bowing as he did, as if he were greeting a duchess. It made the sizzle in her blood pop faster and hotter. "Until tomorrow then, Wind."

"Good day, Mr. Lyncott," she said as her apprentice Tabitha pulled open the back door with an armful of trash. Wendy gave a sharp look to the girl, but said nothing as she walked inside. Her thoughts were on Radley Lyncott the rest of her day.

It made her stitches uneven at times, her work slower than usual, but she couldn't make herself stop—the prince of the neighborhood coming to call on her. But of course, she was a successful shop owner now, she reminded herself. Not a dirty girl running wild in the London streets. She was a proper woman, and it was not so far a stretch to think of such a man.

Or at least it wasn't until that evening, when she was an hour into dealing vingt-et-un. She had a full table, as usual. The men liked her because she smiled. They called her the Green Lady of Mystery because of her green eyes. It had become a game to discover her name or get her to say something tart. Her witty tongue brought them to her table, and she had to admit she enjoyed the freedom to say something cutting. And the sharper her wit, the higher her tips, so she worked at being clever.

She also worked hard at listening. Half the value

of the gaming hell to Damon was not in the money, but in the information. Deep play and a steady flow of alcohol loosened many a tongue, and the Demon paid his dealers well for juicy gossip. And since she cared not who was having an affair with whom, or which lord was embezzling from what fund, she had no difficulty telling such things to Damon if he took money off her brother's debt.

Until tonight.

Tonight's topic was about a lowly sailor now become a duke. The story was simple. The man was descended from a disgraced third son of the Duke of Bucklynde. The rift had occurred three generations back, but the old man had never disowned the son, although he made well known his disapproval of the boy's choice of wife. Everyone in the current generation was waiting until the crotchety nob died to reunite with the disgraced branch.

Then disaster struck. Smallpox went rampant through the ducal seat, wiping out nearly the entire family, the associated village, and a good deal of the neighboring hamlets. It was called a plague, and the area had been isolated simply because no one would risk venturing near.

The sickness had run its course, and it was time to take stock, bring comfort to the grieving, and rebuild the dukedom. But all the men had died.

All except the grandson of the disgraced third son. The man was a sailor, only recently come to port. Imagine, they said, going to bed one night as a poor sailor and waking up the next as a duke.

Wendy smiled at that, as did everyone else. It was

the dream of every poor laborer: the wish to suddenly wake up as a wealthy nob. A beautiful dream, until she heard the man's name.

Radley Lyncott, now the Duke of Bucklynde.

"What?" she gasped, unable to stop herself. "What was his name?"

Everyone's attention abruptly riveted on her. "Do you know him? What's he like? Have you danced with him, Green Lady?"

The questions came thick and fast, but only one man answered her question. It was the Demon, sauntering up behind her.

"Radley Lyncott, my dear. Imagine that."

The men turned to the Demon. "So you know him then?" they asked.

Demon nodded. "Indeed, I do. We were once the best of friends."

That was a stretch perhaps, but not a large one. Meanwhile, Wendy's hands had gone numb. Radley was a duke? Her Radley?

But of course he wasn't *her* Radley. And likely never would be now, if the rumors were true. An aspiring ship's captain could court a dressmaker, but a duke was meant for someone a great deal finer than she. She'd only had an afternoon to linger in sweet dreams of herself and Radley, but in those few hours, the longing had become precious. To have it ripped away so bizarrely—like a random throw of the dice— cut her deeply.

Radley was a duke!

Meanwhile, Damon had his hand underneath her elbow, smoothly lifting her from her seat. "My apologies, gents, but I require the Green Lady's attention for a moment. Sara here will keep you entertained."

Wendy stood. She had no choice, unless she wanted to make a scene.

She tucked her thoughts away, forcing her mind to center on the here and now. She was walking with Demon Damon and could not afford to let her wits go begging.

"Imagine, little Radley's a duke now," he said.

"He was never 'little' to either of us." He'd been older than both of them and taller as well.

"But look how much we've both grown." He directed her to the stairs, climbing until they looked down at the main floor of the hell. The smoke was not yet thick, so they could see the whole area. Damon preened like a king surveying his kingdom. A king and… Her mind stuttered for a moment, but the truth was hard to deny. Standing here like this, Damon proclaimed to the world that she was his woman.

"Listen," he said as he tilted his head to hear better. She had seen him do this often, but had never understood until now. From right here, she could hear nearly everything in the room. The rattle of dice, the murmur of conversation, even the slap of a card punctuated by the bark of a laugh. Or better yet—from Damon's perspective—the groan when a man lost.

There was a rhythm here: a cadence and a beat, like the workings of a great beast. And Damon was the one in charge. He was the one who controlled the lifeblood of money and information here.

Wendy leaned against the railing, feeling the power in a way she never had before. The hell was alive, and she stood beside its brain. Damon didn't even move when he spoke. If she hadn't been looking, she could have imagined the words came from the air itself.

"Have you seen him since he docked?"

"Radley Lyncott?" she asked.

"Yes."

"Yes." She never lied to Damon; it was too dangerous. But she also rarely told him the full truth. "He visited my brother when I was at home."

"Did he know about his inheritance?"

She shook her head. "I don't think so."

"So he saw you before even visiting his mother."

She flinched, startled that he had been that perceptive. "He did not come to see me. He and my brother…"

He waved her into silence, uninterested in her evasions. "Look around you, Wendy. This is my world, and I have two more like this."

And brothels as well. Not to mention a couple of thieving rings. Damon had his hands in any number of pies.

"I have wealth larger than any dukedom, and I'm more powerful than Prinny."

"That's treason!" she cried, stunned that he would match power with the crown, even in words.

He shrugged. "It is the truth. I have more money than the regent, more influence, and a larger circle of people who flow through my doors."

She turned away, disturbed by his words, but excited too. After all, she would never stand beside Prinny and banter with him. But she was here with Damon.

"What has Prinny done for his people?" he

continued. "What does he do that improves any-one's lot?"

She snorted. "What do you do but line your own pockets?"

He turned to look at her, his expression sad. It startled her to see such emotion haunt his face.

"You do not know me as well as you think," he said. "I am not a monster. I never have been."

She shook her head, unwilling to believe anything he said.

He huffed out a breath. "I have never lied to you. I have treated you honestly, and I take nothing from anyone that is not freely given." He gestured to the floor below. "What need do I have to steal? They are eager to spend their blunt."

"What of your whores? I have heard of your initia-tion rooms."

His eyes narrowed in anger. "I have never forced a woman in my life. There are whores enough that come begging to my doors. I give them fair coin and a safe place to work. Food and clothing as well. I even provide for their get."

She nodded, knowing it was true. "The children go to the thieving rings."

"Again, I give them food and shelter."

"But you know what they do."

He sighed as he looked at the floor. But she had the impression he did not see what was below. Instead, he was thinking of something else, remem-bering the past, perhaps, or envisioning a future that she couldn't imagine.

"I have made a place for myself and for countless

others in this world. Prinny has done nothing but grow fat and disparage his wife."

Wendy had no response to that. She knew nothing of politics and cared even less. But she began to see Damon's point. The world was filled with vices. He did nothing but profit from them while keeping his employees safe.

There were other hells in London, but none were safe for a woman to work. In terms of the evil, Damon was perhaps the best of the lot. He was certainly the smartest.

She shifted uncomfortably beside him, unsure of things she'd once thought were absolutes. "You didn't bring me here to talk politics, Damon. What do you want?"

"How is your mother?"

"She is just fine," she answered tartly, mostly because she knew his real question. *Where will you go now that you have been tossed on the street?* "She is packing. We will be sharing the home of..." Her voice trailed away, the truth hitting her hard. They couldn't stay at the home of Mrs. Lyncott. Not if she truly was the mother of a duke now. The woman hadn't liked Wendy when they were of the same social status. Now the social gap was too great.

She swallowed and looked at her hands, trying to hide the panic. They were to leave their home by tomorrow night. Where would they go?

"Wendy?"

She didn't look at him. She knew what he was offering, and more than anything, she didn't want to say yes. She couldn't! And yet, what choice did she have?

He touched her chin, slowly drawing her to look at him.

"Do you have a place to stay?"

"Not yet," she whispered.

His hand was cool on her skin, and she shivered.

"You know I have a place open for you two. Don't let your fear of me put your mother on the street."

She wanted to say she wasn't afraid, but it was patently untrue. She wanted to say she had friends and places to turn to other than him, but she didn't—not for a place to live. Not on such short notice. Meanwhile, he continued speaking, his voice low and mesmerizing.

"You are right to be afraid of me. I am a dangerous man. I have killed men and women without a second thought. But I want you, my Wendy. And when your brother was a fool in my club, I seized on the opportunity to pull you to my side."

So it was true. He had used Bernard to get to her. "I am nothing," she whispered.

"You are a very great deal. Smart, beautiful, and talented. Better yet, you have a practical nature. You see the shadows and don't judge those who are caught in them." He tugged her toward him, and she found herself powerless to resist.

"I don't judge them. But you are the one who creates those shadows," she said, her voice tight with disdain.

He arched a brow. "You don't seriously believe me to be that powerful. I am merely a man. And one who wants you very much."

Her breath caught. Never had she allowed herself to be this near him. Tight enough to smell the mint of his breath above the harsher scents of tobacco and wine.

Close enough to feel goose bumps prickle her skin as her knees grew weak and her nipples pulled tight.

"Look deeper into me, Wendy. See me for the man I am, not the image I project to survive."

"No," she whispered. Or she thought she did. She wasn't sure, as it wasn't a loud word. It certainly had no power to stop him as he closed the distance between them.

He took her mouth, slanting across the lips that he'd already prepared with his thumb. She trembled in his arms as his tongue slipped between her teeth. She was a woman unfamiliar with kisses. In truth, she'd rarely felt a man's touch, and that was usually her brothers' rough hugs. To have two such kisses in one day confused her. To be held in the arms of a man who terrified her was in equal parts horrifying and exhilarating. He wasn't hurting her, and yet his arms tightened around her, and his mouth took control. She had little choice but to obey the orders of his body.

He taught her what to do with her tongue, growling in approval when she began to thrust and parry with him. She felt him shift so that she was pressed backward against the railing, while his body pushed at her from the front. She felt the hard planes beneath his clothing. And she knew enough to be startled by the thick swell against her groin, especially as he pushed it against her in a frighteningly explicit rhythm.

It was that movement that pushed her from arousal into alarm. She tried to break away, but she was trapped. The railing bit into her back, and there was no compromise from Damon in the front. In fact, when she pushed at his chest, he seemed to grow more powerful, more dominating. His mouth slanted harder across hers. His tongue pushed in with more frenzy. And below—sweet heaven—below he was big and aggressive.

Rubbing her up and down with his thick cock, his desire drew a whimper from her. She was trapped, and all her struggles inflamed him. Her senses swirled, her fists beat him, but she might as well have been pounding at stone. It didn't end until he pulled away. Until he eased back enough that she could twist her face away. But his body was still pressed so tight against hers that she could feel his heart pounding in his chest.

"No," she said. This time her voice was louder and stronger.

"Come to my room," he whispered, his own breath short. "I will treat you as a queen."

Her back seriously hurt, arched as she was halfway over empty space. She pushed at his chest, and this time he grudgingly eased back.

"I am not a high flyer," she said. She could not bear to look at him.

"Did I ask to pay you?" he said, the humor in his voice making her cheeks heat. "What I meant—"

"I know what you meant," she said as she pushed harder. He did not move. "The answer is no."

He trailed his thumb along her cheek, and she turned away from the touch. He leaned forward to whisper into her ear. "I had not thought you a coward. Why do you run, Wendy? I will make all your dreams come true."

She snorted, her spine straightening as much as he allowed. "You know nothing of my dreams."

"Really? Shall I prove you wrong? You dream of a safe home for yourself and your mother. I offer you that at fair terms. You wish for a man to appreciate your talents and your intelligence. I do, Wendy. And you wish to know what other women know." He raised his hand and boldly tweaked her nipple. She would have slapped him no matter who he was, but he stepped out of her reach.

She bit her lip, feeling her mind swirl in darkening circles. Her body was aroused—she knew that much—but her heart beat like a terrified rabbit. This man was a demon, and her mind churned in confusion. She didn't want to dance—in the most carnal way—with this devil. She didn't! There had to be another way out.

"I'm going to my table now," she said as she pushed off the railing with shaking arms. He didn't let her go far. She was still caged by his body, but he allowed her to straighten to her full height. Over his shoulder, she caught the sight of his guards standing there with blank faces. She knew that at a single nod from Damon, they would gut her like a fish. "Damon, you've had your fun," she said. "Let me go."

"Where will you go tomorrow? Where will your mother sleep?"

She closed her eyes. She didn't know! And she had no time to figure it out.

He finally bit out a curse. "One month free rent, Wendy. I offer that to no one else. And my men will move everything tomorrow." He touched her chin, his fingers pinching tight as he pulled her to look at him. "Do not play the fool, Wendy. You know, if you refuse me now, I will be angry, and things will go worse for you."

Chilling words, and she felt the blood drain from her face. "And you wonder why I fear you?" she rasped.

"I never expected anything less," he said. "Shall I tell you a secret? You like the fear. It makes your heart race and your skin tingle. It draws you to me as surely as—"

"A moth to flame?"

He smiled. "I was going to say, a woman who knows a man who can satisfy her." He folded his arms. "You are saving your virginity for what? One of those gentlemen?" He gestured disdainfully at the gamblers on the floor. "They are not worthy of you. An altar boy who will bring you posies and kiss you chastely on the cheek?" He rolled his eyes. "He will bore you and then betray you by cutting his association the minute he learns of what you did here."

"I have done nothing but deal cards."

He flashed a feral smile. "That is not what I will say."

She felt her cheeks heat. It was true, and she had known what he was doing when they'd walked up here.

Meanwhile, he shifted to look laconically over the floor. "I believe I shall rent the flat to—"

"I will take it," she pushed out. What choice did she have, really? "For a month. Free of rent." She swallowed. "With my thanks."

He sketched a mocking bow. "But of course. My men will be at your home first thing in the morning to help you move." Then he waved a negligent hand at her. "You may go back to your table now."

She left, but her steps were slow and her mind whirled much too fast. What had she done?

Four

RADLEY WAS WHISTLING AS HE CROSSED INTO THE AREA where he'd grown up. He was blocks away from his mother's rooms, but home was as much about the neighborhood as the place where he slept. He noted the small differences as he moved. One building had been painted. Another looked to have been scorched by a fire, but still stood. The biggest differences were in the people. It had been nearly eighteen months since he'd been here last. That was a long time for the neighborhood children who seemed to have grown like weeds. And they were all running toward him as if he had a treat.

He did, of course, but not on him. They would have to wait until tomorrow for his surprise.

"It's Mr. Lyncott! 'E's here!"

"Mr. Lyncott! We've been waiting ever so long!"

"Mr. Lyncott! Bet you're surprised, ain't ya? Ain't ya? Imagine, you a nob!"

Everything was spoken in a screaming rush, the children bouncing and running while women and a few men popped out of their doors.

"Mr. Lyncott! Welcome home."

"Couldn't have been for a nicer gent. Don't you forget us—"

"Don't forget me!"

"You remember, don't you? How I helped with—"

On and on it went, until he was rather dizzy. Certainly, the neighborhood always welcomed him home. They liked his tales of foreign lands, and all longed to see what new treasure he'd brought. But this was unusual, even for him. Old men he hadn't seen in years were struggling from their seats to come see him. To shake his hand and bid him to remember them.

And that was nothing compared to the women smiling warmly, showing off their assets in a way that made him blush. What was going on?

"I'm not a captain yet," he said, answering one child's question. "Still just a first mate."

"No, you ain't! Not anymore!" said one of the ladies with a throaty laugh.

There was more talk. Something about being a duke, but he laughed that off. Neighborhood gossip was notorious for getting things wrong, and no amount of denial or correction would change what people believed.

So he laughed and waved them off, promising to show them all his new treasure later. Then he mounted the steps to his mother's lodging. Given the trail of people, all jabbering at once, he shouldn't have been able to hear Sadie. But the gin sot who kept her eye on everything that happened in the building wouldn't let him pass through the front door without adding her particular form of address.

"Welcome 'ome, Radley. Just off the ship?"

He acknowledged her politely enough, not because he wanted to encourage the connection, but because it wouldn't do to antagonize her. It would make his mother's life all the harder.

"Just home, so if you'll excuse me. My mama—"

Sadie touched him on the arm, her expression lascivious as she squeezed his biceps. "I always been good to you. Looking out after your mama and all. Don't you forget me, you hear?" Her expression darkened. "'Course I know things too. Things that you don't want spread about."

Radley frowned, startled by her veiled threat. What secrets did he have? And why did she think anyone would care?

He disentangled himself from her clutches smoothly, irritated when he feared that her sharp claws would rip his coat. He saved the fabric—barely—then didn't even bother bowing as he headed up the stairs. Then he frowned when he realized that Sadie had followed him. She was slower on the steps than he was, but at his look, she flashed him a grin. Then she tugged her neckline lower.

He winced at the woman's sorry state. Certainly, he'd availed himself of many a whore back when he'd first started sailing. But that had never been his first choice. Strong drink was his vice, not women, and only when he was on liberty.

He turned away to knock loudly on his mother's door. "Mama? It's me, Radley. Home from—"

His mother hauled open the door. She was standing there in a new gown, her hair pulled into a neat coiffure. And when she saw him, she burst into tears. He blinked, rather startled, then immediately dropped his satchel to enfold her in a warm hug.

"There, there, I'm home. I'm safe."

Her response was unintelligible as she gasped and shuddered. He held her tightly, his gaze taking in the new silver tea set at the same moment he noticed two gentlemen setting aside their cups as they pushed to their feet.

Radley's brows drew together, furious that these two men—whoever they were—had upset his mother.

"What has happened here?" he demanded in his most authoritative voice. It was a tone designed to carry over a violent storm at sea, and it made the two men jolt.

And then as one, they bowed deeply before him.

He stared, confused by such an obsequious reaction, especially as his mother controlled her sobs. She stepped back, wiping her eyes and shaking her head.

"No, no. I'm all right," she gasped. "I just so h-h-happy." She gave him a trembling smile. "You're home!"

He nodded, his gaze still on the two gentlemen. They had the look of solicitors, one old and the other barely controlling his excitement as he shifted from foot to foot. Radley's gaze moved to his mother's beaming face, and his disquiet grew. Were these the solicitors who had left their card with his employer? And where did his mother get the money for a new dress, a silver tea set, and…

His eyes narrowed. Fresh flowers? In a vase on the table? They had never had fresh flowers. It was too big an expense!

"Mother," he said slowly.

"It has finally happened," she said as she wiped her eyes. "You're a duke, Radley! We… I'm… Oh darling, you've inherited the title just as I always knew you would."

He stared at her, his mind stuttering at her words. His first thought was that the toll of near poverty had finally gotten the better of her. Her mind had broken, and these men were here to take her to Bedlam.

That was his first thought. The rest of him couldn't help but replay the many words he'd heard while walking here. Whether or not it was true, the neighborhood certainly thought he'd stepped into something huge. But it couldn't possibly be that he'd inherited the title. He was ninth or tenth in line for the dukedom.

More likely was that the old duke had finally died, and the next one was doing his best to reconnect to the lost branch of the family. That would mean reaching out to his mother in Radley's absence.

"Don't worry," he said softly to his mother. "I'm home now. I'll sort it all out."

"But there's nothing to sort," his mother cried happily. "You're the new duke!"

He smiled, hating that she kept saying that. It couldn't be true.

"Mother," he said gently, "Miss Drew and her mother will be staying here tomorrow. They have had some difficulty with their rooms and—"

"What? What!" She drew herself to her full height, and with the new coiffure, she nearly made it to his chin.

He smiled as he squeezed her arms. "I know it is sudden, but they are having a problem, and they need a place to stay. So I said they could stay in my room—"

"But they cannot!"

His lips tightened, and he took as strong a tone as he dared with his mother, especially while the two men stood barely three feet away. "They can, and they will. I have promised them. It will not be for long, and you can—"

"No!" she cried. "You are a duke now, Radley! There are appearances to be maintained. Your generosity does you credit, but we simply cannot—"

"Mother," he said, coldly cutting her off. He had intended to inform her as soon as possible, not to discuss it openly in front of strangers. He'd expected his quiet mama to simply acquiesce. Between the clamor outside and his mother's odd words, Radley felt his world shifting on its axis. "We will discuss this at a later time. Right now, I should like to meet these gentlemen."

She huffed, clearly disliking what he'd said, but her good manners stopped her from arguing further. Instead, she turned to the gentlemen in question.

"Radley, I'd like to present you with your solicitors. Mr. Pelley and his grandson, Mr. Pelley. They are from the firm of Chase and Pelley. They have been advising the Duke of Bucklynde for generations. And now, they are here to help you."

Both men executed a deep bow, but Radley simply frowned at them. He didn't dare speak. He was beginning to think that his mother's delusion might not be a delusion. But that couldn't be. This was a fantasy of hers. It had to be. All his life, his mother had cherished the dream that one day they would be pulled back into the ducal fold. She had made no secret of her hopes, of the distant connection between them and the Duke of Bucklynde, and she had made Radley's life hell with the constant keeping up of appearances for something that would never happen.

He was a sailor, soon to be captain of his own ship. The fantasy that he would someday take a place among the aristocracy was ridiculous at best. And yet, here stood Mr. Pelley and Pelley, and his disquiet grew.

"Sirs, as you might imagine, this is all rather confusing."

The elder Pelley bowed deeply. "We've been anxious for your return, your grace."

Radley winced at "your grace" but allowed the man to continue without comment.

"I only heard an hour ago that your ship had finally arrived. Assuming that you would come first to visit your mother, we decided to meet you here. I'm afraid the estate has been neglected in this time of crisis, and there are decisions that need to be made as soon as possible."

He looked at the man, gauging his sincerity and sanity. He judged them both adequate, but the idea was still too preposterous to accept. He knew he was rapidly losing the war against denial, but he clung tenaciously to it.

His mother had always put on airs, and his sister had ended up suffering for it. He had tolerated her insistence on seeing him educated as a gentleman, and for a little while he had allowed his mother's dreams to infect him. As a boy, he'd fantasized about some unlikely event that would confer the duke's honors on him. When his sister had become a victim of a heinous crime, in part brought on by his mother's fixation on their connection to the dukedom, it had taken Radley from boyhood to adulthood virtually overnight. He had chosen a profession and set aside his secret hope, a little regretfully, but with relief too. And now, here were two men and his mother telling him that all his boyhood wishes had come true.

"I'm sorry, but I don't understand how this could be."

The elder Pelley bowed again—really, that was getting rather irritating—then gestured to his grandson. "If we might be permitted to explain."

At a pointed look at the younger Mr. Pelley, the boy—who looked barely into his twenties—gasped and grabbed a satchel. He pulled out a stack of papers, which appeared to have an elaborate family tree upon it. He spread it on the table in front of the settee, then both Pelleys looked at Radley.

It took a minute for Radley to realize that they hadn't yet sat down because they were waiting for him. His mother, of course, had discreetly withdrawn to the kitchen. That was, after all, what a dowager countess would do, right? Which left the three men standing, while the Duke of Bucklynde's genealogy fairly screamed at Radley from the table.

"Very well," he said, giving in to the inevitable. He settled on the nearest chair, his knees feeling incredibly weak, and then waited in all appearance of calm. In truth, his heart was pounding and his thoughts whirled more than a storm at sea.

The next few minutes passed in a numb fog. The

younger Mr. Pelley ran through a long commentary about every male on the ducal tree. He pointed at the parchment as he went, indicating birth and death dates, dwelling in detail on how each man died. In truth, the tale was relatively simple. Smallpox wiped out everyone of significance. Apparently, it had begun as a couple of cases, but spread rapidly. The eldest duke had been one of the first to succumb, and sadly, the cause of everyone else's infection. All the men had stood vigil at the duke's sickbed. Then, one by one, they had contracted the disease.

The youngest heir to die had been a boy barely into his teens. The women weren't mentioned by Mr. Pelley, but Radley saw the dates of each death written in a cold script as well.

Then he counted the remaining females: four, not including his own sister and mother. Four women struggling to hold together a semblance of a life when everything—and everyone—around them had died. He shuddered at the thought.

"I see you are looking at the female names," said the elder Mr. Pelley. "I should like to draw your attention to this one in particular: Lady Eleanor. She's a beautiful woman, trained since birth to be a proper wife, and she is your distant cousin, so there will be no concerns on that account."

Radley frowned, not understanding what the man was saying. What concerns? Why?

"If I may, your grace," inserted the younger Mr. Pelley. "What my grandfather is trying delicately to suggest is that there are a great many duties required of a new duke, but the most important one at the moment…" He cleared his throat then blushed a fiery red.

"The most important," picked up his grandfather, "is a continuation of the line. My grandson and I can take care of the most pressing matters of the estate. We've already hired a new steward and are sorting through the requirements of the land, finding new tenants, and clearing out the last of the sick or dying."

"Clearing them out?" echoed Radley, his voice dropping to a deceptively quiet tone. He knew just what kind of panic sickness could create. He'd stopped sailors from throwing the ill overboard out of fear that the disease would spread.

"Er, yes, your grace. We're moving them to a hospital and… um… burning the homes. You must understand that this illness is—"

Radley waved him into silence. This was more than he could process, but he was not going to allow fear to rule even from this distant location. "Wall off the homes for the moment. Do not burn them until after we learn of their owners' fates."

The younger man cleared his throat. "Begging your pardon, your grace, but *you* are the owner. You can—"

"Not of their crockery, not of their clothing or their mementoes." He rubbed a hand over his face. Bloody hell, this was too much. "Wait to find out if the people survive!"

The elder Mr. Pelley inclined his head deeply. "Of course, your grace. You can rely on us. We will see to it immediately. But if I may be so bold…"

Privately, Radley thought the man had been nothing but bold, but he didn't quibble. He simply raised his eyebrows as he might to an arrogant sailor who still needed to learn his place. Sadly, he had the distinct impression that *he* was the one who had the most to learn.

"Yes, your grace. As I was saying, Lady Eleanor is a beauty of the first order. We believe she should be your highest priority."

Radley frowned. "Is she ill? In trouble?"

"Goodness, no!" gasped the younger Mr. Pelley. Then he flushed a bright red. "That is to say, the lady is all that is to be desired. And she would be an excellent choice for duchess."

It took a moment for his meaning to sink in. Duchess. As in *his* duchess. "You want me to wed this woman?"

Mr. Pelley, the elder, beamed as if he were a rather slow student who had just grasped his sums. "The line has been all but decimated. You cannot imagine our terror these last weeks at the idea that you might have been lost at sea."

"Yes, I'm sure that would have put you in quite the quandary," Radley drawled, but his sarcasm was lost on the two men.

"But as you are not lost and are, in fact, a healthy man, it is incumbent upon you to see to the continuation of such a distinguished and lofty title. You have responsibilities now, your grace. The first of which is to secure an heir. Lady Eleanor is not only well suited to the task, but she can also guide you in your new role." The elder Pelley finished his words with a smug nod, while the younger one added in a hushed tone.

"Please understand that my grandfather would push Lady Eleanor on you simply because of her heritage, but I, myself, have had time to speak with the lady. She is elegance personified. Beautiful, poised, extremely intelligent, and with a generous heart. She is a lady of old, who guides with the most tender of touches and inspires the darkest heart to glory."

Radley stared. "Good God, you've composed poetry for her, haven't you?"

The boy's face heated so much it was a wonder he didn't incinerate right there. "Lady Eleanor inspires many—"

"With her beauty and virtue. Yes, yes."

Again, the elder bowed his head. "If I may, your grace—"

"No, you may not," Radley abruptly snapped. "Let me understand this. The entire ducal line has been decimated, the village wiped out. There is still sickness in the area, and my guess is that the crops have been completely ignored while this plague went through—"

"Yes, your—"

"But in all this horror and devastation, your concern isn't for how the survivors will be fed throughout the winter, how the dead can be grieved or the land managed, but for the lady you have selected to get my heir."

The younger man opened his mouth to say something. Probably defend the paragon Lady Eleanor, but his grandfather silenced him with a touch on the arm. Then the man turned rather pitying eyes on Radley and spoke with soothing accents that were completely infuriating.

"I realize the behaviors of the aristocracy must seem strange to you, but I assure you, the Chase and Pelley solicitors have guided generations of dukes. You can rely on our advice to be sound no matter how strange it might seem. In fact—"

"So you were the solicitors who advised my great-grandfather to cut off his youngest son. Over a matter of a stolen horse, I believe."

"The boy wasn't disinherited. Otherwise, we would not be here today. And it was the boy's choice in a wife."

Radley all but itched to hear the solicitors' version of the story. He'd been reared on his mother's endless tirades about the ridiculous action. By her account, the old duke had been senile and stubborn, a bad combination.

Unfortunately, this wasn't the moment to listen to a recounting of an old argument, especially as everyone involved was now dead. What he had to think about right away was his mother. He now understood about the new clothing, new tea set, new… everything. If what these men said was true—and he was beginning to think it might be—then she had probably gone on a spending spree. What if there wasn't any money behind the title? What if this was an elaborate joke? He knew she was standing in the kitchen hanging onto every word. In her mind, he was probably already wedded and bedded with this Lady Eleanor. She'd always been obsessed with the mores of the upper crust, and she would leap upon the chance to marry him into the aristocracy. It was all too much, and he feared for his mother's sanity, not to mention his own peace of mind.

Then over everything came one loud and particular concern. It was a ridiculous thought, especially given the magnitude of what had just happened. But he couldn't shake the thought, nor could he just ignore it. It was simply this: assuming this wasn't a bad joke, what would happen to his captaincy? And without the captaincy, how would he convince Wendy to marry him?

He supposed a dukedom might have some influence, but he wasn't entirely sure that would be a good thing in her mind. She might now believe him to be above her touch, even though they shared their childhood. Besides, she was the owner of a successful business. Could a duchess still work as a seamstress? He rather guessed she could not.

And why was he thinking about Wendy when people were dying in some northern village that he'd never even heard of before?

"Your grace, if I might—"

"Get out," he snapped.

The man reared back, his mouth gaping open. "Now, see here—"

Radley focused on the man with all his considerable frustration. He didn't know if this was a joke or a bizarre reality, but either way the man could not speak to him that way. He could not wax indignant, nor could he dare to look at him with such condescension in Radley's own home.

"I said, get out. Now. *If* this is indeed truth, then I

shall visit you on the morrow. And we shall see if the current Duke of Bucklynde will retain your services."

"Retain! Morrow!" the elder man sputtered.

It was the younger Pelley who had the sense to quiet his outraged grandsire. "Of course, your grace. I'm sure this has been unsettling."

"But—" continued the elder.

"When you are ready, we are willing to assist you."

Radley was on the verge of telling them to go to the devil. But that, of course, was not appropriate, nor fair. They'd merely been delivering the news. They were not the cause of this total disruption to his life or his plans.

He didn't bother seeing the men out. His mother was there to do that, with all her murmured promise to help her son through this awkward transition. Radley blocked her words from his thoughts lest he become furious with her.

Then ten minutes later, he pushed up from the chair. "I'm going to… the ship." He'd almost said *my* ship, but that hadn't been true even before the damned solicitors had delivered their news.

"But Radley! You have to—"

"Mother, I have to finish one life before I can start the next."

He hadn't accepted the reality of a new life, but whatever the future held, he still had responsibilities to Mr. Knopp. He would finish those first, then turn his face to whatever was in store in the future.

"And then," he added in words too low for his mother to hear, "I'm going to get right, stinking drunk."

Five

"WAKE UP! YER LATE FOR WATCH!"

Radley sat bolt upright in his bunk and nearly knocked his head on the low wood paneling. He almost wished he had when his stomach roiled from the motion and his head pounded as if he had brained himself. Meanwhile, the bellowing continued, making everything worse with each syllable.

"Told you that would wake 'im. Come on lad, I'm over here. Cast up your accounts, and let's get on with business."

He cracked an eye, his legs already over the edge of the bunk. He was late for watch. He had to get moving.

Except... what watch? He focused as best he could, seeing two men before him. The first was his employer, Mr. Knopp, holding out a bucket.

His stomach heaved, but he didn't blow, though it was a near thing. Instead, he shifted his attention to the second fellow. A workingman, by the looks of him, with a pleasant expression and a tankard of what had to be hot coffee. Radley lurched for that and nearly missed. It was only the other man's swift reflexes that had him pressing the drink into the shaking fingers rather than spilling the precious brew all over the deck.

Then he took a long pull. The brew was scalding hot, but he barely noticed in the general misery of his brain and body. Lord, what had he done last night?

"Got yourself good and pissed last night, mate," said Mr. Knopp jovially. Radley winced at the loud tone, but knew better than to speak. Nothing like adding to a sailor's misery the morning after to set a captain to whistling. And even if Mr. Knopp hadn't sailed in over a decade, there were still things that the man enjoyed.

Obviously.

Radley finished the coffee and mutely held out the tankard for more. The captain filled it from his flask and pressed it back at Radley, all but forcing him to drink. He swallowed greedily then nearly lost his stomach.

Water!

"Blahhhg," he said on a choke. He wanted coffee. And failing that—ale.

"Quit yer moaning," Mr. Knopp replied, his voice echoing loudly in Radley's head. "Be grateful it's not worse. When I found you last night, you were well on yer way to being fleeced blind by three whores. Course there wasn't much left of you after you'd been buying everyone drinks for half the night. If you were still under my employ, I'd set you to scrubbing the deck with your tongue."

His mouth could hardly taste worse. Then his mind caught up to what the man had said. *If you were still under my employ.*

"I'm sacked?"

"Sweet God, no," answered the man. "But I can't have a duke sailing the open seas. Besides the obvious danger, every pirate on earth would want to capture you for ransom. Then where would my goods and my ships be but at the bottom of the ocean, thanks to your damned title?"

Radley only heard every third word, but the meaning was clear. It hadn't been a dream. He was really a duke.

Except, he couldn't be. He hadn't the first clue about how to be a nob.

"Sir," he said when Knopp paused to take a breath, "why are you here?"

The man snorted. "Well, I had to check on you, didn't I? After what you were blubbering last night, I had to settle you in yer bunk then go find him." He jerked his head to the right where the other man flashed him a warm grin. "This here's my son-in-law," he said, though he flashed the man a dark look. "Not that I got to celebrate anything, mind you. Up and gets a special license. Barely had time to show up in our Sunday best. Not the way to wed, if you ask me."

The man in question gave his father-in-law a sad shrug. "We are throwing a ball, and you and your lady wife can dance to your heart's content."

"Harumph," he said. "Backwards. That's how you nobs do things: backwards."

He focused on Radley. "And now you're one of them, so I brought him here to help."

The other man extended his hand. "Lord Crowle, your grace. But you can call me Grant."

Radley released a low moan of despair at the title, which only made the man grin.

"Yes, you've stepped in it, to be sure."

Mr. Knopp nodded his agreement. "And there's no denying that your life is upside down now. You're a sailor through and through, but now you'll learn how to sail the sheep."

Both younger men winced, but it was Lord Crowle who spoke. "It's not so bad once you get the hang of it. But he's right. You aren't going to be a sailor anymore."

Radley's chest tightened, which set his head to pounding. Not a sailor anymore? Good God, that was the only thing he knew. The only thing he *loved*. Meanwhile, Mr. Knopp rocked back on his heels.

"Damned shame, too. I was going to give you the run of this boat. See what you could make of it and let you cut a name as a captain." He sighed. "Now I'll have to give it to someone who doesn't love her like you do."

Radley spoke, his words coming out in a harsh whisper. "Don't do that yet, sir. Not yet. There still may be a way. She needs repairs still. I could—"

"No, lad, you can't. And you won't be able to. I'm sure it feels like I'm cutting the heart out of you, but it's the way things are. Many a man would be celebrating the windfall that's hit you. The Duke of Bucklynde. God, who'd have believed it?"

Not him. Not yet. He couldn't—

Mr. Knopp gave a rough grunt, still managing to sound affectionate. "I'll get you more coffee and let the two of you get acquainted. Mind you, he's not so bad as nobs go, and he'll teach you how to do things backwards like them." He snorted as he headed for the door. "Just mind you don't forget how to do things the right way too."

Then the man disappeared. He wasn't as lithe as he'd once been, and Radley heard him grunt as he climbed the ladder. And then Radley was sitting in his misery with a gentleman who couldn't stop grinning.

"What's made you so happy?" he snapped.

"Oh, don't be pissing in my direction. I've got a lovely wife who makes me grin like this every damn day, so don't take it personally." Then his expression sobered. "How much have you learned? About your responsibilities, the state of the tenants?" He leaned forward. "Do you even know what crops you grow?"

Radley let his head drop. He didn't know any of those things, beyond the barest. "I know they want me to marry Lady Eleanor."

Lord Crowle grunted as he dropped onto the bunk beside Radley. "She's not so bad, as uptight shrews go. She had no use for me, of course, but as the feeling was mutual, I didn't really care." Then at Radley's sideways look, the man shrugged. "I've been a scapegrace and an idiot for most of my life. All the smart women avoided me, and Lady Eleanor is no fool."

"I'm not marrying her," he said, the words sounding more churlish than powerful. Damn, his head hurt.

"There you go," the man enthused. "Set down the law right away. Only way to handle those solicitor types. Course, the minute you poke your head into society, you'll be swarmed by every marriageable woman looking to be a duchess. And that's not even counting the other women."

"Other women?"

"In the mood for a mistress? Or a dozen?"

"No!" Then he groaned at the way the word exploded in his head.

Crowle laughed and clapped him on the shoulders. "Don't worry. I'll show you how to avoid them. You'll get the hang of it right quick. It's the estate, though, that you have to worry about. Don't know anything about how the Duke of Bucklynde was situated, but I do know that with all the sickness and the like, the land has been neglected. And winter's coming on."

"I know," he said miserably. "They told me they'd hired a steward."

"Well, there are stewards, and then there are stewards. My brother's the best there is and he'd be able to advise you better than I, but I know the basics. I can help you get started."

Radley lifted his head, squinting past the pain to inspect the happy-go-lucky nob. "What's your game?"

The man nodded his approval. "That's the way of it! Question everybody right now because everyone is going to nibble as much of you as they can get. Well, everyone except me. I'm here trying to make nice with my new father-in-law. He's right that I did things backwards with his daughter. So when he asks me to help a sailor suddenly turned duke..." He spread his arms wide. "I'm here with alacrity to render aid."

Knopp's voice boomed as he stepped into the cabin. "And not laugh too hard at his discomfort. Man's lost the sea, you know. All but drowned myself in drink when I had to give it up." He thunked his thigh right above his knee. "Couldn't walk the rigging anymore. Saddest day of my life."

Radley groaned as his chest tightened to an unbearable pain. Was he really done? Would he never sail again?

"There, there. Have some more—"

Too late. Radley was retching up everything he'd consumed in the last twenty-four hours. If only he could get rid of the events of the last day as easily.

❧

"If you break that, I'll box your ears before you can draw breath to scream!"

Wendy winced as her mother screeched at Freddie. He was only one of three men sent to cart all their worldly goods to their new rooms, but he was the most ham-fisted. He blushed a bright red at her remarks—especially as the other men snickered—but then he focused on hefting her mother's prized possession out the door. It was her treadle wheel for spinning, and it was as large as her mother's short five-foot frame.

"Mind the top, ya dolt! And that crockery—"

"Mama, stop!" Wendy took a breath, her nerves frazzled and her head pounding. She hated leaving their home, dreaded where they were going, and most of all, ached for some nameless something that would make this fear go away. It was foolish dreaming, but she wanted it. And that want made the present all the more difficult. As did her mother's incessant screaming. "Mama, everyone's staring. Let's just get this done without all the noise."

"Noise?" her mother snapped. "I'll not be run out of my home all silent-like as if I were ashamed. We're good tenants, you and me. They've no cause—"

"I know," she said. The unfairness of this had been her mother's only conversation since they'd been told to leave. "I know, Mama. But if you could just let the men work—"

"And break my crockery! Well, I never!"

Wendy started to argue, but then thought better of it. Her mother was expressing her own fears in the only way she knew how: by complaining at the top of her lungs. She wouldn't stop until everything was resolved.

She leaned against the wall, her hand shoved deep into her pocket where she toyed with a scrap of paper. It had one sentence on it plus the date: Lady Ottwell sucked Lord Northcott's cock at the Westfall Ball. It was the only secret she'd gleaned from her time at the vingt-e-un table last night, and she'd scribbled it down this morning. A pitiful secret and one likely known by half the *ton* after last night. Lord Northcott had been crowing about the lady's technique to anyone who would hear. But it was what she'd learned, and so she'd scribbled it down as she did all the tidbits she'd gleaned over the years. After they were settled, she'd add this to her other written notes.

Meanwhile, she stared bleakly at the scene before her. She watched Freddie grab a basket of her clothing. She had precious few dresses, and when the sleeve of one dragged over the side nearly to the ground, she should have leaped forward to save the gown from dirt. She didn't. Suddenly, she was too tired. So she watched with dull eyes, her mind too weary to think. And, in that moment of exhaustion, a familiar voice startled her.

"My goodness, Wind! You aren't one to let the work go begging, are you?"

Radley. So he hadn't forgotten his promise to let her stay with his mother. Lord, how her heart just stuttered when she thought of him now. Of his laugh. Of their kiss. But before she could enjoy the rush of feeling from those memories, the other one intruded. The one where he was no longer just a sailor on leave, but a man with a title.

She closed her eyes, doing her best to hide the pain. They might have shared a kiss. They might have made a go of it. But now, the distance between them was too great. So she straightened off the wall, smoothing her skirt in self-conscious movements. Then she turned to face the new Duke of Bucklynde with poise and dignity.

Sadly, her mother did not have the same reserve. Wendy had barely turned when suddenly her mother clapped her hands in delight. Then she squealed loud enough for the neighborhood to know that a duke had come to call.

"Oo-ee! Look at you. Come to see us just like you promised. Little Radley, now a duke! And 'oo is this fine gentleman with you?"

Wendy had been looking at Radley, at his broad shoulders, tanned face, and bloodshot eyes. He looked weary, and her mother's squeal had him wincing. She recognized the symptoms. He'd likely gotten drunk last night and was suffering for it this morning. She wanted to think ill of him, but really, who wouldn't celebrate becoming a duke? It was all the neighborhood could talk about, and many a man had celebrated on his behalf.

But at her mother's words, Wendy turned her attention to the man beside Radley. "Mama, this is Lord Crowle. He has just married Lady Irene."

"Blimey! Lord Crowle, pleasure to meet you, it is. I've 'eard so much about you from my Wendy. Says you're a right fine gent."

"A pleasure madame," said Lord Crowle as he bowed, his manner neither mocking nor dismissive. It was one of the things Wendy most liked about the man: he treated every person with equal parts charm and respect. That he was bowing so politely now set her mother to giggling.

"Look at us, Wendy dear, getting visited by an earl and a duke. And me, in this ratty old gown." She slapped angrily at the dirt on her skirt. It was, in truth, one of her best gowns. No fool, her mother had known that the whole neighborhood would be around to see them thrown out. So she had dressed as well as she could without looking ridiculous.

"You look lovely, Mrs. Drew," said Radley. He bowed rather awkwardly over her hand, but his eyes were on Wendy, narrowing in concern. "I know it's hard to leave a home," he began, but Wendy waved him off.

"I don't mind leaving here," she said. "One set of rooms is as good as another." She was making the best of a bad business. It hurt to leave her home, even a set of rooms that she'd barely seen, except to sleep. "I'm afraid I left things rather at odds with my mother yesterday," he said as he eyed the cart. "You do have a rather lot of things, don't you? But I can run ahead—"

"We're not going to stay with your mother," Wendy said, her words rushed.

He jolted. "What? Why ever not?"

She opened her mouth to answer, but her mother interjected first.

"Well, that's wot I said. Why ever not, when it would be rude to refuse so kind an invitation?"

"But—" inserted Wendy with a glare at her mum, "I have found us a place now."

"Temporary lodgings," spat her mother as she rolled her eyes.

"Mrs. Lyncott's home would be temporary as well," said Wendy. "And there probably isn't room for all our things either."

Radley didn't say anything, just watched the byplay with his bright copper eyes. Then he looked at her, his skin ruddy with embarrassment.

"I wanted you to stay with us," he said softly. "I wouldn't have minded a bit."

"But your mother would. And…" Wendy shrugged. "It isn't appropriate now."

She saw his jaw clench, but he didn't speak. He knew the truth as well as she did. Then he must have come to a decision because he gestured upstairs. "Is there more to be done? Lord Crowle and I can—"

"Oo-ee. Have a duke and an earl hauling our things about?" cried her mother loud enough so that everyone knew the offer had been extended. "Thank ye, no. We've got it all set now." Then she grinned. "But you be sure to visit us when we're all settled, won't you? Wendy can give you the address. I can't remember it for the life of me, but she says it's nice."

It was. Double the size of their current rooms, cleaner, and with a window as well to look out on the street. She feared once her mother saw the place, she wouldn't ever want to leave.

Radley's gaze was steady. "I should like that very much."

She nearly blurted it out right then, but she was a practical woman. Or so she told herself. The difference in their station was too great. And besides, she had no desire to let him know how much she had fallen into Damon's clutches. Not with the history between the two men. Damon had destroyed Radley's sister—or tried to—and in the most heinous way imaginable. Radley would go insane if he found out Wendy was caught in the man's clutches.

"You shouldn't visit us," she said, trying to speak low enough for him to hear, but not her mother. It wasn't possible, and the woman soon planted her fists on her hips and glared at her daughter.

"Not appropriate?" she mocked. "When we've known him all his life? When he and Henry are the greatest of friends? When you've been such a good friend to his sister? Not appropriate? My girl, you have got to learn that some folks don't forget their friends when they get a windfall."

Inheriting a dukedom was a great deal more than a windfall, but Wendy didn't bother arguing. Instead, she looked at Lord Crowle and saw the sympathy in his eyes. At least this man knew she was trying to do the right thing. A break between her and Radley was inevitable. And a sudden break would be easier than a slow, torturous separation.

But Radley would have none of it. He simply shook his head. "My family owes you a great deal, Miss Drew," he said formally. "I would very much like to call on you in the near future, and it's a great deal easier at your home than at your place of business."

A great deal more discreet, she supposed. But she still didn't speak. At which point, he sighed and looked about. "Where's Henry? He can't keep a secret for love or money."

That was true enough. Which made it fortunate that her older brother was nowhere to be seen. "He's been gone since yesterday evening." She frowned. "I thought he was looking for you."

Radley frowned then rubbed his forehead. It likely ached something terrible. "Oh yes. I remember." Then he flushed a ruddy red. "He found me. But I lost track of him…"

Wendy was glad he stopped speaking. She didn't want to know what brothel the men had ended up in. Meanwhile, Lord Crowle took that moment to tilt his head to the bells ringing in the distance.

"I don't mind standing here, Radley," he said in a low voice, "but if there's nothing to be done, you do have concerns elsewhere."

Radley nodded, his expression frustrated. "Very well." He turned to smile at her mother. "Mrs. Drew, I look forward to calling on you another day." Then

he turned his gaze to her. "And Miss Drew, I shall call
on you at the dress shop. Four o'clock exactly, so that
we can have that walk in the park you promised."

She gasped. "We can't go to Hyde Park now! Not
with you a new duke and me…"

"You what?" he asked. His voice was deceptively
soft. He was angry, though few would realize that
until it was too late. It was only because she'd seen
him at the worst time of his life that she knew how
he went quiet when angry, not loud like most men.
"What are you, Miss Drew, that you refuse to be seen
with me?"

She huffed. "It's not like that, and you know it."

"I know that we arranged to walk this afternoon,
and I will not be denied." Then his gaze softened,
taking on a more appealing cast. "Wind, please. I… I
wish to see you. And I need something quiet. Do you
understand? A simple walk in the park together."

There was nothing simple about a new duke walking
in Hyde Park. Not during the fashionable hour. But
she would pray that most of the *ton* wouldn't recognize
him yet. In truth, this was perhaps the last time they
could do such a thing before he became too prominent
to walk unmolested in the park. "Do not dress any differently," she said, eyeing his worn seaman's clothing.
It was neat, and the coat emphasized the breadth of his
shoulders, but it wasn't remotely appropriate for a duke.

"I won't change a thing," he said. "I swear."

Lord Crowle released a snort. "What if he spills his
tea and gets a stain on his sleeve? He'd have to change
then, wouldn't he? Or worse yet, these London streets
can be treacherous. He could fall and get a tear."

The man was teasing, pointing out the ridiculous-
ness of her order. What woman demanded a man *not*
dress to see her? But Wendy simply lifted her chin in
challenge. "Even better. I like all my callers to sport
tears. How else can I show off my stitching skills?"

Lord Crowle sobered, his expression turning gentle.
"It won't fadge, you know. He'll be recognized—"

"I'll be at the dress shop at four on the dot," interrupted Radley. "And in the meantime, tell Henry
exactly what I think of a man who leaves his mother
and sister to pack up their home without his aid."

He didn't have to explain further. He had always
called Henry to task for a certain lack of industrious-
ness. It wasn't that Henry was lazy. Far from it, actually. But on land, the man was never out of bed before
noon. And as it was just before eleven, Wendy hadn't
expected her brother to help.

"He'll be the one unpacking," she said, hoping it
was true.

Radley's eyes darkened. "And who helps you,
Wind? When your shoulders droop and your eyes
squint against the sun?" He took a step forward, his
words dropping to a near whisper. "I have never seen
you so tired, and it worries me."

She blinked. He was worried about her? The
knowledge hit her broadside. The man was now a
duke, and he had come here expecting to help her
move in with his mother. It was insane, and yet, here
he was, looking at her in a way that made her heart
tremble and her blood heat.

"Radley," she whispered, speaking as she had on
that awful night so many years ago. "Radley, we

must both walk forward, one step after another, the best way we know how." They were the exact words she'd said so long ago, and she saw him startle. He remembered what she had done.

"So, I am to trust that you are strong enough to do what needs to be done?"

She had said the words to him ten years ago, and now she nodded. "Yes."

"I don't."

Two words, spoken flatly, and she stiffened at the insult. "It worked out just how it ought."

He nodded. "Back then, perhaps. But I have seen too much to believe that we are solitary creatures, happier alone."

She frowned, not understanding what he could possibly mean. "Your grace," she said, purposely using his formal title. It made him wince, but he did not react beyond that. "What are your intentions?"

His lips curved in a slow smile. "To cease being a solitary creature. I am tired of it, as I suspect are you."

She all but laughed. "You are one day returned, and you know all about me?" He opened his mouth to speak, but she didn't give him the time. "Men," she answered quickly. "That's who tire me: men who think they know me." Then she gestured to the cart. "I need to go."

He bowed as he backed away, but his fingers seared where he brushed his hand against hers. "I will see you at four, Miss Drew."

She wanted to argue, but she could see the stubbornness in his eyes. In the end, she gave in to the inevitable with a slow, reluctant nod. In truth, she wanted to go. She wanted to walk through Hyde Park on his arm. To laugh together as they once had years ago.

She was on the verge of saying something gracious and happy. Something that would let him know she wasn't as reluctant as she appeared. But then, she chanced to see Lord Crowle's face. He stood to the side, listening intently to every word.

And he was shaking his head as if this whole thing was a very bad idea.

Six

WENDY WAS READY AT A QUARTER TO FOUR. SHE pretended that she was spending her time inspecting Tabitha's work. She cast a critical eye over everything and made sure to scowl at least twice. But the truth was that Tabitha was learning quickly. And now that she had new glasses, her stitches were as neat as Wendy's. Neater, actually, as the girl wasn't chronically exhausted.

"Well done, Tabby," she finally said.

"What?" the girl gasped.

Wendy was a little startled. After all, the poor girl looked like she'd been poleaxed. "You've done a good job. No need to look like the devil just nipped your nethers."

Tabitha stared at her, then flushed bright red. It took a moment for Wendy to realize the effect of her colorful language. For all that she'd been working to elevate her speech patterns, her time in the gaming hells had affected her. She'd never have said something like that a year ago.

"Sorry," she said, feeling her face heat. "I've been

out of sorts lately. And I haven't been talking to you as I ought." She pointed to a complicated dress pattern that the girl had done to perfection. "This is beautiful work, and you should know that I've noticed."

Tabby nodded, then abruptly blurted out her question. "Where do you go? You've been missing at all hours, and I think it's hurting you."

That's what came from complimenting an assistant. Gave them all sorts of uppity ideas about what they could say. She took a breath to lambaste the girl, but stopped long enough to study her assistant. She didn't see challenge in Tabby's eyes. What she saw was honest worry, and that startled Wendy enough that she could hold back her words.

"It is hurting me," she finally admitted. "But it'll be done in just a few weeks. Then everything will get back to normal."

"But where—"

Wendy cut her off with a glare. "Don't you be asking things you have no business knowing. And if you stand around jabbering, I'll think you don't have enough work."

That was enough for Tabby. She ducked her head and rushed to her table where she began plying her needle and thread. Wendy would have exhaled in relief, but another voice cut through her peace. It was Helaine, the designer and co-owner with Wendy of A Lady's Favor dress shop.

"You needn't tell her," Helaine said, "but perhaps you would speak with me." She stepped into the room, her elegant gown and serene expression at odds with the determination in her eyes. "I've just made a pot of tea. Would you care to join me in the front room?"

She phrased it as a question, but there was no doubt she intended to have this conversation with Wendy now. Wendy couldn't, not with Mr. Lyncott due any moment.

"I owe you an explanation," she said, "but couldn't it wait a couple hours? Please?"

Helaine gave her a steady look, and for a moment, Wendy thought she'd get a reprieve. But it only took one long breath before she realized how wrong she'd been.

"You needn't speak at all, Wendy," her friend said, "but I have some things to say." Then she turned and went into the sitting room. It was a lovely area designed to put ladies at ease as they looked at pattern books. Helaine would usually sit with them, looking at one or another while she sketched suggestions for each customer based on their discussion.

And just as the workroom was predominately Wendy's area, this place was all Helaine. In fact, it felt more like a countess's drawing room than the front of any shop. Which, she supposed, was appropriate, as Helaine was now Lady Redhill.

"Helaine—" Wendy began, but her friend shook her head as they sat. Then she poured the tea as regally as a queen. It was only after she had served Wendy, then herself, that she sat back and regarded her friend.

"I'm worried about you," she said baldly. "Your hours have been irregular, even before I got married. The orders are backing up, and you look exhausted all the time. I keep waiting for you to confide in me. I thought that eventually you would tell me or work it out on your own."

"And I am!" Wendy shot back, her anger rising, even though she knew Helaine was simply worried. "In a few weeks' time—"

"And then there was Claire's walking dress."

She frowned, trying to place the gown. "Claire Wickett? I finished that two days ago."

Helaine nodded. "Yes, I know. And here it is." She twisted in her seat and pulled out the cream and gold day gown from a basket beneath the table. She stood as she held it up, shaking it slightly so that the skirt fell cleanly before her.

Except it didn't fall neatly. It bunched bizarrely on the side. Helaine shook it a few more times for emphasis, which was when Wendy realized the horrible truth. She had stitched the gown wrong. Not only wrong, but misshapen enough to ruin the fabric.

"What happened?" she gasped as she stood to inspect the gown.

"Happened?" Helaine challenged. "Do you think this was an error in pressing? Wendy, look!"

Wendy was looking, and no, she hadn't thought that the mistake was anyone's but her own. But even staring at the evidence, she couldn't believe she had done such a thing. She hadn't sewn anything this badly since… ever. Even as a child, she'd been meticulous about her work. She inspected the seams and the fabric. It was possible she could salvage the material. Possible, but not likely—certainly not well enough for the standards of this shop.

"I knew the order was late," she said to herself. "I stayed up all night finishing it." She swallowed. Everything was late, and she'd felt bad about working on orders from their titled ladies before other women like Miss Claire Wickett. So she'd come in after working for Damon and would not let herself leave until the gown was done.

As she stood staring at her disastrous handiwork, the bell over the door rang and in walked Mr. Lyncott. He was whistling as he entered, and his first sound when seeing them was to shift his tune to a long, low note.

"That dress doesn't seem right."

"It's not," Wendy said miserably, while Helaine whisked it out of sight. Then she stepped forward with a cool smile.

"I'm sorry, sir. I'm afraid you've entered the wrong shop. We're a ladies' dress—"

"He's in the right place, Helaine," Wendy said, wondering how she would explain this. Radley wanted to take their walk, But after seeing what she'd done to that dress, she knew she had to check every gown she'd done in the last week at least.

Meanwhile, Radley was grinning, happier than she'd seen him in years. "You look very pretty, Miss Drew. Very pretty indeed."

Wendy flushed in embarrassment at being courted in front of Helaine, and at a moment when she felt so wretched. But she couldn't deny that Radley's words set her heart to fluttering. What a missish girl she'd turned out to be.

"Helaine, please allow me to introduce Mr. L—um,

no it's not that anymore, is it? Helaine, this is the Duke of Bucklynde. Your grace, this is my very good friend Lady Redhill."

"A pleasure to make your acquaintance, my lady," he said as he executed a florid bow. Wendy couldn't help but feel her spirits lighten at the sight. He was being playful.

Meanwhile, Helaine started at the introduction, her gaze scanning his seaman's attire. "The Duke of... oh! Oh, you're the *new* duke! Oh goodness, everyone's talking about you."

He flashed her a rueful glance. "Yes, so I've gathered."

Then Helaine flushed. "Oh, forgive me. My wits have gone begging." She dropped into a proper curtsy. "I am pleased to meet you, your grace."

"I am never going to get used to people calling me that. 'Grace' is a girl we knew as children. Remember her, Miss Drew? Bucktoothed—"

"And a lisp, but the sweetest girl. Yes, I remember."

"Whatever happened to her?"

"Married a sailor, had three children, and not one is cursed with her teeth."

He clapped his hands. "Well, that's excellent then. Sailor's wives are a lucky lot, aren't they?"

She picked up the rhythm of his joke without thought. "Best husband is one that's gone."

They laughed, Helaine included. "Obviously, you two are well acquainted," she said.

Radley answered. "We grew up as neighbors. Her brother and I went to sea together twelve years ago. And Wind here has been a good friend to my sister, Caroline." Then he grinned at Wendy. "Did I tell you? Caroline's engaged to be married. To a Scottish lord, no less. The same fellow she's been housekeeper to these last few years."

Wendy gaped, her breath whooshing out in stunned surprise. "Truly? That's wonderful! That's..." She had no other word than "wonderful." After the events of twelve years ago, Wendy didn't think Caroline would ever marry. "How did it happen?"

"I haven't the foggiest idea. Haven't seen her yet. Spent all day with solicitors. And thank Heaven for Lord Crowle. If it weren't for him, I'd have drowned for sure."

Helaine blinked. "You were with Lord Crowle?"

"Yes. He's son-in-law to my employer, Mr. Knopp of—"

"Knopp Shipping. Yes. His daughter Irene is our purchaser here. I know them both well." Then she stopped speaking to look between the two of them. "And you have come here to—"

"Take Miss Drew on a walk about Hyde Park. She promised yesterday, and I mean to collect."

Wendy sighed. "I would like to but—"

His face fell. "Wind, you can't cancel. I have so much to tell you!"

She shook her head, feeling pulled in too many directions at once. It was too much. She didn't know where to turn.

"Is it because of the dress?" he asked softly.

Her gaze jerked to his, startled to see understanding on his face. Then she chided herself. Of course, he understood. He'd worked all his life. He knew what a badly done dress could mean to a seamstress. This was her livelihood and, at times, the only thing that had kept her sane.

"I'm sorry—" she began, but Helaine interrupted her.

"No, no. I can see that you two have a great deal to talk about." Her voice was calm, her expression neutral. Wendy looked at her with suspicion.

"But I can't—"

"You can," she said firmly, "but not for terribly long. We still have a great deal to discuss."

Wendy sighed. If she knew Helaine, the woman would pick at her until she had the full story—Demon Damon and all.

"Excellent!" cried Radley. Then he held out his arm and walked her to the door. "So did all your things get moved without incident? No broken crockery?"

Wendy shrugged. "I believe so. Henry arrived soon after you left, then he and Mama went to the new rooms. I came here."

They were nearly out the door, but Helaine's question stopped them. "Wendy, wait! What has happened?"

She'd forgotten that no one else knew of her change in residence. She hadn't told anyone because she didn't want them to know she was living in Demon Damon's building.

Meanwhile, Radley answered the question. "She's been forced out of her rooms. Cagey thing, according to Lord Crowle. Said he'd look into it for you. Find out the real reason you were tossed out so summarily."

"What?" gasped Wendy. "No! I—he—" Bugger it, this was a mess! Certainly, she wanted to know the real reason they'd been thrown out, but she didn't want her friends even more embroiled in this disaster. "I will see to it!"

Silence met Wendy's cry, and it didn't take long to realize what had happened. In one explosive outburst, she had shown that the situation was absolutely *not* under control. And that she was unraveling more every second.

"Well," Radley finally said, his voice congenial despite the steel beneath his words. "It seems we both have a lot to discuss on our walk."

Helaine's eyebrows went up, but she said nothing. Neither did Wendy. Not because she didn't have words. She had plenty. Words like "stay out of it" and "I know what to do!" But of course, she'd been saying that for months now, and it seemed as if everything was getting worse.

"It will all be resolved in a month's time, I swear," she said. At least, she expected it would. Or she hoped.

Then Radley turned her so that she was forced to look into his face. His expression was sober, but his eyes shone as he looked at her. In them, she saw confidence and strength. All the things that she so needed. In truth, they were the primary reasons she was drawn to Demon Damon. And yet, here she saw the same qualities in an entirely different man.

Radley touched her cheek, the gesture so intimate and just what she craved. "We will take our walk now, Wind, and you will tell me everything."

She bit her lip. "There isn't much to tell. You already know we had to move."

"You are creating too much chop, Miss Drew."

She blinked. "I don't know what that means."

"It means, dear Wind, that I believe you are the one who will be talking first."

She opened her mouth to argue, but was stopped by Helaine, who had joined them at the door. "And after you are done talking to him, you will return here and we will finish our tea."

Which meant that Helaine would demand to know all as well. Wendy sighed.

"And with all this talking, no one will be sewing the dresses."

"As to that," Helaine said with a grin. "Tabitha has been teaching me. I believe I shall be able to help."

"Oh lord," Wendy moaned. She turned to Radley. "This needs to be a short walk. A very, very short—"

Helaine waved them out with a laugh. "I knew that would bring you back here, if only to stop me from destroying a gown."

✳

Radley stayed silent as they walked along the London street. Approaching someone in trouble was a delicate situation. No telling how that person would react, and Wendy was pricklier than most. So he held his tongue and let her relax, feeling the sunshine and the novelty of simply walking without any objective other than enjoying the day.

He was sure it was a novelty for her, almost as much as it was for him. If he guessed right, she was always running from one place to another, from one task to another disaster. And whereas he knew the value of thanking God for a fair day, his quiet walks had always been on deck, never in a clogged metropolis.

So together, they simply wandered and let the tensions drop into the sunshine.

"This is lovely," she eventually said. "I cannot remember the last time I just walked."

So he was correct. He smiled as he squeezed her hand where it rested on his arm. So small a thing—a lady's fingers resting on his forearm—but it was an intimate statement. She trusted him to lead and she to follow, or so the image projected. If only that were really true.

"I have wanted to do this with you for a long while," he said.

He felt the impact of his words in the slight hitch to her step. Did she truly not know how often he thought of her? How many nights he'd spent yearning for her?

She glanced at him then. He would have held her gaze, but he had to shift to protect her from a rushing ostler. Damned streets were too busy. He wanted to be alone with her! And never more so than when she spoke, her words as much a statement as a question.

"So it was you sending me gifts."

"Henry sent you gifts," he corrected firmly. "It would be improper for me to send you anything as yet. There is no understanding between our families."

She snorted, a rather inelegant sound. "I have never been a fine lady. Your mother put such ideas into your head." Then she sighed. "And in the end, she had the right of it, I suppose. Here you are a duke."

A little glow of happiness heated his belly. He was a duke, and as of this afternoon, that wasn't as horrible a fate as he'd once thought. Before he'd been focused on never setting sail again. He'd lost his captaincy. All his plans were at an end.

But now, he saw new possibilities and knew that he could give the woman of his dreams more choices than he'd ever manage as a sailor, even a captain. And again, as if she'd read his thoughts, she asked about his new status.

"How did it go at the solicitor's office today?"

"Excellently," he said. "I'll tell you about it after you have told me about that dress."

He felt her stiffen even before she spoke. "Why ever would you ask about that?"

"Did Lady Redhill make it? Was that why it was so…" His voice trailed away. He did not wish to insult the woman's skill.

"Disastrous? Ugly? An insult to good fabric?" There was a hard note in her tone.

"Yes."

"No." She sighed. "I did that."

So she was in trouble. There was no other explanation. She'd sewn better when she was six.

He squeezed her hand on his arm. "Tell me what the matter is. I hear dukes can solve all sorts of problems. It's almost magical."

She laughed, but the sound was more bitter than happy. "I wouldn't know. I've never known a duke before."

"Well, you know one now. Tell me what happened. Let me try my new magical power."

She bit her lip, and he could feel the struggle within her. She didn't like sharing her burdens with anyone. Ever since she was a child, she was the one to solve problems. It would be hard to admit she had difficulties that she couldn't fix on her own.

"I have it managed," she finally said.

"Obviously, you don't. Not if that dress was any indication."

"And what would you know about that?" she snapped. "You arrived yesterday and whoosh, suddenly, you're a duke. You don't know the struggles of—"

"Of wondering where your next meal will come from? Of fearing that something beyond your control has taken over your life?" He shot her an annoyed glance. How little she knew of him. "I lived as poorly as you did, except that Mama insisted we keep up appearances. Honestly, I think that made it harder. Starving, when you had to pretend you'd eaten a full meal."

"I'm sorry—" she began, but he wouldn't let her apologize so easily.

"And perhaps I have a title now, though I'm still expecting someone to tell me it's a big joke. But Wind, I am a *sailor*. You don't think I've been at the mercy of wind and sea? You don't think I've clutched the boards in a storm and prayed that God would spare my life?"

She quieted, and he knew he had scored a hit. Obviously, she hadn't thought of him over the years. Whereas he had hung on Henry's every tale of her struggles, she must not have heard anything of his life.

"Wind," he said softly. "I want to tell you so much. But I cannot until I find out what threatens you."

"Nothing threatens me," she said. Then she huffed. "Not exactly." Then, before he could press her further, she simply gave way. "My brother Bernard has gone into debt to…" She sighed. "It doesn't matter who. I have promised to pay it off, and I'm nearly there. But I'm tired. I sew during the day and work… elsewhere… at night."

His belly clenched tight. "What kind of work?" he asked, his imagination creating all sorts of disasters in his mind. She couldn't have… Not…

She looked at him, and her eyes went wide. "Not that," she said. "Not… that."

She turned her face away, but not before he saw the flash of shame in her eyes. So things were desperate enough that she had thought of it. He didn't blame her. There weren't many options for women, and he knew better than most how easy it was to slide into an overwhelming debt.

"I deal cards," she said. "At a gaming hell."

This time his belly clenched, but for an entirely different reason. "Whose hell?"

She didn't answer at first, which was confirmation enough. He tightened his grip on her hand.

"Wendy, tell me. Whose—"

"Damon's hells are the safest places for a woman. He protects us and doesn't force—"

"Don't sing that bastard's virtues to me!" he snapped. "He's a blackguard and a thief—"

"I'm not!" she said before he could vent his old anger. And when he cut off his words, she turned to look at him directly. "I'm not. I'm telling you the facts. It was the fastest and safest way to get the money Bernard owes."

Damn fool brother. Radley was going to have words with the man as soon as he had the time to beat sense into the idiot. Good God, but his mind was burning red with fury. Once he had thought Damon a friend. What a stupid child he had been. Radley had been best mates with Damon's older brother. They were as close as two boys could be, sharing an obsession with the sea. At the time, he'd thought of Damon only as a tagalong, the younger brother who couldn't be shaken. He'd never guessed at the jealousy that seethed inside the boy. It had all come boiling over one night, but not at Radley. No, the man had chosen Caroline as his target, and he had destroyed her life. The thought that Wendy was now working in that man's club had him violent with rage. But he couldn't express that. Not in front of Wendy. But he would fix this disaster immediately, no matter what the cost. "How much do you owe?" he asked through clenched teeth.

"I'll have it paid off by month's end."

Too long, and it didn't matter anyway. "How much, Wind?"

"One hundred twenty-one quid."

He almost laughed. So little an amount, and yet she was destroying herself to get it. He wondered how much she'd already paid. "I will have the money to you tomorrow morning."

"No!" she gasped. Then she all but stomped her foot. "I'll have—"

"It paid off by month's end. Yes, I heard. But did you also hear that I am now a duke? Good God, Wind…" He took a breath, then turned her to look at him. He held her gaze, trying to impress upon her what he'd learned, to let her know that all of it was at her disposal if she needed it. Then, when she had quieted enough to gaze back at him, he said it. The words were so new that he'd never voiced them aloud. But he did now. To her.

"I'm rich, Wind. The old duke was a miser like you couldn't imagine. The money I have now, it's staggering. I could never have earned that much in years as a captain even with rich hauls." He couldn't stop his grin. "I couldn't believe it when I saw the ledgers this morning. The money that flows in and out of the estate is staggering!"

"But you need it," she said, her mind obviously coming to grips with what he'd just said. "Nobs are terrible about paying off their bills. All that money is meant for—"

"Yes, yes. And those are being taken care of. As are the tenants—those who survive—and the new ones. The cash is dicey, but still there is value. There is a *lot* of value."

She blinked, and then her eyes grew hooded. "And you will need it. For good clothes, for parties and improvements and—"

"I think I can spare a hundred twenty-one quid."

She closed her eyes then shook her head. "You can't just give it away," she said.

"I can. And I will. Tell me who you owe this money to—"

"No!" she cried, loud enough to draw attention.

He winced, then began walking again. It was awkward at first, but she fell into step beside him easily enough.

"I will not have you working for Damon," he

ground out. "Nor will I have you beholden to a moneylender." His voice dropped. "Do you know what they do to people who don't pay?"

"I know," she said, her voice a whisper.

Yes, she probably did. "Wind—"

"I will take it as a loan. And I will repay every penny."

Of course she would. She had her pride.

"Tell me who it is. I shall have it paid off tomorrow first thing. And you will never, ever set foot inside Damon's hell again. Do you understand?"

She took a breath, but he felt steel in the sound. "I won't work for him again," she said. "I promise."

"Good. Now who holds your marker?"

"I won't tell you his name. I'll take the money with gratitude, but I can't… I won't let you pay it for me."

"Then let Bernard do it. He's the idiot who started this in the first place."

She flashed him a rueful smile. "Very true. And if it makes you feel better, I'll take Bernard with me. But you will *not* be there."

He didn't like it, but he could see that she would not budge on this. "Who is it?" he pressed one last time. "Why would you take Bernard but not me?"

She wouldn't look him in the eye. "Because you are a duke now, with deep pockets to bleed. I won't expose you to that risk."

He frowned, thinking through her words. He'd never been a man with deep pockets before. He had money enough. More than most sailors, but that wasn't the same as what he had now. He had to admit that she was right to fear. It was one thing to bleed a woman and her brother for a few quid. But if whoever it was realized that she had a duke's money at her beck and call? The blackguard would keep his hooks in her by any means possible.

So she was right. It was safer if she went with Bernard. And maybe some of Radley's friends. "Very well," he finally said. "Keep the secret, but if Bernard has racked up one more penny of debt—"

"Doesn't matter," she said, her tone flat. "I have told him I won't pay. And, in case he doubts me, I have already refused when he borrowed again."

Radley would see Bernard flogged! "How much more?"

She immediately softened her tone. "Just a few pennies for a meal. That's all. But even that—"

"He will not involve you more." He said it like a vow.

"And you will not beat my brother for his sins." She flashed him an impish smile. "That's my job, and I've been doing right well at it these last months."

"Months?" he asked in a deceptively soft voice. "You've been working off his debt for months?"

She wasn't fooled by his quiet tone. "It's done now. Or it will be tomorrow." She turned and gave him a grateful smile. "And I thank you."

He didn't want her gratitude. He wanted something a great deal more than simple thanks. But this was a start. And now, they were about to take the next step, as they'd arrived at Hyde Park. If they hadn't, he might have pushed her into a quiet alley and kissed her. But they were here now, and he refused to let his lascivious thoughts destroy his chance.

Whether she expected it or not, he would court her

like a lady. That meant no stolen kisses in dark alleys. But perhaps, he could give her something else—a glorious afternoon strolling in the park while a duke devoted every smidgen of his attention to her.

She must have seen what he intended. She must have read it on his face because he saw her eyes widen. She licked her lips, a gesture that had his cock tightening. Even more telling was the way her expression softened.

"You're a duke now. You can't be thinking those thoughts about me," she whispered.

His eyebrows rose, a haughty expression he used to mimic as a boy. Back then it had been so he could mock the nobs stupid enough to wander down to the docks. Now he realized, he would have to use it for real. It was as much an expectation of a duke as fine clothes and a massive home. He used it now on Wendy, only to discover that she was unaffected. Eventually, he released the expression to look her squarely—honestly—in the eye.

"I cannot stop what I think of you, Wind. Believe me when I say that I have tried." He stepped closer. "You are my best friend's sister and were too young when I left for sea."

He stroked her cheek then. A single caress that had her breath catching in her throat. This was how they had ended up kissing yesterday. They were on a busy street near the corner of Hyde Park, but he had no interest in changing this course. He would kiss her here for all the world to see.

She saw the intention in his eyes. He watched her mouth part on a gasp. He was already closing the distance between them when disaster struck. He didn't hear it at first. He was too busy seeing the word *yes* on her lips. But then the intrusion became all too clear.

"That's him! Look, Minerva, I'd know him anywhere. It's the new Duke of Bucklynde. Right there!"

Seven

WENDY WAS FAST LOSING THE REASONS WHY SHE couldn't kiss Radley. Why he was off limits. Yes, he was a duke, but he'd always been her better. More socially skilled, with a bigger heart, and generally, much nicer than she was. And, if he were fool enough to kiss her, then she would be doubly idiotic to refuse.

So she was done with saying no. They were standing so close, but now, he touched her, and her skin crackled under his touch. *A lifetime of defenses shattering?* she wondered.

"Yes," she whispered.

Then she felt him jolt, and his eyes narrowed in frustration. He was turning away from her. So tense was his reaction, she thought he was protecting her from a threat. But then, a moment later, she began to doubt. What danger came from three well-dressed young ladies as they rushed forward?

"Your grace! Your grace!" cried one auburn-haired beauty. "Do you remember me? Miss Grace Robin. We met this morning. You had been at the solicitor's office with Lord Crowle and were walking my way."

"Yes, of course—" he began, only to have his words drowned in the woman's breathless rush.

"I forgot to invite you to my ball next week. It's a small affair as these things go. Exclusive. I'm sure it will be a marvelous time. Say you'll come. Oh please!"

She stopped to draw breath, only to have the nearest woman elbow her sharply in the ribs.

"Oh! Oh goodness. I'm sorry, your grace. How rude of me. I'd like to present my two best friends. This is Miss Minerva Maitland. You'll hear me call her "M" because of all the M's in her name." She giggled then the woman on her left pinched her. "Ow! And this is Miss Elizabeth Dandleford. We don't have a nickname for you, do we?" she asked, turning to her friend, then immediately spinning back to Radley with a dazzling smile.

"Ladies, it is lovely to meet you," Radley said with more charity than Wendy could have managed. He even bowed neatly over each lady's hand. "I shall definitely enjoy attending your party. Now, if you'll excuse me, I was heading into the park."

"For a fashionable walk! Of course you were. And it's your first one as a duke, isn't it? That's what we're doing too. Not our first, of course. No, this is our second Season. Each of us, though Lizzy here started late, so it's really her first and a half." She stopped speaking long enough to see that Radley hadn't followed them. Instead, he'd turned back to Wendy, extending his arm.

Wendy felt her face drain of heat as the other ladies stared. After all, it was one thing for the famous new duke to wear a seaman's coat and clothes. It was very different for a seamstress in a drab dress to take his arm and stroll through Hyde Park.

"Your grace," she said as she dropped into a low curtsy. She hadn't meant it to be so deep, but her knees felt weak. "I must get back to the shop."

"Wind," he said as he took a firm hold on her arm. "No, you do not."

"You have been recognized," she all but hissed.

He appeared to think about that for a moment. He might have forced the issue. She saw his jaw firm in a stubborn tilt. But then, the beauty started talking again.

"Your grace? Your grace, everyone is in the park today. It's all well and good for the new duke to dress oddly, but people will be less forgiving of a woman. She's welcome to come with us. I will do what I can to help, but it will seem rather odd."

He lifted his head and turned to look at the woman. It took a moment for Wendy to realize what had happened. After all, except for the occasional visit once a year, she had not seen Radley in a decade. And she had never seen him draw himself to his full height and stare down anyone, much less a society beauty.

"I have all the introductions I need for today, thank you." And with that, he simply turned, settled Wendy's hand back on his arm, and strolled away.

Wendy did her best to quell the surge of satisfaction she felt. He had turned away from three society beauties to walk with her. Then, a moment later, she placed the woman's name and found her happiness fading. "She's beautiful and wealthy. Her father is an important banker, and her mother is friendly with the patronesses at Almack's. You should not have angered her."

"Why not?" Radley answered with a snort. "I'm a duke now. I'm going to be accepted everywhere, no matter what I do or who I insult."

She had to admit he was right. "But there are costs. I don't know what they are, but no one flouts society without consequences."

He glanced down at her, his expression sobering. Then he simply shrugged. "I didn't like her."

"You don't even know her. I'll wager you didn't even remember her name."

His lips curved in a slight smile. "Even so."

Wendy nearly groaned. "And now you're acting like a nob. Dismissing people just because—"

"They're rude and impertinent?"

She shot him a look. "And when did you start using words like 'rude' and 'impertinent'?"

"I learned them before I was out of short coats. Good God, Wind, you know how my mother could deliver a set down at forty paces. Did you think she spared me because I was her son?" He rolled his eyes. "She just never criticized me or Caroline in public."

"Well," Wendy said with a shrug, "at least Miss Robin was badly dressed. Not one of our customers, you know."

He frowned. "Really? I hadn't noticed. I was too busy stifling my yawn."

So he hadn't noticed her clothing? "Not even the white lace ruffle at the bodice to emphasize her *full* nature?"

He flashed her a grin. "Well, some things are hard to avoid seeing, I suppose. Made her look like a great white whale."

"It did not!"

"It did. I was searching for my harpoon."

She smiled, imagining him standing at the front of his ship, a great harpoon in his hands. Would he be shirtless as he threw? Would he look like the sketches of Greek Gods that Helaine's mother had showed her? Wendy had a seamstress's eye for body and form. Glancing at him now, she decided he did look like those images. And she couldn't help the heat that rose inside her at the thought.

"Are you evaluating my clothes now?" he asked, giving his coat a self-conscious tug. "Grant has recommended a tailor, and he says he can teach me how to tie a cravat." He flashed her a grin. "I told him I'd just knot a bowline on a bight. Had to show him what it was, but he said I might start a new fashion."

She looked at him, seeing the laughter in his eyes. It was never far from the surface. "You're happier now. It's good to see."

His expression faded. "I miss the sea, Wind. It's only been two days, but the thought that I'll never step to ship again…" His voice cracked a bit as he spoke, and he looked away.

"But you're a duke now. You can do whatever you want."

His expression turned sour. "Of course I can. So long as I mind the sheep and the tenants, produce an heir immediately, as well as make the social rounds enough to quash any fear that I will destroy England."

She jolted at the idea of his heir, but rather than voice that, she asked about the other part. "Destroy England? How?"

"By being a radical. Or worse."

"What's worse than radical?"

"Newfangled."

"I don't understand."

He chuckled. "Neither do I, but that's what they said. I cannot afford to seem radical or newfangled."

"Who are 'they'?"

"The solicitors. The bankers. Even Lord Crowle, though he laughed as he said so. Course he also agreed that… one of my relations should be able to guide me."

She heard the slight hesitation in his speech, right before he spoke of his relation. It wasn't hard to guess why. After all, he was the last male relative. Otherwise, he wouldn't have inherited the title. Which meant…

"This relation is a woman?"

He nodded, his expression rueful. "Lady Eleanor. From what I understand, she and my mother will get along famously." Apparently, that wasn't a recommendation.

"Is she coming here to London? Or do you go there to see her?"

He grimaced. "She's on her way here. I need to go to Derby soon. For a few days, to understand what I'm supposed to do. But no one wants me there until the sickness is well and truly gone from the area."

She shuddered. "I suppose that's prudent."

"It has nothing to do with me," he said dryly. "As far as I can tell, their biggest fear is that I might die without an heir, at which point, the title disappears."

"Oh," she said, not having thought much about titles and succession. Or, if she had, it wasn't to fear if one went extinct. She was more concerned with making sure she survived to the next week.

He turned to look at her, his expression somber. "They want me to marry her. They keep saying she'll make an excellent duchess."

Her heart sank, but she couldn't look away. He seemed to be trying to tell her something, but all she could think—all she could feel—was an abiding hatred of this Lady Eleanor.

"Will you?" she asked, her voice a whisper.

He reared back. "Course not! I don't even know her."

"That doesn't make a difference among the *ton*," she said, while her heart beat triple time.

"I don't care. She's not the woman I want." He took hold of her other hand. "I came home to court you, Wind. That doesn't change, whether I'm a duke, a captain, or a plain old seaman. I want you."

Her eyes started to burn. Of course, she'd guessed this was what he meant. After all, he'd been sending her such lovely gifts for years. But the truth was, they were near strangers. He didn't know her much more than he knew Miss Grace Robin.

And there was something else too. He didn't know what she'd been doing with Demon Damon either. He didn't know that she'd been kissed by a man he considered a monster, and she'd done it in full view of the entire hell.

"Say something, Wind."

She swallowed, her mind in a whirl. "I say that everything's changing. It's not that you've become a duke, though that's big enough. It's that the shop's doing better, but with all the ladies marrying nobs, there's more work and fewer hands to do it."

"Hire help, then."

She nodded. How like a man to have a ready answer to the statement, but not the feeling beneath. And yet, she was no different, focusing on his solution, not on the whirling turmoil inside.

"They must be trained, and there are some things that can't be done by anyone else."

"But surely, you can't think to give your entire life to a dress shop. You're a woman who should be a wife and a mother."

She shot him a glare. "And surely, you cannot think to give your entire life to the sea. To live day and night on a ship, then come to land only to dream of the moment you return."

He blinked, obviously startled by her words. She knew that was exactly how he felt. That even such a windfall as a dukedom paled to ashes beneath the strain of leaving sailing behind forever.

"But... but it's different for a woman."

"Balderdash," she snapped. "If a man can love his work, then a woman can too." Her words came out forceful and angry, but not because of the argument. In truth, she loved her work, but she did want to marry. She did want a husband and children. Her bed was a lonely place at night, and the temptation to reach for a man—any man—to fill that hole was strong.

He frowned, all but gaping. "You don't want to marry? Ever?"

She sighed. "That's not what I meant."

His expression tightened in annoyance. "Then what *do* you mean?"

He still held her hands, and she felt the warmth even through her gloves. He did that to her: warmed her blood and made her thoughts sizzle and pop. Like water set to boil, he stirred things inside her and made her think of things that she'd long since given up.

"I haven't been able to think these last weeks," she finally confessed. "It's been constant work and no sleep and keeping an eye on Bernard, while trying to fill order after order. Don't you understand?" she asked, her eyes meeting his with challenge and a kind of desperation. "You are stirring things up when I want it to settle."

He was immediately contrite. He tucked her hand into the crook of his arm and began to walk again—a slow stroll in no direction whatsoever. It would have been nice to walk through the park like this, but this was good enough. They had to constantly avoid people, but still… it was good enough.

"I have gone too fast," he said.

"You've been home a day. One single day, and in that time, you've become a duke."

He chuckled, the sound tight, but still filled with humor. "You stir me up, Wind. Around you, I am blown into a gale."

"I don't want a gale," she said. "I want…"

He looked at her when she didn't finish her sentence. He didn't even have to ask the question—it was written all over his face. What did she want? And could he provide it? Then, when he kept looking at her without moving, without wavering so much as an inch, the words were pulled out of her.

"I want another kiss," she said.

He grinned. "That is certainly something I can do."

She nodded, but as he leaned toward her, she held up her hand. "Not here. Not now."

He glanced about the busy street and then nodded. "When?"

She bit her lip. She didn't have to work tonight at the gaming hell. Never again, if Radley loaned her the money, and the thought filled her with giddy relief. Could she really be done with Damon?

"I will be working through the night at the shop," she said. "Will you come there? Late?"

"When?"

She bit her lip, thinking hard. She desperately needed sleep, but her work at the hell had kept her up at all hours. That meant she was used to working late. "Midnight," she said.

He stroked his finger across her lips, leaving them burning. "I will knock twice on the workroom door."

She shook her head. "I will leave it unlocked. Just come in when you are ready."

He flashed her a naughty grin. "I am always ready with you."

A year ago, she might not have caught his meaning. Now, the bawdy comment felt tame. "And I will be waiting." Then she hesitated, hating that she had to ask this, but needing to nonetheless. "And… and could you bring the money then? I want to be rid of… of Bernard's problem as soon as possible."

He pressed a kiss into her palm. "I will bring whatever you need, my Wind."

❧

Radley was whistling as he strolled away from the dress shop. Everything was falling into place. Certainly, there were changes to come. He was a duke, for God's sake, and he still had little understanding of what that meant. But he felt as though he was getting it under control. Mostly, he was learning what he had to learn, and that made everything manageable.

He was a smart man, after all, and he'd never failed when he set his mind to something. The responsibilities of a dukedom would be no different. Neither would his courtship of Wendy.

In short, he was pleased. So pleased that he thought he would visit his new home. It was one more duke thing to accomplish before tonight's seduction. And yes, he decided, it would be a seduction. He was truly primed to follow through on the promise of a kiss. And, if some things happened before the nuptials themselves, then that was the way of it sometimes.

His mind wandered as he strolled to the Grosvenor home of the Duke of Bucklynde. He hadn't planned on visiting yet. It had been too much to process, and apparently, there was a protocol for meeting the staff. But he knew his mother was anxious to move to the glorified address, and so he wanted to see it.

He came upon the house in early evening. The sun was setting, and it cast the building in a warm glow. Many people might have said it was a pretty house, especially with all those orange and rose tones from the setting sun. He noted it absently, his mind simply reeling from the sheer size of the thing.

All that space for himself and his mother. Good God, it was larger than the ship he'd brought in. He'd checked the address three times to realize that the massive edifice was his home. It didn't house multiple families shoved together or an entire ship's crew. Just him, his mother, and... well, servants. Probably a lot of servants, if what he'd heard about the last duke were true. The man had been singularly mindful of his consequence, and nothing said superiority like a household full of servants.

Radley's steps slowed as he wandered up the street. He had no interest in all that weight—servants, protocol, sixteen ways to tie a cravat. It bogged a man down until he couldn't move. But his mother would love it. She was itching to order people around. She'd already started talking about his valet, her maid, a cook, and more.

A footman had just hung the knocker on the huge door and was now polishing it. The man stood on a stool, working a cloth in and around the details of the massive eagle clutching the knocker in its claws. Rather fearsome door decoration with its beak open on a silent scream. Dangerous on a ship. He'd be afraid someone would slip and impale himself. But, of course, they weren't on a ship right now. And come to think of it, there was an eagle in the family crest.

He wandered up, contemplating the bird, when the footman looked down from his perch and curled his lip.

"What you looking at?" he demanded, his tone churlish.

Radley raised a brow. "No need to be nasty, mate. I'm just having a look around."

"Nasty?" the man sneered. "This is the residence of the Duke of Bucklynde, and we don't like blokes wandering around. Now get on with you."

Radley's expression darkened. He'd forgotten

why he never visited this area of town. It wasn't just that the owners were filled with their own consequence, but the servants jealously guarded it as well. Whereas a viscount might grin happily at any passerby, his valet would likely call the watch if the stranger weren't immediately deferential. And that was nothing compared to what a footman might say or do. Apparently, this footman was a prime example of exactly what he detested.

So he leaned back and pursed his lips. "Now, that's not very friendly," he said. "You haven't asked my name or if I have any business here. What if I were delivering something important for his grace?"

"Then you'd know to be at the back door, you cur," the man sneered.

The back door for deliveries and the like. Of course. Stupid that he'd forgotten that. "I'm not delivering anything," he said genially.

"Now, there's a surprise," the footman snorted. "Get yourself gone, or I'll call the watch."

"The watch? I'm not doing any harm."

"You're harming the very air." He sniffed in disgust as he descended from the step. The man was slightly taller than Radley, and he tried to use that to his advantage. He didn't know that Radley could easily best him in a fair fight—or an unfair one for that matter.

Radley shook his head in disgust. "I'm a first mate, and you would be wise to mind your tongue around strangers."

"Or what?" The footman bunched his fists threateningly.

"What's the meaning of this?" interrupted the

butler. Just in time too, as Radley was considering decking the preening footman.

He turned his attention to the older gentleman. The man had dark hair and narrowed eyes, but was otherwise unremarkable. Certainly, he looked dapper enough in his livery, but beyond a superior tilt to his chin, he seemed as unremarkable a man as any that might be found throughout this city.

Radley frowned. "This man is threatening me with the watch when all I did was walk to the door to have a peek at this fine knocker."

The butler frowned, his gaze moving between the two, before landing on the footman. "Joseph, what's the meaning of this?"

"He's a scurrilous man, no doubt planning to rob us blind in our sleep."

Radley laughed, allowing a full measure of scorn to slide into his voice. "Scurrilous? Robber? You deduced all that from my proper attire and polite conversation?" He turned his attention back to the butler. "Do you allow the staff to be rude to strangers?"

The butler's brows shot up, but he didn't become obnoxious. If he had, Radley would have sacked them both. Instead, the man came back with a stiff but rational response. First he addressed the footman.

"Joseph, please wait for me inside. Thank you." Then he turned to Radley. "Now, if you will please explain to me if you have any business here, sir, I will see what I can do to assist you."

Radley allowed a soft smile to curve his lips. "Will he be disciplined? Or is this a normal attitude for the household?"

"I don't see why that would concern you. Now, I repeat, sir, what business do you have here?"

"No business at all. I came to have a look around." He would have ducked in the doorway then, just to see if he could get away with it. He didn't because the butler was blocking the way with the obnoxious Joseph a step behind him. He focused on the footman, wanting to see his face when he said his next words. "I'm the new duke, and I'll need a good reason not to sack you both."

In truth, he had no intention of firing the butler. The man had not shown himself unfair... yet. But it would all depend on the next conversation.

In the meantime, young Joseph's face curled with disgust. "As if you could be—" he began, but the butler silenced him with a hiss.

"Well, this is most awkward," continued the butler. "I'm afraid I can't acknowledge anyone as the new duke, you understand. Not when he's expected tomo—"

"Tomorrow at two. Yes, I'm aware. Big presentation, my mother can't wait. But I thought I'd pop around early just to see."

"Seelye," came a female voice from inside, "is something amiss?"

Both men straightened visibly. Radley did as well. It was hard not to when such a cultured voice filled the air. It sounded lovely, actually, and very proper. So he wasn't at all surprised when the butler turned to address someone Radley couldn't see.

"I'm not sure, my lady. This gentleman claims to be the new duke."

"Really? Well, step aside. Let me meet him!" There

was some excitement in the unseen woman's voice, and Radley found himself smiling as the footman and butler reluctantly gave way so she could step forward. It wasn't that they were being rude. They wanted to protect her. Radley approved of such an attitude, of course, but he wasn't going to let it stand.

He pushed forward a bit—well, as much as he could, given that the butler still tried to block his way—and then he simply grinned at his cousin. "Cousin Eleanor, I presume."

"Oh goodness," the woman answered. "You look exactly like Uncle Charles." Then she looked at the butler. "Surely you see it. Think of the portrait in the upstairs gallery." Then she turned back to Radley. "Do look stern for a moment. And put your hand underneath your coat like this." She gestured by putting her hand near her nicely shaped right breast.

Radley obliged by doing just that. Then he finally got the reaction he'd been looking for. The obnoxious footman went pale as a ghost and sputtered. The butler drew himself to his full height and bowed deeper than necessary.

"Welcome, your grace. I apologize for the confusion. We had not been expecting you. And I can give you no reason at all for retaining Joseph."

Radley arched a brow. "Throwing him out so easily?" He wasn't sure he approved.

The butler didn't so much as blink. "It is naturally your decision, your grace."

"But you know the man and his work. I'm just the new employer. Do you not defend your own staff?"

Then the hapless Joseph spoke up with a snarl. "He

wouldn't defend me to the dogs. And a pox on you all!" Then he spun around and stomped away.

Radley was busy watching the dramatic display, trying to decide what he thought of it, when he chanced to look again at his cousin. She had gasped at the man's words, her face going pale. What the devil?

Meanwhile, the butler responded immediately. "Lady Eleanor! Please, come sit down."

"No, no," she said, obviously forcing a trembling smile to her lips. "Don't be ridiculous."

The butler would hear nothing of it as he gently cupped the lady's elbow. A bit of fatherly doting there, Radley guessed, as he watched the older man. Meanwhile, the lady turned her eyes on him. "You must think this all very odd."

"I think my life since returning to London has been very odd."

She smiled, her color slowly returning. "Well, come in, please. Let us show you around your new home."

It was at that moment that Radley realized two distinct things. The first, the reason for the lady's sudden pallor when the footman had said "a pox on you all." Not very original as insults went, but as nearly the entire ducal family had died from smallpox, it was likely a cruel and deliberate curse.

The second, Lady Eleanor was perhaps the most elegantly beautiful woman he'd ever seen.

Eight

"WELL, YOU'VE CERTAINLY STEPPED IN IT," HIS COUSIN said with a chuckle. "Mind you, I expected it. Just not so soon."

Radley didn't respond to Lady Eleanor's comment. His mind was locked on her stunning beauty. She was like a Grecian statue come to life—blond hair, blue eyes, and a stature that was just shy of being too tall. She moved with innate grace, and when she smiled, he felt a physical ache from standing near such beauty.

"Your grace?"

He blinked, coming back to himself with a start. "Um, sorry." He had stepped into the front hallway. The butler was waiting patiently for his hat and coat, and Lady Eleanor had glided back far enough to give him room to enter. But beyond that, he had done nothing more than gape. "This is a lovely, er, home," he managed.

She laughed, the sound light. "It's your home, your grace."

"Er, right." He forcibly brought his thoughts back in line. "Then it's a ponderously huge home that is entirely too dark."

The butler visibly stiffened. "Too dark, your grace? We have practically every candle in the larder burning."

That was true and exactly the point. As a sailor, he was extremely wary of any fires on board. And growing up poor, even the expense of one candle was often counted as too much. And yet, everywhere he turned, he saw candles burning, as staff alternately gaped or cleaned. He counted a dozen flames in the near parlor. Not to mention four maids and two footmen. Good God, how huge was his staff?

Meanwhile, Lady Eleanor looked around. "It is after six, your grace. One cannot expect strong sunlight now."

"Of course," he said, trying to frame his thoughts. It wasn't that the place was too dark—merely that it was so big. And big required lots of candles. Especially with a large army of servants cleaning every surface. "What is everyone doing?"

"We are cleaning, your grace," said the butler stiffly. "For your arrival tomorrow."

Oh right. Then he sniffed, stunned that the place smelled sweet. Of course. Beeswax candles, lemon-scented polish, and clean air. Suddenly, he understood why he appeared inappropriate to Joseph. After all, his coat was nicely made for a sailor, but it carried the scent of the docks. And though his boots were well cobbled, nothing could mistake the London mud that he tracked onto floors that had obviously just been polished.

He flushed at his dirty attire. "Perhaps I should return tomorrow as expected then. Sorry—"

"Don't be ridiculous!" Lady Eleanor cried. "You are here now. Formal presentations are all well and good, but one can't learn a house during something like that. Come. Let me show you about. Mind that you remember to be impressed with it tomorrow, of course."

He smiled, relaxing despite her beauty. "I'd like to, but..." He glanced at his boots, hating that every smudge of dirt showed on this white marble floor. Who would ever think to pick white for a floor?

The butler cleared his throat. "Perhaps if you wouldn't mind, your grace, I can have a footman polish your boots. Thomas, I believe, has been anxious to try a new cleaning solution."

Radley looked at the man, uncertain if that was a joke. Either way, he had little choice in the matter as Lady Eleanor clapped her hands. "An excellent idea. Then I can show you about while the cook prepares us a light meal. Have you dined, your grace?"

Radley kept forgetting that "your grace" referred to him. He kept looking around for someone else to answer. "Uh... well no, but..." But he'd thought to pick up a meat pie on his walk home.

"Mrs. Bardsley—she's the cook—has the most divine sauce for lamprey. I've specifically asked her to make it tonight just for me. It's my favorite. But there ought to be plenty for two." She glanced at the butler. "Do you think she will be able to accommodate his grace?"

Seelye bowed. "I am sure she will be most honored."

"Excellent. And please convey my thanks," Lady Eleanor added with a beatific smile.

"It's really not necessary," began Radley, but his cousin cut him off in an undertone.

"She's been trying new recipes for weeks, just to impress you. Don't you dare say *no* now."

Radley swallowed and dipped his head. "Uh, a small meal would be fine," he said. "But only if she can manage it."

"Very good, your grace," intoned the butler before he glanced significantly at one of the maids in the parlor. The woman dipped a quick curtsy and disappeared, presumably to take the message to Mrs. Bardsley. Meanwhile, Eleanor grabbed his arm and was about to lead him down the hallway.

"Now, the first thing you must see is the portrait of Uncle Charles. I'm ever so anxious to see if my memory is correct."

He took a step forward, only to stop when his boot rang out on the marble floor. "Oh bother." He barely remembered to change the word to "bother" rather than say something a great deal cruder. "My boots."

"Oh my, yes," said Eleanor.

Then at Seelye's gesture, Radley sat on a nearby chair and awkwardly pulled off his boots. He cringed at the dirt and the smell, while a footman suddenly appeared at his elbow. Presumably, footman Thomas. The poor man would be cleaning something better left in the rubbish bin.

"Perhaps it would be better to leave them—"

"And disappoint poor Thomas?" Eleanor interrupted, her voice showing a hint of censure. "He's simply desperate to try out that cleaning formula, remember?"

Radley looked to Thomas, who managed a strained smile as he bowed nearly to the floor. "It would be my honor, your grace."

It couldn't possibly be, but Radley merely sighed. The nobs always did things strangely, and now that he was one of them, he supposed he needed to act the part. Still, he couldn't resist adding an apology as he passed his old boots over.

"They're not meant for fine polish, Thomas. Just knock the worst of the mud off."

He meant it as a kindness, a way to tell him not to work too hard at boots that would likely be thrown out as too coarse for a duke. But the moment the words were out, the footman's face fell into disappointment. "Of course, your grace."

Meanwhile, Eleanor stepped closer. "But if Thomas wants to spend his time cleaning, then you'd be most pleased, wouldn't you, your grace? If he expressly wishes to?"

Radley wondered if the woman was daft. What man desperately wished to spend his time cleaning another's boots? But the message was clear in her heavy stare, and so he nodded slowly.

"Well, of course. If he, um, wishes."

"Excellent!" she cried. He was fast learning that "excellent" was a favorite word of hers. Then she held out her hand. "Now come. Let me show you the upstairs gallery."

Radley pushed to his feet, his stockings looking even worse on this floor than his boots. They were sailor's stockings, darned a dozen times over, except for the hole over his left big toe where he hadn't gotten around to it yet.

"Uh—"

"Come along, Cousin. You simply must see Uncle Charles."

So he did as he was told. He stood, she placed her

hand on his arm, and they walked up a huge staircase to the second story. She chattered about the London weather, her conversation verging on boring, while the butler trailed after them.

"I don't think he trusts me," Radley murmured.

She laughed, the sound musical, for all that it was false. "He's just being careful," she responded in an undertone. "You aren't bamming us, are you?"

He looked at her, wondering if she were naive enough to believe he'd confess a lie. "I don't know how to answer," he finally admitted. "Of course, I'm not fooling anyone, but I begin to wonder if I've stepped into another world."

"One where sailors become dukes?" she quipped.

"And servants are desperate for more work."

She grinned. "Oh, no one wants more work, I assure you. But they do want to make sure they continue working. And that requires your favor. Now that you've sacked Joseph, every member of the staff from Seelye down to the lowest scullery maid will look for a way to impress you." She squeezed his arm. "I did say you'd stepped in it, didn't I?"

He frowned, trying to remember. Oh yes, she had at the very beginning. "But I don't see how—"

"Joseph is an obnoxious prat and always has been. Oh certainly, he knows his place among our set, but among the lower orders, he can be downright nasty."

Radley frowned. "Sounds like he should have been sacked years ago."

Lady Eleanor guided them down a long hall. "And so he would have, except that his father is butler at the ducal seat, and the man once saved papa's life when he was an idiot and fell into a pig wallow."

"Who saved whose life?" he asked.

"Joseph's father saved my father's life."

"And that makes it impossible to fire Joseph?" He understood the value of loyalty, of one family's bond to another's, but aboard a ship, a man either did his job, or he was left behind next voyage.

Lady Eleanor shrugged. "Joseph is the eldest son of a family that has served us for generations. One doesn't sack that kind of tradition, no matter how badly he polishes the silver."

"But now, I have."

She flashed him a wistful smile. "You have. Which means Joseph is right now packing his bag and deciding which nefarious lies to spread about you to his family back home."

"His family of servants. Who serve me…"

"Yes, of course. Which means you can count on cold food and damp sheets when you arrive there."

"And yet here, everyone will be tripping over themselves to please me?" He stopped to look back at Seelye, wondering if the man would agree with all this nonsense. Apparently so because the butler dipped his head.

"Yes," continued Lady Eleanor. "Because if Joseph can be sacked, then there is no security for any of them."

He frowned. "There's no security for any man or woman who does his job badly."

"How democratic of you," Eleanor said. He could tell by her tone that it wasn't a good thing. Meanwhile, she had stopped next to a huge portrait of a man and his hunting dog. At Radley's confused look, she gestured to the rather dour man. "Meet your great Uncle Charles."

He frowned, trying to sort face and form from the dark image. Seelye brought candelabra forward, and together, all three compared the portrait to Radley. Well, he thought with a huff, there did seem to be some resemblance. Assuming, of course, he added a couple stone in weight, especially in the jowls.

"Well," he finally said. "That's rather... disturbing."

"Don't worry," Lady Eleanor said with a laugh. "Uncle Charles was a likeable fellow, assuming one talked about hunting. He was also a favorite among the ladies when he was younger, or so he claimed."

"I believe," inserted Seelye in ponderous tones, "that the tales of his charm grew as he aged."

"As is true for all of us, I'm sure," Lady Eleanor returned. Then she looked back at Radley. "I see it in the nose, of course, but definitely in the eyes."

Radley narrowed his eyes to see more clearly, but it was hard. After all, he didn't have a mirror to compare. He could only look at the man and wonder if he would age to look so stodgy.

"Oh yes, my lady," Seelye intoned. "I see it exactly now."

"What?" asked Radley. "Why now?"

"Because Uncle Charles had terrible eyesight, especially toward the end."

"Couldn't see the muzzle of his gun. Made for dangerous hunting."

He didn't have an answer to that. Instead, he took the candelabra from Seelye and paced slowly down the hallway, looking at the half-dozen portraits filling the space between doors. Were all these people his relations? He couldn't see the resemblance in some, but in others…

"That's your great Aunt Matthew."

He frowned. "Matthew? For a woman?"

"Well, no. Actually, her name was Matilda, but the story went that her twin couldn't say such a big name. Started calling her sister Matthew, and the name stuck."

"Blimey," he breathed. "That's ridiculous." And yet, it was funny too. "Tell me more. Tell me about all of them."

She tilted her head back. "Well, there are diaries you should read. I'll find them for you. But what do you know already?"

He looked at the very feminine form of his great Aunt Matthew and released a low chuckle. "Absolutely nothing," he said. "Papa never spoke of it, you understand. And my grandfather grew ill when I was young. All I know of the family came from my mother, who isn't related. She learned it from the society pages." He wandered to another picture, this one of a younger man sitting near a sextant and a telescope. Was he related to him?

"That's my father," she said softly. "He had quite a passion for astronomy."

"Did he sail?" he asked, gesturing to the sextant.

"Often. He traveled to Africa to view the stars from the bottom side of the earth, as he put it."

"I should like to meet him," he said. "I have been to Africa a few times, and it is a world unto itself." She didn't respond, and too late he realized what he had said. Obviously, if he had inherited the dukedom, then her father was dead. He turned, horrified by what he had said. "I'm terribly sorry. I wasn't thinking."

"Nonsense," she said, though her smile appeared strained. "I'm sure this is more bizarre to you than it is to us. And I assure you, it is very strange for all of us."

By "all of us," she must have meant herself and the servants. Seelye seemed to think so as he dipped his head. "Just so, my lady."

He looked at them, studying both closely. Their posture, their expressions, even the way they breathed. In the end, he exhaled his disappointment. "Neither of you thinks I am the true heir."

Lady Eleanor's eyebrows rose in the most disturbed move he'd seen her make so far. As for Seelye, he simply looked at the ceiling, just as his former captain used to look at the stars.

"Actually," said Lady Eleanor gently, "I believe you. And I think Seelye is coming to as well."

"Really?" challenged Radley. "Then why did you bring me here to dusty portraits in an unused hallway? It had to be to get me away from the staff."

"Oh, you are absolutely correct in that," returned Lady Eleanor with a serene smile. "Even you must admit that you're not quite up to the usual ducal flair." She didn't have to point out his stocking feet for him to be excruciatingly aware of his lack. But that didn't stop him from folding his arms and shooting her a dark look.

"I have sailed all over the world, fought for cargo, killed pirates, and even commanded a crippled ship as it limped toward home. I have stared down mutineers and wielded a whip until the deck ran red." He dropped his voice. "And I remember the men who laid down their lives on my orders and those who would do so again at my word." He looked pointedly at the portraits lining the hall. "Can any of them say the same?"

"Yes," returned Lady Eleanor with steel in her tone. "Every duke since William the Conqueror has served the crown."

She began itemizing the accomplishments of his forebearers, as if each word were a dagger thrown at his face. She spoke of men of letters and others of science. Of wives who were models of grace and stewardship for the next generation. Far from being offended, he listened with rapt attention. This was where he came from. These were the people who sired his father and grandfather. He felt a fierce stirring of pride at all the things he'd never heard.

The shame did not come until her last words. They were spoken darkly and with a condescension that was as cool as she was beautiful. And they cut him deeply.

"And not a one," she said, "ever saw fit to strip off his boots to show the world the hole in his stocking."

He waited to respond. He'd long since learned that a rash tongue would never serve him well. So he took his time, allowed the shame to course through him long enough for it to fade, while anger stepped into its place. Then he drew himself up to his full height and spoke with equal coldness.

"I have a hole my stocking because the last duke cast out his own son for the audacity of loving the wrong woman. You didn't ask me about my grand-mother. Though my grandfather passed when I was young, my grandmother lived until a few years ago. She was a lovely woman, generous and kind. She rarely spoke of her husband's family, and what she said was simple." He arched a brow, waiting for her to ask. In the end, she did.

"Was she bitter?" Lady Eleanor finally asked.

"No. Just sad. She said the old duke missed watching his son grow into a fine man. He never met his grandson who was a scholar despite his lack of an elite education. And, of course, he'd missed knowing me." He shook his head. "I can't imagine cutting a child out of my heart. I don't think I would have respected the man very much."

She didn't answer for a long time. Then she said, "Your great grandfather was not the last duke."

He frowned. "What? But—"

"My father inherited the title for six days." Her expression wasn't so much sad as sculpted from stone. She was chiseled perfection, and yet, her beauty left him cold.

"My apologies," he said with a mocking bow. "Of course, that makes all the difference."

"It makes no difference whatsoever. They are all dead, your grace. Except me and a few others."

He looked away, suddenly ashamed. Nearly every-one she'd ever known was gone, and a stranger stood in her father's stead. It had to be difficult. He rubbed a hand over his face, trying to think. And in that moment, the worst remark popped out of his mouth.

"They want us to marry, you know."

He saw her flinch. It was the tiniest movement, but he saw it nonetheless. Then, when he didn't fill the silence, she lifted her chin to look at him calmly. "It makes logical sense," she said.

"It makes no sense whatsoever. Marry a stranger for the sake of a title? You may put a great deal of stock in that, but I certainly do not."

Her head tilted, and he would swear that he saw shock on her face. But it was so hard to tell. This woman revealed herself in the tiniest fragments of an expression, as fleeting as a single raindrop.

"There is a great deal for you to learn. I can teach you much, but not respect."

"Respect, my lady?" he said, barely keeping a sneer from his voice. "I respect a great many things, but—"

"Nobility, apparently, is not one of them."

He rocked back on his heels as he studied her. Was she furious? Was her jaw clenched? Her eyes narrowed? He couldn't tell. In the end, he simply shook his head. "I do not think you and I will suit."

"No," she said stiffly. "I do not believe we will."

He looked down the hallway, seeing the huge dark faces of his ancestors and Seelye's stiffly formal stance. Was he truly supposed to fit in among these people? Worse, to lead the family and the estate as he'd once led his ship's crew?

It boggled his mind. This could not be what God intended. And yet, here he was. Again, he studied these two, and understanding sparked. "You two have been told to train me, haven't you? Just as I was ordered to court you, Lady Eleanor, those impertinent solicitors have told you to bring me up to snuff."

Seelye reared back as if struck. Lady Eleanor's reaction was much more contained, but on her it was as loud as any outburst. She walked two paces so that he looked directly into her face.

"No solicitor would dare give such an order to me," she said. "And it would be highly inappropriate for them to speak with Seelye at all." Her lips tightened. "Which only goes to show how little you know of us."

"Of course," he said as he took the next logical step. "No orders were needed. You knew your duty as does Seelye."

Neither one had a response. Radley looked at his stocking feet. He saw the hole in the toe and the coarse yarn that scratched his feet and made him hate shoes. And yet, as uncomfortable as it was, as cheap and threadbare as it was, it suited him better than anything in this house.

"I do not want to be here any more than you want me," he finally said. "I was going to captain my own ship and sail to India for spices." Then he lifted his chin. "Would you prefer I recant the title? I can do that, can't I? Give it up?"

She went pale, and Seelye rushed forward. At first, Radley thought the man was nearly violent in his reaction, but then he belatedly realized that he had stepped forward to catch Eleanor should she faint. He'd cupped a hand under her elbow to keep her standing. Radley tensed as well, worried by her unnatural pallor.

It took her a moment to recover. She took a few deep breaths and lifted her arm out of Seelye's hand. "I'm fine," she said in a weak voice. Then she repeated it with more strength. "I am quite well, thank you." She turned her eyes onto him. "I do not know if you can refuse the title, but I would ask you…" She swallowed. "I beg you not to do so."

He frowned. "But you don't want me as the duke."

"I don't want the title extinct either!"

Ah. Damned by faint praise. "So I am better than nothing."

She huffed out a breath. "You are a great deal more than nothing. It has yet to be seen if you can help the people under your care or destroy them."

He stiffened. "I meet my responsibilities."

She gave him a serene—and rather cold—smile. "Then you and I shall get along famously."

He matched her pose. "I doubt that, Lady Eleanor. I truly do."

Oddly enough, that brought out her smile and again, he was struck by her beauty. Poised, elegant, and as cold as stone. Except when she smiled and warmth touched her eyes. "This has been the first step in our dance, your grace. Absolutely nothing is certain at this point."

"Radley," he said, startled when the words left his mouth. After all, he needed all the authority he could muster with these people. If they did not call him "your grace" at every turn, they would likely think of him as a rough sailor forced into their midst. And yet, despite all logic, he insisted on the informal address. "I am your cousin Radley."

"Then you must call me Eleanor."

He nodded, wondering if he should kiss her hand. He stepped forward to do just that when Seelye cleared his throat.

Radley looked up, wondering if the butler objected to the abrupt informality between him and his cousin. But then Eleanor smiled.

"I believe our dinner is served."

"Really?" He looked at Seelye. How had the man known? No footman or servant had slipped into the hall to inform him. How could he possibly know what the state of their dinner was?

Eleanor must have understood his confusion. "I find it best to not question these things. Servants have their own magic, which is completely mysterious to us above stairs. You will learn to simply rely upon Seelye's accuracy."

For a man used to running a ship's crew, the idea of such a mystery disturbed him deeply. On board, he had known every aspect of his subordinates' tasks. He might not have checked everything or seen it accomplished, but he knew how it was done and could, if necessary, do the work himself. Always.

Seelye bowed formally. "If you would follow me."

Eleanor waited, obviously expecting Radley to offer his arm. He did so, feeling awkward next to her elegance. And then, all three proceeded downstairs to dine.

"I suppose I shall have to buy new clothes," he said with a sigh. He hated the business of clothes—the measuring and fitting and all that nonsense.

His cousin's musical laugh filled the stairway. "Cousin Radley, clothes are the easiest of things that you are about to buy."

And on that ominous statement, they settled in to dine.

Nine

WENDY COULD NOT BELIEVE HOW MUCH WORK SHE was getting done. And not just quick work, but perfect stitches, smooth seams, and even decorative touches. She was focused, as she hadn't been since the early days of the dress shop.

And the reason for such industry? Radley. She knew that he would be there by midnight, so she had to get everything done by the time he arrived. So she worked like the wind, and she smiled as she did it.

Then midnight came and went. Ten after. Twenty after. Twelve-thirty. Her hands slowed, her stitches became uneven, and exhaustion crept into her muscles. She set the work down.

Where was he?

The workroom door pushed open. There stood Radley, his face flushed, his eyes bright, and a grin of excitement stretched his face.

"Wind!" he cried as he rushed forward. Except he wasn't all that steady on his feet, and his hip banged one of the tables. "Bugger," he cursed under his breath.

"Shhh!" Wendy hissed as she leaped to steady him.

Fortunately, he found his own balance soon enough. But a noise from above had her glancing at the ceiling. "Helaine's mother lives above the shop." Hopefully, the sound came from the shop cat, but one never knew.

He put his hand to his mouth and nodded gravely, though his eyes danced with merriment. Wendy sighed. He was foxed. Deep into his cups, by the look of it. But at least he wasn't a mean drunk. Instead, he appeared to be one of those interminably happy drinkers.

"What have you been doing all this time?" she demanded. She tried to keep the shrewishness from her voice, but the disappointment was like a cold knife lodged in her throat. Didn't he know how much she had been looking forward to his visit?

"I have discovered the most amazing thing," he said. His words didn't slur badly, but she noticed anyway. "The duke has..." He frowned then corrected himself. "I own the most incredible brandy."

She leaned her hip against her table. They were separated by yet another table in the workroom maze. "And where was this brandy?"

"At *my* London home." He thumped his chest with obvious pride. "In Grosvenor Square!" He slowly worked his way around the table, moving with a drunk's care. "I'm supposed to go there tomorrow with Mum. Formal presentation and all that rot. But I wanted to see it tonight."

"I see. Didn't it upset the staff, you showing up a day ahead?"

He nodded. "I sacked a man because he was rude. And the butler, Seelye—" He rolled his eyes.

"Protective old codger, but we managed to work things out."

"No doubt," she said dryly. "Probably at the end of the first bottle."

"Yes," he said, not catching her sarcasm. "The wine is first rate too! Eleanor says that's the one thing the old duke always made sure of: best drink. The wine cellar is as big as a frigate's hold!"

She straightened. "Who's Eleanor?"

"My cousin," he said. "She's the one everybody wants me to marry."

The cold in her throat expanded through her heart. "So you've met her," she whispered.

He nodded gravely as he maneuvered to stand in front of her. "Beautiful girl. Makes my eyes hurt, she's so beautiful."

She blinked, her eyes burning unexpectedly. "Really?"

"But we don't suit," he said. "She's too…" He waved a hand vaguely through the air. "Ducal." Then he giggled, repeating the word. "Ducal, du-cal, duck all."

She frowned as she thought back to all the gossip she'd heard. Some had centered on which of the duke's family survived, and it included one Lady Eleanor. The descriptions of the woman had all mentioned her beauty, but many referred to her as a cold bitch. She ought not be so relieved by the description.

But here was Radley, smelling of brandy and spice, as he closed the distance between them. He set his hands on her hips and stepped closer, so that she had to look up to see his face. She might have run, but she'd trapped herself against her worktable.

"Now," he said with a grin, "I believe I promised you a kiss."

She held up her hand, stopping him when he would have claimed it. "I don't kiss drunks," she said firmly.

"Aw, don't be like that," he said, as his lips moved across her hand. He started at the tips of her fingers, nipping lightly, before teasing the pads with his tongue. Against her will, her fingers relaxed, opening slightly so that he was able to isolate her middle finger enough to suck it inside his mouth. She gasped at the feel of his tongue swirling around her finger, at the rough scrape of his teeth, and the hard suction that pulled her whole body toward him.

She fought the urge, though her blood simmered with desire. He was so handsome as he looked at her, his copper eyes bright with devilry as he teased her hand.

And as she struggled within herself, one of his hands snuck around her hips. Before she realized what he was doing, she was pressed flush against him. Her arm was trapped between them, and he kept sucking her finger, while below, she felt the hard press of him against her pelvis.

"Radley," she whispered. "You're drunk."

He pressed another kiss into her palm. "I suppose I am." He lifted his gaze off her hand to look into her eyes. "But not just on drink. It's you, my Wind. Do you know how many nights I have dreamed of you? Of holding you like this?" He stepped her further back, pinning her against the table. Then his hands began to rove up from her hips.

She could barely move, but his hands found her

breasts. So many sensations, while his fingers searched for her nipples, and his hips ground against hers. She was dizzy with what he did to her, and as his mouth nibbled her cheek, she felt her knees grow weak. She couldn't think, until some rational corner of her mind had the strength to push against his chest and knock one of his arms aside. Not far, but enough to ease the distracting rub against her nipple.

"Radley, no." There was power in her voice. It got stronger as she turned her face aside. "I'll not kiss you when you stink of drink."

"I think you will," he said, his lips an erotic tease against her jaw. Even his breath heated the air against her ear, fanning the flame in her blood to an inferno. "I have something for you," he said. "Something that you want."

He twisted slightly, reaching into his pocket with his free hand. The other squeezed and shaped her right breast. His hand was clever for all that his motions were clumsy. He lifted her breast, his thumb unerringly finding the point of her nipple. And with every pass of his nail across the raised bump, her blood sizzled and her belly clenched. She tried to push him away, but there was no metal in her arms.

Then he pulled back enough to hold up a purse before her eyes. It was bulging with coins, and he grinned as he held it there. "It's for you. It's the money I promised."

She didn't move, his words effectively dropping ice into her veins.

"Come on," he said, as he jingled it before her. "They'd shut the doors to the bank before I got there, but they opened them for me. I'm a duke now, and so they had to!"

She swallowed, her mind pulling back far enough to see what was happening, as if she were a fly on the wall. Here was a man, his voice thick and his body slow from drink. He had cornered a woman against a table and was now offering her coin with one hand, while the other rooted at her teat.

The image made her sick. That she was the woman, and Radley was the man, made it even worse. Hadn't he been the one who insisted on propriety? On courting her like a gentleman?

She cursed and gathered her strength. Then as hard as she could, she shoved him aside. He was two-stone heavier than she, but he hadn't expected the violence of her reaction. He stumbled sideways. Not completely off her, but far enough that she could escape. She did so clumsily, and she heard her gown tear where it had been caught between him and the worktable.

Then he recovered, his eyes wide, while the purse dropped to the floor with a heavy thud. "Wind?"

"Don't call me that!" she snapped, not understanding why—of all things—she objected to that. "My name's Wendy."

"But you're my—"

"I am nothing to you!" she said, choking back her sobs. "Nothing but a whore for you to pay and—and—" Her words were choked off as she pressed a hand to her mouth.

"What?" he said, gaping. "You asked me to come! You said you wanted a kiss!"

She had. She did. But not from a drunken aristocrat.

She wanted Radley the gentleman. The prince of her neighborhood, who had protected her from bullies and thanked her so sweetly when she helped his sister. She wanted that boy from her memory, not this drunken cad.

She drew back, her eyes burning from unshed tears. "Go home, Radley. I don't want to see you like this."

"Wind—" he began, then corrected himself. "Wendy, please. I thought you wanted…" He swallowed, cutting off the words, but not before his meaning was clear. He thought she wanted to rut for the price of his purse.

She knew she was exaggerating. She knew that wasn't how things were between them. But the similarity was too close, and she could not reconcile the two. Not with him drunk and the purse lying half spilled on the floor.

She bit her lip, her eyes drawn to the dull sheen of coin. She needed that money. With it, she could finally be done with Damon. But the thought of bending down to pick up the purse now made her nauseous. Her one kiss with Radley was so pure in her memory, like a bright moment of sunshine on a dark day. She couldn't taint them both with this. That kiss was the only beautiful thing in her life. She couldn't sour it. It would crush her.

"I don't want the purse," she said. "I've found another way to pay off Bernard's debt."

His expression darkened. "How?" He took a heavy step forward. "How, Wendy? There's nothing a moneylender will take but hard coin or barter."

His tone left no doubt as to what that barter would

be. He thought she was spreading her legs to save her brother. The idea was laughable, given what they'd just been doing, and suddenly, all her fury came blazing out. Hot and passionate, the words burned as they left her mouth, but that didn't stop her.

"You think I'm that cheap? That I'd sell myself to any man for this?" In a quick swoop, she picked up the purse and threw it at his face. Drunk as he was, he still managed to catch it. "Get out! Get out now!"

"What's the meaning of this?" came another voice—Helaine's mother, Lady Chelmorton, as she stepped into the room. One glance showed the woman was in a bed robe, but she had a hot poker in her hands, raised to strike.

Wendy turned to Radley. He'd gone pale at the sight of the older woman, but his eyes blazed with fury. He held up his hands in surrender, but his gaze was trained on her. "You *asked* me to come."

"And now I'm asking you leave," she said. Then she added two words, spoken in a sneer. "Your grace."

He flinched. She'd said the words in the same mocking tone they'd used as children whenever they referred to a useless prig of an aristocrat. He straightened to his full height as he walked around the table toward the door. Lady Chelmorton followed, poker still raised.

He made it to the door but stopped to add his last piece. "That's right," he said. "I'm a duke now. There'll be dozens of women begging for my attention—"

"Then go to them!"

"But I don't want them, Wind. I want you." His eyes darkened. "But I won't wait much longer."

She took an angry step forward. "You haven't waited at all. You've been home a day!"

He sketched her a mocking bow. "Even so." Then he hauled open the door and disappeared into the dark.

❧

Radley woke with a deluge of water on his face. He choked, then reared up while sputtering and coughing. That was a mistake. Rearing up, sputtering and coughing, all of it—a huge, huge mistake. His head pounded, and his stomach heaved. It was only by sheer willpower alone that he kept his stomach contents inside his miserable body.

Someone was speaking. Actually, more than one someone. Females. But the words would not steady in his head, and God knew, he had no desire to open his eyes. He held his head in his hands and prayed that the world would stop spinning.

In the end, a male voice cut through the female gibberish, silencing the women, and he was never more grateful than at that moment. A few seconds later, and the noises resolved into words.

"We're going to be late! And he can't go there looking like that!" Female. Shrill. Oh yes, Mum.

"Give the lad a moment. He's used to mustering at the sound of a whistle. He can manage a shave and a clean shirt by two." Male voice. Slight Scottish brogue. Who the hell was that?

"He needs more than a shave. He needs a bath and a delousing." Female voice. Softer than the first. He smiled. His sister, Caroline!

Then her words penetrated, and he squinted at his sister. "I do not have lice!"

In answer, his sister folded her arms and smiled. "He stirs! My goodness, Radley, you're not dead after all."

He bloody well wished he were with the way his head pounded. Then the man stepped forward. He was a handsome, rugged man with scars on his hands and a simple coat made of fine cloth. And he extended a flask.

"Here. This'll help." Rad took it greedily, unstoppering it and tipping it to his mouth, while his mother sputtered her objection.

"He doesn't need more drink! Good G—"

"It's not what you think," the man interrupted, but he needn't have, as Radley nearly spewed the vile concoction. He would have thrown the flask across the room, but the bastard gripped his forearm in a wretchedly strong grip. "It's horrible, I know, but it'll help settle your stomach. You don't think the Scots know about a morning head? Come on. Drink all of it, or I'll leave you to the women."

He cracked his eyes and glared at the man. But even though the big Scot took up most of his vision, he could still see the prim features of his mother and sister to either side. Choosing the lesser of evils, he reluctantly put the flask to his mouth and choked down the stuff.

Meanwhile, the man turned to smile at the women. "See. He's waking now. Go on, ladies. I'll see to him from here."

His mother spun on her heel with a sniff and

stomped—bloody hell, she must weigh a ton—out of the room. His sister sighed, shook her head, and left quietly. Thank God for that, but of course, one of her disappointed sighs cut deeper than any number of elephants clomping through the rooms.

Radley finished the last of the flask and handed it back to the man who had dragged up a chair. And when the hell did he get a chair in his room? Had his mother been shopping again?

He sighed and let his head hang. It took a moment, but he finally was able to manage a hoarse whisper. "Who the hell are you?"

"Ah, right. I'm Gregory Murray, Earl of Hartfell, and the man deeply in love with your sister. I'd have my ring on her finger by now, but your relations had to get themselves killed. She's the sister of a duke now, and we've got to do things proper. Wedding's planned for the end of the season. Is that acceptable to you?"

Radley forced his head up to inspect the man now seated before him. He looked decent enough. Wealthy too, and with a title. It was a great deal more than he'd ever hoped for his sister, but he didn't say that. Instead, he managed an awkward shrug. "Don't know you. Don't know if my sister likes you." Then his surly side couldn't resist adding one last jibe. "Don't bloody well know what you're doing throwing a bucket of water on me while I'm sleeping."

"Ah, well that was your mother. Claims she's been trying to wake you for an hour or more. Finally, sent round a desperate note to your sis. Once I understood the nature of your illness, I had my valet make this brew." He waved the flask. "Tastes like sewage, but I swear, it'll make a man of you in about an hour."

"I'm already a man," he snapped. "Have been for years."

"Pardon the correction, mate, but you're a bloody drunk right now, with a sore head and an ill temper." He tucked the flask away, then—damnation—pulled out another. At Radley's groan, he laughed. "We're going to get you shaved and bathed. Then you'll finish this second flask before you put on those lovely togs your mother set out for you."

"Like hell I will."

"You will because you'll be craving it. Trust me, I know. And then, we'll go to your new London home. Step lively, we haven't a lot of time. The women will have the bath ready by now."

Radley wanted to argue, but he knew better. He didn't have to see a clock to know that it was already late in the morning, possibly afternoon. So with a grudging nod, he pushed unsteadily to his feet.

That's when he saw it: the purse. Not his regular purse, but a fancy one that had been filled with coins. It was the purse that he'd tried to give Wendy, but she'd thrown at his face. He frowned, trying to remember the details of the evening. He remembered brandy. The best damned brandy he'd ever had in his life. Then he remembered rushing to see Wendy, and...

He groaned. It all came back in a rush. He remembered accosting her in her workshop. He'd pulled out the purse, just like any Jack paying for a back-alley tumble.

He didn't really remember the words they'd

exchanged, but he didn't need to. He could well guess. And then, he'd taken his purse and his dignity—if a drunk could have any dignity—and walked straight to the nearest pub. All that coin that should have gone to her was spent on drink.

Had he really drank a hundred twenty-one quid last night? Apparently so, because the purse was empty, and his head pounded. He collapsed onto the bed with a groan.

"The bucket's right there," said the Scot. "Don't be getting my togs dirty. Neither of us would hear the end of that."

Radley shook his head. He wasn't going to be sick, though he felt ill enough. "I'm a bloody idiot when I drink," he said.

"Well, that sounds like a tale," drawled the Scot. "But we haven't the time. If we take much longer, the women will be back at you."

He bit back a groan, knowing it was true. "Fine," he ground out, as he forced himself onto unsteady legs. "Let's get me ready to present to my massive staff. Though I don't know why we bother. They've already seen me unshaven and in holey stockings."

"What?"

Radley peered at the man. "The old duke has—" He swallowed and straightened. "*I* have an excellent wine cellar."

The Scot laughed. "You can tell me all about it after you shave."

With a nod, Radley began to clean himself up. It was slow going at first, but he managed it. He also asked for the second flask because he did, indeed, crave it by the time he'd finished his bath. The Scot showed himself to be a decent fellow. He didn't crow over the request, but handed it over with nary a word. He also kept Radley's mother and sister on the other side of the screen, since his bath was in the main room, and he even disposed of the dirty water without a word of complaint.

Such restraint wasn't in Radley's nature as he dressed. He looked about the rooms as he moved and saw over a dozen new purchases. So when he was fully clothed in new clothes, courtesy of his mother, he was able to confront her face to face.

"What are all these new things?" he demanded as he pointed to the new tea set, the shiny copper kettle, her new gown, and feathery hair pins.

His mum drew herself up to her full stature, which was nearly as tall he was. "I'm the mother of a duke now. You can't begrudge me a few new items."

"But where are you getting the coin?"

"Coin? Heaven's Radley, you're a duke now. We can buy on credit."

He gaped, already seeing where this was going. "How much," he rasped. "How much did you buy on credit?"

She shrugged. "As if I know! Radley, we can finally have everything we've always wanted!"

Radley swallowed, his head pounding. Certainly, he was wealthy, but he knew his mother. If left to her own devices, she could beggar the crown. He had to find a way to moderate her spending now. So he straightened and spoke in a commanding tone.

"No, Mum, we can't. *You* can't. There are expenses

and an entire village starving for food. I've spent the money we have already. It's gone up north to the people there. Plus there's an army of servants at the house who need pay." The bankers, in fact, had warned him repeatedly yesterday. Not just once when they joined the solicitors, but again that evening, when he demanded the coin for Wendy. There wasn't ready blunt. Not for him or his mum. And there wouldn't be a lot for months to come. He had "assets" they said, not "cash."

"But that's the beauty of credit," his mother said. "You don't have to have the coin now.

"But you have to pay eventually, mum."

"And eventually, you'll have the money."

He shook his head. The woman wasn't listening, and he didn't know what to do about that. And worse, he didn't have the heart to restrict her. When they were growing up, he'd seen her take the food off her own plate to give him. He'd watched her darn socks and cut up her own dresses to patch a hole in his pants. And now, finally, they had money for food and clothing. They had a house full of nice things in London and servants to meet their every need. How could he begrudge her these purchases?

"No more, mum. Not a single thing more."

She flashed him a happy smile—one that had been so rare when he was a child—and then bustled them to the door. "Come along. The carriage is already here."

He frowned. "Carriage? What carriage?"

His mother huffed. "Well, we can't arrive at our new home on foot, now can we?"

Radley winced, knowing that yesterday he had indeed arrived there on foot. "But—"

"I sent a note telling them to send the carriage at one thirty. It's a quarter to two now, so I'm sure—"

"I'm sure the horses have been cooling their heels for fifteen minutes, while the entire neighborhood sits outside to watch."

His mother didn't answer, as she was busy adjusting her hat above the feathered hairpins. But he saw her smug smile and knew the truth. After years of derision at her superior airs, his mother had finally gotten her wish. She was the mother of a duke now, and this was her way of rubbing everyone's nose in it.

"You've been lording it over the whole neighborhood for weeks now, haven't you?"

"Come along, Radley, Caroline. It's time to move to our new home."

Radley grimaced but didn't argue. His mother had earned the right to crow. So he bent to pick up a huge trunk, when his mother abruptly hissed.

"Put that down, Radley!"

He dropped it, startled.

"You're a duke, for God's sake. You don't carry and haul trunks. You have footmen for that."

He blinked. He'd been carrying and hauling for his mother ever since he could walk. But one glance at his sister's slow nod had him rethinking. He *was* a duke, after all. Why not let a servant carry the thing? It was bloody heavy.

So he straightened and nodded. "Very well," he said. "Let's go."

The women filed out, his mother leading the way. He didn't have to see her face to know that she wore an air of superiority in her expression. Caroline went next, while the Scot hung back, waiting for him.

"You ready for this?" he asked.

Radley didn't answer at first. Instead, he took a moment to look behind him. Not just at the rooms, but at his entire life up to this point. Was it all gone then? Would he never return to the life he'd known and loved? He knew the answer already, but it was hard to believe—harder still to want it.

"Can a man be ready for this?" he asked.

"Never."

"Then I suppose it doesn't matter."

The Scot grimaced. "You'll find your way. There are many who will help you."

Radley nodded. Of course, there were. After all, there had been a whole pub's worth of men willing to help him celebrate his new status. There were solicitors anxious to marry him to his cousin and bankers fired up about not spending his money. He had yet to travel to the ducal seat to meet the people getting the bulk of his cash in foodstuffs and medicines. And that didn't mention the people of the *ton* who would likely trip over themselves to help him in other ways he couldn't yet imagine. Marry their daughters, invest in their schemes, and give voice to their politics.

"I was going to be captain of my own ship."

"And now, you're a duke. Some would say you traded up."

He sighed. "I'm not one of them."

"No," said the Scot with a strange expression. "No, you're not. I quite like that about you." Then he shrugged. "Well, come on. No use delaying the inevitable."

"Right." So he straightened his shoulders and headed out. Then the oddest thought hit him as he left the room. He needed a woman on his arm. And not just any woman, but Wendy, with her calm practicality and steady voice. He needed his Wind because without her, he feared he would founder.

He touched the Scot's arm. "How long do you think this will take?"

The man pursed his lips. "A couple of hours to view the whole house and meet the staff. Then there's settling in. I've insisted your sister move in with you, you know. She needs to live the life as sister to a duke before she agrees to be with me."

Radley blinked. "That's right decent of you."

The man didn't respond beyond a tight shrug. "The staff will want to feed you. A meal fit for a king, most likely. Then, there are your requirements—selecting a valet while the ladies pick their maids. And—"

"When will I be able to leave, do you think?"

"You're the master. You can leave when you like. But it wouldn't be good form to depart at all. Not today. The staff would take it as an insult."

He cursed under his breath. He couldn't wait that long to talk to Wendy. He had to see her today. "How late, do you think? When can I escape?"

The man grinned. "It won't be so bad—"

"When?"

The smile faded. "After dinner. Eleven, probably."

Too late. Much too late to see Wendy. She'd likely be asleep, and he couldn't go banging on her door, demanding to see her. Not after the mess he'd made of it last night.

Damn it, he had to find a way to see her. Today. Then he had an idea.

"You said a dinner fit for a king?" Or perhaps, a queen. "Do you think I could invite someone to join us?"

"Just one? Certainly."

Excellent. He was going to get his Wind back. And he was going to do it in style.

Ten

THE FOOTMAN ARRIVED AT THE DRESS SHOP mid-afternoon. His loud and ponderous voice reverberated through the door between the front parlor and fitting area.

"I have a message for Miss Wendy Drew from his grace, the Duke of Bucklynde."

Wendy jumped at the sound of her name. She was in the middle of fitting a matronly baroness and had pins in her mouth. Fortunately, Helaine was also there. Wendy looked to her friend, trying to hold back her panic. She had no idea how to handle such a situation. She was on her knees, for God's sake, and most customers didn't even like talking to her. They preferred all discussion to be with Helaine, the dress designer, while Wendy silently obeyed commands. How would the baroness react to a message from a duke?

Fortunately, Helaine had an answer. She clasped her hands and appeared mortified. "I'm so sorry, baroness. I can't imagine what is—"

"A message from a duke!" the woman squealed. "The new duke? The one everyone is talking about?"

"Uh…" Helaine looked to Wendy, who nodded miserably. "Yes, I believe so."

"Send him in! Oh, send him in! I'm decently covered, aren't I? Do I look acceptable? Is my hair—"

"You look wonderful," Helaine said. "That color compliments your complexion to perfection." And it did. Helaine had quite the eye for color and design. That's why they were the premiere dressmakers to the *ton*. Meanwhile, she glanced at Wendy, silently asking if she was ready.

Wendy had found her feet and set the pins into a cushion, but she was anything but ready. Really, after last night's disaster, what could Radley be thinking to send a messenger? What could the man possibly say that would make up for what he'd done last night?

Meanwhile, everyone was waiting on her, so she gave a reluctant nod. Helaine opened the door to reveal a young footman in the blue and gold livery of the Duke of Bucklynde. He held a dozen hothouse roses in his grip, which he extended to the room at large.

"Miss Wendy Drew?" he asked.

"That's me."

He turned to face her and executed a deep bow. "His grace sends these with his compliments."

"Ooooh!" squealed the baroness as if they had been given to her. Meanwhile, the curtain that blocked off the workroom twitched. No doubt Tabitha and Lady Chelmorton were peeking through to see what was going on.

"Um, why don't I take those?" inserted Helaine, as she grabbed the bouquet. "There's no card that I can see."

The footman continued, his voice booming through the room. "His grace wishes to express his deepest apologies for any slight and wishes to make amends over dinner tonight. Would you honor him with your presence this evening at his London home? A carriage will be sent at eight."

Wendy stared at the footman. Had there been a question in there? If so, he had rolled right over it. Meanwhile, the baroness squealed again.

"Dinner with his grace? How exciting! Is he throwing a dinner party? How many people are invited? Have you known his grace long? Oh goodness, do you think he would come to my musicale? It's next Tuesday. I could introduce him to some very influential people. What do you think? Would he come?"

Helaine held up her hand, thankfully silencing the baroness. "Wendy?" she asked softly. "Do you wish to dine with his grace tonight?"

Wendy bit her lip and looked at her dress. She hadn't the clothes to wear to an evening with a duke. And beyond that, she was supposed to work at Damon's hell tonight starting at eleven. "I—I can't," she whispered.

"You can't!" gasped the baroness. "But you must. He's the *new duke*!" She said the words as if Wendy didn't know exactly whom they were talking about.

The footman nodded, as if he had expected such an answer. He bowed deeply then spoke again. "His grace feared that you might decline, so he bid me give you this." He extended a pristine note in an envelope so fine Wendy feared to touch it. But as Helaine had her hands full with the roses, Wendy had no choice, unless she wanted the baroness to snatch it up. So she took the missive and silently ran her finger over the engraving—the ducal crest, bold and beautiful, on white linen.

"Well? Open it!" exclaimed the baroness.

Wendy's hands shook, but she managed to open the envelope to see another engraving of the ducal crest, this one three times as large. Then she opened the missive.

> *Dearest Wind,*
>   *I know you are angry with me and rightly so. I behaved abominably. If you were a woman to want gifts, I would shower them on you. But you are not, so I must rely upon my meager charms to convince you. Please come to dinner tonight. I wish to apologize. I wish to see you. And even worse, I need your strength behind my sails. This is all strange to me, and I fear I will founder without you.*
>   *In desperate hope,*
>   *R*

Wendy read the letter three times, pausing only to take a deep breath.

"Well?" asked the baroness as she craned her head to see.

Wendy folded the letter closed and held it tight to her chest. She didn't know what to think, but she knew what she felt. *Hope.* A sweet, seductive, undeniably sneaky hope that moved straight through her fears to warm her soul. It was the dream that whispered through every girl's heart that she would marry the handsome prince and live happily ever after.

The revival of such a silly dream was as painful as last night's crushing disappointment when her prince had turned out to be just another drunk man wanting to get between her legs. And the two feelings—hope and disappointment—fought each other until she didn't know what to do.

Thankfully, her best friend was there, compassion on her face as Helaine took her hands. She didn't try to read the letter. Her gaze was trained on Wendy's face.

"What does he want?" she asked quietly.

"To apologize. For being such a beast yesterday."

Helaine smiled. "But you are afraid to believe that he could be sincere. Especially as most men are completely useless."

To the side, the baroness released a sigh. "Well, that is certainly true."

"But you know," Helaine continued, "many men are quite good. My Richard is wonderful. Samuel adores Penny, and even Grant has made Irene incredibly happy. All are good men, and all of us are happy. It could happen for you too."

Wendy didn't realize she was shaking her head until Helaine argued with her.

"Yes, it can. Isn't he the one who sent you presents all these years? The silk shawl, the carved ivory box— all under your brother's name."

Wendy nodded, her throat too tight to speak. Didn't they understand? She was too busy, her life too chaotic, to add a maddening aristocrat. A duke, no less, who said he was lost without her.

She didn't know how to respond to such a heartfelt plea. No one in her experience had ever spoken like that. They all demanded things from her or told her what they intended. Only Radley with his gentle touch and earnest eyes ever said words like that. Radley, who had nearly overwhelmed her last night, against the worktable when he was drunk.

"I don't know what to do," she whispered.

The baroness snorted in disgust. "You go to dinner, silly girl. Let him apologize. Good heavens, men never apologize! So, if you've found one who does—snatch him up! Or at least go to dinner, so you can live the experience once in your life."

Helaine's lips twitched at the baronness's impassioned speech, but she didn't laugh. Instead, she squeezed Wendy's hands. "Go to dinner, Wendy. What harm does it do to hear what he has to say?"

The harm wasn't in the evening, but in the time afterward, when she had to rush away to Damon's gaming hell. How did she explain that? "I… um… but, is it proper? I am an unmarried woman without a chaperone."

Helaine started to answer, but the footman cleared his throat, effectively silencing everyone. Then he spoke again, as if he were speaking heaven's proclamation. "His grace also expects his mother, sister, future brother-in-law, the Earl of Hartfell, and Lady Eleanor to be in attendance."

Wendy straightened at the mention of Lady Eleanor. She would like to get a look at the woman, and this was the perfect opportunity. She looked to her friend. "So, it's proper?"

Helaine nodded. "You can bring a maid along if you like."

As if Wendy had a maid to follow her around. "But what would I wear?"

"What about that gorgeous gown you wore to my ball? The green one that brings out your eyes."

She did look lovely in that. But she'd have to change before going to the hell. That dress was much too revealing for dealing vingt-et-un.

"Oh, say yes!" cried the baroness. "Before I say yes for you, slap on a green gown, and go in your stead!"

Everyone laughed, effectively breaking the tension. So with a pounding heart, Wendy turned to the footman. "Please relay my thanks to his grace. I shall be ready at eight."

He bowed deeply. "Excellent." And then he withdrew, backing out so obsequiously that Wendy fought a hysterical giggle, while Helaine squeezed her hands in joy.

"You shall have such a wonderful time, Wendy," she breathed. "You'll see. It will be delightful."

"Well, of course, it will be delightful," the baroness huffed, waving her hands. "Now go on. Go get the dress so I can see it on you."

Wendy blinked, abruptly confused. "But baroness, your fitting—"

"Tut tut. Don't you have another girl who can set the pins? Go on. I want to see this green gown!"

Wendy didn't have to call Tabitha. The girl pushed through the curtain, the movement awkward, as she was setting her glasses on her ears. "I'd be happy to set the pins."

"I guess that's settled then," Helaine said with a laugh. "Go get the dress. Let's see if it still fits."

And so it was done. The pile of work yet to do, the baronness's fitting, even the shipment of new silks that Irene brought in an hour later—all was secondary to dressing Wendy in a gown that turned out to be loose. Obviously, she'd lost weight. So Tabitha was set to tucking in the seams, while Lady Chelmorton did the hard work of filling a tub for Wendy to bathe. And even Helaine remained late to dress Wendy's hair. Then, just before the carriage arrived to whisk her away, Penny arrived with a pair of slippers to which she had added a stitched flower along the sides for decoration.

Then everyone stood back to smile as if she really were Cinderella heading to the ball. "It's just a dinner," she whispered.

"We know," said Helaine, her tone light.

"It's just a dinner," Helaine's mother continued, "with a duke who sent you roses and wants to apologize." As Lady Chelmorton had nearly witnessed what had happened the previous night, she was the one who should have objected the most. Instead, she was giddily happy and couldn't stop fussing with the wrap she set around Wendy's shoulders. "All men get drunk, you know. And he did just land two days ago. It's important to be gracious as you forgive him. Make him work for it, of course, but he did send you roses."

"Coo, and he's a duke," murmured Tabitha. She had Wendy's pile of stitching in her lap and was plying her needle with skill. The sight should have reassured Wendy, but part of her still tightened in anxiety. It was stupid, really. She was worried that Tabby couldn't do the work well and afraid the girl would prove too good and would replace her.

Wendy pressed her hands to her cheeks, trying to cool her flushed face. "I can't think," she whispered.

"But that's the beauty of it," Irene said with a laugh. "You're not supposed to think tonight. You're supposed to feel. Enjoy! Make the duke kiss your hand and implore you to forgive him."

"Then be gracious," said Lady Chelmorton.

"But not too gracious!" inserted Helaine, and they all laughed at the slightly bawdy suggestion. "Hold out for a ring."

"And then we'll all be calling you 'your grace'!" cried Tabby.

Again, everyone laughed, Wendy included, though the idea of becoming Radley's duchess was... was... what? A giddy dream? A terrifying possibility? She didn't dare hope, and yet, she did. Her, a duchess! And when she stepped out to the gleaming blue and gold carriage, Wendy felt like a duchess indeed. Two footmen hopped from their perch—one to open the door, the other to set down the step and hand her inside.

Her friends stood watching, and Wendy caught sight of Helaine pressing a handkerchief to her eye. Was she weeping? Wendy felt tearful herself, but she didn't dare release a tear. It would smudge the kohl darkening her eyelashes.

Then the carriage started its ponderous trek through the London streets. She leaned back against the squabs and thought of what was to come this night, of all the advice she had been given, and of what she would do.

She didn't know. She couldn't sort out how she felt, much less plan a course of action.

In the end, she simply closed her eyes. Tonight would be magical, she decided. Tonight, she would be Cinderella on the way to the ball, even though it was just dinner. And if Radley wanted to kiss her again… Well, she would decide then what she would do and not think more about it now.

But, of course, she did think about it. She did think and dream and wish all the way to his home and up the steps. And then, everything came crashing down when she saw the stunningly beautiful Lady Eleanor about to kiss Radley.

❦

"I feel like I'm being strangled," Radley groused to the room at large as he tugged at his cravat. How did people stand these things? The tight shirt was bad enough, but add to it a cravat, waistcoat, and coat, and he was afraid that he would drown. He couldn't move in all this damn finery, couldn't grab a rope, or save himself, if he were blown overboard. Yes, he knew he wasn't on board. He was, in fact, in the drawing room before dinner, waiting with his whole family for the dinner bell. He wasn't even outdoors, but logic had little traction against years of training in going barefoot and shirtless on board.

"Stop fiddling," Lady Eleanor scolded as she stepped before him.

He stood in front of the fire, too nervous about Wendy's arrival to sit down. Plus he was afraid he'd split his pants if he so much as bent his knees.

So he'd stood there by the fire and fidgeted with his clothes.

"Goodness," his cousin huffed. "You're worse than a boy in short coats." She slapped his hands away from his shirt points and tried to smooth his cravat into place.

On the settee, his mother laughed. "Good luck keeping him properly dressed. I'd no sooner tie his shoes than he had his coat off. Then, when I made him put that back on, I'd find he'd toed off his shoes."

"Ridiculous to truss a man up like a Christmas turkey," Radley shot back.

"I couldn't agree more," intoned Gregory, his Scottish burr more pronounced with his grumble.

"Oh hush," Radley's sister shot back to her fiancé. "You look very handsome."

Eleanor smiled as she touched his face. Her hand was cool, but her blue eyes sparkled. "I couldn't agree more," she said. "Very handsome indeed."

Radley froze for a moment, his body and mind stuttering at the feel of his cousin right there touching him that way. He knew it was an intimate gesture, knew too that it wasn't really an invitation. Due to the magnitude of their obvious differences, she wasn't really open to marrying him. He had no idea if it was primarily a sacrifice to the family honor or pure female interest, but either way, she was giving him a mixed message. And he couldn't stop himself from being all too aware of the apparent invitation. She was a beautiful woman. He was a red-blooded man who had been months at sea. Of course, he reacted, even as his mind recoiled.

She was not the woman he wanted. Beautiful as his cousin was, he had no interest in her charms. And yet, the realization came too late as his sister suddenly squealed a greeting.

"Wendy! My goodness, look how beautiful you are!"

Radley turned. Eleanor's hand was still on his cheek, but he brushed it away. And then he saw her—his Wind—looking like a green goddess stepped from the sea. Her gown was a shimmering emerald, her wrap a frothy cream, and her eyes shone bright. Too bright, he realized belatedly, as if there were a sheen of tears as she stood framed in the doorway. Her gaze was trained on him. No wait. She wasn't looking at him, but at Eleanor as the woman swept to the door.

"You must be the lovely Miss Drew. Welcome to Bucklynde House. We're so pleased that you could join us for dinner."

Radley frowned, his thoughts too slow as he struggled with what irritated him about his cousin's actions. She was being gracious, drawing Wendy into the room and introducing everyone one by one. It took him too long to realize that she was acting as the perfect hostess. Acting as *his* hostess, as if they were already a pair.

Damn it, that wasn't what he wanted, but he didn't have time to stop it, especially as Wendy asked about Caroline's engagement. His sister started talking about her courtship with Lord Hartfell, details that he guiltily realized he didn't even know, and then his mother stepped forward to kiss Wendy's cheek.

"You are a dear girl for coming," she said somewhat stiffly. "And I hear your little shop is doing well."

"Shop?" his cousin asked, clear shock in her tone. "Do you work?" No one could miss the implied disdain in Eleanor's voice at the word "work," and finally, Radley found his opening.

"She owns A Lady's Favor dress shop." He moved forward and quickly grabbed Wendy's hand. As he brought it to his lips, he tried to make the gesture warm, to re-establish the intimacy he'd once managed so effortlessly. But she pulled away, her manner reserved.

"Your grace," she said, as she dropped into a curtsy. She couldn't have hurt him worse if she'd slapped him.

"Wind," he whispered, "you don't ever have to curtsy to me."

She flushed as she looked away, turning instead to greet the damn Scot. "Lord Hartfell, it is a pleasure to finally meet you. Caroline has told me about your scientific work. It sounds quite fascinating." She started to bend her knees, but he stopped her with a laugh.

"Wist lass," he said, obviously exaggerating his accent. "If ye curtsy ta me, I'll have ta kidnap ye with me claymore and carry ye off to me highland lair."

"Oh stop." Caroline laughed. "He thinks he's charming when he does that. He doesn't realize that no one can understand a word he says."

Wendy didn't have the chance to respond as Radley's mother returned to the previous topic. "Wendy was a student of mine many years ago," she explained to Eleanor. "It's sweet that she and Caroline have remained friends." She made it sound as if the two girls had simply passed each other in the street a few times, when that couldn't be farther from the truth. Wendy and Caroline had been good friends despite Radley's mother's attempts to keep all the neighborhood children at a distance.

"How lovely," said Lady Eleanor, her tone as dismissive as his mother's.

Then Radley stepped forward, his voice stern. "Actually mother, Wendy—Miss Drew—was never your student. She has been our friend for as long as I can remember."

"That's not true," said Wendy, her voice soft, but firm.

Radley jolted. "What? Of course—"

"I was your mother's student." She turned to look at him directly, meeting his eyes for the first time since she'd walked into the room. "In return for helping your sister find her first position."

Radley frowned, unable to understand a word. And, in the face of his awkward silence, his mother explained.

"You don't remember, Radley, because you'd already shipped off—"

"I didn't ship off until after Caroline…" He swallowed down the bile that always rose in his throat when he thought of that time.

His mother sighed. "Yes, until after Caroline found *employment*." Her disgust over the word was more than evident.

Fortunately, his sister was able to speak. "I didn't *find* employment, mother. Wendy did it for me, and I have thanked God for that every morning since."

"As have I," said the Scotsman as he lifted Caroline's hand to kiss it. "Otherwise, we might never have met."

The two shared a look so intimate that it came close

to being indecent. Meanwhile, Wendy took up the last of the tale.

"And in return for my help, your mother tutored me in the ways of being a lady."

Lady Eleanor stifled a soft laugh. "Truly? She is the one who taught you? As a kind of *barter* arrangement?" There was nothing overtly cold in the statement, but Radley felt the flush of anger heat his face.

"Not everyone is gifted with everything they have, Cousin. Bartering is a way of life for most people. I just…" His gaze shifted to Wendy. "I just hadn't realized that was the price for your assistance." He nearly choked on the word "price." He'd thought she'd helped his sister out of kindness. And perhaps, out of feeling for him.

"It wasn't like that, Radley," his sister inserted. "She helped—"

"It was," interrupted Wendy. "I wanted to better myself. Your mother was the only teacher available to me. I helped Caroline in her goal to escape. Your mother helped me in my goal. An even exchange."

He understood it then, though the words were never said out loud. He knew his mother had a thorough dislike of the common classes. Certainly, she taught polish to young girls as a way of bringing in money. But she only taught girls with pretense to money and family—clergymen's daughters, girls from younger sons of titled lords. The same people who hired his father to tutor their sons would give their daughters to his mother.

But she never would have condescended to teach Wendy, whose family had neither money nor status.

The only way she would have done it was if Wendy bartered by finding Caroline her first position.

His gaze shifted to his sister, the shame of a horrible night long ago washing over him. If only he hadn't been such an idiot. If only he'd protected his sister, rather than drinking himself insensate while that bastard Damon Porter got hold of her. If only—

"My face is up here, brother."

His gaze jumped to Caroline's eyes. He hadn't realized he was looking at the high-necked bodice that covered her scars. It was where his gaze always went when he thought of what she must have suffered. Damn that bastard Damon—

"Stop it!" his sister snapped. "I am well content with my life." She glanced at the Scot. "Ecstatic even, because I am in love."

"And loved in return," the man said.

She smiled. "And loved in return. Do not bring back something long gone." She spoke to Radley, but her eyes traveled to her mother as well, then eventually, landed on Wendy. "You are a dear friend, Wendy Drew. I wish I'd found more time to spend with you these last years."

"We both have been busy—"

"Perhaps now I should say what has lived in my heart for the last decade. Thank you, Wendy. Thank you for everything. You saved my life and my sanity. And because of you, I eventually found love."

Wendy smiled, her cheeks pink, and her eyes shining with moisture. "I did nothing but push you on your way. You did all the rest." Then the two women embraced, their arms tight around each other. Radley watched, his heart surging with pride.

Then Eleanor spoke, her voice holding the tiniest hint of censure. "Well, I can certainly tell that I have missed a tale."

"It is a long-dead tale," he said firmly, his gaze on his sister. Hopefully, she could read the apology in his eyes. "And we shall leave it behind us."

Caroline nodded as she and Wendy separated. "And now that Wendy is here, we have a party indeed. You will never guess what Cook has made for us tonight. Duck with a special spice! I hear she is famous for it."

Eleanor smiled. "My father tasted the sauce in India on a peacock. He was so enamored of it that he forced the chef to part with the recipe—and a satchel of the spice—and brought it back home. We have been enjoying the secret ever since."

Wendy turned, a frown on her face. "Your father *forced* a chef to give up his secret?" Her tone was clipped.

Eleanor blinked, obviously surprised to come under censure, no matter how mild. "Well, he didn't threaten the man with a pistol. At least, I don't think so." She shrugged. "I suppose he simply paid an exorbitant amount for the secret."

"Of course, that must be it." Wendy's tone was tart, and again, Radley felt the air turn prickly. He sighed. He wasn't surprised that Eleanor held some prejudice against Wendy. After all, his mother couldn't wait to rid herself of any connection to their untitled, impoverished life.

But that Wendy would poke at Eleanor was a disappointment. After all, she was used to dealing with obnoxious aristocracy, and Eleanor was being relatively polite. And really, who cared about how the cook learned what sauce? So long as they all ate soon, he would be content.

Then, as if in answer to his prayer, Seelye stepped into the parlor and rang a silver bell. The man could have said the words aloud. Dinner is ready. But apparently, this was how dukes were told to dine—with a silver bell and an imperious look.

Lord Hartfell clapped his hands in delight then offered his arm to his fiancé. Eleanor stepped in front of Seelye and turned to Radley, an expectant look on her face. His mother moved into a position behind his sister with Wendy taking up the spot last.

What the devil were they doing?

"Radley!" his mother finally said, exasperation hissing through her every word. "We form a line to go into dinner."

They did? Oh right! His mother had insisted on such nonsense when they were children. Mum and Dad went in first, and Radley had always partnered with his sister.

He took a step toward Wendy, but his mother cleared her throat in irritation. At his confused look, Wendy explained in a quiet voice.

"The line forms by rank. As a duke, you partner with the highest ranking lady." In case he didn't understand, she pointed at Lady Eleanor. Then would come Lord Hartfell partnered with his fiancée, the future Lady Hartfell. Next would come the mother of a duke, and last of all—of course—was Wendy, who had no pretenses of a title.

He bit back his complaint. Even aboard ship, there was dining protocol, so he should have remembered this. Naturally, there was something ten times more elaborate among the aristocracy. With a silent curse, he offered Eleanor his arm. She took it with good grace, then Seelye bowed before leading them into the dining room.

And in such a way began the most miserable meal of Radley's entire life.

Eleven

WENDY FELT LIKE A HORRIBLE PERSON, BUT SHE REALLY enjoyed watching Radley have the worst dinner of his life. The food was excellent, of course, but what made it so terribly funny was watching the poor man constantly corrected by his mother. Having lived through the same experience years ago, she was sympathetic to how frustrating it was to be chided on everything. How he sat, how he held his fork, how he spoke.

Everything began with: "Radley, you're a duke now. You can't…" The list of things he couldn't do was endless. And even though she spoke in a low tone, with only six at the table, they could hear his mother's words and witness Radley's increasingly angry growls.

"You can't slouch in your chair."

"You can't start eating. You have to wait for the ladies to begin."

"You can't slop your food in your mouth. A proper gentleman takes small bites."

"You can't tug at your cravat."

"And don't mess with your hair! Do you want people to think you're distressed? A duke is never distressed!"

"Really, you must know you can't talk down the table as if you were shouting on deck. You converse with the people on your left and right and no one else."

That was apparently the last straw. He slammed his fist on the table and glared at his mother. "Damn it, I will bloody well speak to whomever I want at my own bloody table!"

The room went silent at the explosion. Every eye turned to him as he glared daggers at his mother. In the end, the woman sniffed.

"Very well, Radley. You have everyone's attention. What is it you'd like to say?"

He swallowed and looked up and down the table, but his desperate gaze latched onto Wendy. "Uh, er. Apologies for my language, ladies. Um... Miss Drew? How do you like the, um, the..." He waved at the dish in front of them. She thought it was some type of fish, but really didn't have a clue. Neither, apparently, did he. "The... this dish?"

Wendy's lips twitched. Really, she was horribly mean for finding his discomfort funny. "I find the food most excellent, your grace. You are fortunate in your cook."

"Er, yes. Quite good."

Then again, there was silence as everyone stared. No one dared speak. They couldn't resume their proper conversations with the people on their left and right. Not with Radley being so adamant. So everyone looked to him while his face flushed so red that she imagined she could feel the heat all the way down the table.

"So, um, would you... uh... care for more?"

His mother gasped. "Really, Radley, you're a duke now! You can't offer a person more food. That's the servant's—"

"Mother! If you mention my title one more time, I'm going to... to... I'm going to belch when I meet the Prince Regent. I'm going to do it big, loud, and stinky, and I'm going to tell him that *you* said it was how one greeted a prince."

His mother gasped. "You wouldn't!"

"I will! I swear it!"

The two glared at each other for the ten seconds it took Wendy to lose control of her laughter. She fought it, of course, but it bubbled uncontrollably. It burned her nose and came out more of a snort than a laugh. But it was enough.

Lord Hartfell was next, as he tried to shift his chuckle into a cough. He failed miserably. Everyone knew he was laughing. Caroline punched him in the arm, but her eyes were dancing.

She was the one who broke into open laughter first. And once she fell, everyone else did too. Radley laughed loudest, and even his mother chuckled, though her laugh was more a reserved smile.

Then Wendy chanced to look to her right at Lady Eleanor. The woman had taken the hostess's seat at the base of the table. She was smiling, her laughter sweetly musical, but it was her eyes that were arresting. When she laughed, her eyes sparkled, her face warmed, and everything in her moved from coolly elegant to vibrantly alive. Good God, she wasn't just beautiful. She was mesmerizing. And she was looking at Radley. All that warmth and vitality was focused exclusively on him.

Wendy's gaze shifted to Radley only to see her worst fears confirmed. He had noticed. He was staring in shock at his cousin while his laughter faded, and his jaw grew slack in astonishment.

It didn't take long for others to notice. After all, most everyone had been looking at Radley, so when his eyes became riveted to his cousin, they all turned. And as time ticked on, Wendy watched Lady Eleanor grow softer. Her chuckles faded to a beatific smile that remained sparkling with humor. And Radley—damn his eyes—simply blinked a few more times in obvious confusion.

Then slowly—as if by force of will—he shifted his gaze to look at Wendy. His expression turned apologetic, almost guilty, and her heart froze in her chest. What was he trying to say to her? That he was shifting his attentions to his cousin? She'd only just accepted that he was courting her, and now, had she already missed her chance?

For the first time, she wondered if she shouldn't have been angry with him last night. But he'd been late and drunk and...

No! Of course she shouldn't have allowed that disaster to continue, but was it all over now? Before they'd even begun?

She swallowed, trying to fight tears that she had no business shedding. She looked at her plate while the laughter died. To her right, Lady Eleanor called for the dinner plates to be removed and dessert served. Then Caroline picked up the conversation, asking Lady Eleanor about the Season to come. Radley's mother wasted no time in declaring that he would throw a ball after he was officially recognized as the new duke. His groan of disgust was drowned as the women began planning.

Well, all the women except Wendy. After all, she wouldn't be able to attend, would she? Not if Radley's attention had shifted away from her. If she was lucky, she'd be asked to sew some of the gowns, and that would make the shop more prosperous, so that was good. She tried to find contentment in that.

She couldn't manage to do anything but stir her flan around with her spoon and sit in silent misery. She was never more grateful than when Lady Eleanor declared that it was time for the ladies to withdraw. The gentlemen stood, of course, but when Radley went to escort the women, his mother stopped him.

"The ladies withdraw while the men drink port and smoke cigars. After a proper time, they join us."

Radley huffed a breath, obviously annoyed at the difficulty. Wendy didn't see more because Caroline came to her side and touched her arm.

"I haven't told you how lovely you look," she said.

Wendy frowned. "Yes, you did. You said it the moment I arrived."

"Oh," she blinked. "Did I? Well, you do and…"

"And you wanted to talk to me, didn't you? Is it about your wedding? You know, Helaine will design you a beautiful gown."

Her friend flushed a pretty pink. "Of course, I know it, and of course, I plan on having you do my entire trousseau."

Wendy smiled. "I'm glad—"

"But that's not what I wanted to say."

They were walking to the parlor, Radley blocked from view behind his mother. Wendy shouldn't have tried to see him, but somehow, she couldn't stop herself. And at that moment, her friend huffed out a breath.

"*That's* what I want to talk about."

Wendy blinked. "What?"

"The way you keep looking at my brother."

"I don't—"

"You do."

Wendy bit her lip. They were speaking in an undertone, both wanting to keep the conversation private. In the end, Wendy said the words that were now like stones in her belly. "He's meant for Lady Eleanor. He told me so."

Caroline grimaced. "Well, I don't know about that. What I want to say is that…" She sighed. "Well, that I don't mind. I'd love to have you as a sister-in-law, but…" Her voice trailed away as her expression became apologetic.

It didn't take a genius to know where the statement was going. But I don't think Radley and you would suit. But I don't think it's going to work. But it wouldn't be proper or right.

Wendy's heart plummeted to her shoes. She hadn't thought it could drop further, but obviously, it could. And Caroline's defection hurt worse than she could have guessed. So she did what she always did when something hurt. She straightened her spine and focused on the one thing that had never deserted her. Sewing. So she put on a false smile.

"Helaine will design a lovely gown for whomever

he picks." She would have said more, but that was all she could force from her tight throat.

Caroline took a moment to understand her words, and then she tsked with such irritation that it startled Wendy. "That's not at all what I meant! I want you to give it time. He's just returned to England and suddenly has a title. He was always scatterbrained on land as it was, and now, there are responsibilities—"

"Of course, there are. Your brother is a duke, and I wouldn't dream of—"

A man's voice cut through their whispered words. "I did *not* hear the word 'duke' again, did I?" Radley stood in the doorway, near enough—obviously—to have overheard something of what they said. And, if there was any doubt, he had planted his hands on his hips and glared at his sister. "I am done with being a duke today, thank you." Then, as added emphasis, he ripped off his cravat.

"Radley!" his mother exclaimed, "you can't!"

"I can, and I will." He pulled off the starched linen and held it out to the nearest footman. "Pray dispose of this, will you?"

The footman bowed deeply. "Of course, your grace."

Then Lord Hartfell laughed and tugged at his own cravat. "I think that's a capital idea. Can't stand the things myself. I hope you start a fashion trend."

Caroline twisted away from Wendy. "Really, Gregory, don't encourage him."

"You ladies have no idea how tortuous these tiny scraps of linen are."

"As opposed to whalebone corsets?" his fiancée shot back. "You must be joking."

"Caroline!" her mother gasped. "We don't mention—"

"Oh Mama, can't you see that it's done for tonight?"

The woman crossed her arms over her chest and frowned at the entire room until her gaze landed on the perfect Lady Eleanor who sat so pristine on the settee. "My lady, help me? Please explain that the Season has already started. We have a pile of invitations and more coming in every hour. Tell them that it's scandalous when they undress at home. Worse, it sets a precedent for when they go out. And they cannot imagine how awful it would be to behave badly in public."

"Actually," drawled Lord Hartfell, "he's the new sailor duke. I believe he's expected to be somewhat rough around the edges. Makes him more dashing, I think."

Radley's mother pursed her lips. "There's rough, and then there's disgraceful." Her tone made it clear that her son landed firmly in the "disgraced" category.

"Mama," Caroline began, but it was Lady Eleanor who put an end to the spat.

"I think his grace has made vast improvements in a short time. After all, he's wearing shoes today."

Radley chuckled. "And my stockings don't even have holes."

"What?" his mother gasped. "What did you do?"

Lady Eleanor laughed. "It's nothing, truly. Cousin Radley visited last night, and his attire was even more casual than today. Plus it allowed us a chance to try on some of my father's old clothes. And as you can see, they fit him very well."

"Except when they choke me," Radley groused.

Everyone chuckled. Everyone but Wendy. So that's where he had been last night when he was so delayed in coming to her. He'd been here, trying on clothing with Lady Eleanor. Could the evening get worse?

"Wendy?"

She blinked. That question came from Caroline, who was looking up at her. Up? Lord, what was wrong with her? Apparently, she'd stood and taken a step toward the door without realizing that she was fleeing. But now that she'd started the motion, she knew she had to leave anyway. She had to get home in time to change before going to the hell. She was not appearing there in *this* dress. It was too distinctive.

"I... I'm sorry everyone, but I'm afraid I must leave. I... uh..." Her gaze landed on Lady Eleanor's serene smile. Damn the woman for being everything that Wendy was not: beautiful, rich, and a lady of leisure. "I have a great deal of work."

"Oh, how tiresome," the lady said as she rose from the settee. "But we're ever so grateful you could come tonight, aren't we, Radley?" She might as well have called him her husband, given how easily she took on the role of his hostess.

Radley didn't answer, and in the silence everyone turned to look at him. He was standing there, anger in every line of his body as he glared at Wendy.

"Radley?" Lady Eleanor prompted.

In answer, he turned to the butler. "Seelye, fetch my coat, would you man? I believe I shall escort Miss Drew home."

"That's not necessary—"

"You don't need to—"

"You have a carriage. You are a duke now."

The voices rang out, Wendy's included. Radley didn't acknowledge the speakers. Instead, he turned to the Scotsman. "Gregory, I hope you and I can talk more sometime soon. Over cigars maybe. I believe I own some fine ones."

Lord Hartfell grinned. "I believe you do. And I should be honored to join you."

Then Radley turned and executed a fine bow. "If you will excuse me. I am off for a walk."

"Not so deep, Radley. A duke doesn't bow like—" The rest of his mother's words were cut off as he grabbed Wendy's arm and all but dragged her out of the house. He barely stopped long enough for her to collect her wrap from Seelye's outstretched arms.

"Thank God," he said as they finally stepped outside. He took a deep breath, lifting his face to the sky. "Sweeter than the docks, but nothing beats the open sea."

She knew he was referring to the scent in the air, and she realized anew how much he'd lost. Even as a boy, he'd wanted to be a sailor.

"I'm sorry," she murmured.

"Hmm? Oh, Mama is always like that. I'll pick it up eventually, and she'll settle down."

She smiled. "No, about losing the water. I know you love it."

His expression stilled. "Maybe I'll buy a ducal yacht." He smiled and looked at her. "I'll call it Wind."

"A rather plain name, don't you think?"

"Not with the figurehead I intend to commission." He winked. "Shall I have you bared to the world or dressed in a green silk that appears one splash from peeling away?"

She flushed, the admiration in his eyes unmistakable. But rather than address the idea of her as a figurehead, she slipped into safer territory. "Do you have the money to buy a boat?"

He shrugged. "Not the kind of boat I want. All the ready cash is going to help the village in Derby. Though I'm sure I have enough to commission a toy one. Come to think of it, I could probably carve one myself, if I set my mind to it."

She thought back. "You used to carve boats as a boy, didn't you?"

He laughed. "A few. Sank like a stone. Not to mention all the blood I shed nicking my fingers with the knife."

She didn't speak. They were walking at a leisurely pace. In the distance, a church bell rang ten o'clock. She ought to get a hackney, she realized. There wouldn't be enough time to walk home, change, and then get to the hell before eleven. But there wasn't a hack nearby, so she allowed herself to relax in the night air.

It was lovely walking like this, just the two of them. Her hand was on his arm, and the breeze touched her cheeks with enough air to cool her heated face. She let herself enjoy the silence a little longer. A moment more.

She sighed. She was a fool, and Caroline was right. This couldn't work. As annoying as his mother was, she knew the one thing that Radley refused to understand. He was a duke now, and she didn't have enough assets to balance that fact. She wasn't beautiful enough, rich enough, titled enough, or any of those things that might make a marriage possible.

"You don't have to walk me home," she said. "It's a long way, and now that you've escaped your mother, you can go anywhere. They'd never know."

"But I want to walk with you." He said nothing more, and so they fell into silence. Until they rounded another corner. "I'm always an idiot when I drink, Wind. I can't apologize enough for what an ass I was last night."

"You were," she acknowledged, "but I understand." And she did. He was a man, not a fairy-tale prince. He had flaws, and his life had been turned upside down. Even as she said the words, a part of her ached with disappointment. She didn't want him to become a normal man in her eyes. She wanted him to remain the perfect prince.

"Every stupid thing I have ever done has been because of drink. If I hadn't been drinking that night, then that bastard Damon would never have gotten hold of Caroline."

"Not true," she said firmly. "Damon would have found her eventually. He is like a dog after a bone, and nothing will stop him when he wants something." She shuddered when she spoke, wondering if that was to be her fate as well—initials carved into her chest. That's what Damon had done so many years ago to Caroline. He'd carved DP into the woman's chest, and she would bear the scars until she died.

"I should have killed him. I still think about it, and I wonder why I didn't slit his throat that night."

She flinched. "You shouldn't have! You know that! If you had killed him, you would have hung for murder. Even then, he had powerful friends. The only reason you escaped gaol was because you shipped off."

"I abandoned my sister to a monster. Perhaps I should have hung." He didn't mean it. She knew that he was voicing what all men say when they are posturing. And yet, part of him still lay trapped in the events of that horrible night.

"Shall we look at what happened?" she asked, challenge in her tone. "Look at how it might have gone differently?"

He turned, his eyes narrowed. "I don't want to—"

"It all began when you became friends with Damon's older brother, Ethan. Would you change that? Would you stop that friendship? You were boys with a shared love of the sea. Day and night, you went to the docks. If you weren't trying to sneak aboard, you were at the pubs, listening to the sailors' tales."

She saw him smile in memory. "Ethan died, you know. Fever. Ah, but he was the best mate I'd ever had."

"Exactly. You two were inseparable. It was only Damon's jealousy that made it ugly. A younger brother who couldn't tag along."

Radley winced. "We weren't very kind to him."

"He wasn't very nice to you. He spread rumors about you. He always tried to make you look stupid."

"Boys games. I knew he just wanted to join us, but he didn't care about the things we did. So we hid from him. Told him one thing and did another." He sighed. "It was cruel."

"There was darkness in him even then," she said.

"No—"

"Yes." Even as a child, younger than all three boys, she'd known that Damon could turn spiteful. That he had the devil's own genius for playing pranks. She'd never been the victim of it herself, but she'd guessed even then. A girl who had been mean on Monday had her whole wash splattered with mud on Wednesday. A boy who refused to share his toy soldier found it destroyed the next day. No one could ever tell who did it, but Wendy guessed. She had been one of those children perpetually on the fringes, watching what happened in the neighborhood. And, while others wondered who could be responsible for such terrible acts, she had guessed the source. And had done nothing.

That was her secret guilt. She had known what was going on and told no one. Who would listen? She was a little slip of a girl, barely into her teens. Besides, she had enough to do learning to sew for her witch of a mistress.

Meanwhile, Radley wasn't willing to release his own regret. "Even so. What brother—"

"Celebrates the night before joining the navy?" She squeezed his arm, turning him to face her for emphasis. "That was your party. You and Ethan were leaving in the morning. Of course you would celebrate. Of course you would drink."

"But I shouldn't have let her walk home alone!"

Wendy hadn't been there that night. She'd been sleeping in the dress shop workroom where she'd been apprenticed. But even she knew the truth of what had happened. Even if she hadn't heard it directly from Caroline days later, she would have guessed it nonetheless.

"Your mother never would have allowed Caroline to go to the pub that night. But she had a habit of sneaking out, as did we all."

"But—"

"Don't you see? Damn, you are so blind sometimes!"

It was her curse more than anything that had him stopping in the middle of the walk. "Wind?"

She huffed out a breath. "Don't you remember what Damon was like? How charming he was? How the girls swooned for his crooked smile?"

Radley frowned as he tried to think back. But he had been a young man at the time, obsessed with sailing. If it wasn't somehow attached to a boat, he didn't notice it. After all, he'd barely acknowledged all the girls pining after him. Why would he see the girls looking at Damon?

"I don't remember," he finally said.

"Of course you don't," Wendy answered. "Trust me. He could be charm itself." And his seductive skills had only gotten better over the years.

"But—"

"Radley, stop! You were having a party. Ethan was there, drinking and celebrating right there with you. Do you not understand how younger brothers and sisters wished to be part of that?"

He shook his head, his expression somewhat lost. "I suppose I don't."

He was an eldest son, and he had always had a place in the world. Handsome, a distant connection to a duke, and two parents who brought in money to keep them from starving. He didn't know what it was like to be younger or poor. To want to be a part, but be blocked out.

"Damon wanted to get even with you. Caroline was losing her older brother to the sea. Of course, they would find each other. And, of course…"

"He would hurt her."

She grimaced. The details of the evening were hazy. She had heard it directly from Caroline herself after the rescue, but even that had been interspersed with tears while shame hid the rest.

Damon had taken Caroline to a secret place, an evil room where women could be restrained. He had tempted her initially, promised her a surprise, and since she hadn't wanted to go home, she had agreed. By the time they had made it to the place, she had been fighting him. But he was bigger and stronger, and he chained her up. Wendy didn't know the words that were exchanged then. Caroline was no shrinking violet, and whereas she hadn't been physically strong, the girl had likely fought viciously with her words. And Damon had still been young enough that words could hurt.

He hadn't raped her, thank God. But he had done something arguably worse. He'd carved his initials in her chest deep enough—rubbing salt in the wound as well—so that it would scar for life.

Radley had returned home that night to discover that his sister had never made it home. He had gone immediately in search of her and had kept looking throughout the next day. He'd never joined the navy as he'd planned that day. It was well into the afternoon when a whore who had reason to be grateful to their father had slipped away to tell them of Caroline's location.

They'd found her and broke her from her chains. That night Radley had beaten Damon to a bloody pulp. He hadn't killed the bastard, and quite a few people had wondered why not. The crime against Caroline had been hideous, though of course, most people believed it had been her fault for walking with the man in the first place. Still, Radley was well within his brotherly rights to kill the blackguard who had done it, or so everyone said.

Wendy knew differently. Even filled with a righteous fury, Radley was no murderer. He might have killed when pirates attacked his ship, but self-defense was different from vengeance. Even as a furious teenager, Radley had not been one to kill.

She valued that, and she would not see him regret something that made him a prince and not a common thug.

"If you had killed him that night, you would have been sent to gaol and hung." He had been questioned. In fact, someone powerful had pushed for him to be gaoled and hung anyway, but as Damon survived his beating, there had been no cause. "Caroline would still bear her scars, but she would have lost her brother as well. Your parents would have grieved two children, not just one, and your death would weigh on Caroline's conscience. Do you recall how fragile she was at the time? Do you think she could have stayed strong if she knew her mistake cost you your life?"

Radley looked away. "He is a scourge and—"

"*He* is irrelevant." She spoke the words with conviction, but she wondered what her own life would be like right now. If Damon were dead and gone, would she be free of fear? Or would she be paying off her brother's debt to someone infinitely worse? "You needed to help her, and so you did."

"I didn't!" he huffed. "You did. You found her a position. You spirited her away when Mama would not see the reason behind it. And you—" His words choked off.

"And I saw that you followed your own dreams on board a merchant ship. Yes, I did." It had been the only way she could assuage her guilt at being silent. At not warning Caroline—her friend—about how stupid it was to pine after a handsome face.

He stopped and looked at her. "Should I have stayed?"

"To what end?"

"To keep my father from dying of grief."

She snorted. "Your father was proud of you. He died of apoplexy, and you couldn't have stopped that." She shook her head. "Why would you regret building your own life? Why would you think that shutting yourself away in guilt and shame would have helped anyone?"

Those were the exact words she had used back when she was sixteen. The exact words she'd said when she'd forced him to join a merchant vessel and take her older brother with him. She'd promised him that she'd look after Caroline, if he watched over Henry. And then, because she was manipulative, she'd gone and struck her own bargain with his mother for lessons in acting the lady.

"You were right," he finally admitted.

"And Caroline is fine. They're in love, you know. She and Lord Hartfell." She said it wistfully. That was the one good thing to come from this evening. She had seen how much love flowed between those two. "I think they will be happy together."

He must have heard the wistfulness in her voice. Either that, or he knew the loneliness that came from pursuing one's dreams to the exclusion of all else. He touched her face, and his expression turned intense. "I was an ass last night, Wind. A terrible boor, and you were right to throw me out. But if you can forgive me, then I should like to try again. I should like that kiss now, if I may."

She swallowed, her heart beating fast in her throat. She wanted to find out if he meant to court her or simply bed her. She wanted to ask about Lady Eleanor. She wanted to know so many things, but she didn't dare ask. She didn't think she could stand the answer.

So she simply nodded. Right there in the street, she nodded and lifted her face.

"Not here, Wind. I should like to do it in a proper way."

She arched her brow. Even she knew that any kiss was not proper. He flushed, obviously knowing what she was thinking. Then he shrugged.

"I used to dream about you on watch. Every night, I would stand at the helm and dream about you beside me. Or perhaps, the two of us at the prow."

She smiled, caught by the image. But she had two brothers, so she knew that his fantasies had not been nearly so tame. And that, of course, made her smile even more. It was a wonder that this man desired her enough to dream of her.

"We weren't just standing, were we?" she asked.

He shook his head, his gaze wonderfully dark and intense. "Come to my ship with me, Wind."

She blinked. "What?"

He shrugged. "The ship that would have been mine. The one that I would have captained. I want to show it to you."

"I would like that very much," she said, "but—"

He kissed her then—swift and hard—effectively swallowing her objection. Then he waved to a nearby hack that she hadn't noticed. Before she could do more than gasp, he was tugging her inside the dark carriage and settling her close to his side.

She thought of Damon, of the gaming hell, and all that she ought to do. And then he touched her waist, his fingers quick and deft, as they caressed her up and down. All other thoughts fled.

Twelve

Radley pulled her tight against him, taking advantage of the dark interior of the carriage to bring her close. He would have let her go if she fought him. If she pushed to the opposite seat, he would have released her instantly. But she didn't, and so he acted like a cad and tucked her close.

She smelled wonderful. In a city of every scent in the world, Radley decided that hers was the best. Lemon and honey. And something that was hers alone. Until he caught the vague whisper of tobacco in her hair. Must be the carriage, he thought. She would have no reason to be near anyone who smoked.

His hands were around her waist. He slipped beneath her wrap to stroke the elegant fall of green silk that was her dress. "Did I tell you how beautiful you are in this gown?" he whispered.

"Yes," she said, the word a breathy gasp. He felt her hand touch the back of his, stilling the steady rise of his fingers toward her breasts.

He chuckled. "That's my Wind," he said. "Ever practical. Simple question, simple answer."

"Did I tell you how handsome you look?" she asked.

He thought back. "No, I don't think you did."

"I've never seen anyone more uncomfortable in his clothes," she said. He barked out a laugh as she continued. "But you wear them so well, Radley. You will look every inch the duke in coats fit to you. And they won't pinch so very much."

"Everyone wants to dress me," he groused.

"I know the best tailor in London. He will fit you to a dream and not cost too much." She squeezed his hand. "He is young, but very good."

He pressed a kiss to her forehead. "I shall go to whomever you suggest, provided he doesn't make me wear these ridiculous waistcoats." He tugged at the buttons digging into his belly. "Pants and a shirt. Maybe shoes. These things, I understand. But waistcoat and coat, cravat and starched points? Whatever for?"

"For fashion," she answered. "And because you look wonderful in them." Then she twisted in his arms, bringing her face close to his. In the gloom of the carriage, he could barely make out her features, but he didn't need to see to know them. He had been picturing her face every night for years now.

"Wind," he whispered. "May I have that kiss now?"

He thought he saw her smile, but wasn't sure. It didn't truly matter. He was going to kiss her no matter what. But since she didn't say no, he leaned in, easily bridging the distance between them. He touched his lips to hers, savored the yielding softness of her mouth, and then pushed himself farther, seaming her lips with his tongue.

She teased him, touching her tongue to his.

Tentativeness at first—like the caress of a gentle breeze—quickly kicked into a storm. Their tongues tangled, and he felt his blood stir hot. His cock went from thick to stone hard in the space of a breath. He pushed closer, angling his body over hers. She gripped his coat, and the feel of her pulling him closer was all he needed to push her backwards against the squabs. A moment later, he was lying atop her, his hips grinding against her.

She ripped herself apart from him then. She twisted her head, and they broke the seal of their mouths. Her breath was a harsh rasp against his ear, but no more rapid than his own. Her hands were no longer gripping his coat but pressed flat against his chest. He had gone too fast. He didn't need her sudden stillness to tell him that. And yet, it was so hard to stop. She had filled his dreams since his first night aboard a ship.

"I'm sorry," he said as he dropped his forehead against hers. "I keep meaning to be careful, to go slowly, but…" He closed his eyes, but that did nothing to shield him from her scent.

She pulled back enough to look him in the eyes. "But what? What do you want, Radley?"

"You."

"Why?"

He laughed, the sound almost strangled. So simple a question, but so complex an answer. He had to settle for a simple, partial answer. "Because you're you, and I need you."

She sighed and pulled back. "You're so confused, you don't know what you want."

"Horseshit." He pulled her face back to his when

she flinched at his relatively mild curse. "I have commanded men in storms, I have fought in battles, and I
have grown from the boy you remember. I am a man,
and I know my own mind."

"But do you know mine?" she asked. "You know
nothing of me. You remember the girl I was, not who
I have become."

He nodded, knowing it was true. "Then tell me
of the woman you are now." He smiled as he settled
against the squabs. "We are finally alone, and we have
the entire night. Tell me everything."

She was stiff at first, holding herself away. But in
time, she relaxed enough to settle beside him. He still
had an arm wrapped around her waist, but he didn't
pull her tight. He was content to have her beside him.

"What do you want to know?" she finally asked.

"Start with your day. What do you do when you
first rise?"

"Groan and cover my head with the blanket.
Mama usually makes me get out of bed, and I often
say mean things."

He laughed, picturing the scene. "No one speaks
to me in the morning unless they have to. Some have
been known to leave a mug of coffee and back away."

She sobered. "No one would dare wake you
now. You're—"

"No, I'm not," he said sternly, before she could
say the dreaded word *duke*. "For tonight, I am simply
Radley, and you are—"

"Wendy."

"—my Wind." He squeezed her. "You shall
always be that to me, no matter how much you

object." Then he sobered. "You don't object, do you? Not truly?"

She softened against him. "No, not truly. Sometimes, I wish I could disappear into the wind and be blown far away."

He didn't like the sound of that. He didn't like the idea that her struggles were so many that she wanted to disappear. Right then, he resolved to fix whatever he could. No matter what happened between them—as man and woman—he would see her brother's debt paid. He owed her that much at least.

"So, after your mama drags you from bed, what do you do?"

"Dress and rush to the shop. These days, I'm always late."

He kept asking questions, his interest in her life genuine. It amazed him how much she accomplished in a day. Moreover, it stunned him how casually she spoke of running a successful business. She wasn't just a seamstress. She employed at least three other people and had business arrangements with a half-dozen more. She managed bills and goods, trained at least one apprentice, and still had time to work off her brother's debt.

She didn't speak of that, refusing to talk about it no matter how much he pried. Instead, she turned the conversation back to him, asking about his days. It was an easy shift. They had arrived at the docks and climbed into a small rowboat to take them to the ship. She was clearly excited to be on the skiff, her eyes shining, and her hands trembling as he helped her step aboard.

"I've never been on a boat," she said, her voice tight with anxiety or excitement, he couldn't tell which.

"I will keep you safe," he promised. He noticed that she was wrapping her arms around herself. It was colder here on the water, and so he shrugged out of his coat and settled it around her shoulders.

"Thank you."

"You must tell me," he said against her ear. "I will keep badgering you until I know about Bernard's debt."

She shook her head. "Tell me everything about your boat."

He grinned, allowing her to distract him because he did love talking about the ship. "She's a clipper ship, and you can see that she's been badly damaged. There should be another mast in front, and we had to patch the hull in three places."

"Three? How did you not sink?"

"They were small holes, thank God, and I am a good sailor."

There was a watch posted, of course, but all the men knew him. It was an easy matter to call out and have them drop a ladder to climb aboard. Not so easy was helping her climb in a dress. He hadn't anticipated the problem, but was grateful when she had no choice but to hike her skirts. He shielded her, of course, and sent a dark glare at the owner of the skiff. He would have no man ogle her but himself.

But when he had done all he could to manage her privacy, he allowed himself to enjoy her trim ankles and muscular calves. She was a strong woman, his Wind, for all that she was petite. What would it be like to feel her legs wrap around him? To be pulled inside her sweet center while he lost himself in her wildness? His balls ached at the thought, and because he was so distracted, he did something he hadn't done since he was a boy. He slipped on the ladder.

It was these damned ducal shoes. They weren't even his, but his grandfather's ancient pair. Barely worn, horribly out of fashion, and the worst possible things for climbing a ladder while ogling a beautiful woman's legs. It was only his strong grip on the rope that kept him from falling into the drink.

He recovered quickly enough, managing the last part without incident. His crew noticed though, and he caught more than one smirk as he dropped onto the deck. They knew what he'd been doing as each had likely been trying to see Wendy's legs as well. Fortunately, they didn't have the vantage point from above, or he might have to sentence them to draining the bilge for their impertinence. Illogical, he knew, as he was as guilty as they, but Wind was his woman, and they would know it now or be off his ship.

Except, of course, this wasn't his ship and never would be.

He stifled a sigh as he took her arm, then glared at the nearest men to vent his bad temper. They all tugged a forelock and backed away. All except the leader of the watch, who reported smartly.

"All's quiet, sir," he said.

"Good," he answered. "Man your posts. I'm just showing m'lady around. She wanted to see a ship so I thought to show her the best."

"Aye, aye," came the chorus all around.

There were three on the watch, and each man

slipped into the darkness to leave him to his seduction. Every man had been guilty of bringing a woman aboard at one time or another. There were all sorts of private spots on a ship this size, and as the man who had sailed her to port, he had the captain's berth. They knew what he was about, and he felt some shame about that. Wendy wasn't a typical flyer—not to him, nor in any other meaning of the word. And yet, he had brought her here for exactly what they believed—so that he could touch her in private. And if the kisses became more, then he was not opposed. He meant to marry her, and so he would take what she would give without apology.

Meanwhile, she shifted awkwardly against his side. "I'm not anyone's 'm'lady,'" she whispered.

"You are to me," he said firmly. Then he guided her around the clipper, talking easily about his life aboard ship.

She said all the right things as he showed her about. She was impressed that he would easily climb into the rigging and gasped at the height of the crow's nest. She touched the wheel and marveled at the power he would need to steer in a storm. He told her tales of danger—leaving out the worst details—and she trembled as he pointed to one area of the ship or another.

Then he brought her to the prow, stepped her up at the very tip, and held her there while he whispered into her ear. "Do you know how I came to call you Wind?"

"You have always called me Wind."

True enough. "But there was a moment that burns in my memory, a time that made it more than just a nickname for a child." He enveloped her with his arms, pressing his body along her backside as he spoke. "Do you remember watching on the pier as your brother and I sailed away? Do you remember how you looked or how long you stayed?"

She didn't answer, but he didn't need her to.

"I remember every moment. You stood there as long as I stood watching."

"It wasn't long," she said, proving that she did remember the day. "None of you were allowed to stand and watch."

She was wrong about that. In truth, the captain had let them stand there longer than most. It was his kindness to the men, as it would be long weeks before they saw another woman, and months before they could speak to their loved ones again. But Radley didn't argue. Instead, he let the memory flow.

"You wore a blue dress, the color of the sky on a pristine day. It was your Sunday best, and you wore it that day."

"My big brother was leaving. Of course, I dressed in my best gown."

"You waved at first, but in the end, you stood there watching. A vision in blue with a straw bonnet that blew back from your face. Then you took it off and let your hair blow free."

"I didn't take it off," she huffed. "It *blew* off, and I barely caught it. The wind was terrible."

It was a perfect sailing day, but he remembered her gown pressed against her curves, her hair streaming behind her, and her green eyes wet from tears. He hadn't been able to see her eyes, of course. Not from the ship, but when she'd kissed her brother good-bye, he'd seen them. Spiked lashes, green eyes, and a silent look to him, pleading that he watch after her brother.

It was a ridiculous notion as both he and Henry were as green as her eyes. They hadn't been able to take care of themselves, much less each other. But the faith in her eyes when she'd looked at him had made him feel ten feet tall. And he'd made a vow then that he would be worthy of her faith.

Then she'd turned from her brother to say good-bye to him. She'd held his hands and looked into his eyes. Neither spoke a word, but the agreement was there.

Take care of yourself, she communicated. *Live your dream and be happy.*

I will, he had promised in silence. *And you do it as well.*

Not a word out loud, but he knew what she wanted. And he had done so. He had lived what he wanted, save one thing. He had not returned home to claim her. Not until two days ago.

"Someone on board asked who you were," he said, returning to his tale. "You were so beautiful in that blue dress. Henry answered with your name, but it was hard to hear. The other man thought he said Wind."

She twisted slightly in his grip. "You call me that because some sailor was going deaf?"

"I call you that because you looked like a goddess, standing there. I could see you painted in the sky on a sun-streaked day with your hair streaming back. Your chariot would be the north wind blowing strong." He tightened his hold and pressed his lips close to her ear. "And because all sailors pray for a good wind, I did too, and she always looked like you."

She didn't answer, but he could tell she was affected by his words. Her body stilled, but she was molded so tight to him that he felt it when she let her weight fall against his. Then she touched the back of his hands, pressing her palm flat as she held him against her. But like the wind, she never said a word that he could hear. She just touched him while she kept her secrets hidden.

"Did you never think of me?" he asked, startled to find the question on his lips. "In all the years, did you never..."

"I did," she answered, "but not the way you think."

When she didn't elaborate, he tried to stop his questions. She was the kind of person who closed up when pressed, but he couldn't hold back. He needed to know if she had longed for him, as he had wanted her. "Was it the presents? Did you know from the beginning that they came from me?"

"No. I wondered, of course. It was possible, but not likely."

"Not likely!" he snorted. "Why ever not?"

"Because you were beyond me, even then. Surely you remember how the girls pined for you? Handsome, smart, and with a laugh that could charm a bird from the trees."

He tried to remember. "Mostly, I remember the water, the boats, the stories."

She laughed as she dropped her head back against his chest. "You boys are so blind sometimes." She twisted to look at him. "Do you not know what it is like for poor girls? We work endlessly with our mothers, and as soon as we are able, we apprentice. Sewing, laundry, kitchen or maid service, if we are lucky. The only escape is with a man who will provide a good home." She sighed. "Duke or not, you were always going to provide for your wife. You cared for your mother and your sister. We all saw that."

He flinched, remembering too well how he had failed to protect his sister.

"You did," she emphasized. "All the girls wanted you, myself included."

"Because I would provide a good living?"

"Because you laughed, Radley. Because you always had a kind word for even the lowest among us. Because you were handsome and had a distant connection to a duke. And because you treated us well and gave us all hope that we were special to you."

"Is that how you felt?" he asked. "Special to me?"

She snorted. "I wished, I pretended, but even then, I knew the truth. I was one of many. The only reason you remembered me was because I helped Caroline."

"Is that what you think?" he asked.

She nodded. "Of course."

He stepped away, but kept hold of her hand. "Come with me. I have something to show you."

She moved easily, but her steps were slow. "Where are we going?"

He smiled. To his cabin. Perhaps to his bed, or perhaps not. He no longer cared, but he would kiss her soon, and he would not do it in full view of the watch. "It won't take long," he promised. Then he chuckled. "I promise you are safe."

"I am not afraid."

Perhaps she should be. His intentions toward her this night were hardly honorable. "Then come."

A moment later, they stepped into the cabin. He lit the lantern then shut the door. His trunk was still here, and he pulled it open. The item he sought was not on top, but neither had it dropped to the bottom. And when he brought it out, he set it on the captain's desk for her to see.

She gasped at her first glimpse. And then, as he showed her all of it, she pressed a hand to her mouth in shock.

Thirteen

WENDY'S HEART BEGAN TO THRUM IN HER THROAT, and the heat in her skin made her shrug off Radley's coat as she looked. He'd sketched her. Not just once, but dozens of times. Dozens of drawings, one after another, of herself standing on the docks. Sometimes she waved at him, at others she was standing with her hair down and her gown pressed impossibly against every curve of her body.

He stood beside his work, silently turning page after page. She saw herself sitting as he'd described—a goddess on a cloud of white. Other times, it was her face or her eyes. Once, just her mouth pressed tight, but with a curve to her lips. He drew her often like that. Her chin lifted as if in defiance, and her lips curved upward without a full smile.

She looked to his face, trying to understand what he meant.

"You were special to me from the very beginning," he said.

"No," she whispered. "I became important the day you left."

He frowned, considering the words. "I saw you before. I remember you."

"But not like this. Not..." She swallowed. "Not sketched from memory."

Of course, it wasn't a perfect likeness. Her chest wasn't nearly so full, her legs not so long. In fact, his goddess was at least a foot taller than she was. Her neck was long, her skin flawless.

"I sketched you the first night on board. I didn't have a book then. I drew you on everything—wood, paper, scraps of sailcloth. And everyone called you Wind."

She didn't know how to react to becoming a goddess to an entire ship's crew. She didn't know what to think of such devotion from a man who'd been so little in her mind these years. Of course she'd thought of him. Of course she remembered him. But as a fond dream given up sometime between childhood and adult responsibilities.

"Radley," she whispered, "this is not me."

"No," he said as he stepped around the table to touch her cheek. "You are much more."

"I—"

"Your chin is always lifted because you are determined. Sometimes I make your eyes narrow because you see things that others do not. You knew that I had to leave home because I would only become bitter in London."

"Henry needed something to do, and you were my means to get him responsible work."

"And even as his younger sister, you saw what he needed—what we both needed—and you made us go."

She winced. "You give me too much credit."

"Whose idea was it to start a dress shop?"

She looked at him. "It was mine."

"Of course it was. Would Helaine have done it without you?"

"She needed a push. She didn't see her own value."

"But you did. And you made her take the leap." He touched her chin. "You are more amazing than you realize."

She believed him. When he looked at her like that, she believed everything he said. She had been the force that pushed him and her brother into sailing. But she did nothing more than *see*—see where they needed to go. She was the one who began the dress shop, but that was for her own sanity. She hated toiling for weeks on end with little coin to show for it. The money went to whoever owned the shop, and so she had been determined to get a shop of her own. Finding Helaine had been a stroke of good luck. Capitalizing on the woman's talents had been a mercenary trade for her own good, not Helaine's.

"I am not as good as you think," she whispered.

"Perhaps you are even better."

"I barter," she said. "I traded on Caroline's tragedy to get the lessons I wanted."

"You saw what she needed and got what you both wanted. That is a talent, not a failing."

She laughed. "The priests might not see it that way."

"But I do, my Wind." His fingers trailed into her hair.

She had a moment to decide. A moment to fight the descent of his mouth. She didn't.

Never would she have another chance. Never

would a man cherish her as Radley did now. She knew they would never marry. The circumstances of their lives were too far apart. At best, she could hope to become his mistress.

And, at that moment, mistress did not seem like so terrible a fate. Mistresses to dukes were feted throughout the ton. They were scandalous, to be sure, but they had lives that were often better than the wives.

If she were to choose her fate, then she chose this one. To be cherished right now by this man. To give her virginity to someone who saw her as a goddess. How many women could say such a thing?

She had no idea where her life would take her, but for this moment, he was the best man she would ever have. Tonight was the best moment in her life. She would take all she could, and she would be grateful.

His mouth touched hers, and she opened herself to him. His tongue thrust inside, and she arched her body into his. His hands brushed her wrap off her shoulders, and she wished her gown and corset could be dispensed with as easily. And when he pulled back to look into her eyes, she whispered one word.

"Yes."

She watched his eyes widen as understanding hit. Then, before she could draw another breath, he scooped her up in his arms. Suddenly, she was flying—or at least it felt that way—and her laughter rang, as she'd never heard herself. When had she ever made so happy a sound?

She twined her arms around his neck and pressed her lips to his. He more than met her, and their tongues began the thrust and parry with which she had become familiar. Then he set her on the feather bed, sinking in as he followed her down.

She felt his thighs first, hard and strong, pressed tight against her legs. Her skirt was in the way, but the pressure had her knees spreading anyway, giving him room to settle deeper—harder—against her.

His hips came next, his cock a hot thickness that was a shocking intrusion. Never had she felt anything like this, and it was pressed against her pelvis. But as his kiss continued, she felt herself move against him. There had been no conscious decision to press, but her body was fast taking over. She moaned when she had no idea why. She pushed against him to feel that hard heat push back.

He kept his upper body off her, his weight on his arms, but the air between them felt like a furnace. Or perhaps, more accurately, a brand. She would never again think of kissing without remembering this sizzling heat on her chest and the grind of his cock against her.

Abruptly, she twisted her head away, gasping as her mind came to grips with what was happening. She'd said yes, and yet, she had no true knowledge of what they were about to do. She'd heard of the mechanics, of course, but this *feeling* was more than she could handle.

She said nothing, but he seemed to understand. He dropped light kisses to her cheek, her jaw, and then nuzzled her neck.

"I won't hurt you," he said softly, between tiny bites. "I swear you can trust me."

She knew better than to believe that. Even if she

didn't know tales of girls who'd made that mistake, she'd listened to men brag of their conquests at the gaming hell. And yet, as much as her mind told her to stop, to keep herself pure, the rest of her believed. At a core level, she knew Radley would be true. And so, she turned her face back to him.

"Tell me what to do. I don't know what to do."

He chuckled. "That's my Wind—always doing something. But in this…" He pressed a soft, slow kiss to her lips. "I'll do the work." He grinned. "Trust me."

He didn't say it as a question, but she answered it as such. "I do."

He grinned. "Remember those two words, Wind." Then, before the significance of what he said hit her, he set his mouth to hers again.

She was busy kissing him, losing in the duel, as he touched every part of her mouth in a deeply intimate way. She barely noticed that he shifted his weight to her side, sliding to lie beside her. She meant to object, but she hadn't the time. A moment later, she felt his hand flowing over her belly, up to her breast. Her corset kept her from feeling more than his heat and a little pressure, but it was enough to set her chest to tingling.

But he didn't stop at her breast. Instead, he flowed upwards to stroke her bare neck and the flesh above her bodice. It was a slow caress, done with the calloused pads of his fingers, and the feeling was so exquisite she broke from his kiss to focus on his hand. Long, sweet strokes, meandering circles, and the frustrating constriction along the top of her bodice.

"Shall we take it down?" he whispered against her ear. "Shall we loosen the corset to let you breathe?"

She nodded, not able to speak, but he was lifting her so that he could find the buttons of her dress. The pins in her hair bothered her, so she pulled them out, letting her curls tumble about her shoulders. Her hair had never been more than something to pin up or tie away, but as her locks tumbled over her shoulders, she felt every curl brush across her bare shoulders.

"Beautiful," he whispered as he ran his fingers through one cascading curl. "Like honey in sunlight." Then his finger slid to the skin above her right breast. "In a pot of purest ivory."

She bit her lip, the awe in his voice making her heart swell and her body sway toward him. She did not like being this vulnerable—that mere words could make her melt—but there was no denying his effect on her.

He'd pulled her gown to her elbows, revealing her corset and shift. She shrugged her arms out of the restriction, then tugged at the ties of her corset. A moment later, she was able to take a deep breath as he lifted the heavy thing away.

But he had large hands and nimble fingers. As the corset lifted away, he pulled at her shift. She could have stopped him, of course. She could have held onto it, but instead, she rose enough that he could pull it over her head. And with that motion, her gown slipped down too. Before she realized the full extent of what she'd done, her dress fell, her shift lifted away, and she half stood, half crouched before him, completely naked.

She dropped down to sit on the bed, her cheeks flaming, and her hands widening over her groin before he caught them. With one hand, he clasped the fingers from both hands and drew them to his lips.

"You're beautiful."

She swallowed, but didn't say anything. This was so new. But more than that, too many thoughts were bouncing around her brain. She couldn't contain them all, neither could she grab hold of one to speak. Which gave him time to brush a hand over her face.

"Close your eyes," he said.

She did so as his fingers brushed across them.

"Set your hands here." He pressed them to the mattress on either side, a little behind her body. That meant she was seated there with her chest exposed.

She bit her lip, her heart thumping hard in her throat. And then, suddenly, she felt him. His mouth, his lips, his tongue on her right nipple.

She cried out at the suddenness, but within a second, she relaxed into the wonder of it. He sucked on her breast, and she shuddered at the exquisite feeling. A stroke of his tongue followed by suction, and her whole world shrank down to what he did.

She felt her head drop back. Her breath was quick and shallow, then when she felt his hand on her other breast, shaping and squeezing, she gave herself up completely to him. Her body was his, and she arched her back to give him better access. Then he pinched her other nipple, and she felt her belly clench—a sweet tightening and release done within her stomach and her thighs.

Then he eased off. His mouth left her breast to trail kisses across her skin. He lifted off her while his right hand continued to tease her other nipple. But all too soon, that stopped as well. She opened her eyes in confusion to see him looking at her.

"Radley?"

"Don't move. Just…" He swallowed. "I want to remember you like this. You are so beautiful."

She sat upright unconsciously, but he touched her cheek, silently urging her to lean back again. She went slowly, resting her weight on her arms. Her breasts felt five times larger, and her nipple was cold from the wet of his mouth. Both peaks were straining so tight they ached. And her heart beat hard in her throat. And, all the while, he was watching her, his eyes so intense.

"Your hair," he whispered, "a wild tangle. Your cheeks flushed and your lips…" He trailed a finger across her swollen mouth. "Cherry red and tasting like fine wine."

She licked her lips, feeling his heat as it made every part of her swell. He groaned at the sight even as his gaze slid lower.

"Your skin is like the finest ivory, only impossibly soft. And you smell like lemons and Indian spice." Then his gaze fastened to her breasts. "You are shaped so… so pert."

She blinked, not understanding what he meant. Then he touched her, lifting one breast as he stroked a thumb across her nipple.

"Enough to hold, and the peak lifted for me." He looked at her face. "Drop your head back. Please. And lift…" She did as he bid, and he sucked in a breath. His hand fell away, and he just looked. "So perfect."

She swallowed, her body a wanton thing under his

gaze. For the first time, she felt a confidence in her body, a wildness that he brought out in her.

Then, as if mesmerized, he stared as he stood. Without lifting his gaze from her body, he stripped out of his waistcoat and shirt. Glorious skin was revealed, a golden hue with a light dusting of hair. Muscled contours, dark nipples pulled tight, and a narrow waist. He unbuttoned his falls with quick motions.

He paused before he pushed them down, his gaze going to her face. "Have you ever seen a man before? Like this?"

She shook her head slowly.

"Would you... would you like to see?"

She nodded.

"Would you like to touch?"

Her gaze leaped to his face, but that didn't stop her from nodding her yes.

He stepped back, breaking the connection of their gazes as he pushed off of the rest of his clothing. Pants, smalls, shoes, stockings—everything. Soon he stood before her as naked as she.

And now she got to see golden skin turned whiter around lean hips and a tight bum. She saw the corded knots of his thighs along with a thick scar down his left leg. She wanted to ask, but she hadn't the breath. And besides, her gaze went to the thatch of wiry curls and the thick stalk of his cock.

It was darker than she expected, but still pleasing. It jutted toward her, bobbing slightly as he shifted to stand directly in front of her. And she could see the drop of moisture on the tip.

"Touch me, Wind. You won't hurt me."

She couldn't go directly to it. Instead, she touched his belly, watching in surprised fascination as his muscles rippled beneath her stroke. Her other hand stroked his thigh, needing to touch the white scar.

"Pirate blade," he said, his voice thick. "In the battle for this ship. The cut wasn't deadly, obviously, but it hurt like the devil. And it's healed clean."

She followed the trail of the scar upward, horrified by the wound that had caused it. He spoke as if it were nothing more than a slight scrape, but she knew the wound had been serious. He was lucky to have survived.

All those thoughts flowed through her mind, but they carried only a little part of her attention. She looked at his cock, needing to know more, to understand what they were about to do.

In time, she touched it. The hand on his belly slid lower, while the one below reached higher to cup him. She hadn't even remembered that men had a sac beneath, but now she knew. Now she touched.

His breath became rough as she explored, but he didn't move. His cock bobbed as if in approval, but there was no more. He let her learn in her own time, and for that she was grateful.

Then she felt his cock. The thick stalk first, and she was surprised by the stiffness. She hadn't thought flesh could feel like steel beneath the velvet skin—so thick, so hard, and yet, so hot. His heat pulsed against her hand. Or maybe, that was his life, his blood, his seed waiting there to implant in her.

She glanced up to his face. He was looking at her, his eyes burning with intensity. His jaw was rigid, and his belly twitched as she touched him.

"Grip it," he said, his voice raspy.

She did, wrapping her fingers around him and squeezing. He released a groan, and when she looked, his eyelids fluttered. Had she done that? She tried it again, tightening her fist and pulling slightly. His breath caught, and his mouth opened on a gasp.

She meant to release him, not sure what she had done was right, but he stopped her. He wrapped his larger hand around hers, tightening as he had her push down toward his body.

"Like this," he said.

She did what she instructed and was pleased to hear his breath rumble in his chest. Then he released her hand while she repeated the motion. Once, then twice more.

He groaned in pleasure, then had to brace himself with a hand against the wall. She smiled, thrilled at the power she felt. He was trembling from what she did, his breath was short, and his eyes were glazed. And all because she held him gripped in one hand.

She worked him harder, understanding that this was what he wanted, but he abruptly stopped her. He took her hand in his and gently pulled her away.

"Not yet," he said. "Not like this." Then he touched her cheek, lifting her gaze to his. "You have never done anything like this before."

It wasn't a question. If anything, there was triumph in the statement. She answered anyway, shaking her head slightly.

"Then you must trust me to keep you safe. You must do exactly as I tell you."

She nodded. She had made that decision long before.

"Slide forward," he said. Then to help her, he stroked her flanks until he gripped her hips. He was so strong. He had no trouble lifting her and pulling her to the edge of the mattress. Then he stepped between her legs.

She had fallen backward, but not the entire way. Her weight was on her elbows as she looked at him in alarm. He was so big. And she…

"Trust me," he said softly. Then he leaned down and kissed her, silently pressing her down.

She went easily, and soon she was lying on her back while he kissed her neck and her breasts. Her attention was on his mouth and his tongue as they stroked her skin, but she still felt his hands on her thighs. She knew he had stepped between her spread legs, that he kneaded the flesh over her hips, and then deeper into her bottom.

He captured one of her nipples again, sucking hard, and she squeezed her legs together in reaction. She felt him tremble there, his thighs a hard presence between her legs. She felt air at her most intimate place and a wetness beyond anything she'd experienced before.

Then, while she was gasping at the steady pull on her nipple, she felt his hands shift from her hips. His fingers slid across her belly and down. Then his thumbs slipped between her folds.

It was a slow progression, steady and inevitable. She knew what he intended, knew where he was going, and thought to cry out. Something. But she had no breath and no ability to form words. He was tonguing her nipple, alternating between a stroke and a nip, before sucking her hard. By the time his thumbs slid between her folds, she was arching off the bed, her body on fire.

She felt the slickness there, the wondrous pressure as he slid deep, pushing her open, widening her legs, and... inside! His thumb was inside her! It felt good, she thought, the word so inadequate to what was happening. The words that sizzled through her mind were "deeper" and "more." And "oh yes."

She had no breath to say any of it, but he must have heard. He must have known because he did as she wanted. He pushed deeper inside, then pulled out and up. He slid his thumbs across her folds and then higher.

She cried out when he hit an amazing place. Her body seized up when he brushed over it the first time. Then he rolled across it again, and she was gasping as her body writhed beneath him.

He kept working her, deep inside, then a steady roll over her peak. She became a wild thing beneath him. She had wrapped her legs around him and was pulling him tight. Finally, wonderfully, he fell forward. Not on top, not weighting her into the mattress, though that was what she wanted.

Instead, he moved his fingers lower. With deliberate movements, he widened her folds before he pressed himself lengthwise against her. Not inside, but along her cleft.

Heat. Pressure—thick and hard. That was what she knew of him, and she tightened her bottom so that she could rub him as he had been rubbing her. He was braced on his hands then, his body pressed hard against her below, but still off her above.

"Yes, Wind. Just like that. God, yes!"

He was moving as well, pushing hard against her, while she clenched her legs in a rhythmic pull. She arched as he ground down. She heard his breath stutter but no more than hers. And the heat between them built until she thought her skin was crackling from the fire.

Harder. Faster.

She felt him lose control. His thrust became a jerk.

Powerful.

Wild.

Yes!

The explosion in her body consumed her. A detonation that began in her belly but radiated through every part of her body. Her spine arched back, her ears popped, and her toes clenched impossibly tight. And all through her was such bliss, like a boom of joy that went from her into him.

While she was crying out, he shuddered against her. He held there, thrust as hard as he could go, while her body rolled with blast after blast.

They rode the waves together, him rocking against her, pulling yet another contraction from her. Again and again, while she filled with joy. Pulse after pulse of sweet, wondrous joy.

And when the waves subsided, when he groaned and slid to the side, she was glowing with happiness. The heat on her skin, the power of his touch, all combined to make her boneless as she had never been before.

Her heart swelled, her breath caught, as he adjusted their positions so they were lying on the bed. Then he curled around her, spoons nestled together with the heat of his breath along her neck.

Yes!

Was this love? she wondered. Had it finally happened? This was joy, she knew. This was happiness. But was this love? Was she in love?

She wanted to ask him if he felt the same. If he knew the sweet, simmering delight that tingled in her body. And she wanted to know if he was asking himself the same questions. Were they in love?

But she couldn't put voice to that yet. It was too new, and she was too easily pushed into rationality. He was a duke. She was a seamstress.

She was his mistress now, she supposed, and that brought complications. Weren't those women completely at their lover's beck and call? Didn't they live where the man chose, doing what the man wanted?

Would he want that from her? What of her job? What of her responsibilities?

What of—

"Shhh," he said against her neck.

"What?" she gasped.

"Just… shhh. Let me hold you."

He tightened his arms, nestling her even tighter. And then, with a grunt, he grabbed the blanket and tossed it over them both. He was a banked fire all himself, and yet she welcomed the intimate cocoon of fabric and man.

"You're thinking very loudly," he said. "I'm afraid to ask what you're planning."

She frowned. "I wasn't planning anything."

"You're always planning something," he murmured. "I remember you as a child, always watching, always thinking. And when I asked, you had a plan for something. How to run faster. How to make a fire better. How to sew a dress better. How a woman should walk to make the gown prettier. Always something."

She smiled, knowing he was right. After all, there were a million ways to do things better, if one just looked. And as a child, she had always been on the outside looking in. Looking and thinking and planning.

"Shhh," he said as he nuzzled her neck. "This is the sweet part."

She frowned. "Sweet?"

"This is the rest part, the hold tight and doze part." He nipped lightly at her shoulder. "This is where I fill my dreams with you before the rest."

She tightened. "The rest? There's more?"

She felt him smile against her shoulder. "Rest now. More in a moment."

She tried to twist to see him better, but he didn't give her the space. "What moment? What—"

And then she felt it. His sigh against her shoulder at the same moment his hand glided down her belly, until his finger pressed slowly, firmly, inevitably between her folds.

"Very well," he said, though she could hear the laughter in his voice. "We'll go to the next part now."

"What—oh!"

He stroked her again, pushing between her legs with steady, building pressure.

"Lift your knee," he instructed.

She did, and he slipped his knee beneath hers. With an easy motion, he pulled her leg up and opened her, while he was still wrapped around her. Then he held her hard against him with one hand while the other explored in earnest.

"I want to feel you again," he said, while her breath shortened to a quick pant. "I want to do everything again."

"What?"

"I want to feel you and see you and hear you as you do it all again. Right now. For me."

She had no breath to voice her answer, but he knew it anyway. *Yes.*

"Come for me, my Wind."

Oh yes!

Fourteen

"Sir!"

Radley jerked awake at the anxious voice from the hatch, but he didn't move his body. He would do nothing to disturb Wendy's warm body, as she lay curled into his side. Sadly, the steady pounding on the cabin door had her stirring in his arms.

"Sir, Mr. Knopp is aboard! He's coming down here!"

"Now?" he gasped, shifting to throw the blankets off. He needn't have bothered as Wendy did it for him.

"Here?" she squeaked.

They leaped to pull on their clothes. He tried not to be distracted by the creamy bounce of her breasts or the smooth curve of her backside. How he longed to return to the bed and the sport there. His cock thickened, but he quickly subdued it beneath his pants. He was pulling on his shirt when he realized that she needed help.

"Hold there," he said in a low voice. "Let me help."

He made quick work of her corset ties then aided her with the green silk gown.

"My hair. Oh heavens," she cried as she twisted it into a high knot.

It didn't stay. She had no ribbons to hold it, and her pins were scattered about the room. He scooped up two and passed them to her, even as he pulled on his shirt.

And then, they were out of time. He heard his employer's voice outside the door as he spoke to the sailor standing guard. "Come on, boy, step aside. I need to speak with Radley."

"He's waking up, sir. I was about to get him a cup of coffee, sir. Would you like—"

Radley had just enough time to shoot an apologetic look at Wendy before the door opened. She didn't see his expression. Her face was turned away. And then, he stepped to the opposite side of the room in the vague hope that Mr. Knopp wouldn't look her way.

It didn't work. The man already knew there was a problem, so the first thing he did when crossing the threshold was look around. He saw her immediately, and his expression tightened. Then his gaze locked onto Radley's.

"Morning, Mr. Lyncott. Didn't know you'd be using your berth."

"No, sir. It was a… um. I wanted to get my things, and I… uh…" *Shite.* He was no good at lying.

"I see," the man said, a wealth of disappointment in his tone. The words cut him, and he all but hung his head in shame.

He thought the worst was over, but then Knopp turned to Wendy. "Good morning, Miss. If you would just head up…" Knopp frowned then jerked slightly in shock. "Miss Drew? Is that you?"

Wendy's head snapped up, shock and horror in her expression. Bloody hell! Did she know him?

"M... Mr. Knopp?" she stammered.

"Aye," the man answered, as he turned glowering eyes on Radley. "Bollocks, man. I never thought you one to..." He grimaced. "It's damned disappointing, man. I thought better of you."

Radley stiffened, even though he knew he deserved every word. Still, his pride was pricked, and he heard himself answering in the tone of all embarrassed young men.

"It's not... Sir, she's still a virgin."

He saw Wendy's body jerk. Did she think they had done the full deed? He mentally slapped himself for being a fool. Wendy was not some dockside chippy. Of course she didn't understand the particulars.

Meanwhile, Mr. Knopp's face tightened with fury. The man was angrier than he'd ever seen, and Radley instinctively straightened.

"And you think that excuses you?" Mr. Knopp said, his voice low and cold. "You make everyone think less of her, and you have the gall to claim innocence?" He stepped up, straight into Radley's face, his larger bulk intimidating. "A title doesn't give you the right to be cruel."

Radley's eyes widened. Cruel? His gaze jerked to Wendy's, whose face was bright red with shame. How had he been cruel?

"Duke or not, you've destroyed her reputation. What will her mother think when she returns home dressed like that? What does she expect now that you've been with her?" The man huffed out a breath. "Damn it man, think! Bad enough when you were a first mate with a bright future, but you're a duke now.

You can't give in to temptations without suffering consequences. And it won't be you who's paying!"

Radley stared, his mind working too damn slowly. He hadn't meant to be cruel, but he certainly hadn't thought about what he'd done to Wendy's reputation. And what would her mother think? And her brother!

Damnation, Henry was his best friend. Would Henry bang on his door demanding satisfaction? Certainly, Radley intended to marry Wendy, but... Good God, he'd planned to court her slowly, and now, he'd gone and shamed her.

Radley rubbed a hand over his face, his gaze returning to Wendy. She wasn't looking at him. She was standing so still he wondered if she was even breathing. Why wouldn't she look at him?

He took a step toward her, but Mr. Knopp froze him with a glare. Then the man stepped between them, touching Wendy with a tenderness that shamed Radley for its gentlemanly courtesy. "Miss Drew, please allow an old man the pleasure of escorting you home."

She looked up, her eyes shimmering with wetness. She was crying? Bloody hell, what had he done?

"N-no sir. There's no need—"

"There's every need. I shall worry about you otherwise. And Irene would never forgive me."

Irene? His daughter—ah! Irene was the purchaser for the dress shop. That's how he knew Wendy. Not that the information helped. "Sir, I can—"

"No, you can't." The words were hard and implacable. Then the man huffed, his gaze gentle on Wendy. "I was young once too, my dear, and a father.

Allow me to act as such to you this day. As a kindness to me."

Spoken so sweet and elegant. He watched Wendy drop her head. She might have started to curtsy. "Thank you, Mr. Knopp."

"There, there, young lady." Then he glanced behind him. "And you will stay here." The words were an order. "I have something I wish to discuss with you. I've written it up. Was going to double check it this morning before showing it to you. Now you can do the work."

Radley didn't bother to argue that he was no longer employed here. It would be too disrespectful, and besides, he was curious what the man wanted. So he responded as if he were still first mate. "Yes, sir!"

Knopp flipped open his satchel, pulled out a few sheets of foolscap, and passed them over. "Look it over. Then come to my house tomorrow morn. We'll discuss it then."

Radley gave him a sharp nod. Meanwhile, Knopp gently placed Wendy's hand on his arm. "Come along, my dear. You can tell me all about how your shop is faring. I hear only a few details from Irene, you know, and that is all about what bargains she has found. I should love to know the end use for all those things she buys."

"Of course, sir."

They moved toward the door. Radley had been dismissed—or disciplined, depending on one's view—and was, therefore, of no more consequence. But he would not be so disregarded. Not by Wendy. So he stepped before them, blocking their exit. It was rude, but he had no interest in ending the most glorious night of his life in this way. He had to speak to her, if only to convey his thanks.

"Wind," he began, his voice rasping through a suddenly tight throat.

"Miss Drew," his former employer corrected.

He cast a frustrated look at the man, but was forced to acknowledge he was right.

"Miss Drew," he said, his words and his tone more formal by necessity. "May I call on you later? This afternoon? For our walk—"

"No," she said softly.

He felt the blood leave his face. She would not see him? But why—

"I haven't the time," she said, her voice tight with her own frustration. "I was supposed to…" She choked off her words.

He guessed she was going to say work. That she'd been supposed to sew a frock last night, and now, needed to spend the time stitching. He tried not to be resentful. After all, he knew she was a working woman in the most honorable sense. But couldn't she set aside her work for him? He was a duke now. And he wanted to marry her. As his duchess, she need never work again!

She must have read the frustration on his face. She must have guessed his thoughts because her tone turned hard. "I can no more ignore my sewing than you could forget to trim a sail. Don't ask me to choose. You might not like my answer."

He winced. She was right. He could not ask her to ignore her business. He knew that, but it was so damned hard to wait on her attention.

"Of course," he said, fighting to sound earnest. "Tomorrow then?"

She looked down.

"I shall call anyway," he said, rather than hear her refuse again. "We should talk about…" He glanced awkwardly at the bed they had shared. "About the future."

Her eyes widened, but he couldn't understand why. Did she truly think he would spend a night with her and not plan to marry her? It angered him that everyone assumed him a cad.

"I… I shall wait upon your call," she finally answered. Simple. Demure. And correct words. But his belly tightened in anxiety. There was something missing. Some secret Wendy held tight to her chest that made her anxious.

But there was no more time. Mr. Knopp was tired of waiting, so he patted her arm. "Come along, my dear. The docks will soon get much too crowded for my tastes."

In other words, the longer they waited to leave, the more people would be aware of her indiscretion the previous night. Damn, why had he not thought of these things himself? Was he so used to light skirts coming on and off the boats that he classed her in the same vein? It wasn't true. He'd never thought of her in that way, and yet, he'd treated her exactly the same as any tavern doxy.

Bloody hell. He wanted to run after her, somehow make it right. But she and Mr. Knopp were already out the door, and what could he say to mitigate the damage? Nothing. So he held his tongue when all he really wanted was to curse.

Then his gaze chanced to fall on another one of her hairpins. He picked it up, spinning the thin piece of metal in his hand. It was a simple thing with no more decoration than a vague ripple. This was something a poor seamstress would own—pure function—except perhaps, that vague yearning for more in the ripple.

It was a fanciful thought, but one that gripped him. His Wind was a simple creature by necessity. She worked. She lived. And she was completely untouched by anyone but him—he was sure of it. When she had come apart beneath him, she had been a wild creature completely unschooled. Her reactions had been pure and honest in a way that made his chest swell with manly pride. She was his completely.

Yes, he was impatient to get her in his bed, to complete what they had begun last night, but he had time. After all, if she had no room in her life for a duke, then he could be sure no other man was sniffing at her door.

He grinned as pressure eased from his heart. He had spent the last ten years fearing that another man was courting her, that someone else had caught her fancy. That while he was away making his fortune, someone who lived right next door had seduced her.

Now he knew it wasn't true, and that made him giddy with relief. "I can be patient," he said out loud. The words steadied his nerve and hardened his resolve.

He would go slow. After all, he wasn't shipping out ever again. He had all the time in the world.

The ride to her home was the best and the most
excruciating moments of her life. How a ride with
Mr. Knopp could compare to a night spent with
Radley, she didn't know. Except that she wasn't
ready to dwell on what they'd done—and not done.
In truth, it was rather shocking that she was apparently still a virgin. What she'd felt—what they'd
done—had been so earth-shattering that she knew
she'd never be the same. It had to be the shift from
virginity to fallen woman. It had to be, and yet, he'd
said she was still innocent.

Had it been a lie? She was ashamed to admit she
didn't know. There had been no pain, but she knew
some women claimed that their first time had been
easy. So she didn't think about it—couldn't handle it
just then—which made her focus on Mr. Knopp, as
reassuring as it was horrible.

He was kindness itself. Fatherly, as she had never
known since her own father disappeared when she was
seven. He'd been impressed, they believed, grabbed
and dragged to work on a boat where he probably
died. So she had spent her adolescence wondering
what it would be like to have a man look at her as Mr.
Knopp was now doing.

Answer: it was excruciatingly bad. He was polite,
asking about the dress shop and what she did. He patted
her hand and seemed to smile, even though there was
sadness in his eyes. A distinct melancholy—or was it
disappointment—and she twisted inside at the shame.

By the time the carriage stopped, she wanted to run
inside and hide under her bed. And yet, perversely, she
longed to throw herself into his arms and feel a fatherly

man hold her again. Instead, he touched her hand, stilling her movements.

"If you might indulge an old man for a moment, Miss Drew?"

She paused, turning back to look into his steady gaze. "Sir?"

"Do not sell yourself cheaply. You are worth far more than you realize. And it does us men good to be reminded of that. Frequently."

She blinked, overcome by tears. What he said was so simple, and yet, it rocked her to her soul. How had she forgotten that? Wasn't she the one who always said to get payment first, to barter the deal on everything, no matter how inconsequential? And yet, Radley had kissed her, and she had given up everything. No questions, no hesitation, just a simple yes. Yes, I will give you everything.

What had happened?

"Thank you," she whispered. She wanted to say more. She wanted to throw her arms around him and sob out her fears and confusion. She wanted to sit and ask questions, getting answers without judgment. She wanted such a thing, but she barely knew this man. He was father-in-law to a friend who worked at her shop.

Still, she squeezed his hand. "I will not forget your kindness, sir." It was the best she could say.

"My dear, don't forget what I said."

"I won't," she vowed. Then she had to get out and climb the steps to her new home. She stepped through the building's front door, listening for when the carriage left. It was a small gesture, but the driver waited until she stepped into the tenement house before departing. That tiny kindness had made her feel cherished as never before.

She was still flushed with the warmth of that moment when she found her way to her new home. She'd only been here once, so it took her a bit to remember which was the correct door, and even longer to find her key.

Eventually, she did, and she pushed open the door. Soon enough she would face the questions that last night had created. She would also think of the work that waited. But for now, she would think of Mr. Knopp and the way he had treated her like a daughter.

She started humming, a tune her father used to sing to her. She had not thought of it in such a long time.

"Did he hum that to you?" a cold voice asked, cutting through the gloom in her main parlor. "Or were you the one singing as he fucked you?"

Fifteen

WENDY KEPT FROM SCREAMING. IT WASN'T A CON-
scious decision. Inside, her thoughts were one long
shriek of terror. But outside, her body froze as she
looked at Damon. He was sitting at ease on the parlor
settee. His long fingers dangled—one hand off the
armrest, the other stretched across the back—and each
hand held something terrifying.

The right toyed with a tiny scrap of foolscap with
writing on it. Her writing, her note, her private
thought. He had read it. And a single glance at a
stack of pages beside his legs told her he'd found all
her notes.

She swallowed, the motion thick in her frozen throat.

What the other hand held was oddly less terrifying.
A thin stiletto twisted in his nearly lax grip. Like a
moth dangling from a web, it twirled and flashed dully
in the sunlight. She didn't need the reminder that
Damon was deadly, but she saw it, nonetheless, and
took its warning.

"What are you doing here, Damon?" she asked, her
voice hard with bravado.

"Waiting for you," he answered quietly. "When you didn't show for your shift last night, I grew worried. Imagine my surprise when I discovered that you were with that bilge rat."

She didn't acknowledge his statement, taking the time instead to pull off her wrap and set it carefully on the peg. She didn't want to expose more of her body—and certainly not given what she was wearing—but he'd already seen it. She gained nothing by hiding.

"Where is my mother?"

"Out looking for you, I imagine."

She turned back and frowned. "You imagine?"

He shrugged. "I have been here since two this morning, Wendy. By six, she grew uncomfortable with my presence and went out."

As it was now nearly nine, he'd been here for seven hours. "What about my brothers?"

His eyebrows rose. "What about them?"

She wanted to know where they were, obviously, but then realized that it didn't matter. Even if they were here, they couldn't help her. Not when Damon's eyes glittered with anger.

"I'm sorry I missed my work shift last night. It won't happen again."

He didn't speak, and she grew increasingly panicked at the way he sat staring at her. The dagger twisted in his fingers, nearly forgotten. As did the foolscap in his other hand.

"If you'll excuse me, I need to change. I have to get to work—"

"Did he fuck you, Wendy?" he asked. "Did you

scream? Did he do it hard or gentle? How much did
you bleed?"

"I didn't bleed," she said, stunned by the flat hon-
esty in the words that suggested something entirely
untrue. She'd implied that she wasn't a virgin and
hadn't been for some time.

She saw his eyes darken, and the stiletto momen-
tarily stopped twirling. He held it still in two fingers.
One beat. Two.

Then suddenly, it began to spin again. "You're lying."

"I swear, I am not."

"You forget that I know better. You know nothing
of men." His eyes narrowed. "If I fucked you right
now, I would feel your blood wet my cock. It would
slick your cunny and feel like ambrosia."

Her breath caught at his words. It wasn't the crass-
ness of the statement, but that it came out more as a
promise than a threat and included a word she barely
understood: ambrosia. How could such a cultured
word come in the middle of such an ugly threat? It
was only on second thought that she realized he'd
been working to expand his vocabulary, to smooth his
accent to fit in with the cultured elite.

"Get out," she said, wishing there was more steel
in her voice.

"No." He leaned back, completely at ease. He cut
a handsome picture, she realized. He was dressed in
well-tailored evening clothes of better quality and fit
than anything Radley owned. He was immaculately
groomed without a hair out of place. And given the
way he stretched across the furniture, she was aware of
the broadness of his chest and the power in his hands.

That was his intent, of course. He wanted her to see his elegance and his power.

You are worth far more than you realize.

If she hadn't just heard those words, she might not have found the resilience to face Damon. But she had, so she spoke with casual aplomb.

"Sit then," she said. "I need to change." She turned to go to her bedroom. It would make her skin crawl to undress with him in the other room, but she wanted to get out of this gown. She hated that Damon saw her in the dress she'd worn for Radley.

"Interesting reading here," he said before she could take more than a step. "You have sharp ears and a sharp mind."

She stopped, not bothering to look back. She knew what he read. They were notes scrawled on whatever she had handy after she'd learned something interesting. Men in their cups said things that they shouldn't, and she'd heard many an interesting tidbit when dealing vingt-et-un. Bad enough that Damon had read those, but she took comfort that he likely already knew everything she'd overheard at his hell. After all, she'd told him at least half of them. And if she'd heard it, likely, someone else had as well.

More frightening were the other things she'd heard… and written down. The secrets whispered by women in her dressing room while she crawled around their feet setting pins in their unfinished gowns. Most spoke of nothing more scandalous than gossip. Vicious certainly, but primarily unfounded speculations that were on everyone's lips.

Then, there were the few others who had true

secrets. Who whispered to one another because they thought she was too dull or too unimportant to hurt them. She had written those secrets down and hidden them in her bedroom in a chest that... She sighed. That Radley had given her years ago through her brother. Obviously, Damon had gone through her things. And just as clearly, Damon now knew every secret she'd ever collected.

"Does he know?" asked Damon, his words growing softer, so that she had to face him to hear clearly.

"What?"

He smirked. "Does the bilge rat know you've been blackmailing people?"

She felt her jaw clench, but she still managed to force out the words. "I haven't blackmailed anyone."

He flicked a piece of paper at her. She didn't need more than a flash to remember that tidbit. A prominent political known for his Christian rectitude had beaten his wife. Wendy had seen the bruises when she'd helped the woman dress. That, in itself, was hardly remarkable. They were man and wife, after all, and such cruelty was common among couples. What came after was what was damning.

The man had beaten his wife because she'd walked in on him when he'd been bent over and fucked in the arse by his banker. Six months ago, Wendy wouldn't have understood the woman's whispered description. Now, thanks to her time in Damon's hell, she had an intellectual comprehension, even if she was as baffled as the wife at the reasons for such a thing.

But she'd needed no help in recognizing the possibilities in such a secret. Blackmail was only the first and easiest choice. Selling the information to the man's enemies was equally viable. As was the possibility of tempting man and lover into further depravity—for a price, of course.

She hadn't done any of those things, but she had recorded the names of everyone involved. And she had kept the secret in a locked cabinet, like a miser hoarding his wealth. And now, Damon knew something damning about three people who had never set foot in one of his hells.

Damon stood, moving with a dark grace. She'd seen it before, of course. He prowled his hells in much the same way—calm, quiet, but with presence felt long after he wandered on. She never thought to see it in her own home.

She knew better than to flinch away, so she stood her ground, even as he flicked the scrap of foolscap beneath her chin.

"You gather secrets like I do."

She couldn't deny it.

"You lock them away like diamonds, and you take them out to read when you're alone."

She shrugged. There was no shame in what she did. "They were mine, Damon. And now you've stolen them."

He stroked a long finger across her jaw. "You were mine last night, but since you didn't work your shift, I took my payment in other ways."

She moved as fast as she knew how, backhanding his hand away from her face. "Then you have what you were owed," she hissed. "Now get out."

She had a brief second to think she'd won. A short

breath to believe she might get through this encounter with simply the loss of her stash of secrets. But she'd forgotten about the stiletto.

He sliced it down across her chest. He'd probably allowed her to slap his hand away to give him the space he needed to cut her dress in two. It split easily, as did the ties to her corset, and the cotton of her shift underneath. Within moments, her gown sagged off her shoulders, her corset slowly eased apart, and her shift absorbed the tiny drops of blood that spilled where he'd cut too deep.

She gasped. Her sob and her scream caught in the cold pit of her belly long before either could escape.

She jumped back. Of course she jumped away, even though she knew he would follow. A second later, she found herself trapped against a wall with his body slowly, inevitably closing the distance.

She held the dress up with her hands. She tried to clutch it together, even though she knew he might cut it off just for spite. Or lust, she realized dully. With him, there was always lust.

He kept coming closer. Inch by slow inch, until she felt his feet trapping hers. His knees braced against hers, then thighs, thick and corded, pressed against hers. His groin came next, his cock unmistakable where he ground it into her.

She tried to scream—wanted to scream—but to what purpose? Who would save her in his building? She had only met a few of her neighbors, but she already knew they were all beholden to Damon.

Meanwhile, he leaned down to whisper in her ear, and she shivered at the feel of him so close, so intimate.

"Did he say sweet things to you? Did he talk about your beauty as he spread your thighs? Did he whisper that he loved you?"

She closed her eyes, trying to think of a way out. But her mind was slow, and her choices were few. She couldn't run—she'd heard plenty of stories about what happened to people who thought they could run from Damon. They'd died, some horribly. But more than that, she was trapped in a corner. He was bigger and stronger and had a knife, which he used to cut away the shoulders and sleeves of her gown.

"What did you say when he sucked your teats?"

He set the knife tip to her chin. She felt it as a sharp prick that went no deeper. Though, of course, it could. With a flick of his wrist, it could stab through her jaw, straight to her brain.

"What did you say, Wendy?"

"Nothing!" she rasped.

She watched him smile. A slow spread of his lips revealed a flash of white teeth. "Nothing," he echoed. "Of course not. And do you know why?"

She didn't answer. She had no idea what to say, what could possibly save her from this dangerous predator of a man.

"Because he does not know how to make a woman sing. He doesn't know how to find her secrets, how to make her talk."

Her gaze shot to his, and suddenly, she knew what to say. "Secrets? Is that what you think you have from me? Scraps of paper about other people. You know nothing of me."

His eyebrows rose, clearly surprised by her calm

challenge, when he still held a knife to her throat. "Really?" he drawled. "Teach me."

"No."

"Then perhaps I should teach you. Shall I tell you what I have done? For you." He leaned to an inch away from her ear. "What lengths I will go for you?"

She shivered, her belly tight with anxiety, and her groin a hard ridge that clearly delighted him. She wanted nothing about her to intrigue him, and yet, she couldn't deny she wanted to know what he offered. What secrets did he want to share?

"I know where Helaine's father is."

Her gaze leaped to his. Helaine's father was the *Thief of the Ton*. It was an old scandal of a ridiculous crime, but it was one that could electrify the elite. If the scandal were renewed—if Helaine's father reappeared—then the *ton* would revile anything associated with the salacious tidbit.

Helaine would be humiliated, and no one would dare wear her clothing designs. Orders would disappear in a second, and money already owed would never appear. The dress shop would die. And without the dress shop, Wendy had no livelihood.

She swallowed. "I don't care," she lied.

He smiled, a slow lazy stretching of his lips. "Are you sure?"

She nodded, the gesture reinforcing her thoughts. "I am sure." She would find a way to survive. Her friends would help. She could find another job. There was always something.

"Penny cared when her parents died. Irene cared when she was hunted by a madman."

Wendy's mouth went dry as she realized the truth. Damon was behind all the troubles that had tortured her friends. She had certainly suspected it, though she hadn't wanted to admit it. Others had voiced it as well, though there had never been proof. Looking in his eyes now, she knew it was true.

"Why would you do those things?" she whispered.

"Why would you seek to survive without me?"

Her eyes widened. She didn't understand what he'd just said. Why would she try to survive without him? What sense was that question? Of course she would work and live independent of him.

"Do you remember the day you decided to become a thief, not a whore?"

She gasped, reacting on instinct, rather than sense. Heedless of the knife touching her throat, she shoved hard. He rocked back enough that he was forced to set a foot behind him or fall. She took satisfaction in that, even though she now had a thin bloody streak from mid-throat to chin.

"I am not a th—" Her word was choked off when he held up a hairpin. It had been years since she'd seen it. Three jewels glittered in metal shaped like Christmas holly. Two emeralds and a ruby, all small, but no less beautiful. Except something had happened to the emeralds. Where the gems had been set was now empty. Nevertheless, she recognized it immediately.

Lady Strichen's hairpin. The last she'd seen of the thing had been years past. She'd been working in someone else's shop then, and Lady Strichen had been a customer. The woman was a shrew flush with coin, but she clutched her possessions like a miser gripping sand. And she was a demon to please. Her dresses always had some flaw, something that required the dress to be redone and the pay to be cut in half. The bitch that ran the shop allowed it, because she could take the extra coin from Wendy's purse, claiming a girl who made a dress badly should never be fully paid.

It was a system, she knew, one that took the coin from the most vulnerable soul in the process. Wendy had withstood it. She'd been young—barely seventeen—with no power and no alternatives if she was sacked without a reference.

But then came winter. Henry was gone, Bernard was sick with a hacking cough, and her mother was steeped in despair as the food disappeared, not only from their table, but from the whole neighborhood. And then, one afternoon, Lady Strichen dropped her hairpin.

Wendy didn't see it fall, didn't see it catch on her own hem, and didn't discover it herself until later. She'd had pins in her mouth, and her mistress was chatting up the lady as she always did with customers. She'd said nothing as she worked, but the twin emeralds had burned in her mind. Not the ruby, for some reason, but the two emeralds. She'd never seen stones that color before, and her mind was gripped by the idea that gems could be such a rich green color.

Meanwhile, the fitting had continued. Her stitches were disparaged and her mistress called her a thick-headed brute of a girl. The whole interaction filled her with bitterness and fury, and if it hadn't been for that, what happened later might have gone differently. When the hairpin was found missing, the lady had screamed, the mistress had come running, and both ladies eventually blamed her. They had no reason to accuse her beyond the obvious. After all, there were only three women in the room. They were right, of course, but Wendy didn't know it at the time.

They never found it, but it hadn't mattered. Who else were they to blame but her? And the lady demanded she be fired. Wendy had protested then, furiously pointing out that they had torn apart her workstation and found nothing.

It didn't matter. An apparent theft had occurred, and she was to blame. The injustice had burned in her red face, even as it chilled her soul. She was sacked for a crime she hadn't committed. Yet.

Days later, washing her dress, she'd found the pin lodged in her hem. Before, she would have returned it—she knew to whom it belonged. She knew it wasn't hers, and to keep it made her the thief they'd accused her of being.

But she'd vowed to begin a dress shop that would utterly destroy her former mistress. This pin gave her the means.

So she had done it. She'd already met Helaine, but now, she pursued the talented designer with single-minded determination. By the time Helaine agreed to try, Wendy had already pawned the hairpin and used the money to begin A Lady's Favor. And then, she'd quietly pursued every one of her former employer's clients and wooed them over. Well, every one but Lady Strichen, knowing that the shrew would one day come knocking. She had, and Wendy had slammed the door in her face.

And now, Damon held up the hairpin that had

begun her march to success, spinning it before her eyes as if he knew her tale.

"How did you get that?" she asked, though she already guessed the answer.

"Do you think that any woman can sell such an item—in our neighborhood—and I not know about it? I knew the tale within hours."

She shrugged to hide the sickness growing inside. She'd managed, somehow, to bury all memory of how she'd started her shop. That he brought it up now seemed like the devil finally returning for his due. Inevitable. And yet, she refused to pay.

She lifted her chin and affected a calm that she did not feel. "What of it? Certainly, you cannot claim to be horrified by a single theft."

"Horrified? Hardly. I admired you. It brought you to my attention as few people have. A single item of such value, sold so quietly, and for a well bargained price. I wanted to bed you that very day."

She rolled her eyes, stunned by her audacity. "You grow tiresome, Damon. You are not the first to desire me, nor the last. Do you know how many drunken sots sit at my vingt-et-un table and talk about how they want me?"

Far from being repelled, he actually smiled at her jab. "And yet, I will be the one to win you."

She released a sigh, trying to suggest she was bored. In truth, she was terrified at the dangerous game she played. How many people had she heard at the hell? Men who thought they could outwit a demon? Their screams echoed in her mind still. After all, Damon made sure everyone heard the scream.

And yet, she still thought to match wits with him. "Are you done posturing, Damon?" She touched her chin, reassured when the blood that came away on her thumb was not so bad. In fact, the sting from his knife was already fading. "Done cutting me?"

He was on her in a moment, his groin harsh against her pelvis, his hand in her hair. While he trapped her against the wall, he slowly drew her head back. It was terrifying—the way he went so slowly. He fisted his hand in her hair and steadily tilted her back, exposing her bare neck.

She knew what he was going to do long before his lips touched her flesh. She knew he was going to lick every drop of crimson blood, and God help her, she was mesmerized by the hideous idea.

She looked to his eyes. In truth, she had no choice. And in the depths of his pupils, she saw a manic desperation, and it terrified her.

Then he licked. The swirl of his tongue, the rasp of wet coupled with the tender press of lips was both erotic and nauseating. The hard bite of his fist in her hair and rhythmic grind of his cock against her made for an opposition of pain and desire that disoriented her.

How was she to react? Pain and pleasure, attraction and terror—it was everything she hated about her life, and yet it was as true as the coldness in her belly. Was nothing pure? Was nothing simply joy? She couldn't deny the wild beat of her heart even though her chest felt constricted with fear.

Who was *she* to expect simple joy? Love without fear? She was a thief and a liar. She deserved no better than this half-measure of mixed sensuousness and pain.

Then he pulled away. He eased his grip on her hair and allowed her chin to drop so that they faced each other. Eye to eye, he looked at her. Simply looked, and she wondered what he sought in her eyes.

"Fight me," he whispered. "Kick me, scream at me, claw the flesh from my bones."

"So you can overpower me?" she whispered.

"Yes."

"No." Then she said the boldest words she'd ever imagined. "Rape me if you must, but I will not give you what you want."

"I can take it."

"You can force it. But what you want is not here, Damon. I have no love for you."

She felt the words hit him. He had cut her, but she had eviscerated him. His cock shrank against her belly, though his hips pounded against her as if he tried to keep it thick. It was a losing battle as he mauled her. He pressed forward, bracing himself on his elbows, as he trapped her head. He kissed her hard, the grind of his mouth against hers brutal and bloody. She felt her lip tear against her teeth, but she kept her mouth closed.

And then, he stopped. One moment he had been thrusting with frenzy, the next he was frozen into stillness. Not quiet, but absolute restriction, as if he were locked in ice.

Then she felt him shift. His hand pressed against her forehead, shoving her face sideways. She didn't mind at first. Anything to get away from his mouth, but he locked her down with her right ear flat against the wall and her neck twisted.

"You are mine," he rasped.

She didn't bother speaking her denial. They both knew it wasn't true.

"If you move," he said, "you will die." It wasn't a threat. It was a fact, and she stilled in terror.

His forearm held her flat against the wall, her head twisted. His other arm came up slowly, and he took his time to flash the stiletto in the sunlight.

She swallowed, knowing what was coming, but unable to stop him. The Demon would make his mark.

Pain flashed in her earlobe. A pierce that went straight through without mercy. She bit her lip rather than cry out. Then he turned her head. Same position, same warning, as he pierced her other ear.

Then he drew back. He showed her the stiletto, now darkened with her blood. Then he took a step back, finally pulling his body off hers.

She took a breath, almost dizzy with the rush of air into her lungs.

"Hold out your hand," he said.

She knew better than to argue. Whatever he intended was nearly over. To fight him now would be to risk inciting him to greater depths of horror, and there was a great deal worse that she could suffer beyond two bloodied ears.

She lifted her right hand, palm up. He pulled something out of his jacket and placed it deliberately into her hand. She looked down, dreading the sight. It was worse than she'd feared.

The two emeralds lay in her palm. The emeralds from the stolen hairpin refashioned into earrings. Though pierced ears were not uncommon among the *ton*, they were rare among her class. Now, apparently, she was one of the rarified few who had holes made for jewelry.

"Put them on," he said.

She looked into his eyes. "And if I don't?"

He shrugged. "I will kill your brothers."

She nearly choked. He'd said brothers—plural. Both. Not just Bernard, who carried some responsibility for this disaster, but Henry too.

She blanched because she believed him. And so she lifted the earrings and managed to shove them—one by one—into her bloody lobes.

He waited, watching without helping. It was a long wait because her hands were shaking, and she had never done this before. It was painful too. By the time she was done, she was nearly sobbing in shame. Then her hands dropped away, and she looked at him, silently praying that he was done.

"If you take even one of those bobs out, I will kill a brother."

A brother. And she wouldn't even know which one it would be.

She nodded her understanding.

He didn't wait to see her acknowledgment but sauntered to the door. He opened it casually, stepped through, then stopped, turning to look over his shoulder. She had a flash of white teeth and saw the furious glint in his eyes.

"Radley is dead either way."

And then he was gone.

Sixteen

RADLEY WAS WHISTLING AS HE MOUNTED THE STEPS to his new home. The day was sunny, last night had been wonderful, and there was no reason that tomorrow couldn't be equally delightful. Certainly, being aboard a ship—even a docked one—had been bittersweet. But after perusing Mr. Knopp's proposal, he began to think that life as a duke still had joys.

And so he was smiling as Seelye opened the door, only to have the expression slide away as he met the irritated gazes of his mother, his cousin, and his sister. They were dressed to go out, and all three glared with some level of irritation.

"Um, good morning?" he tried.

"It is customary to inform the house when you shall be out for the night," his mother said, acid in every word.

It was? Whatever for?

His mother must have read the question right off his face because she huffed in disgust. "Meals, Radley, and your servants had to prepare your bed, and your valet stayed awake, awaiting your return to help you disrobe."

"I can undress myself." He wasn't trying to challenge her dictate. After all, she knew a great deal more about being a duke than he did. But really, what sense was there in having servants that made one's life *more* difficult?

"That is not the point!" snapped his mother. Then she grimaced. "Well, go on. Hurry up and dress, so that we can be off."

He frowned. Whatever was she talking about? He was looking forward to taking off these high shirt points and damnable shoes for a bit. There were any number of books in the library. He thought he might read one if it was appealing. Books were a rarity on board, and he'd looked forward to discovering what his library contained.

His sister intervened before his mother could vent more ire. "We had time to discuss things last night, and we've made some plans. We know it's fast for you, but this really is important." Her voice was soothing—almost coaxing—but it quickly became clear that he wasn't going to be reading in his library today.

His cousin took up the tale. "The Season has already started, so we're late for these things. It all rolls backwards from the ball. You need clothing before that, a few forays into society—"

Caroline made a minimizing gesture. "Nothing too difficult. Just a musicale and a few visits to the theater. Very easy."

"And then, there are those invitations you've already accepted," his mother huffed. "Really, Radley, you shouldn't have said yes to anything before talking with me."

All three ladies nodded, and he gaped. He didn't recall accepting anything from anybody.

Eleanor smiled warmly at him. "I believe you met some of the ladies at Hyde Park." She rattled off names that he didn't recognize. But he did remember taking Wendy to Hyde Park and not being able to enter for all the...

All the women inviting him to events. Had he told them he'd attend their parties? Just to brush them off? He couldn't remember.

"You're an important duke now," his mother said. "You can't say yes to any ninny who asks. You have a reputation to maintain."

"I don't have a reputation, Mother. I've only been in London a few days. No one knows me."

"*Exactly!*" the woman huffed.

Eleanor stepped forward, touching him lightly on the arm. "What your mother means is that first impressions are extremely important. You want to begin as you mean to go on."

Silence reigned as he tried to ferret out her meaning. A minute later, he still had no idea. So his sister tried to explain.

"You are the newest *cause célèbre*. Everyone wants to meet you. People wander the streets outside just to get a glimpse of you."

Was that what all those women were about? He'd wondered at all the souls knocking him about on the street, angling for a reason to talk. He'd sidestepped them and murmured an apology because that's what men did when a girl stumbles and all but lands in his arms. Then he moved on. Nearly dimmed his mood, but nothing could dent the joy of the last twelve hours.

Well, nothing but his cousin, sister, and mother as they looked at him expectantly. In the end, it was his mother who delivered the marching orders.

"Here is what you need to know, Radley. Your ball is in two weeks, and there is a damnable amount of preparation."

His mother had sworn. Clearly, this was something of importance. He took the cue to stand taller and not argue.

"But before your introduction, you need to have new clothes, new hair, new…" She flicked her fingers at him. "New everything."

He looked at himself and admitted, perhaps, she was right. It would be nice to have shoes that fit. "I shall do that straight away. Tomorrow."

"*Now*, Radley. For tonight's ball."

Now, he was getting annoyed. Truly, how could he understand things when they got their details fouled up? "You said my ball was in two weeks."

"It is," Caroline said with a smile. "But we feel you should get a little experience. Lady Eleanor's dearest friend is having a small party tonight, and we thought to attend."

"It would mean a great deal to her," his cousin said. Then she added in an almost shy voice, "And to me."

"Oh," he said because it was obvious that they expected an answer. "Of course, we can attend."

"But," Caroline inserted with an apologetic shrug, "when was the last time you danced?"

Danced? When was the last time he'd partnered

Caroline in the parlor while his mother hummed? He'd been seventeen. "Um…"

"No matter," Eleanor soothed. "You can make a quick appearance tonight. A courtesy dance with me and your sister—"

"And me!" his mother cried. "I should… I mean I would very much like to dance at least once."

He heard the yearning note in his voice and knew that his mother had likely wanted to dance at a true society ball since she was a little girl. "Of course I shall partner you, mother." Though, damnation, did he remember the steps?

"Then there is no time!" His mother grabbed his arm and all but shoved him upstairs. "We are already behind schedule. You must see the tailor then the dance master. I'd thought to add in a cobbler, but—"

"That is a necessity," he snapped. He'd be damned if he spent the night doing the pretty in shoes that didn't fit.

"Then we had best get started!"

He stood for a moment at the base of the stairs. His gaze took in the expectant glances of the three females, and then he chanced to turn to Seelye. He didn't know why he looked at the man, except that he was the only other male in the hallway. Perhaps there was some sanity to be had from that direction.

"I find, your grace, than in matters of fashion, it is best to allow the ladies to have their heads, while the gentleman follows a pace behind."

He didn't fully understand the analogy, since it regarded horses and not sails, but he supposed the meaning was clear. In this, the ladies were the wind and the sails. He was simply the boatman with a broken rudder.

"Radley!" his mother said, snapping him out of his reverie. "Your valet has your attire ready. Pray tell him to make haste."

He nodded and allowed her impatience to blow him into his day. Then three steps up the stairs, he paused and turned back.

"We are attending a ball tonight?" he asked.

His cousin smiled. "Yes, at the home of Lord and Lady Tindelar. Their youngest daughter's debut. Her older sister is a dear friend of mine from school."

Radley ignored the details to focus on Seelye. "I should like to send a footman to Miss Drew, asking if she would attend as well."

The man didn't respond—for which he was grateful—as the three women made their opinion known in nearly identical choking gasps. Clearly, he'd stepped in it again.

"Is there a problem?"

"Er, no, your grace," Seelye answered in a tight voice. "It is merely that it is unlikely that Miss Drew will have an invitation."

He thought about that. Of course, that was true. Wendy was a seamstress, after all. She wouldn't be invited to a coming out ball.

Then he nodded, his expression shifting to Eleanor. "They are excited to have me attend this function, yes? It will provide a boost to this girl's debut?"

Eleanor's face remained rigidly composed as she dipped her chin. "Every hostess in London would be honored by your presence."

He took that as a yes. "Then perhaps they could see to Miss Drew's invitation." He tilted his head. "Do you know how to arrange such a thing smoothly?"

His mother sputtered. "Y-you can't possibly—"

"See to it, would you Eleanor? Seelye? While I apply myself to making a suitable appearance tonight."

He held their gazes. Seelye's dropped immediately into a respectful bow. Eleanor's took a moment longer, but in the end she, too, gave him a serene smile. "It should be my pleasure, cousin."

Hours later, he realized that he had sold his day too cheaply. Just the visit to the tailor had been a nightmare. Never had he thought to be a living doll, dressed, poked, and pulled like a rag figure caught between two little girls. Except, instead of two girls, it was more like six obsequious men with a strange desire to touch him in places that would result in keel hauling if it were done on a ship.

When he'd finally escaped, it was to the dance master's, where he wasn't touched in those intimate ways. He was flicked. A heel not turned out? The man snapped his middle finger against his calf. Turned in the wrong direction? A backhanded slap to the arm. And once, he'd cursed in irritation, and the bugger had flicked him on the lips.

In truth, he spent the dance session one touch from flattening the curly-wigged fop and storming out. But Eleanor was with him, acting as his partner as she serenely guided him left or right, up or down. Damnation, how did one remember all these blasted turns? His sister and his mother were at a dress shop— not Wendy's, he'd noted with irritation—ordering their gowns. So that left Eleanor to keep him from slugging the prancing dance master.

Once that was done, he went directly to a cobbler, then back to the tailor for a second fitting. By the time he escaped, he was elated to realize they could at last head home. He looked at the mound of packages in the carriage and winced at the amount of coin they'd just spent. Adding in his new wardrobe, the funds the steward needed him to spend at the ducal seat, and the proposal Mr. Knopp had laid at his door—he wasn't sure he could cover it all. But he shoved that thought aside as he dreamed of heading into his library.

Within a moment of arriving at home, he realized his doom. Waiting in the hallway were three tradesmen, all smiling warmly, before dropping into deep bows. They were introduced as (1) the man to cut his hair, (2) the man to instruct him and his valet on appropriate cravat styles, and (3) the man who would explain how to act when in the company of men.

He didn't bother arguing that he had spent most of his adult life in the company of men. Obviously, sailors behaved differently than the elite of the *ton*. Perhaps ballroom conversation was more refined. He wasn't sure, and so he resigned himself to instructions and no reading.

He stopped long enough to address his question to Seelye. "Was the invitation delivered to Miss Drew?"

"Yes, your grace, though I don't believe she was at home."

Radley frowned. "Do we know her address?" She

was gone from her last home, and she hadn't told him of her new location.

"I don't believe so, your grace. I sent a footman to her place of business. That was also the address we passed on to Lord and Lady Tindelar. However, she did stop here. I took the liberty of expressing your desire for her company then."

"Wendy was here? When? What did she want?"

Seelye's eyes flickered with emotion Radley didn't understand. "She was most interested in speaking with you," he said in his very even, very annoying butler tone. "I informed her of your absence, and she was most distraught."

"Good lord," he said, grabbing his hat again. "Why didn't you ask her to stay?" And where the hell could he find her?

"I did, your grace," the man said with only the slightest note of reproof in his tone. "She refused, saying that she would find you at the tailor's."

Bloody hell. "I haven't seen her all day." Had she truly been wandering all over London in search of him? What could have caused—

"She did leave you a note."

And the man hadn't seen fit to mention it the moment he'd entered the house? Apparently not. He waited impatiently as the butler walked to a nearby table and lifted a silver tray. There were nearly two-dozen cards resting there, and Radley snatched them up, rifling quickly through, until he found her message.

It was a simple note: a piece of his own paper, apparently, as he noted the ducal crest on the top, folded in half. Inside, her hand was neat and clear.

Your life is in danger. I'm so sorry. Please take precautions. I will explain as soon as I see you.
Wendy Drew

He stared at it, reading it a dozen times. Whatever did she mean? It made no sense whatsoever. He looked to Seelye.

"She said nothing else? Left no other explanation?"

"No, your grace. Only that I was to see you received it immediately."

Well, he supposed within two minutes of entering the house constituted immediate. Still, the woman was clearly distraught. Though his mother might be prone to dramatic statements like, "your life is in danger," he didn't think Wendy was such a woman.

"She said nothing more?"

"No, your grace."

"Only that she intended to find me at the tailor's."

"Yes, your grace."

"I should go to the dress shop and make sure she's all right." He spoke more to himself than to Seelye, but the butler responded nevertheless.

"My apologies, your grace, but the footman just returned from the dress shop. She is not there."

Not there, but where? He grimaced. Probably at the tailor's waiting for him. But he'd already moved on. Bloody hell, what a mess. How did he find her?

"If it please you, your grace, I can have the footman return to the dress shop. She's sure to return eventually."

He nodded. "Send two. Have them find out where her home is, and make the other go there."

"Of course, your grace. And what should the footmen say when they locate her?"

"They are to escort her to me with all speed."

Seelye didn't respond, except to bow. Radley took a moment to stare out the door. He still had his hat in hand and was poised to rush out. But where would he go? Her shop, of course, but Seelye had just said she wasn't there. Much as he hated it, he knew it was more likely that she would come back here once she discovered she'd missed him at the tailor's. Rushing out now would only mean that he'd miss her again.

With a muttered curse of disgust, he handed his hat back to Seelye. The footmen would bring her back here. The wise thing was to sit and wait.

"Bring her straight to me, Seelye. No delay."

"Of course not, your grace."

Radley turned to head for the sideboard. He wanted a drink after a day of fashion and dancing. Bloody, ridiculous nonsense. He'd gone no more than a step when Seelye's level tone stopped him.

"It if please your grace, Mr. Milton could join you now in your room. He could cut your hair while Thomas prepares your bath."

He stopped, his mind split between Wendy and wondering what he'd do until he found her again. There was little room in his brain for Mr. Milton, his valet, or hairstyles, but he supposed that would pass the time as well as anything. Not as well as a stiff brandy, but it would suffice.

He grimaced. "The moment she arrives, Seelye."

"Yes, your grace."

"Then very well. Come on, Mr. Milton. I believe my room is this way."

The man jumped up, managing somehow to bow and walk at the same time. "Excellent, your grace! I'm sure that's a wonderful idea! I have been thinking, you know, you have a delightful head of hair! What do you say to a Brutus cut? It's all the rage!"

Good God, the man was a rabbit who spoke only in exclamation points. "Shave it bald, Mr. Milton."

"What?" he squeaked.

"All off. Not a hair left. Naked as—" He swallowed his next words as not very ducal.

"But! But! But—"

Radley grinned, though he made sure his back was turned. It wasn't nice to take out his temper on the hapless rabbit that cut hair. "Never mind, Mr. Milton. Pick a style, use your scissors, but remember this—" He turned and glared at the man. "If you ask me one question about what you're about to do, I shall grab a razor and shave myself bald."

The rabbit blinked. "Your grace is joking?" he whispered.

"No."

The man dipped into another bow, temporarily hiding his horrified gaze. "Yes, your grace."

"Glad we understand each other." Then he tromped *past* his library and headed up the stairs.

What the bloody hell did she mean by "your life is in danger"?

❧

Wendy sat and stared at the walls of her old home. No one had rented the rooms. She understood that now. Damon had arranged for her to be tossed out, so that she would be forced to turn to him for lodging.

She knew that without experiencing any niggling of doubt. She could process that as she sat inside her empty home and stared at the pocked and dirty walls.

He had instigated the theft of Penny's home, he had incited a madman to attack Irene, and he had done it all as a way to isolate Wendy. The thought was depraved, and yet it made perfect sense. Damon had systematically tried to destroy everything that allowed Wendy to function outside of his circle. Destroy the dress shop, and Wendy would have no choice but to deal vingt-et-un to survive. Isolate her from her friends, and she would have no one to help her but Damon. Threaten her brother, and Wendy would kiss him in public, even allow Damon to bend her backward over a railing, so that he would not break Bernard's legs as an example to others.

And now, he would kill Radley.

She touched the earrings. Blood had crusted over them, and she winced at the feel as she tugged them free. But before she pulled them out of her ears, she stopped herself. It was bad enough that Radley was at risk. She would not add to the problem by threatening her brothers as well.

It was a ridiculous thought. No one knew she was here, and Damon certainly couldn't have spies watching her in a dark and empty room. And yet, she let her hand fall away, her spirits depressed as never before.

She had been a fool to think she could handle

Demon Damon alone. She who had built a successful business, who had solved problems since she was
able to talk, had arrogantly assumed she could handle
anything, including a demon. And now, he was going
to kill the man she loved.

She swiped her face, hating the tears that wet her
hands. What a useless creature she was. When had she
become so stupid as to fall in love? And not just in
love—that was disastrous enough—but in love with
Radley? He was a duke. She was a seamstress. He was
proper, she a thief. He kept telling her how good she
was, and now she would have to tell him everything.

Everything.

She felt her earrings again, wincing at the pain. And
she cried.

Seventeen

RADLEY WAS BRINGING HIS COUSIN LEMONADE AT THE ball when Wendy was announced. He'd been insane with worry, building steadily to a towering rage, when hour after hour passed with no word. In the end, he'd managed to keep himself from killing his family and staff. In truth, the entire day had been an exercise in restraint. Stand still and be fitted, sit quietly and have his hair cut, wait patiently for a response from his footmen. Nod when his mother showed him her dress and hold the right fork, when all he wanted was to tear apart the city in search of Wendy. He'd have drunk himself through half his brandy, but he wanted to be clear-headed in case she needed him.

He tried to remember that he was a sailor, and all sailors knew that sometimes, the wind blew ill. All he could do was wait it out, watching for the moment to make his move. That moment came barely into the first set at Miss Diane Beckam's coming out ball.

Wendy was announced.

He whipped his head up, nearly dropping the delicate teacup all over Eleanor. Only her quick reflexes saved her from disaster, and he didn't have the courtesy to care. He abandoned his cousin without a word and headed straight to where Wendy stood waiting to greet her host and hostess.

She was dressed simply, the gown made of light blue cotton rather than stunning silk. She looked like the bright blue sky, fair wind after a storm. The thought was fanciful, but then again, it was always that way with her. She was a goddess of the air, and he would always be blown back to her.

So he crossed to her side, or at least, he tried to. He had underestimated how much every soul wished to speak with him, to touch him, to draw his attention to them. He could scarce take two steps before a half-dozen people found an excuse to talk to him. It was maddening. Shoals everywhere, and no way to tack around some of them.

In the end, he resorted to rudeness, roughly pushing away, or simply refusing to stop, no matter what the obstacle. It took no more than ten minutes to get to Wendy, but he'd felt every second like the snap of an untethered rope in a high wind.

And then he caught her. A touch on her elbow, and she settled by his side. He exhaled in relief and saw an echoing release on her face. He also saw that she had been crying, that her earlobes were bleeding beneath emerald bobs, and that her stiffened shoulders meant she was resolved to do a task. Resolved, determined, and terrified.

He saw it all in that one moment when he locked her into his side. He remembered belatedly to greet her properly. He had to remember there were people watching his every move, and now, hers by extension. *Who was she to him?* they whispered.

He bowed deeply, kissing her hand in greeting, as if she were a queen. He watched her skin flush a dull pink before fading back to gray. Like the brief fullness of a sail before the wind stalled again.

"Wendy, what is it?"

Four words, and then he saw something he'd never thought to see. She was lost. He saw tears in her eyes, chaos in her emotions, and a complete lack of coordination. Her hand went to her face, her foot stepped to the side, and her gaze remained on him. And he, fool that he was, just stood there and gaped.

Until a woman jostled him from behind. Good lord, did they not have any other tricks? He had never thought that the words "falling all over him" were literal.

The woman gasped a false apology as she managed to press her thigh against him while flashing her bosom. He gave her no more attention than he would a passing shark. She was of no danger so long as he did not swim in her waters. So while she tried to entice him with her charms, he placed Wendy's hand on his arm and steered her onto the dance floor.

It was a waltz, and he vaguely remembered that such a dance signified something important. Whatever it was, he didn't care. He had her in his arms, and no one would disturb them as he whirled her about the room.

"I can't dance," she whispered. "I don't know—"

"Yes, you do. Just relax, and let me steer." Then he smiled. "Three beats—one two three, one two three, one two three."

They began to dance. She was resistant at first, her steps halting, but in this he was the master. And she needed the support. So he sailed them in and around the couples in the room, and he never dropped his gaze from hers.

"I spent the day looking for you," he said. "I sent out footmen and messages…"

"I know. I missed you at the tailor's and the cobbler's."

"I was with a rabbit of a dance master. And he was nothing compared to the idiot who instructed me on how to talk to men."

She frowned. "You don't know how to talk to men?"

"I don't know how to talk to you, Wendy. What has happened?"

She swallowed, and he felt her tense. But he would not allow her to stop her words. He needed her answers, and so he spun her quickly to disorient her, using the motion to pull her tighter into his arms.

"You can trust me," he whispered. "Tell me what happened?"

"The… The man who… The one I owe money to…" She blinked, and he saw the shimmer of tears.

"Has he hurt you?"

"I… That's not…" She shuddered. "He means to kill you. He told me this morning. He said he would kill you."

Her note had said as much, but it made no sense. "Why? What have I done?"

She shrugged. "I spent the night with you and not him."

He tripped. It was a small misstep, but significant enough that he might have fallen. In this, she was the one who steadied him, and soon he was whirling them around again. "You had planned to…" *Sleep with him?*

"I was supposed to work in the gambling hell." She looked away.

"You swore that you would not work there any-more!" he all but snarled.

She flashed him a frustrated look. "And I didn't! I was supposed to, but I was with you instead."

He felt his blood heat at the memory of what they'd done last night. "But Wendy—"

"I deal vingt-et-un. I wear clothing that… that distracts. I ply the gentlemen with wine and let them ogle my breasts. The money I should have made last night would have gone to the debt. But…"

He released a breath, the tightness in his chest easing. "So you were supposed to pay him last night?"

"Yes."

"And when you didn't show…?"

"He waited at my home. Mama let him in, and he…"

His eyes narrowed. He saw again the blood beneath her earbobs. "How did he hurt you?"

"It was nothing," she said, her grip tightening on his arms. "Listen to me. He means to kill you!"

"So you have said, but I need to know more. How will he do it? What resources does he have?" Simple questions, but he could tell she didn't have the answers. Whoever this bastard was, he had her thoroughly cowed. She was terrified and half convinced that Radley was already dead. "People have tried to kill me before. Not just on the boat, but in market-places and on the docks. Footpads, religious zealots, pirates—all are simply violent men who wish to hurt someone for some reason. Understanding them is the key to ending the threat."

She swallowed and nodded, but still she had no answers beyond the obvious. "He has men who will do his bidding. A knife in the dark. A gunshot when you go riding." She shuddered, her eyes going to his as she whispered. "I'm so sorry. I didn't mean… I thought…"

He squeezed her tighter. "Don't worry. Just tell me his name." The music was ending, the dance slowing. In a moment, they were standing, but he did not release her. "His name, Wendy."

He could tell she didn't want to speak, but there was no choice. The words came out in a whisper, and he read the name off her lips. And in that moment, he knew it had been inevitable. She spoke the one name that still haunted his nightmares, the one man who had ripped away the mirage of his perfect childhood.

"Demon Damon."

❧

Wendy felt the name hit him. She'd worried that he would explode or rage or do any of the things she'd seen him do over ten years ago when his sister had suffered at Damon's hands. She felt his body go rigid, then she tensed to keep him from doing anything rash.

But in that moment, she saw how much he had matured from the boy he'd been. The words hit him, his body stilled, and then she saw a kind of joy hit his face. It wasn't happiness. Far from it. But it was purpose and direction. As if she had given him the direction, and now, he did what he'd always been born to do. He sailed. But to what, if not certain death?

"Radley—"

"Don't worry, my Wind," he said with a fond smile. "The dance is done. Come, let us step to the side."

He didn't give her a chance to argue. He simply took her arm and guided her to the edge of the floor. People tried to stop him, many attempted to gain his attention, but he moved around and between them as if by magic. And when he stopped, they stood before his sister and her fiancé.

"Caroline, would you mind staying with Miss Drew for a while? You may have to escort her home."

His sister frowned, clearly sensing something was happening. "Of course—"

"Hartfell," he said to his sister's fiancé, "if you have a moment, I'd like a word."

He made to leave, but Wendy gripped his arm. "You cannot go. You cannot…" Her voice trailed away because she could see he wasn't even listening. He gently disengaged her fingers and then touched her chin.

"I am not insane, nor am I frightened. Remember who I am now—"

"But—"

"I know how to settle disputes between men."

"He will—" Her voice choked off. She could not be the cause of his death. She could *not*.

"No, love, he will not." Then he pushed her gently toward his sister before turning to Hartfell. "We have something in common tonight. Would you join me?"

The Scot gave him a hearty grin. "I love a little high jinks."

Radley didn't answer, except to move steadily

toward the door. Caroline came to stand beside Wendy, watching them leave with a worried frown.

"Where are they going?" she asked.

To their deaths. She almost said the words, but then she knew she would endanger Caroline as well. What woman would stand still while her fiancé faced a demon?

"It's nothing," she lied. "But I'm afraid I don't feel well. I believe I shall—"

"Run after them to keep them from being stupid?"

Wendy turned to the woman she'd known since girlhood. There was steel there that hadn't existed when she was young. Life had taught her a great deal.

"Yes," said Wendy.

"Then come along. I'll make our excuses to mother, and we'll be off. You know where they are going?"

"I know where they will end up." Then she gripped Caroline's hand, knowing the woman's history. "They are going to confront Damon Porter."

Caroline paled, but there was no backing down in her stance. If anything, she became more determined.

"You call for the carriage. I shall make sure mother and Eleanor stay far away."

And so it was done. Before long they were in the carriage, sitting in silence as they headed for the gaming hell. Wendy worried how her friend would react to confronting the villain from her childhood. But her one attempt to ask had been met with a heavy silence. Perhaps Caroline didn't know what to say. Her expression was flat, her body completely still. When they arrived, Wendy led them inside. She'd worked here for months, so she was able to slip in. She regretted the distinctive dresses they wore and that she lacked the mask she sometimes wore.

"I am called the Green Lady here," she said to Caroline. "Pick whatever name you want, but do not acknowledge your true self."

Caroline nodded, and once inside, they saw Damon immediately. He was in his place on the upper deck, though he did not survey the floor. Instead, he sat lounging in his chair like a tired king reading his accounts. She even saw him yawn, and that was a shock. She had never seen him tired, much less bored, but for the first time in her life, Damon appeared exhausted.

She slowed, her eyes narrowing. What was wrong? What had *changed*?

She was busy looking around, gauging the mood of the room, but there was no time. Caroline had seen him and was climbing the stairs.

"What are you doing? Stay down here!" Wendy gasped, trying to grab hold of her friend. She was too late. And even worse, her hiss was loud enough for Damon to hear.

The man's head snapped up, and he turned to her. His gaze met hers, eyes narrowed, and then he saw Caroline. She saw his jaw drop in shock, and his entire body stilled. Then he sat there, eyes riveted to Caroline, while his guards stepped to block her ascent.

Wendy stifled a curse, then rushed up behind her friend. She heard Damon growl a single word, and the guards stepped away. Then the two old enemies faced each other. Caroline squared off a few feet across from Damon. She stood with her eyes narrowed, and her teal gown seemed to shiver as she trembled.

Meanwhile, the demon slowly pushed up from his seat until he faced her, his eyes still narrowed, but his body calm.

"Perhaps we should go downstairs," Wendy suggested as she touched the woman's arm.

Caroline didn't respond. Her eyes were completely trained on Damon. "Do you know who I am?" she asked.

"I do." His voice was a coarse rasp, but it carried easily enough. "Would you like to sit down? I can have food brought up. Or wine."

She shook her head, finally breaking his gaze long enough to look about her. "This place. It is yours?"

His lips curved in a smile, pride evident in every word. "This, two more, and numerous other businesses. Elite and impoverished alike come through my doors and fight to spend time with me."

She nodded slowly, her gaze steady as she looked across the floor. The evening was established, and every table was full. But in the end, she returned to look at Damon.

"I made the right choice." Her words were dismissive as she turned her back on him. "Come along, Wendy. They are not here."

"Caroline, wait!" he said as he caught her elbow.

The woman's reaction was immediate. Faster than anyone could have expected, she spun back and slapped Damon hard across the face. The sound carried through the hell, like the crack of an axle breaking, and abruptly, the murmurs around them paused. People looked up, card play ceased, and all were poised for Damon's reaction.

He hadn't been slow. He'd caught her arm, but only after the blow. His cheek showed the red imprint of her hand, and his eyes blazed in fury. Around them, she felt the guards step up, ready to retaliate however Damon chose. Once, after closing, Wendy had seen them break a man's hand for a lesser insult.

Wendy had to act fast, but she wasn't sure how. So she did the only thing she could think of, the only action that had soothed drunken players and giddy lechers alike. She touched the demon's face. She couldn't feel the heat of the mark, not through her gloves, but the red was clear enough. She stroked it as if she could brush it away.

"Come, love," she cooed, nearly choking on the words. "You're done with her. Have been for years."

His gaze slowly slid to hers, and she saw calculation enter his gaze. Then they flicked to his guards. "I think the ladies would like some wine," he drawled.

The men stepped back, and one gave the order to a waitress. Meanwhile, Caroline tried to wrench her arm free to no avail. Wendy heard the woman's grunt of frustration before she vented it in the worst possible way.

"I want nothing of yours, Damon. I never have."

Did she not understand the danger? Damon never allowed anyone to insult him. Not in public. The noises from the floor had resumed, but slower, and there was almost no conversation. Everyone watched to see what would happen next.

With trembling fingers, Wendy slid her hand to Damon's fingers. "Wine would be lovely," she said as she stroked the back of his hand.

"Take them off," he said.

She blinked. He was looking at Caroline, but she knew the words were for her. But she didn't understand. "Take what—"

"Your gloves." His gaze finally shifted to hers, and his joy frightened her. He knew something she did not, and it would soon be turned against her. Normally, she would flee. If ever that flash of happiness came into his eyes, she ran as far and as fast as she could. But she would not abandon Caroline. He waited, his gaze turning more confident with every second that passed. "It's been too long since I felt the stoke of your skin against mine."

It had been this morning, and it made her shudder, but she nodded. "You will let her go, yes?"

He smiled, and his fingers went slack. Caroline jerked back, but she didn't go far. Meanwhile, Wendy was busy stripping off the first of her gloves with trembling fingers.

Her skin went cold as the fabric left her forearms, but she forced herself to remain calm, as if she did this every day. And she did, she reminded herself. She showed her bare hands everywhere. And yet, the feel of the fine linen pulling down her hands was as terrifying as if her shift were pulled off her. Not in the way of a woman undressing for a man, but in the way of a small animal slowly enticed into a trap. She knew she was stepping closer and closer to disaster, but she couldn't stop it.

"Slow down," he said, his eyes on her. "You know how I like it."

She winced. He made it sound like she had been

stripping for him for months now when nothing could be further from the truth. But he was making her pay for the insult to his face by having her show everyone that she had surrendered. The stripping of her gloves was symbolic, of course, but it would suffice, provided she gave enough of a show.

And, if she doubted the threat, he flicked his gaze to a large brute of a guard who stood a pace behind Caroline. He was the one who enjoyed breaking bones and would often regale the customers with tales of how it feels to snap the small delicate ones in the hand. He was looming behind Caroline, and Wendy doubted the woman even noticed. Her eyes were on Wendy and Damon, while shock grew in her expression. Damn it, the woman had no idea how much danger she was in.

Plastering on a seductive expression, Wendy slowed her movements. "Of course," she purred, though the words came through thick and low. Not a purr so much as a choke, but it was enough. Damon settled back on his heels as his smile widened.

She stretched up her arm, knowing she had to show it to the gallery below. Then she crinkled the fabric from the elbow to her wrist. A slow, steady push that revealed herself, inch by inch. The cold air made her body tighten, and she became excruciatingly aware that her nipples had pebbled. She was cold, terrified for Caroline, and humiliated to her bones. But, at the same time, she felt an inevitability settle upon her. How many times had Damon said she would gift herself to him? That eventually, she would be his?

She pulled off one glove, the slide of the fabric

feeling like the peel of skin from her bones. The thought was so real she half expected to see her blood dripping on the floor. Nothing so dramatic appeared. Simply white flesh with goose bumps.

Damon crossed in front of her, moving to the bend in the railing, where he had kissed her not so long ago. He leaned negligently there, but she knew he was reminding everyone of the kiss they'd shared.

"Give it to me," he said, holding out his hand and forcing her to step further into view.

She did, extending it to him. His gaze flickered— the only warning she had—before one of his guards pushed her. She hadn't even known the man had moved behind her until she felt the hard shove right at the base of her spine.

She stumbled forward, and Damon caught her. She stiffened quickly, but his grip tightened painfully across her back.

She struggled, of course, pushing back, but he was too strong, and there was still the threat to Caroline. In the end, she relaxed, though only by a small degree. Clearly, the show wasn't just for the men below, but for Caroline. He wanted Wendy to act as his tart before her friend.

"Let me pull off the other," he said against her ear.

She swallowed and looked away. She'd agreed to take off her gloves, but this humiliation wasn't part of the bargain.

"No," she said, her voice cold. Then she ripped off the other glove, stripping it with quick, angry movements before she balled it up and threw it at him. He grinned, not even bothering to catch the thing. Instead, he let it sail over the railing to land somewhere below. She heard the roar of men, then laughter as someone caught it.

God, he'd turned her into a harlot for everyone to see.

"Can we leave now?" she bit out.

"Of course," he said as he let her stomp back. "Though, of course, you're welcome to stay for the rest of the show."

He gestured casually over his shoulder. His back was to the stairs, so she had no idea how he knew. But one look had her stomach dropping like a stone.

There were Radley and Lord Hartfell storming the stairs. Lord Hartfell's gaze was on Caroline, his brows tight with fear. But whereas the Scot rushed to save his love, Radley slowed down. His eyes were trained on her remaining glove as Damon pulled it slowly through his fist.

Eighteen

WHY WAS SHE HERE?

That was Radley's overriding thought as he climbed
the stairs. Why was Wendy stripping off her gloves,
her face tight with fear, as she undressed for everyone
to see?

It made no sense. She was terrified of Damon,
and yet...

"Damnation," Lord Hartfell cursed. "Caroline's
here as well." Then he sprinted up the stairs. But
Radley slowed, his eyes narrowed as Wendy threw
her glove at Damon. Something was at work here,
and he would do well to understand it before he went
crashing up there.

Then it happened. Wendy spotted him, and her
eyes widened in shock. He watched her pale, then
stiffen in bravado. Then his eyes trained on a flash
of white: her glove in that bastard's hand. The man
toyed with it, pulling it slowly through his fist, over
and over.

The need to kill Damon burned in his blood, but he
was a rational man. Murder—even of a monster—took

careful thought, especially when facing the evil in its own territory. So he mounted the last steps slowly, noting the guards, his sister's position tucked tight to the Scot's side, and Wendy, as she stood too close to the bastard.

And everyone looked to him as he topped the steps and turned to face his sister's attacker.

"Ladies," he said without shifting his gaze from Damon's. "Are you well?"

"Perfectly," answered Caroline in a voice that seemed strong enough. "We were just about to leave."

The Scot rumbled his questions, his burr strong. "Are ye sure? Nothing amiss?"

"Perfectly sure," she answered. "I've seen everything I care to see in this place. Come along, Wendy. It's time to leave."

Wendy nodded, but she didn't move. Her gaze turned anguished. "Lord Hartfell, why don't you take her home? I think the air is bad here."

"Can't," the Scot answered. "Seems someone's threatened his grace's life."

He watched the news hit Damon, his body tensing in surprise. "What? Who?" Then his face hardened as he glanced to Wendy. "What did you say?"

She frowned as she turned to look at the man. "You said…"

Radley watched as her face closed down with frustration. He saw her hands tighten into fists, but there was no more protest. Was she cowed? Was she afraid? Or was something else going on?

"Please come over here, Wendy," he said. Whatever was going on, he didn't want her within the bastard's reach.

She started to move, but then froze, her gaze slipping back to Damon, as if asking permission. A second later, he realized it wasn't permission. It was assuming a position of power—one where she kept both men in sight—as she faced the bastard.

"What do you want to end this, Damon? To just... let them all go?"

Damon's expression shifted into dismay. "Negotiating for your lover's life? Sacrificing yourself for him?" He shifted his gaze to Radley. "Sadly, none of it's true. Little Wendy has quite the flair for the dramatic, and I'm afraid we've been victims of her fascination with gothic novels."

She gasped. "That's not true!"

"But of course, it is. Your grace, I have no intention of harming you." He made an expansive gesture. "Welcome to my club. Please feel free to play."

"Stop it!" Wendy cried, and he was sure there were tears shimmering in her eyes. "You told me you'd kill him. You told me! And you hurt Caroline. And you..." Her words choked off.

If anything, Damon looked sad. "I did hurt Caroline, and that is a crime for which I can never atone." His gaze shifted to Caroline. "I offered you wine, did I not?"

"You were going to break her hand," Wendy hissed.

Damon reared back. "Break her hand? Damnation, Wendy, do you hear yourself? How can you expect any rational man to believe you?"

"Because it's true," Wendy said as she shifted to Caroline. "You slapped him, and he doesn't allow that. I've seen him hurt people," she cried. "Everyone knows what he can do."

"Wendy, really," Damon said with clear irritation.

Then Damon pushed off the railing, setting her glove aside, as if it were of no more importance than yesterday's cravat. Radley tensed, ready for anything, but not moving until he understood more of what was going on. And right now, he comprehended little.

"And yes, I do hurt people," Damon admitted. "It's a necessity in my business. But Wendy," he said as he gently pulled her to face him. "I love you. You know this."

"Stop it!" she cried as she wrenched from his arms.

He let her go, his expression infinitely sad. Then he slowly shifted to look at Radley. "I do not know what lies she has told you. I can only say that I would be a fool to threaten a duke." He gestured about him. "I have created a good life for myself here, but it is subject to the whims of society. Should any member of the *ton* take umbrage with me, they could close my doors. Or they could simply take their coin to a different hell. I would be a fool to risk that."

Wendy gaped. "You bragged not more than a week ago. You told me how you meant to end the elite. That you did more for London than Prinny!"

"That's treason, Wendy." He huffed out a breath, rubbing a hand over his face. "Are you so afraid of love that you must make me out a monster?" Again, he tried to touch her, and again, she threw him off. It was a pattern he'd seen before, so Radley disregarded it. His concern was more in the words "a week ago." Just how long had they been having conversations like that? How well did she know this bastard?

He stepped forward and brandished his purse. That

was what delayed him from the ball. He'd had to find enough coin to pay off her debt.

"Wendy said she owed you money."

Damon lifted his hands. "Her brother owes me. She has been helping to pay his debts." He shot Wendy a tolerant glare. "Which could have happened much earlier, if she would work when she promises." He grimaced. "She deals vingt-et-un, and I pay her an excellent wage. Far more than what her talents are worth, but..." He shrugged, as if to say, *I love her. What else can I do?*

Meanwhile, Wendy stiffened. "I have made every shift, save one."

He didn't argue. His expression suggested that he would not stoop to bicker over dates and times. Instead, he looked to Radley.

"It is kind of you to pay off her brother's debt, but I assure you, they both need the lesson. Bernard works for me as well, and he's learning to control his need to gamble. As for Wendy, she likes it here. Pay it off or not, she will be back."

"I hate it here!" she hissed.

"And yet, you have favorite customers who dote on your every word. Men who constantly plague me as to when you will next appear." He looked to Radley. "She loves the attention." He sighed. "And she loves rubbing it in my face as well."

Could it be true? Could Wendy be so different from everything he'd thought? He glanced to his sister. "How easily did you come here? Were you stopped by guards? Anyone?"

Caroline shook her head. "We came in a back

way, and they all know her here. They call her the Green Lady."

As if realizing that he wavered, Wendy stepped toward him, her expression desperate. "Everything he says is a lie. You have to believe me. I've seen him do terrible things. You know what he has done."

He did. Every time he looked at his sister's high-necked gowns, he remembered the scars underneath. But even at seventeen, Radley hadn't been able to bring himself to kill Damon. He'd beaten the bastard nearly dead, but murder was beyond him then. It was still, apparently, because he felt no desire to gut someone who appeared more rational than the woman begging him to understand.

Meanwhile, Damon was speaking, his tone and appearance that of a man burdened by terrible guilt. "I cannot undo the crime I committed as a boy. I was wild and foolish, and I regretted it then, even as I did that terrible thing." He turned to Caroline. "Whatever you want of me, just ask. I will give it to you freely. If I could undo that night, I would. You cannot know how sorry I am."

Radley looked at his sister as she shook her head. "I want nothing from you." He heard the finality in her words. There was no lingering fear, no hatred, and no terrible emotions whatsoever. Just a simple end to something that happened years ago. He could not say the same, and yet, she was the victim. He certainly couldn't murder a man who showed every appearance of regretting his crime.

Damon bowed his head with total humility. "I... I thank you. I never dared hope you could forgive me. I

don't ask it. But that I haven't destroyed your life is…
is a great comfort to me."

The Scot's answer rumbled through the air. "She
does not say it to comfort you."

"Of course not," Damon replied. "I didn't mean to
imply such a notion." Then he turned back to Wendy.
"What do you mean to do now, my dear? Will you
stay and deal? Already, there are gentlemen lining up
at your table."

Radley looked over the railing to the floor below.
There was one table that sat empty, though easily a
dozen gentlemen loitered nearby. Was that where
Wendy worked? Did she entertain such a group on a
regular basis? The very idea made him sick.

His gaze returned to her. She looked like she was
collapsing in on herself. He wanted to believe that she
was exactly as she appeared: a woman under terrible
strain, exploited by a monster. The urge to rush to her
side was strong. But he was beginning to doubt her.
After all, he'd asked her to come to him, but she'd
chosen instead to stand on her own. And there were a
dozen men down there waiting for her. Just what had
she been doing?

"What do you want of me, Damon? What would
it take?" she asked.

The bastard touched her cheek, stroking it slowly
as his fingers went from jaw to cheek to her bloodied
earbobs. "You know what I want, love. Stay with
me." He touched her chin, lifting it to look at her.
"Marry me."

Radley felt more than saw her breath catch, as if
everything had been stilled to a frozen silence. She

just… stopped. So did he. So did everyone there as they strained to hear her answer.

And waited. And waited.

She didn't answer. It was as if she couldn't.

In the end, Damon sighed and looked at Radley. "You do not believe that I am innocent yet. Of course, whatever she's said would be convincing." He tilted his head. "Have you asked about her earbobs? Shall I tell you how she got them?"

Wendy did react to that. She let out a soft moan as she sank to her knees. At first, he thought she had collapsed, but Damon went with her, cradling her as she dropped. Had she fallen into his arms? Did she welcome the man's touch? He didn't know, and his doubt kept him immobile while Damon continued to talk—this time to her.

"Shall I tell him, my dear? It really is better if the truth comes out."

She didn't answer, and so the demon kept speaking as if he'd never paused.

"She stole them. From a customer at her first place of employment. Then she sold them, so she and Lady Redhill could start their shop."

Caroline gasped. "Lady Redhill? But she couldn't…"

"Well, as to that, I believe Lady Redhill's father—"

"Helaine didn't know," Wendy cried. The words were loud, easily drowning out whatever Damon was going to say.

Radley could see that the words were to cover another secret. Something about Lady Redhill—or maybe her father—that Wendy didn't want to get out. But that confession alone told him two things, both chilling. First, Wendy had stolen the earbobs—or done something illegal with them—and second, she had more secrets, more lies that she was trying to cover up.

Radley took a step forward, needing to come closer so that he could see Wendy's face and understand what was going on. "If she sold them to start her shop, then how is it that she has them?" he challenged.

Damon smiled, the expression wistful. "Well, I found out, of course. There is plenty of information that flows through these halls. I discovered the truth, found the buyer, repaid him, and then..." He shrugged, as if embarrassed. "I gave them to Wendy as a gift. That's why she's wearing them now." His gaze lifted to Radley, and his eyes slowly went cold. "She wears them now, your grace, because deep down, she prefers me."

Radley looked to the emeralds, then to Wendy's face. Her eyes were dull, her expression like stone. Was that true? Did she wear the earrings out of love... for Damon?

"He needs to hear it said out loud, my love," said Damon. Then, when Wendy didn't respond, he touched her chin, lifting her face up. "Did I or did I not give you those earrings?"

"Don't make me do this," she said, her voice a hoarse rasp. "You cannot make me—"

Damon's voice hardened. "Tell the truth, or suffer the consequences. You know I cannot abide a liar."

Radley wasn't a fool. He knew there was a subtle threat in the man's tone. Knew as well that they were surrounded by guards. He'd already counted his opponents, but he judged the danger as relatively small. Both he and Lord Hartfell were armed and knew how to defend themselves. Any attack would be a bloodbath, and neither side would benefit. Damon couldn't take the risk. The death of a duke in this public place? That would draw too much attention.

Unfortunately, any fight would mean danger to the women. Radley hadn't liked that risk, but then he wasn't the one who brought them here. Wendy had. Fortunately, he knew the Scot would protect Caroline, just as he would protect Wendy. And again, he returned to the obvious conclusion. Damon was a logical man who ran a lucrative business. He simply would not risk a bloody confrontation now.

So that brought them back to the central question. Was this an elaborate game created in Wendy's mind?

He grimaced, sinking down so that he faced Wendy. "Just tell me the truth," he said. "It is safe."

She winced, and he knew she didn't believe him. He couldn't help that. Afraid or not, he needed to know more. But he was able to glare at Damon.

"Step back."

The man lifted his hand in a surrendering gesture and backed away. Wendy was now on the floor, a woman collapsed into a puddle of shimmering blue.

"Don't be afraid, just tell me. Is what he said true? Did you steal the emeralds?" She'd already admitted as much. She would answer, and he would see how she looked when she told the truth.

"Yes," she whispered, her gaze dropping in what he thought might be shame. "We needed… I didn't have…" She bit her lip. "Yes, I stole them. Helaine didn't know anything about it."

"And you sold them to start your shop?"

She didn't speak this time. She just nodded.

Now came the more important questions. "And Damon found them somehow? He gave them to you?"

She swallowed. "This morning after…"

"After you missed your shift last night. At the vingt-et-un table?" She had told him as much last night. He knew she'd had someplace to be, but he'd wanted her in his bed. In that, at least, he bore at least as much responsibility as she.

"Yes," she said, and he saw her eyes flicker as she said it. Was she remembering what they'd shared last night? He hoped so. He hoped she was thinking of how they'd loved one another and was gaining strength from it.

Now came the real question. "I know I just returned. I know matters are unsettled between us, but we cannot go ahead without settling the past." He glanced at his sister, taking another look to reassure himself that she had moved on from what she'd suffered at Damon's hand.

Without Radley speaking the question aloud, Caroline answered with a firm voice. "I just want to go home," she said. The Scot gave a quiet nod, seconding his fiancée's wish.

So that past was done. Now, all that remained was Wendy.

"You don't have to say you wish to be with me, Wendy. But the man has proposed to you." He couldn't bring himself to say the bastard's name. "If you wish to be rid of him, simply give him back his gift. I have coin to pay Bernard's debt, so you need not fear on that. If you want to leave this place, then take out the earrings."

Her eyes welled with misery. "It's not that simple," she whispered.

"Of course it is."

In the background, Damon made a sharp gesture. Radley had kept an eye on him, so he saw it for what it was. The man was gesturing to his guards. A moment later, all the menacing men on the upper deck had moved away and down the stairs. Damon now stood unprotected. He even spread his hands to show that he had no weapons. And in case there was any doubt, he spoke, his tone clear and almost gentle.

"You are safe, Wendy. No one will harm you no matter what you say, but his grace is correct. I need an answer. All you need do is take out the earrings, and I will know your choice."

She stilled at the man's words, not even moving her eyes to look at him. He was to the side—not quite out of her vision—but Radley was watching. She didn't look anywhere but at a fixed spot seven inches in front.

Frowning, he moved until he was directly in her line of vision. "Wendy. Just take them out."

She couldn't meet his gaze. "I can't."

Two words, but they froze him to his soul. She couldn't. Then her gaze did flicker, and she lurched forward.

"He is more dangerous than you think."

So she was still afraid. Of course she was. He could

see it in her body though all the guards had been sent away. "Have some faith in me, Wendy."

He could tell she wanted to. He saw her take in a ragged breath, but in the end, she stopped. Her breath was cut off, and her gaze dropped away.

"I... can't." She seemed to deflate before his eyes. "Go now, while you still can. You have your answer. Damon will not allow your insult to last much longer."

He didn't move, still too shocked by her choice. That wasn't a problem for the bastard. Damon had heard her answer, even though her words had been barely audible. He knew what she had said, so he knelt beside her, his expression triumphant.

"Come, love, this is a happy moment." Damon gently turned her face to his. She went easily with no more resistance than a rag doll. "We will marry!"

He held her then, their gazes locked for an excruciatingly long time. And then, the unthinkable happened. The man bent his head to hers.

He took his time, while Radley squatted no more than a foot away and watched. The bastard pressed his lips to hers. A soft touch that lasted an eternity. Then more. Radley watched in disgust as the man wrapped his arm behind Wendy's back, slowly drawing her to her feet without breaking the seal of their lips.

Radley moved as well, straightening, unable to look away. Damon and Wendy rose while the bastard deepened the kiss. He must be incredibly strong, Radley thought, to lift her like that—so smoothly—when she was no more than a flopped creature in his arms.

Then he broke the kiss and looked at her with narrowed eyes. "Such is not the kiss of a true fiancée," he rasped. "I have lost patience with you, my dear. Either prove that you want this, or I shall take back the earrings, and you shall see what is left to you."

Radley saw the shudder that racked her body. Saw the release that came from those words. Would she do it now? Would she take out those damned earbobs and throw them at his feet? She had thrown her glove at him, so he knew she had the strength of will. If she were truly afraid, she would.

She didn't.

Instead, she twined her arms around the bastard. Radley could see she was shaking, but he remembered too well how she had trembled in his arms too. How her body had shaken before she finally gave in to his kiss, his touch...

She kissed Damon. Not a slow press of the lips, not a chaste twining of arms and mouths. She kissed Damon with her whole body. She wrapped her arms around his neck, she pressed her groin against the bastard's obvious erection, and she opened her mouth. He wasted no time in restraint. With a grunt of satisfaction, the man wrapped his arms around her and bent her back. Even Radley could see that he plundered her mouth, stroked her backside, and rolled his cock against her.

And so, it was done. Wendy had chosen. The woman he'd adored since he was a young man had chosen someone else. She was—in fact—completely different than what he'd expected.

"Come along, Radley," his sister said as she touched his arm. "There is nothing left here for us."

Radley didn't move. He couldn't unfreeze his

body enough to shift. Then Lord Hartfell spoke, his tone brusque.

"Dangerous to wait. Stupid to remain for no point."

They were right. He had to go. But…

The kiss continued with no signs of stopping. If things went on this way, Damon would have her skirts at her waist in another five minutes. He shouldn't see this, didn't want to see it.

Then the two broke apart. Damon lifted his mouth enough so that both could breathe. Radley could hear the rasp of the man's breath and see the way his body tightened, even as he pressed tiny kisses along her cheek.

Then Damon turned Wendy in his arms. It might have been a casual movement or done with deliberate intent. Either way, he turned her head to the light. The emerald flashed in the lamplight before Damon's lips engulfed her lobe.

He was kissing the earbob. And, as he did it, Wendy released a slow moan. Despair or desire—he didn't know. Nor did he care. He'd built an image of Wendy in his mind. He'd remembered her from that day on the docks when he'd first shipped out. He'd drawn her likeness, envisioned them together, and created a dream with her face on it.

And now, he was shocked when the reality didn't fit the illusion? What a fool he was. What an idiot to think after one week that he knew her secrets.

He hadn't known how she got the money to start her business. He hadn't known to whom she owed money. And he sure as hell hadn't realized she could kiss him with abandon one night then show the same ardor with someone else on the next.

He hadn't known then, but he did now. So with a grunt of disgust, he pulled out his purse. In it were the coins he'd promised. All the money she owed to escape from Damon. The idea disgusted him now. It made no sense, but in his mind, these coins were tied to her. So he tossed them away. A single flick of his wrist, and the purse dropped with a thud.

He knew she heard the sound. Saw her body flinch, but she didn't turn his way. Had he been hoping for more of a response? Some sign of gratitude for the hundred and twenty-one quid he'd thrown at her feet?

He was a fool.

So he turned and left.

❧

Damon kept her locked in his arms well after Radley had left. She might have minded if she hadn't gone numb. If she could feel the way his touch made her skin crawl, if she knew the putrid horror of his tongue in her mouth. But she had blocked her mind out of her body. She had inch by inch let her consciousness climb the walls, until she felt as if she were perched in the rafters looking at the tableau beneath.

She saw herself kiss Damon as if she were a harlot after a coin. She knew when Radley cut free his purse and tossed it at her feet. Payment, she supposed, for his night with her. And she shrunk against the ceiling while Damon caressed her body through her clothes, a foretelling of what he would do to her soon.

Not here, of course. He had been sure to claim her in public, but the intimacies would be in private. The depravities too, she supposed. She had heard whispers of that as well and didn't want to guess at what was to come. Then he finally stepped back. He set her aside as he settled on his couch and smiled in triumph.

"We shall have to announce the banns as soon as possible." He glanced to where one of his guards stepped out from the hidden room. He had three such doors in this upper deck. Places for guards to hide or doors through which to escape should disaster strike. "Is Father Wollet here?"

The guard nodded. "At the hazard table."

"Tell him I require him to announce my forthcoming marriage to Miss Wendy Drew. Write it down. Make sure he understands it is vital that it is announced this Sunday."

The guard nodded and left. Wendy's mind watched the exchange from her perch high up along the ceiling. Her body, of course, hadn't moved from where it stood—swaying slightly—near enough to the railing to be seen by all.

"Aren't you going to ask me why we are to be married?" he asked.

"Why?" she asked, her voice surprisingly clear.

"As your husband, I shall own A Lady's Favor, the premiere dress shop to the *ton*. You have built yourself a luscious place, my dear. My world gives me the secrets of men, but yours has proved quite rich with the secrets of women."

If she doubted his words, he carefully pulled out a few of her recorded secrets. The ones learned from ladies at the shop—the things that women revealed to their closest friends that might not be whispered among men.

"I don't own the shop," she lied. "It's really Helaine's."

It was a fool's game. He knew the truth. She was co-owner, and he was smart enough to turn half of a successful business into a place as seductively poisonous as his gaming hells.

He didn't bother responding to her lie. What was the point? They both knew her evasion for what it was. Meanwhile, he sauntered leisurely to the railing. He looked down at the gaming floor, closing his eyes and tilting his head as he often did when standing there.

"Secrets," he said. "The whisper of secrets amidst the snap of cards, the roll of the dice, and the clang of coins. It is the secrets that I love the most."

She knew it was true.

Then he turned to her, his expression jovial, even though his eyes were hard. "I will have it all now," he said sweetly. "I will have your hand in marriage, your business as my forfeit, and your body for my pleasure. Everything I want."

She closed her eyes. If she had simply taken off her earrings as Radley asked, it would have been a death sentence for her brothers. Perhaps Radley was safe with his dukedom and his fighting skills, but Henry and Bernard were more vulnerable. And they were her brothers.

In the end, she had sold the possibility of a life with Radley for the certainty of her brothers' survival. That had been her choice, and she would make the same one again. But the cost had killed her soul. Not her body. She feared that would continue for a long while yet—that, and her pride, which kept her lips sealed.

Damon came closer. "Think of this. He would have

married you. Radley Lyncott, Duke of Bucklynde, would have made you his duchess, despite all the pressure to marry a society virgin. He wanted you. And do you know why?"

She didn't move. She couldn't, even though she strained with everything to block out his next words. She didn't want to hear because in her heart, she knew it was true.

"Because he loved you. He. Loved. You. And now, he doesn't."

She bit her lip, the reality of everything that had just happened hitting her hard. It began in the pit of her stomach then swelled upward, outward, until it consumed every part of her. But she held it back. If she gave voice to it, then it would be real, and she would be utterly destroyed.

Damon didn't say a word. Not a single word, but he leaned close. He set his hand near her ear and snapped his fingers. A pop, sharp enough to make her jolt. And, in that moment, all her strength shattered.

She screamed.

Nineteen

SHE SAT BESIDE HIM FOR HOURS. DAMON HELD COURT as always. Wendy sat through supplications and negotiations. She barely heard any of it. She simply watched—as if disembodied and sitting in the rafters—as the minutes ticked by.

He played with her hair. She noted that and couldn't stir to fight him. Occasionally, he would tug on her bloody ear. It was a petty cruelty or an attempt to rouse her from her stupor. She didn't even blink. What was a tug when she'd lost Radley?

Eventually, the evening slid into night then early dawn. He pinched her awake. She hadn't realized she'd fallen asleep when she felt an agonizing pain in her nipple. She jolted upright, a cry on her lips. He chuckled, and she curled her arms over her chest. It wouldn't save her, she knew, but she was hurting, and so she did it. Watching the movement, his eyes lightened in amusement.

"You like seeing me in pain," she said.

A statement of fact.

"I like seeing a lot of people in pain," he answered honestly.

"Why?"

He frowned, his mouth open as if he intended to answer, but the words wouldn't come. A moment later, he spoke, but his tone sounded a little lost. "I don't know. I just always have."

She tried to understand but couldn't. "Is there nothing else you enjoy?"

He grinned. "Oh yes," he said, the tone lascivious. But then his expression clouded. "Though it's usually entwined with pain."

She straightened slowly, her mind struggling to find clarity. "Do you like receiving pain too?"

His body stilled, and his nostrils flared. For a moment, she thought she had pushed too far, but then she realized he was aroused by the idea. Then he smiled.

"I shall enjoy our marriage, little Wendy."

She wanted to look away from his dark gaze, but knew that would be a mistake. He would sense her revulsion and her terror. In truth, she didn't fully understand the game he played, but she had worked in his hell for months now. Some whispers reached her ears whether she comprehended them or not. Enough whispers had given her a picture she thought was depraved, even as part of her thrilled to the play of power.

That was the real shock. Her soul was barely back in her body, and it understood a little more of this man who tormented her. Just as she collected secrets, Damon collected power games. Pain was his game of choice, but power—dominance—was the currency. And in such a game, he would give as well as receive.

That was the key to him, she guessed. The driving force, as he looked for a woman who would dominate and surrender in a constant dance of lust and power.

"I cannot be what you seek," she said honestly. "I am not the woman you need."

He stepped forward, looming over her in menace. "Are you sure?" he growled.

She didn't flinch, didn't back down, though she desperately wanted to. "I am sure."

He grabbed her chin in a bruising grip, tilting her face up. He didn't need to. She was already looking at him, but he needed to hurt her while he tried to read her mind. She remained as calm as she could while he glared at her.

"You can be trained," he finally said. "There is promise in you, my dear. Something that can be nurtured."

She shuddered at his words. He was probably right. She might not have all the tools, but her heart beat hard in her throat and her hands were slick. Terror? Absolutely. Interest? Perhaps. A tiny part of her wanted to know more about what he offered. No one else wielded power so effortlessly. To learn such a thing interested her.

It was the cost that horrified her—the immersion in pain that was part of it—her own and another's. Could she swim in those waters and not change at a fundamental level? Probably not. After all, she remembered when Damon had once been sweet. Nearly two decades ago when he had laughed at something fun, at a shared joy untouched by darkness. And now, he didn't even remember that time.

"I don't want to learn," she finally said.

"I don't care," he answered.

And that was also truth.

But something in their conversation must have affected him. Something made him gesture to his guards as he reached for his drink. It was late, even by his standards, but he showed every appearance of settling in for longer.

"Take her home. Make sure she doesn't leave."

Wendy swallowed, feeling his chains tightening ever closer. "I have to work. A Lady's Favor won't be a premiere dress shop for long if I don't sew the orders."

He didn't even look at her. "You're exhausted. Sleep. You can work tomorrow." Then he turned to flash her a dark smile. "Sew your wedding dress."

She didn't answer, her throat too frozen. A moment later, he turned away, and his guards steered her down the stairs. She moved slowly, her body aching with exhaustion. She'd been more tired other times, she was sure, but the problem now was in her mind. And her heart.

Both were sluggish and cold. It numbed the pain, but did little to help her find a way out of this mess. Had all her struggles, all her manipulations brought her to this? Her dress shop handed over to a monster? Her—married to the man? Is this what she deserved?

She walked in a fog. Her rooms were close—an easy walk—but it wouldn't have mattered if they intended her to tromp to Scotland. Nothing penetrated the steadily thickening wall of ice around her soul.

Until there was a blur of movement. She heard the thud of blows and grunts of pain. She stopped to look at the guards when she saw the third drop to the ground, blood seeping from his mouth.

All three guards were down? She stared at their prone forms in confusion. Then her gaze lifted to the man standing over them. He wore rough sailor's garb, but she recognized him immediately. She knew it was Radley, but she could only stare.

What was he doing here? And why had he brawled with the guards? She was still trying to puzzle that out when he spun to her.

"Come on, Wind. We need to go."

She blinked. Why couldn't she think? "I can't. He'll know."

He flashed her a grin, his white teeth flashing in the morning light. "Of course, he will. But not for a bit. Bernard says he's settled in for a dawn of heavy drinking. Says he does that sometimes."

Wendy wouldn't know. She never stayed this long at the hell. Meanwhile, her brother stepped from the shadows. Had he been there the whole time? Probably not. Radley was the one who dropped the guards. By himself, too, she thought with distracted pride. He was a strong fighter. No wonder he defeated the pirates and won their ship.

"Come along, Wind. We have to go." He reached for her then, but she watched his eyes go to her earrings. They didn't hurt anymore. In truth, she'd forgotten they were there, but at his gaze, her knees went weak. She stumbled, and he caught her. "Wind!"

"He'll kill them," she whispered.

"Who?"

"Bernard. Henry. He'll know and—"

"Bernard is coming with us. Henry is taking watch on *The Northern Glory*."

"But—"

"I've warned them. And your mother is already at my home. He can't get us there. Not a duke's residence in Grosvenor Square."

She looked him in his eyes. "You don't know him the way I do."

His expression darkened. His eyes narrowed, and his mouth went flat. She knew what he was thinking—that she was Damon's mistress—but she hadn't the strength to fight him. She'd lost all will when Radley had left. She hadn't realized at the time, but now, she saw that she was too frightened to fight, too exhausted to argue.

"Wendy," he said as he held her upright. "Look at me."

Had she looked away? Apparently so, because he touched her cheek and brought her attention back to him.

"You've spent your life relying on yourself. You managed things for your mother and your brothers. You helped me and Caroline when we had no idea what to do. You built a successful business. Damn it, Wind, for once in your life allow me to help you. Come with me. Have faith in me."

She looked at his face, at the jut of his jaw and the fierceness of his pose. In her mind's eye, she remembered him as a young man first stepping onto a boat. He had that same fierceness then. A strength that had surrounded him like an aura as he headed to sea. Not when he'd been looking back at her—that expression had been boyish and wistful—this was later. After he'd been called to work. After he'd started learning the tasks of a sailor.

She'd stood on the dock and watched as long as she could, and she remembered seeing that power. And now, it was directed at her. Now he looked at her in the same way he'd once stared at the open sea.

"You never fail," she whispered, knowing for the first time—deep in her soul—that it was true. Not when he had that look. Not when he focused on his goal and made it happen.

"So come with me. Unless you want to stay with him."

She shuddered. "I want to be with you."

"Then—"

"But my family—"

Bernard stepped up, his eyes constantly scanning the area. "We can watch out for you, sis. We can do that now."

Radley touched her cheek. "I can do that too."

So it was settled. She found the strength in her legs, found the belief in her heart, and most of all she found Radley's hand. She grabbed it and held on as they took off on foot. Bernard led the way. He wended them through the London streets. She kept track of where they were going, amazed at the byways and alleys that he took. She'd lived in London all her life, and yet her little brother knew better than she did where to step to avoid a clogged street, where to turn to hide in a shadow. The sun was up, though the sky was hazy. They slid through London like a ship silently gliding through fog. And some forty-five minutes later, they arrived at Radley's Grosvenor Square home.

They entered the kitchen, but quickly moved to the main part of the house. The butler was in the front hallway speaking to Lady Eleanor when they came through. The lady gasped in surprise, her eyes going wide at Radley's attire. The butler, however, executed a smooth bow.

"Miss Drew's room is ready." He looked at her. "I can show you up if you like, and a bath can be brought up."

Wendy's mind was quicker now as her gaze hopped from the butler to Radley. "You had a room prepared for me?"

He nodded with a wolfish smile. "I did."

"But when you left…" She couldn't finish the question. She remembered how he'd left. She remembered the sound of his coins hitting the floor. The disgust on his face. And the anger.

"Did you really think I would abandon you?" he asked. "Even then, did you think you were alone?"

She swallowed. She had. She did.

Her brother stepped up. "I was there. I told him the truth."

"And I heard you scream," Radley said. He touched her cheek, turning her to look at him. "Every good sailor can read the wind. We never learn all its secrets, but we understand enough. I never believed you false, just capricious."

She stiffened. "I've never been capricious!"

"Of course not," he said with absolute seriousness. "At least, not to me." He dropped his forehead to hers. "Because I'm a good sailor, my Wind."

She swallowed, unable to speak. Was she really safe here? Was her family truly free of Damon's threat? She didn't believe it. She had yet to set eyes on her mother or Henry, but for the moment, she found faith. Radley would see it through. And so, with shaking hands, she set her fingers on her earrings. It was hard to manage— and a little painful—but she'd never felt better than when she pulled out the blood-encrusted jewels.

Then she mutely handed them to Radley. "I never wanted these things," she said. "But he didn't lie. I did steal them. A long time ago."

She barely heard Lady Eleanor's horrified gasp. Her attention was riveted on Radley's expression as he accepted the bloody earbobs.

"And that's something we will talk about. But not right now." Then he looked at the butler. "Seelye, she'll want to see her mother first. You can set up her bath while they're talking. And after that…" He turned back to her. "You should sleep. We have enough time for you to rest before we begin again."

She blinked, startled to find her eyes burned with tears. "Thank you," she whispered. Inadequate words for the man who had single-handedly gotten them out of debt and given them safe haven. But at the moment, it was all she had.

His grin widened. "I like it when the wind owes me a favor. I mean to collect on it."

She smiled, surprised that she still could. "I drive a hard bargain, you know."

"I know," he drawled. "You always have." And with that, he stepped backward.

"This way, Miss Drew."

And so she went, doing exactly what Radley had suggested, and finding peace in trusting someone to guide her.

Twenty

Radley was still yawning when a discreet knock sounded on his sitting-room door. He was barely out of bed though it was past teatime. He hadn't shaved yet but had managed to call for coffee as he lounged in this antechamber to his bedroom.

And wasn't that a laugh. Who had an antechamber to his bedroom? A duke, obviously. And that was what he was—as powerful a man on land as a captain was at sea. Still subject to the whims of air and sea, but more master of his own fate than nearly any man on earth.

The knock came again, and he roused himself to speak. "Enter." Lord, he needed that coffee now.

The door opened, he smelled the thick brew, and he turned to greet Seelye, only to have the word stop in his throat. It wasn't his proper butler who stood with tray in hand. No, it was his cousin who glided smoothly inside and set the heavy thing down with nary a rattle.

"Eleanor? What are you doing?" Belatedly, he realized he was supposed to stand upon her entrance. He scrambled to his feet, one hand tugging his morning jacket closed. The other went to smooth his hair. He usually felt like an unkempt braggart in front of her. That she'd caught him in dishabille made it worse.

She smiled as she eased down on the settee across from him. "I'm hoping you will forgive this intrusion, your grace. I have need to speak with you, and as I saw Seelye gathering the tray, I imposed upon him to allow me to bring it."

As she spoke, she neatly poured his coffee and passed it forward. He was still standing awkwardly, taking the moment to tie his jacket front tighter. Certainly, he was used to appearing in public with less clothing, but that was on board a ship in the company of men. She was a woman and a well-bred one at that. This had to be wrong. And yet, she was smiling as if this were the most natural thing in the world.

"Um… thank you," he said as he awkwardly took the coffee. He needed the damn thing, and so he sipped it, though it scalded his tongue. Then he glanced guiltily at the stack of family dairies she'd given him. Bloody hell, he'd promised to read them and had done nothing more than set them in the corner, forgotten.

"Pray, sit down. I assure you, it is perfectly natural for cousins to talk casually."

What choice did he have? He couldn't toss her out. So he sat, he sipped, and he waited. Meanwhile, she poured herself a small cup but didn't drink. Not surprising. Tea was her choice, if he recalled. But she held the cup as she sat back and watched him. Just watched him in a way that made him distinctly uncomfortable. As if she were studying him and trying to discern his weaknesses.

"Really, Eleanor," he said as he drained his cup. "I should probably get dressed."

"Nonsense," she said as she waved a negligent hand in his direction. "As I said, I wished to speak in private with you."

He waited for her to continue, but she didn't. She settled pleasantly in her seat with the sun highlighting the gold in her blonde curls. She was, indeed, a beautiful woman, he realized, but much too reserved for his tastes. The woman he really wanted to catch him in dishabille was apparently still sleeping. Which was annoying. Which abruptly snapped him out of his awkwardness regarding his cousin.

"What is it, Eleanor? I'm afraid I'm feeling rather flat this morn—afternoon." Like a ship without any wind, he thought wistfully, as his eyes drifted to the hallway. He couldn't see Wendy's bedroom door, but he'd be able to hear it open.

"I wanted to talk to you about tonight's ball."

His gaze jumped back to her. "What?"

She released a delicate sigh that conveyed benevolent tolerance. "I knew you had forgotten."

Bloody hell, Wendy had been trapped by a madman, her brothers' lives were in danger, and Eleanor was annoyed that he'd forgotten a ball?

"I don't blame you, of course," she said, immediately taking the wind out of his annoyance. "But you did promise Lady Aikin and her daughter that you'd appear."

He had?

"And more than that," she leaned forward, eyes alight with excitement, "Prinny has stated that he will attend."

The Prince Regent was going to be there? He was supposed to meet royalty tonight? He had no idea what to think. It was so beyond his usual frame of thought. He scratched his chin, then silently cursed. He hadn't even shaved.

"I don't think I can attend," he said. He wasn't ready.

"But you've promised. And I think Prinny has said he will come specifically to meet you."

"That can't possibly be true. How would the prince know that I'm…" He knew the answer before he finished the question. If he'd promised to attend then the hostess would have bragged about snaring him. Lord, he hated navigating unfamiliar shoals.

"I see you understand. And now, everyone in the *ton* who can attend will be there. They all want to see you and Prinny meet. You cannot miss that."

Bloody hell, he didn't feel in the least bit prepared for such an event. But he could already see that if nothing else, Eleanor would suffer shame if he failed to appear. Just to be sure, he leaned forward, watching her face carefully as he asked his question.

"And if I don't care? If I don't go?"

She visibly paled, but then gathered herself again. Matching his pose, she spoke clearly. "You would damage your credibility among the *ton*. You would likely anger Prinny, which is stupid beyond reckoning. You have no footing right now, except as a novelty. Why would you make enemies before you've even begun?"

"Enemies? That's overstating things a bit, don't you think?" After all, a real enemy was a pirate with a broadsword. Or Damon—cutter of women—with half the nobles in debt to him. Not appearing at a party was hardly enough to anger any man.

"At some point, you may wish to buy sheep or seed for your tenants. Those transactions are often negotiated between noblemen. Perhaps you wish to connect your land to a canal, or even take someone special to a playhouse. We do not have a box anymore, you realize. It was let go a few years back."

He frowned. A canal seemed improbable, but a visit to the playhouse would be nice. Naturally, a duke could not stand in the gallery. He needed a box or to borrow one.

"Business deals are handled with merchants."

She laughed, the sound light and musical. It wasn't a derisive sound, but one that indicated pure mirth. "You know I once said that to my mother. I recall it distinctly. And then, I spent my first Season in London and learned how malicious society can be. In fact, few negotiations have anything to do with logical business sense."

He had the uncomfortable feeling that she was correct. He rubbed a hand over his face, thinking again that he needed to shave.

"You are already at a disadvantage," she continued, "because you did not go to any of the elite schools." She peered at him. "You didn't, did you?"

"No," he said. "My father was a tutor. My mother as well, for girls. They taught me—"

"An excellent grounding in the classics, I'm sure. But that means you have no boyhood friends."

He had a great many boyhood friends, but none who could help him here.

"Now, imagine if you want to go into politics—"

He held up his hand. "You have made your point, Eleanor. I shall attend this party long enough to bow deeply to the prince before dancing with Wendy. But that is all I can promise."

She inhaled sharply, though she quickly covered it by pretending to drink her coffee. He knew it was a sham, but in this he was determined. Wendy would be at his side tonight. If he had to face the entire *haut ton*, including the prince himself, then he wanted his Wind with him.

Eleanor set down her cup with a click, and he could tell that she was about to battle with him. She didn't know it was useless. He would take her advice on anything having to do with society, but he would not compromise when it came to Wendy.

"Radley, I know you are fond of the girl. Indeed, you have extended yourself immeasurably for her safety and that of her family." She paused, her gaze holding his as she tried to measured his reaction. He gave her none. He simply waited to hear her out. In time, she started again. "You have only been back in London a week, you have barely begun to function as a duke, and you have no idea of the consequences of even the smallest slips in protocol. What you are doing for Miss Drew and her family does you credit, but you must understand that you cannot trust your feelings on this matter. You cannot adequately judge the ramifications of your actions. And you cannot…" Her brows pinched in a worried frown. "You simply cannot do this to the family name. The weight of generations rests on your shoulders, as it will rest on your bride's."

She stopped speaking, again studying his face. He knew what she was asking herself. Would he listen? Did he understand? The answer was "no" on both counts, but he didn't say it. She hadn't asked the questions yet.

She sighed, seeing that he would not be pushed to speak. "Cousin, please," she said, "let me guide you." To add to his discomfort, the pile of family diaries mocked him. There was history there, not just his family's, but England's as well. And yet, he could not give her what she wanted.

"Of course, you are my guide. In a great many things."

Her shoulders drooped, and he knew she understood his implication. In this matter, he would not be swayed. But his cousin was a persistent woman. Her expression softened, and she tilted her head so that the light fell sweetly across her face and hair.

"There are many women anxious to meet you. Beauties, intellectuals, and even bold, scandalous women. Many will be at tonight's ball. Why would you hurt Wendy by throwing those females in front of her? Showing her clearly what she could never attain?"

He tilted his head, honestly confused. "Whatever do you mean?"

Her expression took on a pitying look, quickly masked. It was as if she were speaking to a young child. "Think of it from Wendy's perspective. She hasn't the training, the refinement, or the speech patterns of the *ton*. It's not her fault, of course, but taking her to a ball will expose her shortcomings. How awful to spend an evening seeing what you can never be, reviled at every turn. Oh, no one will be openly rude. They would not risk offending you, but she will feel it—the thousand, tiny stings of disapproval and disgust. It is inevitable, you know. And it will hurt her deeply."

He hadn't thought of that. He hadn't realized that attending a society ball might be painful to Wendy as bitter harpies found ways to wound her. With gentle smiles and refined poses, they would find a way to stab her, he was sure.

Unless, of course, she had a protector. Unless she had someone to teach her how to act and stand as her guide. He would do everything he could, of course, but in this, he was nearly as lost as Wendy. He might turn to his mother, but in terms of experience, Eleanor was by far the better choice. She just had to be willing to perform the task.

He leaned back in his seat as he considered his cousin. At his thoughtful look, he saw her smile in triumph. She hid the expression, of course, covering it with a false sip of coffee, but he saw it. And sadly, his estimation of her character dropped a notch.

Was she truly the best the *ton* had to offer? If so, then he would never look among their ranks for a woman. Meanwhile, he took another sip of his coffee and started his attack with the most casual of questions.

"Do you not think that the aristocracy is rather stodgy in their notions? I know extremely little of animal husbandry, but even I recall that stock must be replenished by new blood, or the entire herd grows sickly."

She gasped. "Surely you are not comparing England's elite to a herd of sheep!"

He was, actually, but he could see the notion would be a struggle for her. Very well, he would take a different tack.

"You have spoken quite eloquently, Eleanor. As always, I am impressed by your poise. You are quite a beauty."

Her cheeks tinged pink as she bowed her head. "Thank you, cousin. You are very kind."

"No, actually, I am not. You are the epitome of refinement, and I have a task for you."

She blinked. "A task? I don't understand."

"No," he said, his voice growing colder, "you don't. You have spent a great deal of time telling me what I should think. Now it is time for you to listen."

"Cousin, I—"

"I am the Duke of Bucklynde, the head of your family, and the man in whose house you reside."

"Of course—"

"I know you value the family legacy and honor. The dukedom has a history that I need to learn, traditions that only you can teach me. And then, there are the societal protocols with which you are so familiar."

She flashed him a quick smile. "Exactly! Which is why—"

"You will cease interrupting and listen to the head of your family."

Her mouth was caught open, but she quickly snapped it shut and dipped her gaze.

"It is too late to mold me into the kind of duke you are used to. However, I do value your input in the societal seas, as will Miss Drew."

She nearly said something then. He knew because

of her quick inhalation, but she wisely held back her words.

He smiled in approval. "I intend to marry her, Eleanor. Now, you may choose. You can stay here as a valued friend and advisor, helping myself and Miss Drew live up to the best of the family name, or you can depart from here."

Now, she was too horrified to hold back her words. "You would throw me out?"

"Isn't that what the previous duke did to my grandfather?"

"No," she rasped. "*My father* was the previous duke, and he never met your grandfather."

Radley didn't respond. What she said was an irrelevant detail, and they both knew it.

"I will have your answer, Lady Eleanor," he said coldly. "Is your family pride stronger than your outrage? Do you help us? Or do you leave and damn the loss of a great family name as it falls to a common sailor and his seamstress bride?"

She flinched. He could tell that the idea of the dukedom falling to commoners felt like a sickness deep in her belly.

"You will not even consider other women?" she asked, her voice barely more than a whisper. "Didn't you hear her? She's a thief! Have her as a mistress, if you must, but marry someone else." Her gaze rose, and he saw the unspoken statement in her eyes. *Marry me.*

He sighed and shook his head, saddened that she didn't understand the smallest thing about how the real world worked. "You have no idea how to survive alone. You have been cosseted your entire life, your every need met. You think that makes you pure. I think it makes you weak. I will not have a bride who crumples at the first sign of adversity."

She shot to her feet, her hands balled into fists. "You know *nothing* of what it takes to be a daughter of a duke."

True enough. "And you know nothing of what is needed to build a business as a seamstress. Or to live when you have nothing, save a will to survive."

She didn't respond. Her jaw was clenched tight, her fists pressed uselessly against her sides. She shook with the force of her emotions, but no words escaped her lips. And for the first time during this meeting, he had no clue as to her thoughts.

They remained this way for a minute, maybe longer. But eventually, she spoke. "Without guidance, you will be a disastrous duke."

He nodded. "I am sure there will be others who wish to teach me."

She blanched, realizing too late how precarious her status was here. To her credit, she didn't seem to care. "I am only trying to help," she said. "You and I are all that is left of the family."

His brows shot up. "My mother and sister would disagree."

"Your sister is about to marry a Scot, and your mother gads about with the eyes of the *nouveau riche*."

He could tell that those were ugly sins in her mind, but he had no understanding of why. "And yet, they are family." He frowned. "Are you so well loved that you would throw away the last of your family because we do not match your standards? Where is the pride in your blood?"

She swallowed, and he could see that she was caught by her own value system. Blood ties were all that mattered. That was, after all, how he came to be duke—and the head of her family—in the first place. It would be the worst sin to abandon him and her heritage just because he was cut from a different societal cloth.

"Winds change, Eleanor. Will you adjust? Or do you sink?"

She swallowed and looked away. But to his surprise, her voice came out strong. "I will adjust."

He grinned, his high estimation of his cousin returning. She was stubborn, but she could change. And with a modicum of grace too, he thought, as she neatly folded herself into her chair.

He was about to say something gentle. Something to show approval and family warmth. Anything that might ease the blow of what had transpired. She never gave him the chance.

"I suggest you call for Miss Drew immediately," she said. "There are things you both need to know before you meet the Prince Regent."

Twenty-one

SHE COULDN'T DO THIS. SHE COULDN'T GO TO A BALL and meet the Prince Regent. The very idea was ludicrous.

Wendy sat in the carriage next to Radley, her hands clutched tight in her lap. Across from them sat that witch Lady Eleanor and Radley's mother. The older woman was practically vibrating with excitement. The ice queen cousin was cool and faintly disapproving as usual. Radley sat, apparently in oblivious ease, while Wendy's stomach knotted like a stitching snarl.

She couldn't do this!

"Remember, the best choice is always to say nothing," the witch cousin said. "Just lift your chin and remain silent. Everyone else will think you extremely clever."

"Or an imbecile," she said tartly.

Eleanor released a sigh of frustration. "I know this is daunting, but surely, some part of you is capable of facing this. Just imagine yourself as a knight-errant facing a horde of monsters. I will be right there beside you, trying to defend your flank."

Wendy took a moment to process the woman's

statement. What the hell was a knight-errant? Monsters she understood, but did the woman really think that a ballroom of society matrons qualified? She'd seen many of those women in their shifts and corsets, with wrinkled fat pouring out every which way. Her imagination wasn't up to the task of making them into monsters. Not after what she'd seen Damon do.

Eleanor leaned forward, obviously trying to be comforting, as she touched Wendy's hands. "I'll be right there to help."

"I just had to choose between my brothers' lives and Radley's. A society ball hardly compares."

Eleanor reared back in shock while Radley's mother gaped. "And you chose to be a duchess over your brothers' lives?"

"No!" She cut her words off, the whole situation too complicated to explain. Meanwhile, Radley reached out and grabbed her hands.

"Henry and Bernard are safe. Your mother too. Why not try to enjoy the ball?"

She grimaced. "You cannot protect them forever."

"I can, and I will." He drew her hand to his lips. "Have a little faith, Wind."

She looked into his eyes. It was relatively dark in the carriage, but she didn't need light to know the contours of his face or the confidence in his expression. And, with her hand in his—even through the dulling fabric of their gloves—she found the way through her churning emotions.

"It will be fun to see all those dresses I sewed."

Eleanor winced. "Pray, do not ever say that aloud."

Radley just chuckled. "I feel my sails begin to fill."

Wendy turned away, but her lips curved into a smile. "I am not the wind, and you are not a ship."

"And yet you lift my spirits, and together we soar."

She felt her skin flush with heat. No one had ever spoken so prettily to her. And, if they had, she would have snorted and called them fools in the most derisive tone she could manage. And yet, with Radley, she flushed like a silly child. It was…

She swallowed. She wanted to call herself ridiculous, but the thought wouldn't form in her head. In truth, she felt young and pretty. She was on the way to a ball with a duke on her arm. And she was dressed in a pale blue silk gown shot with threads of gold. She'd stitched the gown herself, but an accident had stained the bodice and made it unsalable. Helaine had ordered Tabitha to add lace decorations and seed pearls. It was an extravagant expense, but it had been done in an afternoon and sent to the house for her to wear tonight.

In short, she was living every young girl's fantasy. She was going to meet the Prince Regent. A wild excitement built inside, and instead of squashing it by mentally listing everything that could go wrong, she simply allowed the feeling to build. What freedom it was to stop thinking—even for a moment—and experience the joy.

She squeezed Radley's hand and felt his answering grip. Tonight she would simply enjoy. With that thought, the snarl of emotions unraveled. She was still nervous. Of course, she was. But that was secondary to the knowledge that Radley was beside her tonight. And they were going to a ball!

❧

"And who is this vision of loveliness?"

"Aren't you the woman who stitches my hems?"

"Bloody good to finally meet you, your grace. Miss Drew, may I have this dance?"

"Humph. You'd think a seamstress would wear a current fashion, not something so *outré*."

"Miss Drew, you dance divinely. Would you care to take a walk outside?"

"Your grace, let me introduce you to my daughter, a woman of *true* refinement. Nothing *common* about her."

Wendy sipped her lemonade and shifted her weight, trying to ease the pain in her feet. She wasn't used to dancing. Neither was she accustomed to having someone at her elbow every time she turned around. But all in all, a ball ended up being not so overwhelming a place.

Why? Because a ballroom was the province of the women. Certainly, men were there, dancing with the ladies, or huddled in clumps having political discussions, but the real power flowed through the hands of women. And Wendy had managed women since the day she started as an apprentice seamstress. She'd learned by the time she turned sixteen not to feel verbal barbs. After all, once you've been kicked by an irate dowager, an insult to one's gown hardly registered.

As for the men, her last few months dealing vingt-et-un had taught her how to handle them. She danced with them, occasionally flirted with them, and then dismissed them from her thoughts. Easy. Especially with Radley's unfailing presence at her side.

Until the moment the Prince Regent entered the

ballroom. It was as if the air suddenly became electrified as everyone turned en masse to greet their ruler. Wendy barely caught a glimpse of the man in the doorway before Radley touched her hand.

"Are you ready?"

She swallowed and nodded, as ready as she would ever be. It was one thing to handle a bitter countess, or three, another to meet the crown prince.

Radley flashed her a nervous smile. "We can do this together, right?"

She straightened. "He came here to meet you. The least we can do is allow him the honor."

He grinned and brought her gloved fingers to his lips. "Have I told you how beautiful you are?"

She smiled. "At least a dozen times."

"You cannot know how much I mean it."

She flushed, but her gaze never wavered from his face. When he looked at her like that—equal parts joy and possession—she felt mesmerized. Or perhaps, the better phrase was caught and held, like the wind in a sail.

She almost said it then. She nearly spoke the words that had been trembling on her lips all day. *I love you.* She nearly said them, but this was not the place, and they were about to meet the Prince Regent. And besides, she could never say anything when he looked at her like that. Everything in her heated nearly to bursting, and all her words burned away.

"Your grace, if you would follow me please?" their hostess interrupted. "There is someone I should like to introduce."

And so it was done. They were escorted to Prinny. Radley bowed. Wendy curtsied so deep she nearly flattened herself onto the floor. And all the while, her back prickled with awareness of everyone watching.

"Good evening, Bucklynde," the prince said. "You're a difficult man to find."

Beside her, Radley straightened to his full height, as if he were reporting to his superior officer. Which, she supposed, he was. "Your highness, I apologize for the delay. As you might imagine, it's been a rather busy week."

The prince chuckled heartily. "I imagine so. Estate matters and the lot?'

"Mostly, it's all these infernal women trying to dress me up to snuff. Half the time I don't understand what they're saying."

The regent laughed with good cheer. "They are an interfering lot, aren't they? But what a dull world it would be without them."

"Very true, your highness, very true."

"Well, when you want an escape from all that rubbish, pray come visit me at Carlton House. Tuesday next, hm? For cards."

"I should be honored."

"Of course, of course," the royal said as his gaze drifted to Wendy. "And Miss Drew, you are a pretty thing, aren't you?"

She smiled, mentally cataloguing him as akin to a lecherous uncle. Fortunately, she knew exactly how to respond: flattery and a flash of bosom. "I spent hours worrying over how I should appear before you, your highness," she said as she dropped her fan enough to let him look. A moment, no more, and then she straightened. "It is a very great honor you do me."

"No doubt," he said with a laugh, "but then I always like meeting pretty girls."

"Is that the musicians starting up again?" Radley asked. "My dear, should I escort you to the floor?" He gave an apologetic smile to the royal. "She does love dancing, you know."

Wendy glanced at Radley, realizing with a little shock that he hadn't liked how Prinny ogled her and was trying to get her away. And wasn't that nice to realize he was protective?

Meanwhile, the regent looked wistfully at the dance floor. "I enjoy it as well, actually, but these days my knees pain me too much."

And that was that. Beyond a few sympathetic comments regarding the regent's health and another quick lowering of her fan as she turned away, their glorious meeting with the prince was over.

Curiously unexciting, truth be told. And yet, she couldn't suppress her grin of triumph. Radley had been invited to Carlton House—a sure sign of approval from the prince—and she had not embarrassed herself. And when Radley swept her onto the dance floor, she nearly laughed with sheer joy.

Only one more thing to do, she thought. One more choice, and it had been made days ago, during their first kiss outside the dress shop. It had only taken this long for the timing to work out. She would do it tonight, if only this interminably wonderful ball would end. Another hour perhaps, and then she would do it.

It actually took more than an hour. Nearly three, to be exact. There was dancing and a midnight buffet, but after that, it was over. Lady Eleanor decreed that it was never good to stay overlong at a ball because it gave the impression of desperation. So they left after the food and listened in the carriage as Radley's mother chattered about every person she'd met.

No one else spoke. There really wasn't room amidst all Mrs. Lyncott's excited exclamations. Lady Eleanor managed to nod once and declared the evening "acceptable." Neither Wendy nor Radley said anything, though both were grinning. The evening had been a success. They had royal approval!

Then they were home. There was another half hour of chatter with Bernard and Wendy's mother who wanted to know everything. Then finally, she was allowed to retire. A maid helped her undress and uncoif. And wasn't that a relief to get the heavy coils of hair off the top of her head? Then the maid buttoned a pristine, white night rail to her neck before helping her climb into bed.

The woman took the candle and left. Around them the house quieted as even the mothers went to bed.

Half an hour more.

Fifteen minutes more.

Five…

Now.

Wendy slipped out of bed, opened her door, and walked through the dark hallway to Radley's room. She didn't even knock, but quietly turned the knob before slipping inside. A candle burned by his bedside, but he wasn't using it. She saw him lying in bed, his arms behind his head as he stared at the ceiling.

At least he had been. By the time she shut the door

behind her, his gaze was on her, and she felt that heat swell in her belly. Fire and desire.

Her words burned away as she crossed the room until she stood beside his bed.

He looked at her, his gaze dark as his nostrils flared. Then, without a word, he flipped the covers back.

He was naked as he lay there. She saw his flat stomach, his corded thighs, and the hard stalk of his organ lifted toward her.

She moved toward the bed beside him, but he stopped her. He touched her arm and waited until her gaze locked onto his.

"Are you sure?" he asked, his voice rasping through the darkness.

Her nipples tightened at the sound. Odd that his voice could be as sensual as a rough caress across her breasts.

"I owe you everything," she whispered.

He recoiled. "This is not a debt. I won't have you—"

"I love you."

She saw her words hit him. His eyes widened, and his fingers twitched where they rested against her cheek.

"Say it again," he rasped.

"I love you."

There was no more waiting. He surged upward and claimed her mouth with his. Hard, possessive, and so powerful, his kiss did everything she wanted and more. He took her in that kiss, grabbed hold of her, and drew her to him in a way that she could never escape.

And that was only the beginning.

Twenty-two

WENDY HAD BEEN KISSED BEFORE. SHE AND RADLEY had done a great deal more than this, but something was different this time.

He held her firmly with one hand cupping the back of her head. He had large hands, and so his fingers threaded through her hair until she felt caught in a net of warm fire. He wrapped his other hand around her waist, lifting her onto the bed so that she lost all control of her position. She tried to put one knee on the mattress to steady herself, but his bed was so high he had to carry her. As he tightened his hold—his mouth never leaving hers—she lost connection to the earth. She was lifted and caught as if she truly were the wind in his sails.

And then he made it more.

He brought her to him, pulled her on top until she lay against his naked torso. She felt the hard planes of his chest, the rigid thrust of his organ, and the shift of his muscles as he moved his hands across her back, then through her hair.

She felt these things distantly, myriad sensations

that composed the background of what he did. Her main focus was on their mouths, fused as his tongue thrust inside.

There was power in his push—different than any she had known before. Dominant, possessive—it claimed her but in the way of a man claiming a god as *his god*, his being to worship. Or perhaps, she should say goddess. He owned her as his goddess, his every caress an act of exaltation.

She had no idea how to respond, no thoughts beyond pleasure and joy. But even as her mind labeled the thrust and parry of their tongues, her heart sang its own tune.

It was a simple song with one word: love. It had a tempo that echoed in the rapid beats of her heart. It had a harmony in the way she intertwined her body with his. Her tongue rolled around his, her hands found purchase on his shoulders, reveling in the heat of his skin. And even her legs slipped between his, pressing her hips against the thrust of his pelvis.

And the music had a melody that sang in her veins as she broke from his mouth to push away. Her shift in position ground her groin against his, and she heard his hiss in pleasure. He hadn't let her go far—high enough to look at him in the moonlight. Apparently, the man liked to keep his curtains open, and the light bathed them in silver. And while she looked, she found enough space to gulp in air and to use one hand to tug at the buttons of her night rail.

He stopped her fumbling fingers, stilling them as he whispered. "Let me take it off you. Please."

She could hardly say no. After all, she was too

clumsy, and her position prevented her from real progress. So she let her hand fall away as his fingers replaced hers.

He used one hand, but he was more in control than she. While his left hand gripped her hip, his right undid button after button down her neck and between her breasts. The fabric gaped open, and as he worked, he stroked the exposed skin. A brush here, a caress there. She felt her body tremble as he touched her.

Then he ran out of buttons. In truth, the opening went barely below her breasts, but it was enough for him to brush his entire hand inside, to stroke her from belly to neck.

She still was pushed up, her legs and groin heavy against his heat, while her arms kept her torso elevated. That meant she had little leverage to move as his hand roamed freely. At first, he kept to the narrow passageway between her breasts, but before long, his hand spread, his fingers stretched, and his path meandered.

He used his knuckles and the back of his hand then twisted so that the pads of his fingers touched her. All in the lightest of strokes, and every caress left a tingling fire in its wake. Her breasts soon became hot, her nipples aching. He squeezed those tips. First one, then, eventually, the other. A pinch, a twist, whatever seemed to strike his fancy, while the heat of his touch seared her.

Her breath grew short and her head heavy. Before long, her forehead dropped until it touched his. He smiled, looking at her before taking her mouth again. A steady catch, a slow penetration, then thrusts that had her arms giving way until she once again lay fully on top of him.

This time when she broke away, it was so she could catch her breath. She turned away, but his fingers found her face. He stroked her hair from her eyes, touched her flushed cheeks and swollen lips.

"I cannot stop touching you. I'm afraid this is a dream."

"Do you often dream of women coming to you at night?" She meant it as a joke, then belatedly realized that all men fantasized these things.

"Not women," he said. "You. Night after night, I dream of you."

Then, before she could respond, he abruptly lifted her. Never would she have guessed that he was strong enough to pick her up and set her to the side. She scrambled to get her knees under her, and he held her aloft as he waited. And then he slid his hands down her sides to the hem of her night rail.

She shifted slightly, letting him pull the fabric away from her legs. But as she moved, the shoulder of her gown slid down her left side. The fabric caught for a second on her breast, but her ragged breath allowed it to drop. Her breast was exposed, and his gaze settled there.

"You are glowing," he said as he touched the curve of her breast. "Your skin in the moonlight. It's like alabaster." Then he abruptly brushed the other side of the gown away. "I will adorn you in pearls and rubies, but they will never come close to your beauty."

"Radley," she whispered, "I don't want jewels. I want you to touch me."

His eyes flashed dark, his expression hungry. "Of course, my lady."

She was about to protest the title. She was no lady, not in any sense. But at that point, his hands shifted to her arms, holding them at her sides. Then his mouth touched her neck at the notch in her collarbone. His lips at the base of her throat, and as if by magic, her head dropped back, exposing all.

He licked her there, and then he nuzzled her neck. His hair tickled her jaw, his lips soft and his teeth rough. She smelled his scent—a spicy sea salt—and had no words to frame how perfect that was. As if that scent were her home.

His mouth moved lower as she arched into his kiss. He took his time, holding her still as he sucked her nipples. First one, then a nip, before transferring to the other. Soon her entire body trembled, and her nipples were a dark, wet red.

"Beautiful," he breathed.

She opened her eyes, feeling dazed and slightly annoyed. Didn't he want more? Her legs shifted restlessly, and she tried to escape his grip. She wanted her night rail off. She wanted to touch him. She wanted to express what she felt.

"Radley," she murmured, his name a throaty moan. "More." She felt him smile against her breast, but there was no change in his actions. He continued that leisurely circle of her nipple before sucking it into his mouth. She gasped, but it wasn't enough. So when he pulled back, her breast escaping his lips on a pop, she jerked her arms free. Then before he could react, she pulled her night rail off.

She was naked and unashamed. In truth, the fire he had stoked in her body gave her an authority she'd never felt. So she leaned down and took his face in her hands, and she spoke one word as a command.

"More."

His nostrils flared, and his hands slid to her rib cage below her breasts. He tightened his hold and slowly lifted her. She unfolded her legs as he gently laid her on her back. Then he pushed into the breach, gently widening her legs as he settled himself atop.

He placed himself carefully, a groan rumbling through him as he rubbed against her. It was what he had done before, and her eyelids fluttered at the roar of sensation. But again, it was not enough.

So she squeezed his arms, her hands wrapped as far as possible around his thick biceps. "Not like this," she said. They had done this before, and he'd said she was still a virgin. She wanted to be claimed in every way. This was her decision, and she would not accept anything else. "Not—oh!"

He was rubbing against her, sliding his cock over her most private place. Her body shuddered, the wet slide incredible. But it was not what she wanted. It was not enough.

So she grabbed his ears, turning him to look at her in the most forceful way she knew how. She could tell she'd startled him as his entire body stilled. That gave her enough time to lift her knees, to arch her back, and to shift. But it still wasn't enough. His weight was keeping her too restricted. And his every breath had him rocking against her enough to make her body tighten with hunger.

"Take me," she whispered.

"Marry me," he returned.

Her breath caught, but his gaze remained steady. His expression was fierce, and even the slow press of his groin stilled. He meant it.

"You don't need to propose," she said. "I will be your mistress."

His jaw hardened, and his eyes blazed. "Marry me."

Did he think she would refuse? She would give him anything. And she would say yes now, knowing full well that he would change his mind later. It didn't matter. She loved him. She would give him whatever he wanted.

"Yes."

He swooped down for a kiss—hard and possessive. She opened to it, and she lifted her knees, doing her best to ready herself.

Then he slowly raised himself up, his forehead pressed against hers. "I can wait," he said. "We needn't do this now." But as he spoke, he tilted his hips. His cock slid between her thighs until it pressed against her wet core. She trembled even as she tried to lift herself onto him. She wanted him to take her. She wanted to be owned by this man in the most primal way.

"I can't wait," she said. "Radley, please."

He pushed in slowly. A thickness and a heat sliding inside. He groaned, and she looked at his face. His eyes fluttered, and his mouth opened on a gasp that he stopped mid-breath. Then he pressed in a little more.

Oh! He was big. It felt good, but… a lot. A lot to feel, a lot to push inside, and a lot of time to wonder if he was too much.

"Radley…" she whispered.

His gaze was on hers, his eyes dark and fierce. Then he thrust. Hard, quick—a sharp pierce of pain shot through her abdomen. She cried out, startled and shocked. She had known there might be pain. Of course, she knew, but Helaine had told her it was nothing. Penny had said so too.

"Wendy? God, I'm sorry. Is it bad?"

She swallowed, feeling him deeply embedded. He pushed up on his arms, keeping his weight off her— for which she was grateful. But as he looked at her, as her body stretched and accepted him, she began to settle. Where she'd been tight with tension, she relaxed. Where her body had arched in withdrawal, she shifted to accommodate. In fact, every piece of her rearranged itself around him.

So this was why virginity was so important, she realized. Once given to a man, everything reorganized to accept him, to surrender to him, to be with *him*.

"I'm yours now," she said with awe.

He swallowed, and she felt him pulse inside her. He didn't mean to. She could tell by the way his eyes widened and sweat beaded on his brow.

"I'm trying to stay still, Wendy. But… should I pull out?"

She stroked the hair off his face. Time felt suspended. Her blood simmered, her body stretched impossibly tight, but her happiness made everything softer. And joyous.

"Don't go," she said. "Show me the rest."

"Are you sure? I can't go slow."

She shifted her hips. It wasn't a conscious decision, just a movement that happened. But the second she shifted, pleasure began to build inside her. He groaned, the sound rumbling into her.

He leaned down, kissing her fiercely. She responded with a fire all her own as she held his face and dueled. And as they fought—tongue to tongue—his cock withdrew.

She tightened her thighs, not wanting him to leave. Her belly was caving in from the emptiness, and she squeezed to keep him in place. It didn't help. He was stronger, and his tongue possessed her with a new frenzy.

Then he stopped. He broke the kiss enough for their breaths to rasp in the tiny space between them. His cock was nearly out, his body poised on the edge.

He thrust forward. The impact was hard, and her body seemed to burst with the power. She gasped, her back arching.

That was wonderful!

He'd frozen above her, and when she opened her eyes, he was studying her with a worried frown.

"Wendy?"

"Do that again."

He did. He pulled out slowly, torturing her with the incremental compression of her belly. But this time she knew what he was doing, knew that the further back he went, the more—

He slammed forward again.

She cried out as pleasure burst through her.

"Again!"

This time was not so slow. This time his control seemed as ragged as his breath. He seemed to jerk half out, then nearly all the way. And then...

Yes!

"More!"

He complied. He did everything she wanted without her even asking.

He thrust into her over and over. She threw her head back, she angled her pelvis, and she gripped him with every part of her.

Slam after slam, while her body tightened, and her vision shot through with white sparks.

More—

Yes—

Detonation! Her body seized, hovering on the edge, before everything exploded in a wave of pleasure. He felt it too—he must have because he cried out at his deepest thrust. He shuddered while another explosion rolled through her. Heat and fire.

Pleasure and joy.

And underneath it all—love. An ocean of love.

Twenty-three

"YOUR GRACE! YOUR GRACE!"

Radley came awake slowly, the lethargy of a sated body holding him under much too long. That, and the tart, lemony scent of Wendy filling his nostrils. He was wrapped around her, her body spooned against his belly, and her glorious hair spread across the pillow they shared. His nose was pressed to her neck, and he nuzzled her, his cock stirring enough to distract him from whatever had woken him.

"Mmmm," he said.

"Your grace!"

He frowned, the noise disrupting his lustful thoughts. Not for long. Wendy stirred against him, but the damn knocking began again.

"What?" The barked question startled Wendy into full alertness. She gasped and stiffened, but he held her still. "Shhh,"

"Your grace, a Mr. Knopp is at the door. He says it's an emergency."

Radley jolted with surprise. "I'm coming! Get him whatever he wants."

A lifetime aboard ship had trained him in dressing with lightning speed even at... he groaned... barely after six in the morning. Wendy, apparently, had similar training. She was out of bed as well, pulling on her night rail nearly as quickly as he.

A damned shame to cover all that beauty, but Mr. Knopp wouldn't say it was an emergency lightly. Radley had on pants and grabbed his shirt when he saw Wendy pause, her eyes wide. It took him a moment to realize what she was staring at: he'd strapped on his daggers—two long ones set in special holsters that crisscrossed his chest.

"It's a precaution," he said to reassure her. "I'm sure they won't be necessary." In truth, he'd grabbed them out of habit, not intention. But having now noticed them, he wasn't going to take them off. He simply covered them with a shirt, though damn, these stupid ducal shirts were too long. He'd have to cut slits in the sides for better access to the knives. Or rather, he'd have to do that if he were going into a fight, which he wasn't. Because, of course, this wasn't aboard a ship, and they weren't about to be attacked by pirates.

He finished buttoning his shirt, then stepped forward to touch her shoulders. "It's habit that made me put them on, nothing more."

She nodded. "But there's an emergency. At six in the morning."

"Go back to bed, Wind. I'll wake you if—"

She stiffened. "I will join you downstairs in a moment. I usually wake at this time anyway."

That might be true, but not after they'd spent most

of the night making love. Neither had more than a couple hours of sleep at best. Not that he could regret the reasons for their exhaustion. He stroked her cheek then couldn't stop himself from pressing in for a kiss that ended too soon.

"If you must," he finally said, "but I must go." Then he went to the door, opening it a tiny crack to peer out. The hall was empty so he pulled it wide. She moved quickly to her bedroom, slipping inside without a backward glance. He didn't have time to worry about that. She had said she'd marry him. She'd said she loved him. They had their whole lives to work out the details of their relationship, and right now, his former employer waited below with an emergency.

So, with a last longing look at her door, he turned and rushed downstairs. He found Knopp and Seelye in the parlor. Mr. Knopp was sitting down, a delicate teacup in his shaking hands. Seelye stood discreetly nearby, holding another cup for Radley.

"Good man," he said as he grabbed the steaming coffee. He downed it in three gulps despite the burn then silently held it out for more.

Meanwhile, Knopp pushed to his feet. "There's been an attack on the clipper. It's gone. The men too."

Simple. Direct. And it completely blanked Radley's mind. "What?"

Knopp waited a moment, his shoulders drooping. For the first time, Radley saw the man's age, vitality fading before his eyes.

"It happened just after one. I got the news a few hours later. Been trying to find the men on watch. If any escaped, mayhap they went home. I went by

Henry's place, but no one was there. Do you know where his family is?"

"Here," Radley whispered.

"What?"

Radley fought to keep his mind moving, his words clear. "His family. They live here, sir." Then he looked at Seelye. Had Henry appeared sometime in the night? It was an illogical thought, but he was grasping at straws.

The butler gave a discreet shake of his head. And, in that moment, Wendy appeared. She was dressed in a simple workwoman's gown of faded green. Her hair was tied neatly back, and her face seemed freshly scrubbed. But her eyes were too wide as she looked at the three men before her.

Radley went to her side, touching her arm to guide her to a seat. She didn't need help, of course. She didn't know the news yet, but he needed to touch her. He needed to understand. He needed to...

"There were five men on watch," he said as much to himself as Knopp.

"Yes."

"And you found...?"

The man cleared his throat. "Uh, perhaps the details can wait."

Of course. Wendy didn't need to hear the gory aftermath of a battle, but...

He looked at Mr. Knopp. "They were all trained men. Fighting sailors. And I warned them!"

Knopp's eyes abruptly narrowed. "You warned them? You knew what was coming?"

"Yes! No! Bloody hell!" He rubbed his hand over

his face. Which was when Wendy tightened her grip on Radley's hand. She hadn't fully sat down yet, but now, she straightened to her full height.

"What has happened?" Her voice was calm, but there was steel beneath.

Mr. Knopp deflated again as he looked at her. Worst part of an owner's job: talking to the family.

"Miss Drew, I have terrible news."

"Henry."

"The clipper was attacked last night. It appears as if Henry was lost."

She closed her eyes. No sound. No cry. Just a single tear—then more—leaking from her eyes. Radley rushed to reassure her.

"We don't know what happened. There is still hope."

Mr. Knopp cleared his throat, the sound tight and angry. Radley looked over and saw the reason on the man's scowling face. He didn't believe Henry was alive, and therefore, saw no reason to give Wendy false hope.

But they were trained fighters! And they'd been warned. How could they have lost? Damn it, they'd survived battles at sea against the worst pirates spawned on earth. How could they have lost while at dock in London?

"No," he said firmly. "I don't believe it."

"Radley!" Knopp snapped. "Damn it, man, do you think I'd lie about something like this?"

"No, sir! But… But…"

"Contact Mr. Morrison," interrupted Wendy. "That's Penny's husband. He's a Bow Street runner—"

"Already did. He's there now at the dock, but…"

The elderly man stepped forward, gently taking Wendy's hands. "Miss Drew, you must understand. There's been no mistake."

"But you came here," she said softly. "Why?"

"I was looking for Henry. On the slim hope that he escaped."

She looked to Seelye, and the man was forced to shake his head again. It was a futile exchange. They all knew Henry wasn't here.

Meanwhile, Radley's brain had finally started working. He looked to his butler. "Wake Bernard. Get him down here. I want to know exactly what he said to Henry, what he saw."

"I'm already here," said a low voice from the hallway. Everyone looked over to see Bernard, his face haggard as he stepped into the room. "I heard Wendy come down. I... followed." Then, before Radley could ask, he started answering questions. "I told him exactly what you said. That Wendy was in danger, and she feared for his safety. That he was to stay on board and keep watch. That Mama, Wendy, and I would be here." Then he looked to his sister. "I tried to explain about the Demon. I tried to tell him the danger..."

Wendy looked away. "He didn't believe you. Not really."

"No."

"No one believes," she said, her voice dull. "Until it's too late." And then, it was as if her strength had left her. Her knees softened, and she simply folded into herself. If Radley hadn't been right there, she would have fallen to the floor. But he caught her. He guided her into the chair. And then, he finally understood.

She wasn't surprised. She'd seen the depth of Damon's violence. Bernard had too. They'd tried to tell Radley, to tell Henry, to tell someone, but that was the way with civilized monsters. No one believed that such an evil could exist. No one thought it possible until it was too late.

Meanwhile, Knopp touched his arm. "Who is Demon Damon? And why the hell would he burn my ship?"

Not a simple question, and not something he meant to answer in front of Wendy. So he quietly shook his head, then glanced to Bernard. "I'm going to the boat. You will stay here and protect them." He looked to Seelye. "Are there men here who can defend themselves? Weapons?"

Seelye's jaw went slack, shock written in his every line. Radley simply glared.

"I underestimated this bastard once." Twice actually, given what had happened to his sister so many years ago. "I won't do it again."

Seelye's stance firmed up as he gave a crisp nod. "I believe there are some men I could contact."

"No. We'll use my men. I'll give you the names and what to say. Bring me paper and ink. I'll write down the names for you."

The butler left to do as he was bid. Meanwhile, Radley turned his attention to Wendy. She sat there unmoving, barely breathing. Guilt and shame twisted in his gut. To think he had been in bed seducing Henry's sister, while the man had been fighting for his life. Against Radley's foe! Goddamn, it couldn't be. It just couldn't!

And yet, looking at Wendy, he knew she had already accepted it. How much had she suffered at this bastard's hands that she could so numbly believe in her brother's murder? Good God, why hadn't he listened when she warned him? Even his message to Henry had been nearly casual. *I'll protect your family. You keep watch on the boat.* He hadn't believed Damon had fighters who could take down a boat at dock. The idea was ludicrous, but all he had to do was look at Wendy to know it was true.

She was the strongest woman he'd ever known, and yet, she became silent in terror with Damon. And Radley had simply brushed it off as womanly ignorance.

He was a fool. And Henry had paid the price. Wendy was still paying. And his sister had suffered a decade ago.

He crouched before Wendy, gently drawing her eyes to his. "I'm going to the docks. I have to... I have to see it for myself. You're safe here. Bernard is going to stay, and there are men coming to protect the house. You won't be harmed."

She blinked, then her eyes slowly narrowed. It was a subtle change. He saw her slow inhale of breath, only to see her release it in a controlled exhale. Nothing unusual, but this was his Wind. And he knew a calm before the storm.

"Yes," she said calmly. "Bernard should stay with mother. She will need him."

"And you," Radley said clearly. "He is staying with you."

She blinked. Once. Twice. Then she lowered her eyes. "Of course. With me as well."

A lie. Damn it, a bald-faced lie. He had no idea what the woman planned, but she was thinking of doing something.

"Wendy, you need to trust me."

She raised her gaze, her eyes blazing with fury. He winced, knowing what she was thinking. She had trusted him yesterday. She had come to his home, she had dressed as a duchess, and she had gone to a ball. And after that, she had gone to his bed. And all the while her brother had been fighting for his life.

She had trusted him, and now, her brother was dead.

"You're right," he said, even though she hadn't spoken. "I was a fool. I—" His voice choked off. "But I can..." He was going to say he could fix things, but he couldn't. Her brother was likely dead. "I should have listened better. I should have learned more."

"You should have believed me when I said it was too late. I should never have gone with you."

"Wrong!" He gripped her hands tight enough to make her wince. "You belong with me." Then he gentled his grip, but his words were no less fierce. "We can figure this out. But hear me, Wendy. You will not go to that bastard. You will not sacrifice yourself."

"No, sister, you will not." That was Bernard, his voice hard and—when they turned to him—his face tight with fury. Radley had seen that look before, that moment when a boy shifted into manhood. Bernard was the baby of the family, cosseted too long. No more. The child had become a man.

Wendy sighed. "Bernard—"

"This was my debt, my problem, and I drew you into it." His voice cracked, but his stance remained strong.

"And did he trick you into it?" she asked. "Was your drink tampered with? The game false?"

He watched as Bernard's jaw firmed. "I still played. I still lost. And I still ran to you—"

"You had to come to me. Mama doesn't make any money."

Radley fit the pieces together. Damn, he was thinking too slowly! "So it has always been about you?" he asked Wendy. "You think Bernard was tricked into debt to get to you?"

She nodded.

"But why?"

Bernard snorted in derision. "You draw pictures of her for ten years, send her gifts through Henry, and you still ask? Damon has been here all that time. He has seen who she is and what she can do. Of course, he wants her!"

Radley felt his face heat in shame. The boy was right. "But that's a lot of work to get a woman. A lot." Certainly, Wendy was worth it, but... it was hard to comprehend. Unless, of course, trickery was part of one's character. If it were simply a matter of course to taint drinks and fix games, then it would be no more difficult to target Bernard than it would be to order lunch. And, if that man were also capable of murder, the only question was how Wendy had resisted so long. How had she kept herself and her family free for as long as she had?

He was about to say as much when the knocker sounded. Seelye had barely finished setting down the paper and ink, and so now had to rush to the door. Radley and Wendy straightened, already following. In their minds was the hope that Henry had somehow—

Not Henry. A man with wild hair and a dirty coat of good quality. He was halfway to handing his hat to the butler when he caught sight of Mr. Knopp, who had also come to the doorway in hope.

"Ah, there you are. Haven't the best news, I'm afraid, but I've been thinking as I made it here. Been a devil of a lot of fuss for you, Miss Drew. You're a handsome woman and all that, but there's something more. Obsession never focuses without reason. Why you, I ask. And how can we turn that against him?"

Radley frowned, his mind quickly placing the man. "You must be the Bow Street runner."

"Samuel Morrison, your grace. And you're the secret admirer turned duke." He stepped forward with his hand outstretched. Unfortunately, he still held his hat, so Radley ended up taking the crushed thing and passed it to Seelye.

Meanwhile, Mr. Knopp stepped around Wendy. "What did you find?"

"Hmm? Exactly what I thought. Fourteen dead— your men and theirs. Ugly fight that. The fire was started with the usual implements—nothing special there. Witnesses aren't talking, but it's pretty clear who's behind it."

Mr. Knopp frowned. "Demon Damon."

"Yes." The man's steady gaze turned to Wendy. "It's past time to tell me the rest, Miss Drew. I've worked out that he was behind my Penny's trouble with the shop, and we know he set that madman onto Irene."

"He threatened Helaine too," she whispered. "He knows about her father."

The runner nodded. "Damon knows secrets, so it's no surprise he knows about the *Thief of the Ton*. And he's done all this to isolate you from your friends."

Radley felt his eyes widen. He'd had no idea the depth of the problem. The man had been attacking her friends too? For how long? Good God, it sounded like this had been a slow game that took months, if not years!

"But that still doesn't answer the question," continued the runner. "Why you, Miss Drew? What does he want from you?"

In the most animation she'd shown all morning, Wendy threw up her hands and all but wailed. "I don't know! I've never known!"

Mr. Morrison's eyes narrowed. "Bloody mess there on your ears. How'd it happen?"

She touched her lobes, her hands trembling as she visibly shrunk into herself. Radley reached out and tucked her tight to his side. She resisted at first, but in the end, she was too exhausted to fight. Even so, she didn't speak.

In that moment, he understood his mistake, understood what needed to happen to fix it. So he pressed a kiss to her forehead and spoke in a low, soothing tone. "I was wrong, you know, to say you should trust me."

She flinched, and he rushed ahead before she could misunderstand.

"You've spent so long fighting this alone. I wanted you to rest, to give the burden to me. That was wrong. I didn't understand the magnitude of the problem. I didn't know..." His throat tightened against the grief. Henry was his best friend. "I thought I could take care of it," he finally said. "But we are strongest together. You can't give the problem to me. You have to work with me."

"And me," said Bernard.

"And a whole lot of us, I should think," inserted Mr. Morrison. Mr. Knopp nodded in response. Even Seelye dipped his chin in agreement.

Radley flashed them a grateful smile. "See?" he said to Wendy. "Let us figure this out together."

"Start by telling me about those bloody ears," pressed the runner.

Wendy let her hand drop from her face. "He likes pain."

Bloody bastard. Radley lost a few moments of time in the rush of fury that flooded his body. Not a problem for Mr. Morrison, apparently, as the man tilted his head. "What kind of pain? In what way?"

Bernard growled. "In the stabbing women kind of way. And carving them up."

"Tch! That's not specific enough," said Morrison as he stepped forward. He tried to disentangle Wendy from Radley to draw her aside, but there was no way that would happen. Instead, he allowed the man to precede them back into the drawing room. Then he followed with Wendy still held tight in his arms. She wasn't trembling anymore, thank God. And when she spoke, her words were stronger and more thoughtful.

"Not just giving pain," said Bernard, his tone thoughtful. "Everything must be mixed with pain for him to enjoy it."

"So giving *and* receiving," said the runner.

She nodded. "He said..." The trembling began again, but she finished her sentence. "That I have promise. That... I could be trained."

Mr. Morrison waved that off with a distracted air. "Anybody can be trained to enjoy pain." Then he turned to look at her. "But I can see what he means."

Radley stiffened. "What the bloody hell do you mean?"

It was Mr. Knopp who steadied him, stopping his explosion before it got started. "He means that she's smart, and she gets people to do things. And anyone who can manipulate people knows the temptation to hurt them too."

He knew it was true. After all, he'd captained a ship, been first mate for years, and before that... well, before that he'd always had people following him, doing his bidding. He'd never wanted to hurt them, but he knew the temptation. When he was angry, when they'd done something idiotic.

Looking at Wendy, he saw that in her as well. It was something they had in common. Though he'd been a golden boy with money and status—at least in their poor neighborhood—she'd been a girl on the outskirts. As poor as they came, with only her wits and her will to survive. How much stronger must be her desire to strike back, to hurt others as she'd been hurt?

"But you're not like that," he said softly as he pressed a kiss to her hair. "That's not who you are."

She looked at him, fear in her eyes. "Are you sure? I can... I can understand the need."

His lips curved into a grim smile. "That, my Wind, is different. And entirely normal."

"When did you hurt him, Miss Drew?" asked Mr. Morrison. "What, specifically, did you do that hurt him badly?"

She shook her head. She had no idea.

But Radley did. It was there in a blinding stroke of clarity. "You helped Caroline. You got her out of the neighborhood."

She looked at him, her brows narrowed in confusion. "But how does that hurt him?"

"He branded her. He didn't rape her. He carved his initials into her chest. Everyone knew what had happened. Even though he discarded her, she would live daily with everyone knowing that she was his."

Mr. Morrison snapped his fingers. "Of course. You took away his trophy." He glanced at Radley. "How is your sister doing now?"

"Um... better than ever. She's engaged to Lord Hartfell."

The runner released a huff of exasperation. "There you go. Obvious really." Then he gestured to the butler. "Fetch my hat, will you? I've got to report this to the constable. Let me know when you have your plan. I'll make sure he and his men are in place."

He started to head to the door when Bernard stepped in front of him. "Please explain to those of us who might not be as quick."

The runner frowned. "Hmm? Oh right. Well, what did you miss?" Bernard opened his mouth, but Mr. Morrison kept talking. "Years ago, Damon brands the woman he wanted. My guess is she didn't want him.

He was humiliated, so he takes his revenge by making her relive his dominance every day of her life."

"Caroline did *not* want him," Wendy said. "Said he could rape her, but she would never love him." She shrugged. "I said the same thing before he did this to my ears."

Morrison nodded. "Clever you," he said. "Got you out of the rape, but then he brands you. Is there some significance to the ears?"

"Yes." The one word did not encourage him to ask more. Fortunately, the runner took the hint.

"Anyway, back to Caroline. She's a walking, talking testament to his power back then, but in steps little Wendy. You are younger than she, are you not?"

She nodded. "Younger than everyone except Bernard."

"Yes, so here you are, a little slip of thing, and you arrange for Damon's trophy to escape the neighborhood. Gone is the walking testament to his power. Worse, off goes the outraged brother to sea. Your doing, I assume?"

Radley nodded, along with Wendy. "Not only that," he said softly, "you got Henry out too and arranged for lessons for yourself."

Morrison chuckled. "Right clever of you to take his statement of power and turn it into a means for your advancement. That must have been the icing on the cake. Made you into a right tasty morsel, and you, no more than a girl."

"I didn't do it for that. I just… saw an opportunity."

"You helped," Radley stated firmly. "You saved her, saved me and Henry, and you bartered for what you needed." He touched her chin, turning her to look at him. "It's when I first fell in love with you. Even back then, I knew how incredible you were."

"Just so," agreed the runner, as if he'd been right there. "And Damon too. How many people have defeated him? And so neatly?"

Bernard answered. "No one. No one challenges him the way you do, Wendy."

"And he failed to isolate her. The shop is doing wonderfully. My Penny is happier than ever." He leaned forward, a twinkle in his eye. "Increasing too now. Going to be babes running around that shop soon."

"What?" Wendy gasped. "Congrat—"

"Yes, yes. Happiest news of my life after the day she said yes. As I said, Penny's happy as any soon-to-be mama."

Mr. Knopp spoke up. "My Irene has found her love. Baby's due in the fall."

"Which means that you, little Wendy, have done nothing but thrive, while his efforts to hurt you have failed."

"They haven't failed," she gasped. "They—He—"

Radley tucked her tight against him. No one needed her to say the things she'd suffered at Damon's hands. Henry's… disappearance… was only the worst in a long list of horrors.

Mr. Morrison's tone softened. "Of course, it's been terrible, but I was speaking from the Demon's perspective. From the way he sees it, you have succeeded at every turn, and it has only fueled his need to possess you."

Radley understood it then. Or at least he

comprehended the depth of the problem from an intellectual perspective. Emotionally, personally, he couldn't calculate the costs to Wendy or her friends.

Rather than speak, he gathered her into his arms, lifting her into his lap as he cradled her close. She was all but limp. She was hurt and feeling powerless against such a monster, but he would not let that stand.

"You're not alone anymore," he said. "I'm here."

Mr. Morrison snorted. "Can't crumple now. We're at the endgame. And we've got a right good hand, don't we?" His tone was brusque, but Radley could hear the encouragement in his words. "Got a duke and his men, Mr. Knopp and his fleet of men. I'm off to apprise the constable, and I'd guess your sister's Scot will want a piece, not to mention Lords Crowle and Redhill. This Demon has hurt us all."

"But how?" she said. Her voice was low and filled with despair. "How do we end this?"

"Well, I should think it's for the fighting men to answer that." He looked to Radley and Mr. Knopp. "My job is to figure out the pieces. I've done that. Will happily consult in the planning. But, all in all, I'd think you should look to your duke. I think he's already got an idea."

Radley raised his eyebrows in surprise. The man was right. He did have a plan.

Twenty-four

Damon

I will marry you. Tomorrow at two o'clock, Father Wollet's church. But know that I have conditions.

—W

WENDY PRESSED HER LIST OF DEMANDS INTO THE neatly folded note. Then she sealed the envelope and handed it to her brother. Bernard hesitated as he took the missive, his young eyes troubled.

"Are you sure you want to do this? The duke—"

"Still doesn't fully understand what's happening. He's a sailor, not a London kingpin."

"But he's got a right smart plan."

She nodded. It was a good plan and simple enough to work. They had to get Damon into a public place with his men around him. Then someone would goad him into attacking. The Demon was a patient, calculating man, but some insults no man could bear. Not in front of his men. And once Damon attacked, he could be killed. While the constable looked on as witness, Radley would defend himself, and Damon would die.

"It's still his plan," she told her brother. "We are changing the location, that's all."

Bernard shook his head, dismay in every line of his body.

Wendy sighed. "It takes an even exchange on both sides to make a bargain. Radley and I won't ever work out. It can't. Not with him a duke and me with nothing."

"He loves you. You love him. That should be enough."

She looked at her baby brother, at the determination and the hope still in him. How young he looked sometimes. Or perhaps, it was that she was so old with all romantic notions crushed from her. "It is not enough," she said. "You know that as well as I."

He opened his mouth to argue, but she cut him off.

"This is what I want. But I need you, Bernard. I can't do it without—"

"I know my part. But I never thought it would be to do this."

She touched his face, seeing maturity where before she had seen only softness. "Thank you."

"It ain't a good thing," he said, his voice rough with emotion.

She echoed his tone, bringing back her accent from their old neighborhood. "It ain't a bad thing neither. It just is."

He nodded once. Then suddenly, she was wrapped in his arms. Like hard bands of steel, they wrapped around her as he buried his face in her neck. "I'm sorry, sis. I'm so sorry."

She hugged him back, her eyes wet with tears. "You heard what Mr. Morrison said. This thing started when you were ten. It had nothing to do with you."

"But if I hadn't gambled—"

"Then he would have gotten Mama to do it, or he would have found another way. It's not your fault." Then she straightened. "But you can help me fix it."

She watched his face harden with resolve. "Henry wouldn't let you do it. If he were here—"

"But he isn't. You are. And you know this is the only way."

He nodded, his expression troubled. But it didn't change the resolve in his face.

"I love you, Bernard," she whispered.

"Well, you know I love you," he said, his tone surly. "Only love can make me do something this stupid." Then he gave her a last look before he left, his movements surprisingly quick and silent.

Which left her alone in her bedroom to stare at the night sky and brood. The day had progressed in slow, torturous agony. She'd had to tell Mama the news that Henry was missing. Then she'd had to sit and watch her mother grasp at every possibility that her eldest son was still alive.

Maybe he was at his woman's place. Had anyone gone there? Maybe he'd escaped the fire. He was an excellent swimmer. Maybe he hadn't been on the ship at all. Every knock at the door, every shuffle down the hall, brought her head up as she strained to see if Henry had magically appeared.

He never did. Then Radley had returned from the docks. Wendy knew the truth the moment she'd seen his face. His body sagged with every step, and his eyes were rimmed with red. The conclusions were inescapable. Henry was dead, Radley couldn't save her, and so Wendy had made her plans.

And now, everything was set in place. She just had to wait for Damon's response. He would be at the church with a special license. She knew him that well at least, so she sat and brooded.

She barely heard the knock on her door. Her eyes were trained on the hot coals in the fireplace. The way the flames danced before her eyes made her mind go blank. So she stared, and she didn't even respond when the door opened.

"Wind?"

Radley's voice broke her out of her blank state. She didn't know whether to be grateful or angry about that. But one look at his drawn expression, and her own misery faded. The guilt was so stark on his face.

"Radley," she whispered as she stood. "Oh God, it's not your fault. You warned him."

He stepped into the room, hesitated, and then wrapped her in his arms. She hadn't realized she'd crossed to him until she felt him enfold her. He wore no coat or waistcoat—just his shirt and cravat, pulled askew. So when he enfolded her, there was little fabric between them, and God, his warmth was exactly what she wanted. She hadn't known she was so cold until he pulled her into his heat. Even better, when he held her, she felt lifted. Not just in body, but in her heart too. Simply by touching her, he made everything easier because she was not so alone.

"You didn't come to dinner," he said against her hair.

"I couldn't face everyone. Mama finally fell asleep, and so I came here."

He tightened his grip for a second. "I'll go if you want to be alone. Tell me what you want. I'll do anything—"

"Just this. Just. This." She buried her face in his chest, hearing the steady thump of his heart. He kissed the top of her head, tucking her tighter against him. And they stood that way for a long time.

Then he shifted, quietly picking her up before crossing to her chair by the fire. It was a large chair done in feminine lines. When he sat in it, the wood creaked, but held. And when she made to lift off his lap, he tightened his arms.

"You're going to stay here and eat something," he said firmly.

She smiled but shook her head. "I'm not hungry." Her stomach was tied in knots. Seelye had brought a tray earlier, but it sat untouched.

Radley reached for an apple slice, apparently meaning to force her to eat, but she stopped him with a touch of her fingertips on his arm.

"I can't. Really. It won't stay down."

He shot her a worried frown, which she ignored as she curled against his shoulder. She wanted to be in his arms. She just wanted—

"We don't have to go through with the plan," he said softly. "Not right away."

She flinched. "I've already sent the letter to Damon. Bernard took it an hour ago."

"You told him you wanted to talk? You told him to come to your old home? In the old building?"

"Yes," she lied, feeling swamped in guilt.

"That's all you need to do. He'll pick the time, probably early afternoon tomorrow. Long enough to get my men in place. The constable will be there too—plus Crowle and Hartfell. We'll catch him then."

She nodded, knowing that Radley and his men would be at the wrong place. "What will you do?" she asked. She needed to know that more than anything. So much hinged on his answer.

He didn't respond at first, but she heard his heart speed up and knew that he was afraid to tell her. But in the end, he spoke, his words clear and deliberate. "He is a monster, Wendy. He hurts people, and he carves up women. I was a fool for not killing him years ago."

"No," she said, straightening to look him in the eye. "There was still hope for him even then, I think." Then when he pressed his lips together, shaking his head, she changed her thoughts. "Very well. Even then it was too late, but what about you? What would have happened if you'd killed him then?"

"You would not have spent the last year in terror of that bastard."

"But you would have changed." She felt herself grip his shirt as she struggled to compare the boy he'd been then with the man he was now. "I remember when I heard about what you'd done to Damon. I heard that you'd beaten him to within an inch of his life, but you hadn't killed him."

"I should have finished it—"

"I thought, that's a real man. Someone who thinks about what he does and why. Someone who has control."

He snorted. "It wasn't control. I was blind with fury."

"And yet, you stopped."

He tugged her back to lie against him. "I stopped because I couldn't do it. I couldn't kill a man, even in rage." Then his tone strengthened, and she heard the steel in his voice. "I can now."

She shook her head. "I don't think you can. Not in a temper. Not in—"

"Wendy, I will kill Damon tomorrow. He has gone too far."

No, she thought silently, he wouldn't. "One of the things I love about you is that you think before you act. And when you have decided—"

"I do what is needed."

Yes. Just as she would. "We are a pair in that," she said, "but I don't think the way you do. I weigh advantage and bargains. You thought of justice and hoped for atonement."

He threaded his fingers through her hair, stroking her locks as he thought about her words. "I love that in you. You turn a disadvantage into profit. I think you take any weakness and make it work for you."

Her belly clenched at his words. Not the admiration in his tone, but that he used the word "love" in such a way. He loved something *about* her, not that he loved her. And after tomorrow, would he be able to say that?

"I love that you have honor," she whispered. "I don't think I ever will."

He jerked, startled. "What do you mean by that? Of course you have honor!"

She shook her head. "You said it yourself. I barter.

My honor is a good bargain—one in which both parties benefit. And failing that, one in which I benefit."

"You bargain for survival. And to help your friends and family. I'll wager everything I own that you have never cheated a customer."

She sighed. "You would lose. I stole Lady Strichen's emeralds, remember?"

He nodded, and his expression tightened. "Have you done it again? Ever?"

She bit her lip, unable to answer. And as the clock ticked away the seconds, he adjusted her so he could look into her face. So she confessed her sin. Not the big sin that had yet to happen. Not her coming betrayal, but the last shame of her past.

"I collect secrets," she whispered. "I hear them, you know, from the ladies who come to the dress shop. I write them down and look at them from time to time."

"Secrets?"

"Who is sleeping with who. Who did a favor for someone they shouldn't have. And, best of all, who has money and how they got it." She flashed a smile. "Most society women have their own money, and it isn't always given to them by their husbands."

He stared at her a moment, and then his eyes danced with merriment. "You amaze me. I never would have thought that important."

It was important and valuable. And he would not be alone in underestimating what women know.

"Did you blackmail anyone? Did you use the secrets?"

She shook her head. "No, but I have thought about it." A great deal.

"Of course you did. It would be hard not to. But as long as you never do anything with the information, I have no quarrel with you. It is simply bits of knowledge you acquired." He touched her chin, tilting her so that he could kiss her lips. "I care about actions, Wind. And you have done nothing wrong."

Yet. She had done nothing wrong yet. He didn't know she was about to cross that line irrevocably. Fortunately, he didn't give her time to speak. Any urge to confess was drowned beneath the touch of his lips against hers, the seeking caress of his tongue.

She opened immediately. More than anything else, she wanted him to touch her again. Now. Tonight. Before everything changed tomorrow.

Then he pulled back, his eyes dark and his hands damnably still. "If this is too soon…"

She grabbed his shirt, snapping off two buttons as she crumpled the fine linen in her fists. "Love me," she said. Then she yanked him forward with all the fear and desperation and grief that twisted inside. "Love me!"

He smiled and touched her hands. He didn't understand that her last words were a command. Or maybe, he did, because his expression gentled to something so tender she had to stare. It was so different that at first, she couldn't process it.

"I do," he said. "I already do."

She stared, and eventually, sputtered a question. "W-what?"

He chuckled. That he could laugh after this day was a joy. A pure joy that when she felt as if her whole world was collapsing, he found the words to shore everything up.

"I love you, my Wind. And if you will let me, I will love you for the rest of our days."

She laughed, the sound watery. "I'll settle for tonight."

"I won't." He dropped his forehead against hers. "You've promised to marry me. I haven't forgotten."

Neither had she. But tomorrow he would likely rescind that offer. "Just now, Radley. I can't think about tomorrow."

His hand was on her cheek, brushing away the tears she hadn't realized were wetting her face. "Don't think, love. Just kiss me."

Exactly what she wanted to hear. So she kissed him with all the mix of emotions that churned inside. He took it all into him—the pain, the fear, and most especially, her love—and gave back such adoration he stole her breath away.

He toyed with her tongue, letting her tease him until that moment when he took control. He dominated her, owning every part from teeth to tongue to the roof of her mouth. And then, a growl rumbled through him, low and hungry. The sound thrilled her, and she wrapped her arms around him, pulling him tighter against her.

Then she was weightless, her mind wrapped in his kiss while he stood, carrying her in his arms. She barely noticed except when he set her gently on her bed. He tried to pull away then, but she'd wrapped her arms so tightly around him, he couldn't break away.

He'd managed to separate their bodies enough that his hands could roam. Shoulder to chest to hips, his large hands stroked her. Then while she moaned her hunger, he found the buttons of her dress. An excellent idea, she thought, as she shifted her grip to finish what she'd started on his shirt. But as she tugged at his cravat, he choked and pulled back.

"I'll get that," he rasped.

She laughed, a real laugh, on today of all days. "I love you so much."

"I love you too," he answered as he pulled off his cravat. Shirt and trousers came next. She wasted no time either as she shrugged out of her gown then set to work on her corset. He helped her, being faster than she. He loosened her ties, then he tossed the thing aside while she pulled off her shift.

Naked. They were gloriously naked. And he looked at her as if she were a goddess, yet he was the one who appeared Adonis come to life.

He caressed her cheeks, brushing the wetness aside. "No more tears, love."

Had she been crying?

"Don't leave me," she said, knowing that her words meant tomorrow after her betrayal. After she hurt him in the deepest way possible. "Don't—"

"I'm not going anywhere." Then he gently pressed her into the mattress. He did it with his hands, not his mouth. He stroked her face and neck as he pushed her steadily back. She didn't fall until he took her breasts in his hands.

Yes. Calloused fingers, large palms, and the shape of his hands as he lifted her. Then his mouth came down, and he suckled. Tiny nips accompanied by the swirl of his tongue. Then harder sucks while her back arched.

His mouth shifted to her other breast, but his hands

roved. Belly, hips, then below, where she was wet and open to him. His fingers slid there first, touching her everywhere. He squeezed her thighs and then stroked her petals. He pushed her knees wider apart with his hips, and she felt the briefest brush of his cock—there, then gone.

"Radley, please."

He lifted from her breast, a last hard pull, making her cry out as lightning sizzled from her nipple to her groin.

"It was just last night. You must be sore."

She blinked, his words making no sense. She only knew the desperate thunder of her heart and the emptiness between her thighs.

"Love me," she cried again.

"I do," he said with annoying calm. Then he kissed his way down her belly.

She didn't know what he was doing, and truthfully, she didn't care. Radley worshipped her body as he gently lifted her knees onto his shoulders. She had a moment to frown, wondering what he was doing, and then she knew.

Oh God, she knew what men had laughed about at her gaming table. She knew what women whispered behind their hands. She suddenly understood how a man's tongue could give the most amazing caress ever. He licked her open, and he thrust his tongue inside. And then he suckled an incredible place just as he had done to her nipples. That place was like a lightning rod, a spot where every stoke shot white-hot fire through her body. And when he sucked her there, she bucked like a wild thing.

The detonation sent her soaring. No thoughts, no worries, just bliss. Sweet, silent, pulsing bliss.

Until she drifted back to earth. Until she opened her languid eyes and felt him settle beside her on the bed. He pressed a kiss to her lips then tried to roll her against him, spooning, as if for sleep.

She frowned, then shook her head. "No," she managed, her voice a throaty purr.

He paused, obviously startled. "What?"

"No, Radley. That wasn't enough."

"What?"

Fortunately, he had snuggled close to her hand, where it lay lax on the bed. It took only a shift of her wrist before she gripped his cock and squeezed. Just a quick pulse, but it was enough to catch his attention.

"I said, not enough."

His eyes widened, and then she squeezed again, pleased when she heard him groan.

"I was trying to be respectful," he ground out. "I thought—"

She interrupted him with his own words. "Don't think. Just kiss me."

He did. And while he kissed her with deep, thrusting strokes of the tongue, she pulled his hips around by his cock. He made sounds as she did it, half whimper, half growl. Then he broke off their kiss.

"Easy there. It's a sensitive organ."

It was thick and hard, and when she rolled her thumb over the tip, he shuddered and his eyelids fluttered.

"Have I hurt it?" she asked, knowing she hadn't. From what she'd heard at the gaming hells, these organs were singularly indestructible. Then she softened her touch and waited for him to open his eyes. "I want to carry your baby, Radley. I want..."

She swallowed her next words. She couldn't voice what she felt, except in her own thoughts. *I want a reason for you to know me after tomorrow. A reason for you not to abandon me.*

He stroked her brow. "We have plenty of time."

"We have tonight," she said. "Please."

He settled between her legs, his cock teasing her entrance, going only so far, and no farther. "I should have used a French letter yesterday. I wasn't thinking—"

"No," she said as she stroked his sides. It was the only part of him she could reach just then. "I want to be the mother of your child."

His eyes lighted up with an intensity that stole her breath. "Yes," he said. One word, and then he thrust.

She cried out at the invasion, even as every part of her stretched. She squeezed him with her thighs then wrapped her legs around him. She wanted to speak. She wanted to tell him how perfect this was, but her words had left her. All that she knew was *him*.

Him as he slowly pulled back.

Him as he tightened his thighs before slamming forward.

Him as his strokes became harder and faster, and his face pulled tight.

Him as his eyes held hers, as his breath grew short.

Him.

Him.

Him.

"Radley!"

Ecstasy.

And after that, a single thought: *this was love, and it would be gone tomorrow.*

Twenty-five

HE LEFT BEFORE DAWN. WENDY TRIED TO KEEP HIM with her and succeeded for a bit. All it took was a single kiss, and he returned to bed. The morning's lovemaking was slow and tender, and all the more devastating for her, knowing that it was their last time.

Eventually, he had to leave, and so he kissed her and whispered, "It will be over tonight. Then we can begin our lives together. Plan our wedding, name our children, anything you want, starting tonight."

She kept her tears back long enough for him to leave. Then she sobbed until her belly ached, and her throat was raw. But even that had to end. So she rose, dressed in her ugliest gown, and announced loudly to anyone who wanted to listen that she was going to work at the shop.

Seelye gave her a searching look then ordered the carriage. Thankfully, he didn't speak. She had no idea what she would say if he did and felt like she was a breath away from shattering anyway. So she left and spent all that time in the carriage, praying that she wasn't destroying everything, even though she knew she was.

She didn't go to the shop. She couldn't face everyone there. So she loitered at a nearby park, and though the timing was critical, she waited until the last moment to arrive at the church. This was hard enough without waiting for Damon to appear. She slipped into a side room meant for brides and changed into the dress she had waiting. It was a plain white gown with a blood-red sash—a matching ribbon wove through her hair. Nothing elaborate, except for the hidden pocket along the side. Then—finally—Father Wollet knocked on her door and told her it was time.

She took a breath, then forced herself to begin. She left the room and walked all the way around so that she entered the church from the back. No one took her arm, and there was no father to give her away, as she walked up the aisle in a church filled to bursting with people. There was no music, no decoration. Simply a church full of people she didn't know.

A lot of people, she realized with shock. She had expected Damon to invite his most trusted lieutenants, but not the nearly hundred and fifty people who stuffed the pews of this modest church.

They were all of a disreputable ilk, from the tarts who worked in his brothels through titled lords who frequented his hells. She caught sight of the man who ran the pickpocket ring and a bishop with a drinking problem. And they all stared as she walked slowly up the aisle.

She looked about and tried not to falter. Sweet heaven, she'd never felt so alone. This was her wedding, and no one she liked had attended. Not her mother, nor her brother, nor anyone from the dress shop.

She hadn't wanted them here. In truth, she was too ashamed of what she was doing to see anyone she cared about here. But it made everything so much harder.

The altar was lit, and Damon stood there looking resplendent in his dark clothing. Everything he wore was black. *Everything.* Even his linen shirt and the black onyx pin for his cravat. His eyes gleamed as she approached, and his grin flashed white. Likely, he saw that she wore the damned green earrings. She had gotten them back from Radley on the excuse that she wanted to return them to where they belonged. He hadn't questioned her, thank God, and she hated having the things touching her, but she had to do this.

"You look beautiful," he said as she finally made it to Damon's side. "We match perfectly."

She didn't answer, but she knew what he meant. White and black, with her blood-red ribbon as accent. Then he completed the picture by handing her a bouquet of pale white coriander, the flower of lust.

"I am a lucky man today."

She gripped the bouquet and dipped her chin. She didn't trust her voice to speak. He smiled, his eyes glinting with humor, as if he took pleasure in her anxiety. And then he held out his hand.

"Shall we?" He gestured to the altar where Father Wollet waited in his vestments, his florid face looking waxy as he weaved on his feet. Apparently, the good father wasn't feeling well.

"N-no," she said, her voice breaking on the word. Then she took hold of herself. This would never work if she looked like a timid flower. So she straightened her shoulders and dropped Damon's hand. He didn't want to let go, but she managed to wriggle free. "Not yet. We need an agreement first."

He raised his eyebrows. "Come, come, I agree to your terms, but let's not bore these people with the details."

She frowned and purposely raised her voice to carry throughout the church. "Since you chose to invite these honored guests, they ought to know the specifics behind our wedding." Then she flashed a smile. "And I won't be saying, 'I do' without it."

"Anything you want, my dear," he said with a beautifully executed bow. And as he straightened, he pulled out her written conditions. "Shall I read it aloud?"

She shrugged. She cared not if he read it aloud, so long as he signed it. But Damon had a flare for the theatrical, so he turned to face the assembled guests.

"My lady love's first condition of our marriage is as follows: no harm will come to her family, friends, or their loved ones through me. Namely, the Duke of Bucklynde, his family, or any person who works at her dress shop." He listed the names she had written. "Then she adds the names of her dear brother and mother."

"Do you agree to that?" she asked.

"Really, Wendy, do you think me that blood-thirsty? I would never want to harm anyone, least of all, one of your friends."

She nodded. "So you agree to the forfeit then." She noted that he hadn't read that aloud, so she stated it. "If it be proved before an officer of the law that you willfully caused harm to any of those listed persons, then you forfeit all your many businesses to me."

"My dear—"

"Do you agree?"

"Yes," he said, though the word carried an abundance of condescension. No doubt he was thinking that as a married couple, whatever came to her, would go right back to him anyway. He was right, of course, but she didn't quibble.

"Excellent. Next condition," she prompted with a mocking smile.

He lifted the paper. "Number two. I will receive ownership in A Lady's Favor dress shop." He looked up and blew her a kiss. "Which is the premier dress shop of the *haut ton*. In return, I shall gift my lady love with partnership in all the gaming hells. Equal halves, I believe."

She nodded. "I want to be trained in your business, Damon. I want to run them alongside you."

"Of course, my dear. You do realize that it will all be mine upon our marriage."

She did. "But your word that you will teach me and allow me responsibility of half your hells within a year." And, more important, she needed everyone to know that they had struck this bargain. That she was, indeed, his heir apparent, at least for now.

"Five years."

"Three."

"Seven years."

"I am leaving you the brothels. I want nothing to do with them." She lifted her chin. "Two years, or I turn and walk out now."

He grinned. "Three years, and you learn the brothels too. And you train the woman of my choice at the dress shop."

She blinked coyly. "You don't want to learn it yourself?"

"And violate that sanctum of female frippery? Nonsense, my dear."

She took a deep breath, weighing the bargain, then nodded. "Agreed."

"Excellent!" He glanced at the congregation. "Such a woman I am getting. You cannot imagine how stimulating she is."

Laughter followed his bawdy comment, and Wendy cursed the blush that heated her cheeks. Such a mild comment, and yet, she felt the shame of allowing him to say such things. Still, she held her head high as she pulled ink and a quill from her pocket.

"Shall we sign?" she asked.

"Not quite yet," he countered. "I have a condition of my own."

Of course he did. She tilted her head, waiting to hear what he wanted.

"You agree to be trained—by me—in the sexual arts. My rules, my *mastery*."

She opened her mouth to argue. In truth, once they were wed, he would have rights to do whatever he wanted, but she would fight him, and they both knew it. So, before she could get a word in, he raised his finger to stop her.

"No arguments, no fighting. You will report to my training location three nights a week from dusk until dawn."

"No," she whispered. The very idea repulsed her.

"If you do not, I will chain you there tonight and not let you free until I deem you appropriately broken."

She blinked, seeing the determination in his gaze. And the excitement. Either way, he would break her. At least this way, she would be free four days of the week, or as free as any wife could be.

"Agreed," she whispered.

"I am sorry, my love," he said in a carrying voice. "I'm afraid the others couldn't hear you."

"*Agreed*," she all but shouted. Then she held out the ink and quill. He took it then crossed the pulpit to sign.

She followed him slowly, her steps dragging, as she fought her decision. Did she really want to do this? Could she carry through?

He scrawled their terms and his signature with a flourish then held out the quill. She stepped forward, seeing that he had added his condition to her list. There it was in stark black ink: her promise to allow his mastery over her. The idea made her nauseous. But this was the only way she could keep Radley safe. Keep her friends and her family alive. It wasn't a guarantee, but it was the best she could do.

So she signed.

Then as she picked up the agreement, he whisked it away. "Not so fast, my dear. I think I'll keep this." He tucked it inside his jacket.

"No, I want it."

He smiled. "Perhaps we should leave it in the care of the dear bishop," he said, as a man in the pews stood and crossed to Damon. "He's also the man who signed our special license to wed. We want to be sure everything is legal, now don't we?"

"Of course," she mumbled, her heart beating

painfully in her throat as she stared at the bishop. The man was one step below the Archbishop of Canterbury, and he was here at her wedding. Was there no end to Damon's reach?

Apparently not, for the cleric took hold of the document.

"You can thank your brother Bernard for reminding me about a special license" continued Damon in a cheery voice. "I'd almost forgotten, until he asked if such a hasty arrangement was legal." He chucked her under her chin, and she had to restrain herself from biting his finger. "But then, I know how eager you are to grace my bed."

Again, the bawdy laughter floated around her. She ignored it, finding it easier this time to block it away. Perhaps that was because Damon had taken her arm and had steered her toward the altar. He even remembered to press her bouquet of flowers into her limp hand as he smirked.

This was happening, she thought dully, as they took their position in front of Father Wollet. She was marrying Demon Damon. Right now.

She didn't hear the Father's words. The sounds blurred together. Damon had to prompt her— apparently, more than once—to say, "I do."

A minute, or an eon, later, he pushed a ring onto her finger. A signet ring, she realized, one that he had created for himself. She narrowed her eyes. Good God, it was a parody of a shield of honor with a demon in the center on a field of blood.

Charming.

"So it is done?" she rasped. She looked to the priest. "We are wed?"

The man nodded. "It is done."

Which was the exact moment a commotion began at the back of the church.

Twenty-six

RADLEY GROUND HIS TEETH. IT WAS A TERRIBLE HABIT, one that gave him headaches and made his jaw ache unbearably. It only happened in those interminable hours before a battle. Like now.

Where the hell was Damon?

He had his men scattered about the old neighborhood, hiding in shadows or in people's homes, scouting for any sign of the bastard or his men. Meanwhile, Radley waited in the darkness of Wendy's old flat, grinding his teeth and counting the seconds.

Had Damon found out about the plan? Obviously, he had, but how? And besides, he knew Damon. Even if the bastard had figured everything out, he'd still be here just to taunt Radley.

So what was going on?

A knock sounded on the door, and Radley tensed. He had his sword in his right fist, a dagger in his left, but he didn't move. Something was off about that knock. It wasn't bold enough to be Damon's.

Another knock, and then the doorknob twisted.

"Don't hit me. Damon's not coming." Bernard's voice. Damn it!

Radley crossed the room and jerked the door open. He'd barely seen Bernard's face before he set his dagger tip to the man's jaw. He wasn't going to kill the man, but he was angry and needed to express it somehow.

"What happened? Is Wendy all right? Where's Damon?"

Bernard swallowed, his body frozen, half in and half out of the room.

"Tell me!" Radley bellowed.

"They're at the church getting married."

"What!" It was all that he could do to stop his fist from twitching enough to pierce Bernard's jaw.

"I'll take you there, but we have to be quick."

Radley jerked his weapons back, slamming them into their scabbards with barely leashed fury. He didn't bother speaking to Bernard. The man knew Radley was poised on the edge of lethal violence. So with a quick nod, the man turned and led the way. He was fast, thank God, and before long, the two of them— plus a trail of Radley's men—were running through the London streets to the church.

Bernard slowed as they got close, but Radley barely paused. He hadn't wanted to think about what Bernard had said—hadn't wanted to believe it—but the questions had circled, even as they ran through London. Why would Wendy do this? Why would she marry that bastard? Why couldn't she trust him to handle it? Even if today's plan hadn't worked, he would have figured something else out. But not if she married the man! How could she do this?

He had no answers and wouldn't until he could see for himself what was going on. So he ruthlessly shoved all doubt aside. With a flick of his wrist, he ordered his men to surround the church. Whatever was going on inside, he'd be damned if the Demon left the church alive.

Not now. Not after marrying her.

Why had she done it?

He stomped to the entrance and dragged the heavy doors open. What he saw inside made his heart go dead. But what he *heard* made his entire body freeze in horror.

Wendy stood at the top of the aisle, her face as ghostly pale as her white gown. She'd dropped a bouquet of flowers on the floor beside her feet, so nothing prevented his view of a heavy ring on her finger. He didn't have to guess whose ring it was. Damon stood beside her, his expression twisting into one of pure hatred.

The reason for the man's anger came in the form of Radley's sister. Caroline was walking up the aisle, speaking in a loud voice as she moved. And even though her voice practically throbbed with emotion, her body was calm, her elegant figure straight and proud.

"Thin like a quill and weak. I was a girl at the time and knew nothing of men. I remember wondering if he meant to poke me with that? Like a pin. But it was too puny." She waved a hand at him. "That's why he carries knives, you know. They're thicker than his cock."

Snorts of laughter erupted around the church, quickly stifled when Damon surged forward.

"Kill her," he rasped.

Wendy jerked on his hand. "You can't! You promised!"

He shoved her aside, and she tripped and fell backwards against the altar. "I will do as I bloody well please." Then he drew a pistol from inside his jacket. Radley jerked, rapidly evaluating his choices. There wasn't time to dive in front of his sister before the blackguard could sight and fire.

Meanwhile, apparently oblivious to the threat, Caroline kept advancing, her words ringing through the room. "And he had a smell, you know? Like rancid meat. Are you sure he still has a cock, Wendy? It may have fallen off by now."

Radley took three steps forward, moving to protect his sister. Too slow, too slow! Especially as the congregation started to rise. Two thugs noticed him and immediately intercepted. He knocked them down easily—not drawing blood yet—but there were too many between him and Caroline. He had enough time to look up, grateful to see that the Scot was suddenly there. He stood in front of Caroline, his expression dark, and a... was that a claymore in the man's hand?

"I think that's enough, love," the man said, his voice low, but strong enough to be heard.

Radley looked from him to the altar. Damon had his pistol pointed straight at the Scot's heart. Damn it, now Gregory would be shot. That was hardly better! Radley let out a roar and burst ahead, but the chaos was absolute. Everyone in the congregation was on his feet now. Many drew weapons, while others shrank back. And damnation, Caroline was still talking. No, she was laughing!

"You think killing me will stop the truth? Good lord, all the whores laugh about it, even the little ones—the boys too weak to fight you. Is that why you use them? Because they are small enough to make it feel tight on—"

There was more. She was relentless as she steadily pushed forward. Radley shoved ahead as well. He had to protect his sister. He had to get Wendy out of the way. He'd seen her already back on her feet and stalking toward Damon with murderous intent. And damn it, the Scot could only protect one side, and that claymore was impressive, but bad for fighting in such close quarters. Damon's men in the pews were fouled by the people in the way, but that wouldn't last long.

A fist came at Radley from his right, and a knife flashed on the left. He lost track of what was happening ahead as he fought in earnest. This was close-quarter battle—restricted by the pews. And to his shock, these were skilled fighting men, as used to their blades as their own arms and legs. He barely ducked a short sword before he let his fury burn into his actions. There was no holding back, not against these men. But even though he fought like a demon, he knew it was too late. There were too many skilled street fighters between him and the two women he cared most about.

And still, his sister's voice rang loud and clear. In truth, it was the only thing that kept him grounded, though he wondered about her sanity.

"The doctors say he has frog cock. It smells like sewage, it's green, and it croaks when you poke it."

What the hell was she doing? Then he caught sight of a few more people. Not men heading for him, but others along the side. Bow Street men, by the look of them, keeping the street fighters away from Caroline.

It was at that moment he realized the truth. This was his plan, damn it. He had intended to taunt Damon to attack. He'd meant to be the one to gut the bastard. But apparently, the fight had shifted here. And it had put Caroline at risk as she all but begged Damon to kill her.

He couldn't cut through the crowd fast enough. With a muffled curse, he leaped up on the back of the nearest pew. Solid wood, but it required delicate balance. Fortunately, he was a sailor used to climbing ropes in icy storms. This was as solid as open ground to him, and gave him the advantage of seeing the battle clearly.

Caroline was almost at the altar rail with the Scot standing before her, trying to protect her. But he was one man, and there were five ugly men hedging him in. The claymore held them back, but that wouldn't last long. Bizarrely, no one had touched his sister, and now, he saw why. She wasn't just protected by the Scot. There were others around her too. Footmen? Men who weren't true fighters, but they were holding their own for now.

His gaze cut to the altar, where Wendy stood a half-step behind Damon, his face mottled with rage. His pistol was up, and his hands were steady as he sighted on Caroline. He didn't have a clear shot, but apparently, that didn't matter. Radley had a second at most. Any moment now, the men would back off the Scot, and he or Caroline would be shot through.

So Radley threw his dagger. It was a quick throw out of desperation, and it cost him as a man close managed to grab his leg. He twisted away, but suffered a slice along his thigh before a downward stroke of his sword ended the tussle. But it cost seconds, and in that time, a shot rang out.

Damon had fired.

Then the room seemed to detonate as a half-dozen shots came from all sides.

Everyone in the pews froze or cowered. Radley strained to see what had happened.

Damon was dead, but not from Radley's dagger. His throw had been good, lodging deep in the man's belly. It would have killed him eventually, but not immediately. No, what killed the man was a thin stiletto shoved through his neck and still held by Wendy. Or perhaps, it was the bullet hole through his face, thanks to Bernard, who now stepped out from the side vestibule. Or perhaps it was the half-dozen bullet holes riddling the man's body without ever touching Wendy.

Radley looked around him, making sure that the people in the congregation weren't fighting—they weren't—before he looked to the walls of the church.

He saw Lords Crowle and Redhill, each priming a pistol. Mr. Morrison was putting his own weapon away, a grin on the thin man's face, while an older man beside him grunted in satisfaction.

"I think that's got things well in hand, don't you, constable?" the runner asked.

"Sit everyone down, boys," the constable said loudly, "while we sort things out."

And so it was done. Everyone slowly settled

into a seat—or was forcibly guided to one—while Radley stood on top of a pew and watched with slack-jawed astonishment.

The men were there. Not only the husbands of Wendy's friends, but the constable's men, and... He blinked as he looked at one of the men protecting Caroline's back. "Seelye?"

The man snapped his head up. "Ah, there you are, your grace. Bloody good throw."

What did he say to that? "Er, thank you."

Then his eyes traveled back to Damon's body, where Wendy now slowly stood. Blood stained her dress, and her eyes were wide, but she remained poised and quiet. Her brother had crossed to stand behind her until silence pounded from all sides.

Apparently, that was too much for the cleric, who had been cowering behind the altar. The man pushed up from behind his hiding place, his florid jowls quivering with terror.

"She did it! She brought madmen into my church! And she k-ki—"

"Killed the madman? That she did," barked the constable as he climbed over an unconscious man and headed to the front. "Seems to me that we were all attending a wedding when suddenly, the groom orders a woman killed. Killed, and right in a church." He glared at the assembled people. "Good thing I'm a friend of the bride here. Kept things under control, didn't we, Miss Drew?"

Wendy opened her mouth, but the constable didn't give her a chance. "Oh blighter, you're not Miss Drew anymore, are you?"

Radley's belly clenched as she paled, but she raised her gaze to his. "No, Constable," she said in ringing tones. "I'm Mrs. Porter now, recently widowed." Her gaze dropped to the assembled crowd. "And now, sole owner of Demon Damon's property."

Radley's jaw went slack as the truth finally became clear. This hadn't been a wedding. This had been a coup d'état! Wendy had married and then killed Damon in order to take over his businesses. And while Radley stood there gaping, Wendy leaned down and pulled her stiletto out of Damon's neck before calmly wiping it on her gown. Then she looked at the assembled people.

"Does anyone have any problem with me stepping into my husband's place?"

There were quiet murmurs, the shifting of feet, but no one said a word. Meanwhile, the constable nodded in approval.

"I should say not, Mrs. Porter. We all saw you wed, right and tight. We all heard him order Miss Caroline Lyncott's murder. And you most helpfully dispatched the villain. I, for one, thank you for your service and would like you to call on me should you or your brother need my assistance."

Mr. Morrison stepped forward and gave her an elegant bow. "Bow Street at your service, ma'am."

Lords Crowle and Redhill were in the process of tucking away their pistols, but they waved cheerily from opposite sides of the church. "Seems like a capital idea," said one. The other grinned his agreement.

Then Lord Hartfell tucked Caroline close to his side. He didn't speak, but she did. "You saved his life, Wendy. I cannot thank you enough."

Then it was one statement after another, first from the bawds, then from the less savory men who had been scowling in the pews. They voiced their support of her, while she nodded like a queen in her bloody gown, taking their vows of loyalty—for that's what they were—as her due.

Then everyone was silent, even the sniveling priest, while Wendy turned her gaze to Radley. She didn't speak, and neither did he. Radley was still struggling to absorb everything that had happened. Last night she had said she loved him. She had opened her body and her heart, and he had done the same. They had talked about their *children*, for God's sake. And yet, not twelve hours later, she was another man's widow and owner of half of Soho.

And into the silence, his sister crossed to his side and tugged on his trousers. "Do come down, Radley. It's really not done, standing on the pews."

"It's really not done, inciting a riot in one either."

She waved an airy hand. "Everything I said was the truth."

He gaped at her, but then caught the flash of blonde hair tucked neatly beneath a hooded cape. It was another woman, slender and composed, as she sat next to Seelye. "Eleanor!"

She flipped the hood back, her eyes shining. "Yes, your grace?"

"What...? Why are you here?"

"She asked me." She waved at Wendy. "She asked me to witness this, so I could tell the *ton*. And I have to tell you, she's magnificent. I thought she was beneath you. I thought she was beneath us all, but Radley, don't you see? She's a bloody Borgia! My God, she fits the dukedom better than anyone I've ever seen!"

He blinked, staring at his cousin in shock. "You called her a thief. You hate her."

"Not anymore. Do you know what kind of money she will bring to the dukedom? And if you thought a little murder would put me off, then you have not read our family history. Really, Radley, I have asked you to read those diaries. Did you think they were made-up stories?"

He didn't answer. He didn't know what to say. And so, he turned to the woman he loved. She remained poised at the front of the church, her hands tucked neatly together, the bloody stiletto now in her brother's hands.

"Wendy," he whispered. "Why didn't you tell me?"

She swallowed. "You'd have stopped me. You never would have let me marry him."

Too bloody right. "But—"

"A good bargain is equal on both sides," she said loudly. "I've said that before, and you've agreed."

"Yes. But what does that—"

"You're a duke, Radley. I'm a nobody seamstress."

He practically rolled his eyes. "This is not the act of a nobody. This is—"

"Balance. I've ended the threat. And now, I have something to offer. I have money. Property and businesses."

"You already have a business," he said. That wasn't what he meant to say. He meant to point out that taking ownership and keeping it were entirely different things. But he couldn't get those words out, though she must have understood because she answered his unspoken worry.

"Bernard will run the business," she said. "He knows a great deal more than you think. And besides, I now have friends who will help."

Morrison waved a hand. The constable grunted as he tugged on his coat lapels. "She means to keep things honest, your grace, and I mean to help her. Me and my men."

He didn't need to see the other lords nod their agreement to know that should Wendy need it, she had a great deal of aid. Meanwhile, she stepped forward, picking her way carefully past Damon's body before coming down the aisle. He leaped down from his perch when she was halfway there. He had no interest in towering over her. He wanted to know that she was safe. And that she...

"I have all this now," she said softly, when she came within arm's reach. "And I want to give it to you." She lifted her chin. "I want to marry you, Radley, but I had to make the bargain equal."

He shook his head. "It was equal. It *is* equal, Wendy. I don't want this. I just want you."

She nodded, as if she had expected those words. "You need to know." She took the edges of her skirt and spread them, making the bloodstains on the white so clear. "This is me, Radley. I'm not the pure woman you've drawn in your books. I'm not a frightened seamstress afraid of a demon. And I'm not the wind to your sails. I'm just me." She shrugged. "Bloodstains and all. Just me."

He stepped forward, touching her face. "And I love you. I always have."

She shuddered, her eyes closing as she wavered on her feet. He grabbed her, afraid that she would fall, but she'd already steadied herself. "I love you, Radley. Are you sure—"

"I have never been more sure of anything. You amaze me, woman. I am in awe. And I love you."

He kissed her then. Deep and purposeful, he possessed her mouth, wrapping his arms around her, while she surrendered. The church erupted into cheers, but he barely heard it. All he wanted was this woman, right now.

Eventually, she pulled back. Eventually, the cheers quieted. And then he heard his cousin shushing everyone. He frowned.

"Eleanor?"

"Finally!" she huffed. Then she dropped her hands on her hips. "Are you finished kissing?"

Not really, but he wasn't going to quibble. Not when she was gesturing to someone at the side vestibule. A moment later, an elderly man stepped out wearing ecclesiastical robes. He grimaced as he looked about him, horror and disapproval in every line of his face. But he walked steadily forward until he faced Eleanor.

"Lady Eleanor," he began, his tone stiff with anger. Which was when, apparently, Wendy recognized the man.

"The Archbishop of Canterbury!"

Good God, it couldn't be! But Lady Eleanor pulled out a piece of paper, briefly showing it to all assembled.

"A special license to wed. Right now. Right here."

"What?" Radley exploded.

Then there was a touch on his arm and a whispered voice. It was Bernard, his words low, but the meaning clear.

"It's a show of strength, your grace. It won't be easy to hold things together, even with everyone here. But with your wedding happening over Damon's corpse, officiated by the archbishop himself..."

Radley didn't need him to finish. He understood the symbolism of what they were doing. After all, it wasn't just sailors who were superstitious. And having the Archbishop of Canterbury here was like bringing God into Soho.

He shook his head. "How did you manage this?"

Wendy frowned. "This was your idea. Every piece of it." She gestured around. "I only shifted the location. After I married—"

"This next part—" interrupted Lady Eleanor. "That was my idea. As was bringing Seelye and the footmen. Now, it's time, cousin. Will you have her?"

He laughed, suddenly feeling as if he'd found his land legs. They put him right where he belonged—at Wendy's side. So he laughed, as he scooped her up in his arms. Everyone parted as he strode forward, and the poor archbishop had to rush to get to the altar.

"I thought I'd miss the sea," he said as he finally set down his bride, "but I believe you are as challenging a mistress as she ever could be."

Wendy gave him a soft smile. "You want this, Radley? Truly want—"

He touched her cheek. "Every sailor's dream is to marry the wind."

"I love you," she said.
"And I love you."
And then—ten minutes later—they said, "I do."

Read on for a peek at an original novella from
USA Today bestselling author Jade Lee

Available for download now

the
Groom's
Gamble
A NOVELLA

"BREATHE DEEPLY, LADY ANNE. RELAX YOUR MIND.
Let me see through you to the Great Beyond." The
words were sonorous, the intonation mesmerizing.
Caroline Lyncott would have been caught just by his
tone—if the man didn't have duck feathers dangling
from his ears.

Caroline pulled back from her hiding place behind
the door frame. His lordship would have a fit if
he knew what was happening here. Lord Hartfell
and Lady Anne were brother and sister, but a more
opposite pair could not be found. Whereas he was a
man of science, his sister was fascinated by all things
occult—and most specifically, by the gypsy with the
waterfowl accoutrements.

If nothing else, Caroline thought with a smile,
the view was intriguing. Somewhat like watching
a monkey colony at the zoological gardens. In the
center sat a handsome, dark-haired man with kind
eyes and hands that moved too quickly for the eye to
catch. Made her wonder what he hid up his sleeves.

Lady Anne sat before him in a muskrat cap. Caroline narrowed her eyes. Unless that was a beaver hat. Hard to tell from this distance. Then, in a circle around them, sat the preening biddies, seven members of the aristocracy with an interest in the occult, plus all the servants peering in from the door.

The only question now was whether she stood as part of the colony or as a curious human visitor. She was still pondering the question when the butler, Mr. McTavish, crowded in. "Flimflam and folderol," he muttered. "If his lordship were home, he'd put a stop to this right quick. Just how much is that gypsy fleecing my lady for?"

Caroline smiled and tried to take a compromising tone. As housekeeper here, it was her job to soften the jeers of the outspoken male before he could clash too loudly with the female staff and disturb the main attraction in the parlor. She was used to the task. This wasn't the first time his lordship's scientific attitudes and her ladyship's esoteric studies had collided in one way or another. Sure enough, before she could say anything, Lady Anne's maid, Marta, spoke up, her voice tight with anger. "The gypsies have powers—always have. And who's to say how a body grieves their loved ones? If he can give her peace—"

"By emptying her wallet?" Mr. McTavish interrupted.

"By speaking with her dead sister," the maid shot back, "and you've no cause to criticize."

Mr. McTavish opened his mouth, ready to lambaste the girl where she stood. But Caroline stepped between the pair. "His name is Stefan Pike, and he's only charging a guinea," she said. "Lady Anne can afford it."

"Doesn't mean she should be throwing it away." Mr. McTavish glared at the room in general. "She should pay me the guinea. I'll tell her that her sister died quickly and misses her terribly, but hopes my lady can find happiness without her. It's damned gypsy thievery, I tell you."

Mr. McTavish had any number of diatribes on how England was going to the dogs.

"Oh, go on with you," grumbled the maid as she squeezed closer. "Let the rest of us watch in peace."

Mr. McTavish rolled his eyes, but after a last dismissive look at the parlor, he walked away. Going to the wine cellar most likely, while the rest of the house crowded around the parlor doors. And it was the whole household, Caroline realized with a bit of shock. With Lord Hartfell away, there was less work for everyone, which meant that the cook, two maids, and one footman all watched the entertainment from the hall. And who could blame them? If nothing else, the gypsy knew how to put on a show.

Truthfully, she wanted to watch too. She needed to know what drew Lady Anne so strongly to this man. He'd apparently followed her from Berkshire to London—something unheard of with the Romanies—and that spoke of a deeper connection to Lady Anne than was proper. But delving into the lady's personal life wasn't the job of a housekeeper. And besides, Caroline had work to do: receipts and orders to organize, and all the day-to-day tasks of running a large

London establishment. But mostly, she needed a little time to herself in her room. Handsome gypsies were delightful, to be sure, but her thoughts generally wandered elsewhere. Lately, she had discovered a secret attraction to his lordship's slight Scottish burr.

And didn't that just make her the biggest, dumbest monkey of the lot? His lordship was a good man and a fair employer. It would be the height of folly to indulge in girlish dreams that could never be realized and would endanger her position as housekeeper. She might be single and female, but she was *Mrs.* Lyncott here because such was the way with all housekeepers. And it helped remind her that romantic fantasies had cost her dearly before, so she would not indulge in them now. With that in mind, she tamped down her desires as she headed for her room in the topmost corner of the house.

She was on the second floor, climbing toward the third, when she heard the noise. A slight thud followed by a muffled grunt. This was the bedroom floor, and no one should be up here now. His lordship wasn't due home until late tonight, and her ladyship was downstairs, along with all the staff.

The dog, perhaps? Trapped where she shouldn't be? Turning, Caroline walked down the hall, listening intently. Most rooms were empty—the nursery hadn't been used in years—but Caroline checked each. Nothing disturbed. And no more sounds either. Had she imagined it? It wouldn't be the first time her daydreams had gotten the better of her.

She knocked on his lordship's door, opening it quietly when there was no response. There was Sophie, a golden retriever, just now lifting her head.

She'd been sleeping by the banked fire, waiting for her master's return.

"Not yet, my girl," Caroline said as she stroked the animal's head. The dog was old but still affectionate, and all the staff loved her. In fact, Sophie was the one thing everyone in the household agreed was absolutely perfect. "He'll be home soon. I promise."

Then she heard it again. Another noise, and this time from her ladyship's bedroom. Caroline strode forward. Not bothering to knock this time, she shoved open the door to Lady Anne's room and saw a rough-cut man with dark hair and thick hands. He'd knocked over a lamp—that was the thud she'd heard—as he rifled through her ladyship's jewelry.

A thief! Caroline drew breath to scream but hadn't the time. The man was quicker than she thought possible as he sprang across the room to grab her by the throat.

She released a sound, but it came out more a squeak than a scream. She shoved him with her hands, but he was too strong. Then he dragged her into the room, pulling her quickly and solidly, despite how she tried to scramble backwards. Her hands were fists now, beating him about the head and face, but they had no effect whatsoever.

She was going to die here, she realized in horror. Killed by a gypsy thief with no one to discover her for hours. His hands were tightening around her throat, and even worse, he started speaking to her. Crooning as if she were a wild animal.

"There, there now, my girl. Can't have you screaming—" His words were cut off by barking.

Sophie!

The old dog came scrambling around the corner, her back paws sliding as she lunged at the man holding Caroline.

The thief cursed, blocking the blow with his forearm and ripping the top of Caroline's dress in the process. But it was enough to ease the pressure on her throat, especially as Sophie grabbed onto his arm, growling and shaking.

Caroline slammed her fist into his face. Her hand exploded in pain, but it didn't matter. She could breathe! She hauled air into her lungs, though it burned like fire. Beside her, Sophie and the thief were struggling, growls and curses filling the air. She wanted to help—especially when she heard Sophie's high-pitched yelp of pain—but all her concentration was on dragging air into her lungs.

"What the devil!" exclaimed a loud voice. His lordship?

Caroline looked up to see the Earl of Hartfell storm into the room like an avenging angel. He swooped down on the thief, punching the man with a blow that seemed to echo in Caroline's head. So loud, so powerful, and yet the bastard didn't go down. Instead, the gypsy managed to throw off Sophie, sending the poor dog flying against the wall with a whimper, before slamming forward against the earl.

Caroline tried to call out. She was struggling to her feet, though her legs felt weaker than pudding. If only she could scream, but all she managed was a harsh rasp.

It didn't matter. The thief was all ugly face and massive fists, but the earl was ready. He blocked the man's blow, then… bam, bam, bam! Three punches, and the blackguard crumpled to the floor.

He dropped right in front of Caroline, blood seeping from his thick lip. She would have screamed if she'd had the breath. Instead, she just stared, horror and gratitude at war within her. The man was down.

The earl was beside her in the next breath, his hands gentle as he supported her. She'd barely managed to get to her feet, unsteady as she was.

"Are you all right? Mrs. Lyncott?" When she didn't answer, his hands tightened. "Caroline!"

She opened her mouth to speak, but again, all she could manage was a harsh rasp.

The earl's expression grew worried as he gently tilted her head to inspect her neck. "Don't speak. It's not crushed. You can breathe, can't you?"

She nodded, then made the mistake of trying to swallow and winced.

"Bet it hurts like the very devil. You need a doctor." Then he twisted around and shouted, his bellow loud enough to be heard throughout the house. "McTavish! Henry! Someone get up here immediately!"

Now there was the true call of the colony head, she thought with a near-hysterical giggle. One command and immediately came a rush of heavy feet. Even poor Sophie responded with a weak bark. Caroline turned enough to see the old dog struggle to her feet. Her teeth were bared as she stood unsteady guard over the unconscious thief.

"Good girl, Sophie," the earl said as he smiled at the dog. "Very good girl." Then he turned back to

Caroline. "Why don't you sit down, Mrs. Lyncott? Right here."

She wanted to refuse. Indeed, she shook her head, but she felt so unsteady. Fortunately, he insisted, and so she all but dropped onto the bed. Meanwhile, people appeared at the door: Henry, Marta, then Mr. McTavish.

The earl began issuing orders the moment they arrived, his voice hard and clipped. Rope to restrain the thief, a doctor sent for, and the watch summoned. Marta went to the dog, cooing over the animal as she pronounced her merely bruised.

Then came one more order, spoken in a tone that brooked no argument. "And bring me that charlatan gypsy immediately. Clap him in irons if you have to, but I will—"

"No need," came Mr. Pike's voice. "I am here."

And a second after that came Lady Anne's horrified gasp. "Oh no! Caroline, are you all right?"

The earl stepped forward, his eyes blazing as he glared at Mr. Pike. "She was nearly strangled to death. If I hadn't been just coming home, she would have been murdered." Fury radiated in his voice, and it was the only thing that kept Caroline from collapsing as the reality of what had happened began to sink in. She wouldn't think about it, she told herself. Monkey colony, she thought. Nothing of import. Just monkeys jumping around doing inconsequential monkey things. And if she felt any fear, all she needed to do was focus on the solid strength of the zookeeper. His lordship towered in her thoughts as the voice of civilization in a very dangerous world.

"Is that your man?" the earl snapped at Mr. Pike.

"Yes, I brought him here," the gypsy answered, his voice thick with disgust. Surprisingly, the hatred wasn't aimed at his lordship. Mr. Pike stepped into the room to tower over the now tied-up thief. "On the recommendation of my cousin, the damned idiot."

"Your cousin!" the earl nearly exploded. "You brought this man here—"

"Yes, and as such he was my responsibility." Mr. Pike's jaw clenched as he glared down at the thief. "I swear that he will answer for his crime."

"He certainly will," the earl said. "The watch will be here in a moment."

Mr. Pike looked as if he was going to say something, but then he gave a quick nod. "So be it. He will answer to your justice, as will I. But I swear, I had no idea he would do such a thing. I left him with the horses. He wasn't even supposed to come into the house."

"That's true," Lady Anne spoke up. "I heard him say so myself."

"That means less than nothing," her brother retorted, his opinion of the gypsy's word obvious. Then he looked at Caroline, his eyes haunted. His gaze roved over her features to where she held a hand to her burning throat. She didn't do it to hide the bruises. In truth she was keeping her torn dress up to cover scars that were a great deal uglier than whatever the thief had done to her throat. "The doctor will be here in a moment, Mrs. Lyncott."

"I'm fine, my lord," she whispered. It was easier than speaking aloud. "It will heal. There is no need for a doctor."

"The devil there isn't!" Then he flushed. "My apologies."

She smiled. She didn't think anything could make her smile right then, but there he was—an earl—apologizing because he thought a curse was too uncivilized for her to hear. It warmed her enough that she managed to get to her feet. Or at least she tried to.

"Sit back down," he said sternly. "You will not move an inch until the doctor has declared you able to do so."

Meanwhile, Mr. Pike glanced over. "My sister makes a posset that will aid in healing."

The earl nearly growled his response. "We'll have no more of your gypsy nonsense—"

"Gregory!" Lady Anne snapped. "Don't be nasty. He's only trying to help."

Any further discussion was stopped by the arrival of the watchman. Caroline tried to keep track of it all, but there were too many people. In the end, she simply focused on the earl, who was never farther than three feet from her side. He stood beside her as she explained to the constable what had happened.

By the time the doctor arrived, both gypsies were being taken away despite Lady Anne's objections. His lordship declared that Caroline would be seen in Lady Anne's bedroom, and everyone but the doctor and poor Sophie were shooed away.

The diagnosis was exactly as Caroline had expected. Her throat was bruised, and she'd be eating nothing but thin gruel for a day or so, but beyond that she would be fine. In truth, Sophie had fared worse with bruises all over her body, but at least the old girl would get a bone and some fine meat to eat.

The doctor stepped out of the room as Caroline righted her clothing. There was little she could do to repair the tears at her bodice, but at least there were pins to cover her scars. The doctor, of course, had inquired about them, but she had passed them off with the same lie she told everyone: a childhood accident, nothing more. Everyone knew she was lying. One look showed that the marks had been as deliberate as they were disfiguring. No one accidentally gave themselves scars that spelled DP. But the kind ones let her lies pass without challenge.

So when she stepped out of Lady Anne's bedroom, she was able to put a serene smile on her face and nod to both lord and lady.

The earl spoke first. "The doctor said you need rest and soft food. So you will stay in your bed and allow the staff to wait on you."

She opened her mouth to argue, but he held up his hand.

"And no speaking either. Not until you're well."

Lady Anne stepped forward. "I shall tend to you myself. In fact, I shall get a tea tray immediately. I cannot express how sorry I am for this."

Her brother released a "harrumph" while Lady Anne disappeared for the tray. Then Caroline was escorted to her own bedchamber as if she were a veritable princess. She kept trying to tell them she would be quite well, but his lordship would not hear of her saying a word. He insisted on seeing that she made it to her bed, and then he shooed everyone out with the order that she needed to rest.

"Really, my lord," she whispered, but he cut her off.

"Hush, Mrs. Lyncott. No speaking." Then he fell silent as he simply looked at her. Only now did she see how very pale he was. And when he rubbed his hand over his face, she noticed that his knuckles were bloody.

She gasped, reaching forward to grab his hand. The doctor had already left, she knew, but he could be called back.

Meanwhile, the earl looked down as she captured his fingers. He had a large hand with callouses and scars from his scientific experiments. But he was an earl, a learned man of study. He should not have bloodied knuckles.

"What is it?" he asked. Then when she lifted his hands to the light, he chuckled. "Oh that. It's nothing, I assure you." Then he sobered. "I only wish I had done it quicker or arrived sooner. When I think of what might have happened…"

She straightened, pressing her fingers to his lips. She felt the curve of his lips and the moist heat of his breath as it caressed her palm. It had been familiar enough just to touch his hand, but now her heart stuttered, and her belly went liquid.

"I am fine," she whispered. "You saved me."

His mouth twisted beneath her fingers, and he drew back. Then he caught her hands in his. "I rather think it was Sophie who saved you. I would not have run upstairs had it not been for her barking."

She shook her head. "It was you." And when he raised his brows, she shrugged. "It was both of you."

"It should never have happened," he said, his expression suddenly dark and intense. Then abruptly, he squeezed her fingers. "No more speaking, Mrs. Lyncott. There isn't time." They could hear the tread of someone coming up the stairs. "After you are better, I should like it if you came to speak with me."

She looked into his eyes and felt her heart sink to her feet. He was waiting until she was better, of course, but she could read the determination in his dark, angry eyes. He blamed her—in a small part—for the events of this evening. After all, they all knew his lordship's opinion of the gypsies. Any decent housekeeper would have either found a way to prevent those men from coming here or gotten him word of Lady Anne's intentions. She had done neither, so she would likely be expelled from the household.

Fighting the lump in her throat, she nodded slowly. "Of course, but if I am to be let go, perhaps you had best tell me now."

His expression shifted, and she saw raging emotions on his normally impassive face. Anger, frustration, and horror flashed across his face but centered on his mouth. His lips thinned before he gave a heavy sigh.

"Mrs. Lyncott, why would you allow Lady Anne to bring those men here? I believe I made my opinion of the gypsies quite clear some time ago."

She folded her arms across her chest. Did he not understand anything about his sister? "I did not know about the event before yesterday—"

"Yesterday!"

"And it is because of me that she brought them

here. She intended to meet at his vardo or campfire or whatever she called it."

His brows drew downward in fury. "The devil you say!"

She returned his look measure for measure. He was furious, but now that her terror was fading, she had her own fair share of anger. How dare he take her to task for this evening's debacle? Did he not see that no woman could preserve order in this house?

He must have seen the determination on her face. Either that, or realized the stupidity of dismissing a woman an hour after she'd been attacked. He rubbed a hand over his face and stifled a curse. "It is not the time to discuss this."

"If I am to be dismissed—"

He held up his hand, shock in every line of his face. "You are not! I swear that was never in my thoughts."

She exhaled a sigh of relief. One less worry then, at least for today.

"But we must discuss this, Mrs. Lyncott. Neither of us is having the least success in moderating my sister's behavior."

He was having no success. She, on the other hand, had managed to bring the gypsies here. Which—in retrospect—had not been her best idea. The very thought made her knees go weak. Had she truly almost died tonight? The world began to tilt and swirl around her.

"Caroline!"

She blinked, brought back to the present with a gasp. The sound sent fresh fire down her throat, and she clenched her teeth against the pain. He was beside her in an instant, cupping her elbow and guiding her to a seat. She took it gratefully, her heart still beating with too frantic a pulse.

She felt his hand on her face, large and gentle. "Caroline," he said, his voice growing urgent. "Caroline, look at me."

She focused on his hazel eyes and the green flecks she saw there. They made her think of meadows and sweet grass, and nothing at all of monkeys. "Do all Scots have such amazingly colored eyes?"

She watched as the corners of his eyes crinkled with his smile. "Nay, luv, they're all mine." His thick burr sent lovely shivers down her spine, though she could barely understand a word he'd said. Normally, he adopted a proper English accent.

Still, she held his gaze, watching as his pupils dilated, losing the green into darker tones. She raised her hand to touch him in some way. She wanted to know the texture of his skin, the width of his mouth, the feel of a man.

"Here you go," said Lady Anne as she rounded the corner carrying a tea tray. And suddenly, his lordship was two steps away from her. In the blink of an eye, Caroline's view went from the man's eyes to the shiny brass buttons on his coat. She glanced at Lady Anne but saw nothing amiss. If her ladyship had seen anything untoward, she gave no sign of it. Meanwhile, the earl took another step back and executed a handsome bow. "I shall leave you to it then, Anne. Mrs. Lyncott."

Caroline looked up, unsure what to say. Their gazes caught and held, and in the silence she heard a strange sound—a shush, like the wind through the trees or the touch of a hand through meadow grasses. It was quiet and powerful, and yet she could barely hear it, much less feel its caress. She was so focused on trying to understand the sensations that when he spoke, the words startled her. His tone was too formal, too superficial, and not at all the subtle whisper she'd almost heard. "You will tell us if you need anything," he said. "If you are distressed in any—"

"I am merely bruised, my lord." She pushed through her confusion. "I have suffered much worse, I assure you." She hadn't meant to say that, though the knowledge was clear upon her scarred chest. But he didn't know that so she flashed him a smile. "Of course, I will tell the staff if I need something."

He studied her a little longer, as if trying to judge whether she lied. In the end, he had no choice but to withdraw. Caroline turned her attention to Lady Anne, who was pouring the tea, her hands steady though her expression was deeply troubled.

"Don't speak anymore," the lady said. "I am simply horrified by what happened. I cannot express how sorry I am. To think that it happened in our own home. In my bedroom!"

Caroline took the teacup, sipping obediently as Lady Anne settled in a chair across from her. In truth, the hot liquid did feel good on her throat.

"I am going to get you that gypsy tea. I know my brother is furious with me, and rightly so, but I cannot believe that Mr. Pike knowingly brought that horrible thief in here. He expressly told him to stay in the stable. I heard it myself, but…" She swallowed and looked away, but then a moment later, she was looking into Caroline's eyes, her expression pleading. "I am so very sorry," she whispered. "I don't know how to help."

Caroline set aside her tea with a smile. "I am fine, my lady." Then she reached forward and squeezed her ladyship's hand.

That motion was her undoing because it pulled at the pins that held her bodice in place. A single breath later, the tear in the dress fell open to reveal her scars.

Lady Anne's gasp of surprise echoed in the room. Caroline tried to cover herself quickly, but there was no help for it. The woman had seen.

"Caroline," she breathed. "What happened?"

Damnation. What was she supposed to do now?

About the Author

USA Today bestselling author Jade Lee has been scripting love stories since she first picked up a set of paper dolls. Ball gowns and rakish lords caught her attention early (thank you Georgette Heyer), and her fascination with the Regency era began. An author of more than thirty romance novels and winner of dozens of industry awards, she finally gets to play in the best girl heaven: a bridal salon! In her new series, four women find love as they dress the most beautiful brides in England. Lee lives in Champaign, Illinois.